good deed rain

The Books of Ticks © 2017 Good Deed Rain
www .gooddeedrain.com
ISBN 978-1-63587-419-8

Cover illustration and design: Aaron Gunderson © 2016

Interior illustrations by Aaron Gunderson © 1992-95

Writing: Allen Frost © 1991-2009
    (also illustrated p.85 from my original notebook,
    p.173 from *Pie in the Sky* #23, 1993
    p.265 from *Pie in the Sky* #66, 1993,
        refers to p.288 of this text,
    p.339 Phil's shoes from *Pie in the Sky* #11, 1992.)

Apple by TFK!

Production assistance: Fred Sodt

Acknowledgement:
With sincere thanks to Fred Sodt for sharing his talent and
time bringing these many works of Good Deed Rain to light.

The Book of Ticks

The Book of Ticks is a collection of eight adventures featuring Phil Ticks:

*"A Tic is a vision suddenly of memory...
a BOOK OF TICS is..."*

—Jack Kerouac, from *Some of the Dharma*

INTRODUCTION:

Phil Ticks also appeared in another novel I CAN ONLY IMAGINE in 1993. He is a bicycle repairman who works in a cryogenics appliance store. (That book will be published in a separate compilation, due soon.) It's possible he may be hiding in some short stories too. He sure got around.

For 18 years he was my Kilgore Trout. He was a companion and the shotgun-riding ghost in my own real life adventures. Phil Ticks appeared and disappeared on the Pacific Coast. He traveled with me from the fog world of San Francisco, up to Seattle and then down again to Portland for a book. He stayed out of Ohio, but he returned in Bellingham. After three more manuscripts, I let him drift off towards the mountains north of here. Presumably never to be seen again.

Aaron Gunderson's sketches were drawn from 1992-1995, to illustrate Phil's adventures in my self-published magazine *PIE IN THE SKY.* (Most of these pictures were drawn very quickly on scraps, cardboard, napkins, or the company stationery we used.) Aaron's work complements these stories so well they make this book seem like a crazy cartoon. Knowing this publication would arrive one day, I kept those drawings all these years, waiting.

I met Aaron when we worked at the same restaurant in Seattle. Later on, I worked with him again at a comic book factory. We spent a lot of time talking about the old comedians and detective movies, Kenneth Patchen, Frank Sinatra, and *The Fugitive* TV series, on long walks to coffee shops. Those were some tough years and I owe a lot to friends like Aaron who made sure the world stayed an inspiration. This book is filled with dream-movie memory, the names and jokes and places and circumstances are drawn from the day to day.

Although Phil Ticks served as a sort of voodoo doll for me, he was also a lesson. These stories were written by a much younger me who was still learning, not only the craft of writing, but everything else too. So let's not wait a second more, here we go, after 25 years in the planning, I'm very pleased to share this work with you.

Allen Frost
Bellingham, Washington

SITTING ON A BOMB

Introduction:

Sitting on a Bomb is the birth of Phil Ticks. In 1991, I was traveling so close to lost in the John Muir State Park, where the fog really and truly comes up over the cliffs and blows along the winding road. I was reading H.G Wells' *The Time Machine* paperback in a parking lot. The day before, I was sitting on a Sunday street in front of a very old California Spanish church. This book wrote itself, it rolled off the ocean from Japan, right onto the page. And what do you know? Everything seems to be truer today, as time unfolds and here we are in another America, sitting on a bomb.

Contents

There was a breath of wind, and the lamp flame jumped. One of the candles on the mantel was blown out, and the little machine suddenly swung round, became indistinct, was seen as a ghost for a second perhaps, as an eddy of faintly glittering brass and ivory; and it was gone—vanished!

H.G. Wells
The Time Machine

PROSPERITY

There were parades like you wouldn't believe. The flag was everywhere, when he was caught in America after the war.

All kinds of building was going on in the city now the war had been won and he was hired on at a construction site, forming a new bank out of huge gray marble stones. There were other soldiers working there too. Some of them he even recognized from the ruins of liberated Paris and the road to Tokyo. They were all promised a bank account, enough to get started on, with credit for houses and cars and families to put in them.

Phil Ticks worked for weeks there and thought only of making the shadow of the bank taller. In a small crane compartment, he flipped switches, levers and turned a wheel to feed steel to the people on the scaffolds filling in granite around and around the metal frame like ice cubes.

He was making good money too. The union was treating him well. He was pleased with his present life. Everything was paved with gold into the future, long enough until one morning he was seized with terror.

A ghost was waiting for him in the crane control box.

It shimmered, becoming something with shape and then

not, then with substance again.

There was no one around him who could see it too—it was there just for Phil Ticks. Even though it flickered so much, he knew who it was.

Phil had shot the man on an island in the Pacific during the war.

The ghost still wore a Japanese uniform and carried a gun. He was cloudy white, but exactly as he was in that jungle in 1945. The ghost was still a rattle of sabers and bullets and World War Two, but it was past fighting, the haunted shape of him waved for Phil to come closer.

Phil wasn't able to do anything else but move towards the ghost. The land below tilted through the glass. Something in Phil was moving him forwards because, "If you could come this far to see me," he was close now, "It must be important. It must be something I need to know."

He stood next to the ghost and looked to where the finger pointed, out the window of the crane.

America was constructing itself down there, after victory, as people and machines moved across the ground, building and changing the landscape from the past into something brand new.

The ghost wanted Phil to see where they stood. It didn't want him to forget.

*"We are going to defend ourselves alone,
surrounded by an ocean of capitalism."*

—Fidel Castro
October 10, 1991

PHIL TICKS AND THE OCEAN OF CAPITALISM

Phil went a little crazy after the ghost. There was no other way he could have been after that. His life was ripped apart. He lost his job and so much more. He lived close to the reptile of poverty, sunk in a basement room where the cold came down the cement walls and his bed creaked like an old battleship. A dark green painting of a forest and mountain hung on the wall. It was a still life of Transylvania in the 1600s. The window rattled from the jazz and neon of the club next door, footsteps and laughing went by all night long.

When he wanted to eat, either in the morning before work, or in the evening after work, he cooked on a communal stove that was splattered with the remains of hundreds of other meals. He boiled instant coffee and noodles on it every day.

There must be a way to make enough money to get out of this, Phil thought every time he drank the coffee and swallowed it down with noodles. I just can't seem to make any progress out. Being without money in America made for a difficult life—it made life seem like there was no way out. It was all he could do to hope that this would somehow end.

At his saddest, darkest moments, he thought, I'll never fit in with this world, these kinds of people. I know I'm not a part of this lasting. When he looked around himself, he saw no one like him. There were those moments in floating time when he thought he was the only one alive.

Things needed to be made different. It wouldn't take too long now.

HOME ON THE RANGE

Luck was always that spinning beautiful or cruel thing, making life good or bad. Phil decided it didn't have anything to do with the kind of person you were, there was no way he could persuade good fortune towards himself like a friendly white swan.

Unfortunately, everything about him had reached the end of the line: from the clothes that barely held together to cover him, to his mind going in circles, wobbling like a record blanketed with warps. He wore cheap used clothing, he ate out of cans, and he was lucky if he could find enough money for a cigarette. Sometimes he stared for too long at billboards and the signs in the subway. Jobs were revolving doors; he could barely consider himself employed. When anyone stops to think about the life they're living, and what they've done with it, it will happen to them too, he thought. America isn't meant to be questioned; there are no rewards for that.

He had been absentmindedly trying to close the torn cloth over his knee while he stared out the window. I've got to get some thread for this, he realized. But then I'll need to buy a needle too. Maybe a piece of tape will close it?

But luck did eventually seem to turn his way. Like any other circular thing, he had been through his share of the bad already. It only took a few more years. Another decade had to start for it to change.

The first sign that something new was happening for him arrived with her, just when Phil never would have considered himself ready. It seemed like he was afloat, but maybe only barely.

What she saw in that, what she wanted from him, was anybody's guess. Maybe she was desperate and desperateness attracted her. It would have been like asking a woman to share poverty with him; it was the most he had to offer. And anyone who could seem to fall in love with him, he could love. He was tired, there was a difference to her, and she was kind.

On their third date, after a meal of spaghetti, she brought him to her home. It was a small yellow house with a garden of struggling flowers. The driveway took the car into the garage quietly and they stopped.

"This is quite a place you've got, Pearl."

"This is only the garage, Phil."

"Oh, I know. I mean, it's a nice garage. And house too. I like the flowers."

"I'm not much of a gardener. I just give it my best shot. I don't think my thumb is very green. C'mon inside, Phil."

There was a door key under the flowerpot on the step. "Timmy!" she called as she opened the door into the kitchen. "Timmy, we're home!"

Phil was waiting for an Airedale to come bounding in from off a sofa, or a cat maybe, meowing and turning circles slowly around Pearl's ankles.

Instead, a small voice answered her from far away.

About as loud as radio static, the sound came from another room.

"C'mon Phil, I'll show you Timmy. He's my other reason for living." She took Phil's hand and squeezed.

In the other room, a tiny boy was sitting in front of a television, a redwood cabinet with a fishbowl screen of glowing, moving pictures. There were hoots of cowboys and stampeding horses and gunshots and then whispering desert and the narrow gentle breathing next to it.

"Timmy! Oh, he's watching a Western. Nothing can tear him away from one of those programs. Except maybe a Western on the radio…"

"TV's better," the little voice seemed to come out of the machine, only a bundle of wires.

"We won't disturb him til the show's over. You'll like him, Phil. He's a nice kid."

"Is he your son?" Phil stared at the back of the boy, the shad-

18

ows moving from the black and white.

"Naturally."

"Then you're not still, uh, married are you?"

"No…No, not really…His father's doing life in prison, so I can't really be married now, can I?"

"In prison?"

"Oh, don't worry. He'll never get out again. They've really got him locked up tight this time." She wheeled Phil towards the kitchen, "Anyways, let's us have some coffee."

"So, how was marriage?" Phil asked as she felt around the cold dishwater in the sink, looking for two cups.

"Which one?"

"Which *one?*"

"Well, the first one didn't last long. He wasn't really my type. Of course, I didn't know that at the time."

"Oh."

"But it really is a lovely institution, don't you think?"

Phil was watching her hands make coffee.

"It's nice to have someone to come home to. Even if he is a convicted murderer…Well…That wasn't really his fault though. He has a temper."

"Yes," Phil listened to the gunshots and hollering of Indians in the other room.

"So what do you do for a living again?" she asked him.

"Right now I'm a taxidermist."

"Oh, how wonderful!" she smiled. "Can you help me with mine?"

"*What?*"

"I can never figure out all the forms and small print and what it is I'm supposed to declare or not. And I'm no good at math at all! It's so confusing. Maybe you could do it for me?"

"No, Pearl. I'm a taxidermist. I stuff dead animals."

Pearl groaned and her face spoiled. "I hate dead animals! There's a dead rat in our garage. It's been there for a week, but I don't dare pick it up. They frighten me."

19

"Yeah, I'm not crazy about the job either. But you gotta do something."

She poured coffee for them quietly. It swirled in their cups.

He cleared his throat, "But I'm looking for a new racket. I need something with a future."

"I guess I'm lucky," she said. "I've got a skill. That's what you need, Phil. I can type. There are always people who need things to be typed. Right now, I'm typing up a science fiction story. It's about a world all controlled by machines and the people are only numbers. But I don't really get to read it, just type it. Do you want cream with your coffee, Phil?"

"No thanks, I take it black."

"Sugar?"

"No thanks."

"Well, I like mine with lots of milk and lots of sugar." He watched her unload teaspoons of sugar into her cup and turn it white with milk.

A small noise, a parade of mice, scuffled up behind her.

"Timmy!" she cried. "The Western's over? The good guys win?"

"It's a commercial," a tinny voice replied. "Oatmeal Houston's trapped in a mine." Timmy stood there, glassy-eyed, pale face, wearing his pajamas with a silver sheriff star pinned over his heart. The cowboy boots had made all that noise, such as it was, otherwise he could have floated invisibly through the air. He tipped the huge white hat that hid his face. "Hello, pardner," he said to Phil.

"Howdy, Timmy," Phil answered.

The boy turned to his mother, "Ma'am."

"Timmy, would you like some milk and cookies?"

"No, ma'am. Evening." And he turned and went back to his television.

Phil said, "That Timmy's quite a character."

"Oh yes, he is." Pearl smiled. "He just loves Westerns. He watches them all day."

"Doesn't he go to school?"

"He tried, but it didn't work out. Timmy learns everything he needs to know from television. All he wants to do is learn about the Wild West."

"Have you ever given him any books? He could read a lot more about it, how it really was."

"Why? Television *moves*. It's much more real, it captures his little imagination. He can't get enough. Every night I have to carry him to his room to sleep. It's his whole life, why ruin that?"

"Yeah, I guess so." Phil tried his coffee. "I was reading a magazine today that was saying how television will take the place of reading. In the future there will be no need for anything else."

"That's right. And little Timmy is the wave of the future."

"Hmmm." Phil sipped his coffee and drank some more.

THE MARRIAGE OF PHIL

It didn't take long the way things were progressing, before Phil got married to Pearl and her little television son, Timmy. Timmy was given the present of a week in a hotel room with television, while they went into Las Vegas to get married.

The Golden Instant Marriage Flowers Chapel was a small white building with a large sign, next to The Arabian Night Casino and the minister needed help standing, as he reeled through the routine like a strange dance. But he remembered to ask for his ten dollars at the end.

Afterwards, Pearl showed Phil how lucky their marriage was by winning the ten dollars back on a slot machine next door. The silver money poured into her hands, spilling out onto the floor.

They went laughing back up to their room and into bed, playing and touching each other for hours, while Timmy was mesmerized into sleep by the all-night television static pouring into morning.

THE VULTURE

All three of them lived in Pearl's house, where it was quiet outside the city. A field behind the house filled with birds in the dawn.

After a couple days, Phil had settled into the family routine and was enjoying the whole day of getting up in the morning next to Pearl...Sunshine in the windows, eating breakfast together, with Timmy fused by electrical rays to the television screen...Going to work for eight hours, using the phone to talk to Pearl during lunch...Taking the bus home and having dinner around the square red table in the kitchen while Timmy watched TV...Then in a few hours going to bed, to dream, to start all over again when the alarm clock awakened. Phil liked the way it worked.

And taxidermy wasn't all bad. It was important to remember that all life can be brought back from death. Phil learned how to put glass beads in the statue animal's eyes, to make them seem ready to move.

He was working on a vulture, hunching it over, giving it that eager, hungry look. This was something to be proud of, he congratulated himself, never knowing that his luck was about to turn again so abruptly.

Next to the window, he propped it on a branch, and the black feathers glowed with the blue fires from the shipyards.

HELL

That morning, Phil slept in, with their blue sheet wrapped over him, and the ripe smell of the breakfast she had made working on his senses to revive him.

Finally, he rolled over and sat up.

The television, as usual, was on in the other room. Timmy woke up at dawn with the machine.

Phil walked through the kitchen wearing his gray underwear and socks, scratching his stomach. "What's for breakfast, darling?"

Whatever it was had burned itself black in the fry pan and was still cooking. Maybe it was eggs and something else.

"Hell," Phil sighed and turned the gas burner off. "What's going on?"

He poured some coffee for himself. "Pearl?"

The coffee was barely warm. "Hey, Timmy? You seen your mother?"

Through the shooting, Indians dying, was a reply.

"Say it again?" Phil, with no shirt on, stood in the doorway, the gateway to the Old West televised.

The little form seated in front of the TV quietly spoke again, "No."

"That's strange…" Phil walked back into the kitchen.

If he followed the directions on the box carefully, he might be able to make pancakes.

He opened the cupboard and the note taped to the door almost hit him in the forehead.

> *Dearest Phil, I'm going back to Vegas.*
> *Don't try to follow me. I need all the luck I can get.*
> *Take care of Timmy, Love Pearl*

"Back to Vegas?" He closed the cupboard door. "Hell." He went to the icebox. "What is she, crazy?" It was part of his expe-

24

rience with these things to take everything in stride. It was part of his training, he must remain rational and calm at all times. He tried to be unemotional. Imagine a fish. Like everything else, she could leave or return. For now, she had disappeared. It had to make sense that it couldn't last.

Inside the bare icebox was another note.

p.s. I took some food with me. There's breakfast
for you on the stove.   Love Pearl

"Awww, hell." Phil got out a plate decorated with Oriental blue flying birds and he sat down at the table with the burned breakfast pan.

By using the fork as an alternating pick and shovel, he could eat the blackness.

There was a letter on the table. He hadn't noticed it before, even though it was stamped in red, Urgent.

Using the butter knife, he opened it with a slippery tear.

The papers slid out onto his ash breakfast.

He unfolded them, had a sip of cold coffee and read in a silence broken only by faint gunshots.

The house was being repossessed. She had sold the rights to a land developer and he was being given a day to move out.

"Hell," Phil crunched.

BACK TO CAPISTRANO

On top of that, he lost his job at the taxidermist. Orders had dropped. So it was back to the old poverty game, Phil sighed. When times got tough, it was always back to that…Not something to look forward to, like the return of the swallows to Capistrano.

Except now, he had to take care of another person. He had Pearl's son, their son, to care for. Fortunately, Phil reassured himself, as he heaved the big wooden television into the back of the cab, this was all Timmy needed to survive on. If Phil could keep up with the rent, as long as he could do that, the boy would be happy.

The frail, white Timmy kept a hand on the big TV like he could still feel the energy from it, enough to grow pale flowers by.

The cab took them downtown, away from the suburbs, and the house that was repossessed. The buildings got taller and louder.

"I used to live in this neighborhood," Phil said to the boy, who was watching the blank screen so intently. The little blue eye at the center was getting smaller and smaller, disappearing. "Before I met your mother and you…See, that building over there is where I got my food from."

The sights flew by. "If memories could talk, Timmy…" Phil found and lit a cigarette. "They'd sure have a lot to say."

"This is as far as I'm gonna go, buddy," the cabby said. "I'll let you off here. This place ain't safe. I don't like it." The cab stopped at the curb.

"We still have a ways to go."

"Not with me. This is my limit. No further, I ain't crazy."

Phil opened the door and helped Timmy and his television out onto the sidewalk. Phil took from his wallet as little amount of the little he had.

"This is what I think of your cab!" was what he wanted to say, like a movie hero flickering on the pavement, but the cab had already turned around, the wheels squealing away, gone.

"Who needs you!" Phil brought his arm up and down. "C'mon, Timmy, let's go." Phil peeled the television from the boy and carried it in front of himself. A suitcase wobbled on top and the electrical cord trailed.

Timmy had a backpack on and he walked sideways, with his hands on the wooden cabinet, divining images of Roy Rogers and Oatmeal Houston and the Grand Canyon in all its black and white beauty.

A BIG THING OF FEARS

A big thing of fears is all it is, Phil wrote steadily down the lines of the application. I really don't think you could understand how it gets inside your head, all these things: When you can't find a job, when you are so hungry, when there's nowhere to sleep, all the simple things become so hard. Do you think it's possible that we could get rid of all this stuff that makes things so hard for people? Time is short. Don't you think we could be a little smarter than this?

Phil wrote a bit more, about his service in the army, and his medal, filled in the blanks with his job experience, then he put the pen down and handed the application in.

It was more than what they needed for someone to just sweep the steps and street in the mornings at seven o'clock while people went to work, but he got the job and he breathed a sigh of relief. The landlord would ease off his back and the bills could be paid, and there was even some cheap food out of paper boxes and cans to eat.

One night, while cooking supper, Phil was reading a newspaper someone had left behind. Going through the classifieds, he saw:

Wanted: Detectives
Must Be Able to Solve Crime

In the morning, he went to the phone in the hallway, put in a nickel and called for an interview. It rang and a voice welcomed him.

28

TOYBOAT

They shifted around the table and all the smoke from their cigarettes made the ceiling disappear. "We'll let you know. We'll give you a call."

That was the way it would be, they had decided. Now Phil felt he had no chance of becoming a detective, he would have to go back to sweeping, or taxidermy, or something else.

Phil wanted to get away from them, run suddenly away from all of them. Mars would do—that was far enough away from these things. If only he could be like a rocket and keep going up when he said, "Okay..." and stood.

"We'll keep in touch then."

The door was far away.

They watched him as he left, his cheap suit, his secondhand shoes, everything about him should have been defeated with Japan. There was nothing about him that could be seen as the American dream.

The Salvation Army would have kept him in a cardboard box with broken thick records, a scarf, and a torn children's book about earthworms.

As he walked away, he mumbled a tongue twister, caught up suddenly in the impossibility of saying it quickly. "Toyboat, toyboat, toyboat..." That was the best he could do before the words failed him.

He opened the door and went through and when he closed it behind him, he felt like he had gone through another war.

He breathed a sigh of relief that he had survived.

What Phil didn't expect was the phone call from them. He got the job. He got the license, he got the office. He was a detective.

REDIAL

This was why he thought he would make a good detective: he had seen them in movies and decided he could become one too. Movies were always convincing you of something. They hypnotized you and drew you into their world.

Phil was watching the latest mystery film on the huge black and white screen. It was called *Redial*. It was about a woman with twenty sons who were all in the US military. The Navy called her to tell her when one was killed after a ship ran aground. The Air Force called her to tell her the news of her son crashing into a mountain. The next morning, the Army called her up—her son had been shot. The two hours of the movie were filled with the elongated terrible shadows of her running down the hall to the telephone…Over and over again, twenty times.

The film didn't sit well with Phil. He left the theater feeling endangered. Every step on the crowded street had to be put down just right. Walking back to his office would take a long time at this rate.

His office was tacked up against the back wall of a Texaco, like a birdhouse on stilts, and he would sit there and wait, holed up behind the gas station in that seedy room that swayed in the wind.

When he settled into the detective business, he thanked his stars. It was so easy he couldn't believe it! Here he was, with his name painted on a door and everything: Phil Ticks, Detective.

He climbed the many steps, opened the door and crossed the floor and sat behind his desk. He watched the cars pass by in the street below, knowing all the people had mysteries that eventually would lead them to him, mysteries that not even Sherlock Holmes could fathom.

THE CASE OF JOSEPH STALIN

"Since I work at an American flag factory, you think I wouldn't get so much grief about my name. There are probably lots of Joseph Stalins working at factories, right? So why the big deal?"

"Well…" Phil had to find the right words to explain it. That was part of his job. Phil pushed some papers on the table while his client watched him.

"Listen, I'm not a Commie if that's what you're thinking! You should see me on the 4th of July! You never saw so many fireworks!"

"Joe, I have no problem with your patriotism."

"Best country in the world!"

"Right…It's just that…Well, you know how quick people are to judge. They won't even let colored folks eat with them in the same restaurant. See, I think it's just that your name…Well, it brings out a kind of resentment. Joseph Stalin is supposed to be one of our enemies, you know. Maybe you could just solve it by changing your name." He struck a match.

"What?" Joe leaned forward with his cigarette.

"You know, try something a little more American sounding…Like John Wayne, or maybe Babe Ruth or something." He shook out the match and tossed it into the overflowing basket next to his desk. "Think about it. Sleep on it. Give it some more time."

"Yeah…That just might be the answer."

Two days later, Phil got a phone call from a very happy George Washington.

PLAYING THE PIANO UNTIL THE END OF TIME

Darkness, with a warm wind that filled her like a sail when it floated through her dress, brought her up the creaking wooden stairs in back of the gas station, into his office. The woman had bright orange hair and a wake of moths that followed her from the parking lot. As stood waiting for Phil to look up, she said, "I've seen a ghost."

"Oh no."

"Yes. I'm not sure what I should do about it." She entered the room and sat down, holding the armrests while she stared around at everything in the four corners of Phil's room. Everything seemed to be waiting for a garage sale. "I've never really had any experience with anything like this."

She showed him her hands, long gentle fingers, "I'm a piano player. I work at an old folks' home. They have an old piano there and I often play it when I'm done with my job, when I've put everyone to bed and turned out the lights.

"They have a piano downstairs, where it's quiet, in a place next to the kitchen. I play Beethoven and Bach. I practice my scales. It's a big house, no one can hear me."

Phil watched her and the moths that still circled her.

She looked into his eyes and looked further into his eyes. "I was in the kitchen, making myself some coffee to stay awake through the night. I also had a sandwich already made, waiting in the other room, on the piano, on a plate."

She was speaking very methodically, Phil thought. A detective could make sense of these things, but he shivered while she began again.

"I was pouring the hot water, taking no more time than you need to fix coffee and when I returned, my sandwich had somehow moved all the way down the piano. There was nobody else around that late at night, but it had moved.

"I thought, how strange that was and I drank my first cup of coffee and listened to the silence in the room, trying to figure it out…Maybe I played a few notes on the piano…I drank my coffee until it was gone and then I went back into the kitchen to refill my cup.

"While I poured it, I heard the piano playing a very faraway song. It was almost like a radio, but not. I rushed back into the room, but no one was there and the music had stopped." She stared and stared at Phil with her wide blue eyes.

"Well, all ghosts have their purpose," Phil said at last. "There's got to be something they come out of darkness for."

"Oh, I know. You know why I think it was happening? I think it was the music." She said, "I felt like, as I was playing the piano, that someone was watching me. It made me nervous and I started to make mistakes, then I could feel that presence even colder, even more."

"A music lover," Phil offered, playing catch with his pen, tossing it end over end.

She moved her legs. "I found out that a music teacher used to live in the house…Before I worked there…And he died just a while ago."

"He died, but he didn't die," said Phil.

She nodded.

It didn't take Phil long, only a moment to decide what to do. "The solution is simple enough. Stop playing the piano. Try playing cards, solitaire perhaps."

"No," she laughed. "It wasn't only when I played piano. Sometimes I've seen him as a shape moving across the lawn out-side. A glow at night that goes across the grass into the garage… That's the only time I've ever actually seen him, when he looks like colored twinkling lights."

She touched her fingers together, "But the problem is he's not around anymore. He got to be something I would look forward to every night."

For a moment she became her lonely night self and Phil could see her all by herself in the mansion, playing the piano until the end of time, waiting for him to return.

AMERICA IS HAUNTED

Phil wasn't doing anything really, just thinking numbers in his mind: how many cups of coffee he drank today; there were three cigarettes left in his pocket; weren't there twenty six steps that creaked up to his office? The radio just said it was the 8th inning with two men out and runners at first and third and a single could tie the game at six. He pushed a quarter and two pennies into a triangle shape on his desktop.

The fan on the windowsill was humming.

A moth tried to make it through the glass.

It was about time to go to Caspar's Hot Dogs, he thought.

That was when the ghost of that Japanese soldier Phil killed reappeared. He spun like a paper lantern, giving off a green kind of light. He wouldn't let Phil forget.

Phil knew it wouldn't be enough to tell the ghost that he was sorry. It wasn't enough to admit that World War Two was a terrible mistake. Because they both knew America's wars were just going to continue. He didn't know what to say to the ghost. It wouldn't do to say, "Why me? Go flap at somebody who matters, go spook the president!" Phil was just a single person, scared, but in his own small way he was responsible for what America was.

Still, when he saw the ghost again after such a long time, Phil closed his eyes tightly and lay his head down like a dead man.

CASPAR'S HOT DOGS

11:35. The clock ticked through the night and Phil had been asleep on his desk. He stretched and felt hunger. "I need a hotdog," he said to the papers scattered all around him.

So he left his office and hurried to Caspar's. He envisioned the meal as he walked, red, smothered with peppers and spicy mustard, his mouth watering until he was there.

An old Chinese man cupped around his coffee, glowed in the big curving window.

The smell of hotdogs leaked through the silver roof vents.

The restaurant was a perfect stainless steel circle and Phil was going to sit in the exact center.

I'm a lucky man tonight, he thought, as he was paying for the hotdog—he found out that he still had enough money in his pocket for another one. What a great place Caspar's Hot Dogs is, Phil smiled.

Caspar was a tall man with only one hand, but it always pleasantly surprised Phil how fast and skilled Caspar was at making hotdogs.

Always in motion behind the counter, Caspar would balance the hotdog roll on his stump and with the other hand he'd be like sausage lightning, stuffing it all full of food.

While Phil was passing Caspar's good hand the money for a second hotdog, he asked, "Say, Caspar, how'd you lose your hand anyway?" But in that moment of asking, he remembered that Caspar couldn't talk.

Caspar ripped a napkin out of a shiny holder and wrote quickly.

Phil read the message out loud.

Because I was a big target.

Caspar stood there in front of the register with his arms outspread wide, one hand missing, and it was easy to see how

35

all the German machineguns would have had a hard time not hitting Caspar. He made a kind of woo-woo sound to make sure Phil understood.

Phil did. He nodded and took a bite. "Well, these hotdogs are the best!" He flashed a smile full of hotdog. "Keep the change."

OATMEAL HOUSTON

Going back to his apartment, Phil ran into a cowboy in the hallway. Standing on the worn carpet, his broken down slumping figure was like a vision from American history.

"I'm Oatmeal Houston, the famous cowboy," he said when Phil got to his door. "Your kid watches me on the TV."

"I know. He sees more of you than me." Phil got out his key. "All my kid watches is Westerns. It's like he doesn't belong to this century."

"Why would he want to?" Oatmeal Houston's words were long drawls. "At least we had some sense of order and right and wrong in our day."

Phil opened his door, "Yeah, right… Hey, Timmy! Oatmeal's here!" He knew it was bizarre, standing in his doorway with a television cowboy beside him.

"Oh, he knows."

"Timmy? I'm home!" The room was dark. There was no one inside. Even the TV was off. "Where's Timmy? Asleep?"

"Nope. He's not asleep. But he's far away…"

"What are you talking about?!"

Oatmeal Houston, the lone cowboy, moved slowly away from the wallpaper. "He wanted to come with me."

"What are you saying, mister?" Phil knew there wasn't much he could do against the tall cowboy. He had seen him brawl and shoot and he always won. Still, Phil had a gun in his coat pocket, and maybe outside the glow of Hollywood he had a chance to outdraw Oatmeal Houston. "Have you got my boy?" His fingers itched and trembled.

The cowboy shrugged. "He wanted to leave with me."

"What do you mean?"

37

"This is what I mean…" Oatmeal Houston held up a curved piece of glass, a television screen the size of a hand mirror.

All the gray colors, dots, turned into Phil's son, riding a white horse, with black cactus and hills in the background.

"Howdy pardner!' the boy's voice came out of the glass.

"Timmy?" Phil stepped closer, looked up at Oatmeal Houston. "What is this?! Some kind of magic?"

"You could call it magic. Or time travel. It's television, Phil Ticks. It's where I'm from." Then he put the glass away in his coat. "I'll be seeing you." The cowboy started to walk back down the hall, his spurs cutting into the carpet.

"You cheap cowboy!" Phil went for his pistol, pulled it out of the holster below his arm as the fast bullet from Oatmeal Houston's six-shooter knocked it clean out of Phil's grip with a flash of metal and sparks.

Phil held his burnt, stinging hand between his knees.

"See you, Phil." Oatmeal Houston made the long walk to the elevator. He turned when he got inside and tipped his white ten gallon hat. He smiled. The door closed and he was gone.

SHIPYARDS ARE MY SPECIALTY

"What do you know about shipbuilding?"

"Excuse me?"

He looked up and there she was. Just as he had figured from the movies, every detective must have a woman like this. Phil had been expecting this since he became a detective. Actually, he had been hoping this would happen.

Ever since his wife had taken off in their car and he hadn't heard from her in such a long time, he had been more than hoping for the movie-like arrival of a woman like this.

She pulled the door closed behind her and took a gun from her purse.

"Woah, lady!" He eased open the desk. "Take it easy," he soothed, "Let's talk first." Close at hand, he kept a loaded pistol in the drawer, waiting for an emergency like this.

"Can I interest you in a cigarette?" he asked and quickly he went for the gun, knocking a few sci-fi magazines out onto the floor as his pistol came out.

But she was already lighting her cigarette and putting her gun-shaped lighter away in her purse. The smoke purred out the side of her mouth.

Phil held his gun pointed straight at her. He tried to laugh. "Yeah, I like these gag lighters too…My kid collects them." He waved his loaded .38 in front of his lips, being careful not to pull the trigger.

"You shouldn't let your kid play with guns," she said.

Mysteriously, she liked to hang in the dark, her long thin body like a hinge in the door shadow. She was a lot better than any detective movie actress. He couldn't even think of a comeback.

He imagined the camera trained on him and him not able to say anything in reply. The audience was waiting.

"Well, do you?" she said.

"What?"

"Do you know anything about shipbuilding?"

Phil said, "Oh, just a basic knowledge, enough to get by on..." He leaned over and picked up the Martian cover of a magazine and slid it back in the drawer with the gun.

She stared at him.

He said, "It's not my field of expertise, by any means."

She started to look at her long fingernails, eyeing them for the smallest imperfection.

For a moment, Phil thought of her as one of those science fiction princesses, in a tattered gown running away from a Tyrannosaurus Rex.

"I used to work at a construction site though," he said quickly, "I used to make tall buildings."

"Oh yeah?" she murmured.

He nodded. "It was like being in a circus, walking up on those catwalks, way up."

She let some ash fall from her cigarette.

"People look just like ants when you're that far up." He could hear the wall clock ticking. It was a sound he never really paid attention to before.

If this was a film, the cast would have left a long time ago, the set would have been dismantled, and the studio would have gone bankrupt. There would have been nothing left but him standing on a crumbled lot, with the drifting by of occasional newspapers.

It pleased him when she spoke again, broke the silence like a flower. "Well then, it looks like you're my man for the job. I want you to do some spying for me."

"I like to call it sleuthing." He prepared himself professionally before her, straightening his tie.

"Okay, call it whatever you like." Then she smiled so he could see the white of her teeth. "You could say that I represent the government."

She moved towards him, still the shadows stayed with her, and she laid an envelope filled with money on his desk. "You'll have to believe in secrecy with me."

"I like secrets." Phil reached for the envelope. He wanted to thumb through it all.

"Only remember…" She kept her cold hand on the money. "I only pay you for results."

"What do you want me to spy on?"

"That's good," she smiled. "I like that." Against her teeth, the white office walls were even more crumbled, even more gray, collapsing down like smog.

Still smiling, she walked over to the window and became serious in the dark coming from its glass. "That's the shipyard over there."

Rust and silver cranes stood next to the mouth of the brown river, with riveting and cutting metal, sparks and white clouds, while freighters were being turned out into the ocean.

"No problem," Phil said. He would take this case. He suddenly had a lot of money in his coat pocket. "Shipyards are my specialty."

SEAWEED

Phil stared from the blue welding arcs, the reflections of all the machines moving, and he tossed his cigarette at the brown water. He watched it sit there, not even sinking, like a crumpled boat. Nearby, a blowtorch was going through sheet metal.

Someone tapped him on the shoulder, menacing, "You looking for something?"

"Yeah…" Phil answered. He cupped his hands around a new cigarette. "Mermaids."

The fist caught him on the jaw before he had time to put out the match. Phil was hanging half off the pier, in a kind of pain remembered from every other fight he'd been in. The water invited him to fall in with open waving arms.

"There's only one place to find mermaids, wise guy!"

The water, the water with its purple oil slicks and turning flotsam, chips of foam and junk.

If there were mermaids…scaly, half-women, sometimes taking pity on sailors washed overboard, staring with their green fish eyes and reaching wet hands…he could have used one. And maybe he did. Somehow Phil ended up on the rocky beach, between two shipwrecked boats.

His clothes were filled with gravel and seaweed and when he rolled on his side, gallons poured out of his shirt.

Where am I? That was his first thought, followed by, What happened?

The setting sun shined off all the parked ships across the water from him.

The pain in his jaw, the cheap shot, mermaids…Slowly the picture started to form. Not like a detective movie with him fighting off five Nazi goons and uncovering their sabotage plans, this was Phil Ticks, splashed up, half-drowned, clocked for a bad joke.

Phil moved like a starfish, ever so slowly, reaching out with his waterlogged arms.

He thought how good it would be to be dry, eating a sandwich and sipping hot coffee at the counter of Woolworths, leaving the beautiful waitress a tip, a shiny quarter that would mirror her bright smile…only to discover that she was the lovely heiress of Rockefeller millions, and she was just waiting for someone like him to prove human kindness and share in her fortunes.

His jaw was numb. There would be a terrible bruise.

He pulled a cigarette out of his hair and sat up into the swaying mobile of screaming seagulls.

THE SECOND NATURE OF PHIL TICKS

When Phil got back from the beach, she was waiting there darkly at the top of the stairs, like the black fruit of a tree, way up there by the door of his office.

"You go swimming?" she asked. Her mouth was on the turn of a smile, holding only a second from laughing. Her eyes and head were covered by a veiled hat.

"No," he wrung out his hat before her. "I went fishing."

"I hear it works better it you use one of those fishing poles."

"That's what I found out..." He couldn't find his key. He went through his wet pockets again.

He didn't know it was underwater. At that very moment, silently, a fish passed over it. In the water that never stopped moving.

"Looking for this?"

He couldn't believe the way she could hold a key and make it seem like something more—connected to her it was more than for opening doors.

"I found it over the door ledge. That's not a very clever place to hide your spare key, Phil." She became a whisper, "What if I wanted to break in?"

"What are you doing here?"

She unlocked the door and passed him the key, softly, wanting him to touch it from her palm. "I couldn't stand being away from you, Mister Ticks."

He took the key, "Yeah, right!" and moved through the doorway towards his desk. "I need some coffee. You want some coffee?"

"Have you got instant coffee, Phil?"

"Of course." He plugged in the hot water pot. In the desk drawer, a jar of coffee crystals waited. All they needed was the hot water.

She wore a wide rim hat that drooped over her face and bare-ly showed her smile, "I thought so. That's my favorite kind of coffee." Her hand moved in front of her mouth.

"So what exactly are you here for?" He knew all detectives should be aloof.

"Phil, isn't it enough that I'm here?" Posed next to the empty water cooler, she wanted to see what he would say, but after a silence, she spoke again, "I found out something about you."

Only a little light reached her, some pale yellow bars from the window blinds curved on her.

It took him a while, going through drawers and shelves and looking under paper stacks trying to find some cups for their coffee. "Yeah, what's that?"

She pulled something out of her bag and walked towards him. Held up in front of her, it was a map of America and there were X-marks-the-spots on New York and San Francisco.

"You're a detective, right?" she asked.

He noticed the big question mark she tied in the air.

"So you can find things?"

He said, "That's my job."

"Did you find anything unusual at the shipyard?" She slid the map onto the desk before him.

"It's not exactly the friendliest place I've ever been." He poured the hot water into the cups to turn them into coffee. "Their hospitality was lacking."

Almost a coffee smell came from the two cups.

"You could say they were being protective?" she supposed. "Could it be they have something to hide?"

"Possibly…" Not just because she wore sunglasses, he wasn't good at making eye contact. He looked into the dark in the coffee mugs and instant steam instead.

"Phil," she leaned closer over his desk so he could almost see through the shadows she wore, "How much do you believe about what seems to be reality? Are there things you don't think could exist?"

"What, like things that go bump in the night?" He tried to laugh.

"More than that, Phil."

He gave her some coffee. "Try this."

She took the cup and backed away with it. The perfume of her stayed a moment more, then folded.

"You may find this very hard to accept, but we have reasons to believe that there are those in the government, powerful people, people you know from photographs and radio and newsreels, who want to..." She brought the cup up to her lips and drank. "They've so abused their power that they want everything around them. And still, they want more. They want to control people's minds."

The coffee tasted like an aircraft carrier.

Across from him, she waited in the silence he created.

Then Phil said, "What are you trying to get at exactly? That's ancient history. If you want me to solve this, I'll need more than that. Tell me what you know then I can do something."

"I can't tell you everything yet, Phil. We don't even know exactly how it's being done. All we have are clues. What we know for sure, what we have found out, is that these people are putting their plans into action now. In these two cities..." Her finger pointed out to the map that had been waiting on Phil's desk.

"Los Angeles and Boston?" he asked.

"No. New York and San Francisco. Phil, we don't know how they're doing this, but we know where. Right here in our city, in the shipyard."

"I don't know. This is just a little hard to believe." He laughed and spun the map with his hand. "I mean, more people would know about something like this. I don't really see how..."

She cut him off, "Phil, how long do you think America will last?"

"What?" he looked hard at her, at the shadows.

"Everything that you think of as America is threatened by this. If they succeed, you'll be just what they want you to be. You might as well be a machine! We want you to return to the

46

shipyard and find out how this is happening."

She brought out more money and put it on his desk. "But it's more than money, Phil. This is truly about saving this brave land."

"Every day I was in the war, I was fighting to save America. It's second nature to me."

"I'm glad you have such a sense of duty to this country, because that's what we need." She retreated towards the door, "Someone to risk their life for America."

THE BRAIN DEPARTMENT

There was something strange going on at the shipyards. She was right about that.

But maybe this was more than a detective could do.

No, he had to think positive. All anyone needs is a key. You have to know right and wrong. It's all anyone needs to solve things.

He had his own intuition, he didn't need anyone to show him the clues and lead him on. Who was she anyway? Phil thought it would be a good idea to do a little checking up on this client of his. Why she was so eager for him to risk his life at the shipyard, and why exactly did she keep so much in the shadows?

So he changed quickly into dry clothes and hurried after her, following her trail from his office.

She moved along the sidewalk, through the pools of broken streetlamps. Her silhouette was always a cat of a shape and Phil had to almost run to keep up with her.

Not far from the docks, she stepped through the blue neon into a bar. The door and a blast of music closed behind her.

Phil wondered what someone like her would be doing in a sailor bar called The Anchor. There was broken glass in front of it and a merchant marine was passed out in the alley. The blue anchor shape sign buzzed and crackled from overhead.

Phil opened the door and went inside.

He joined a crowd of people and loud music under heavy smoke. The bar was surrounded and curtained by sailors from all over the world. They all had different uniforms on. A fight was brewing in one corner of the room.

Over in a dark booth with her back to Phil, his client was talking to a huge pirate of a man. Phil thought it was plain to see something was going on between them. She kept making shapes with her hands and touching him.

Phil took a good long look at her boyfriend, the scars and tattoos, his thick skulled head and black eyepatch. He was a dragon next to her. "So this is the kind of man she goes for?" Phil wondered, "She may not be so smart after all." From where Phil stood at the doorway, he could hear the sound, through all the crowd and noise, when her friend cracked his knuckles and drowned another beer. "At least he can't be much in the brain department."

Phil thought it would be a good idea to get close to them, eavesdrop, so he slid himself up against a pillar covered with the scrimshaw graffiti of sailor's drunken knives.

By holding himself very quiet and not moving, he hoped to become as much a part of the post as she could be a shadow.

For ten minutes he listened to her monster retelling a fight in the Philippines. As victor, he had carved her initials in the other man's back. "Oh Knarr, did your really?" she asked. It went on like this until Phil gave up and turned his attention to rolling a cigarette.

That was the last thing he remembered.

PHIL TICKS UNDERWATER

Dripping water fell on his forehead. It ran down his eyelids and nose, into his mouth, down his chin and dripped again into more water. The tears of water and a ticking sound.

Phil found himself waking in this place, most of which he couldn't see, it was just so dark.

There were dim poles overhead with seaweed and barnacles that went up into more darkness above.

Trying to move, something tugged at his chest. A wire connected him to a smooth metal curve, a tube about five feet long, with rounded ends. The wires fed into a plate stuck over his heart. He ripped it off and yelled. It had been taped to him.

Now it was quiet, there was no ticking.

Just the water made its sounds.

This open place smelled of the ocean. He was half lying on the tube in a pool of black water. His head ached. "Who knocked me out? Who put me down here? What is this thing?" Phil couldn't even budge the tube it was so heavy, or maybe it was bolted to the water.

He got unsteadily to his feet.

Slabs of metal, ripples, discarded nails, more rusty things, dim outlines, were scattered in the half light underwater around him.

He splashed his way forward and noticed the water was getting deeper, it was up to his knees.

The light had to be coming from somewhere though, and he waded back into the shallows. The metal tube gleamed there and he stepped over and saw a shadowy corner ahead. The seaweed edges of it reflected light. The corner took him to a stairway and he went up, holding to a slippery green handrail that had lived through many tides.

Up the steps, Phil crawled into the moonlight falling on the wooden dock.

He was stunned. "I was under the shipyard?" Manhattan

stood across the water, tall with electricity. Once again, he would be going back home drenched, riding the subway in a wet pool.

PHIL TICKS FOR PRESIDENT

In his dream, she was no longer a person at all. She came at him a shapeless dark thing, moving like black spilled ink that could speak with her voice. "Haven't you realized it yet, Phil?" she hissed. "This country isn't governed for the people, by the people. Haven't you noticed that there might be some reason to worry about that?"

"Listen, if you're trying to recruit me for the overthrow of our country, you've come to the wrong person! I fought for this country."

"Sure, Phil, and you fought the world to make sure that some people will be able to have all they want."

"Listen, I don't have to believe any of this! I'm not going to let you ruin my idea of America. I can be whatever I want to be in this country. I can be a detective because that's what I want to be. I could be president if I wanted!"

She was laughing at that. That struck her as funny, "Phil Ticks for President of the United States of America!" She kept laughing, all the while the dark of her moving, encircling him.

The only way out of it was to wake up.

He opened his eyes.

A branch was clawing on the window glass. Phil didn't know what to make of the dream. It was a part of his imagination.

The night, after a while, turned back into a happier dream of chickens and Phil was stacking them like stairs, leading them all up into space.

PORTRAIT OF PHIL TICKS AS CHARLIE CHAPLIN

That morning it was raining. She always picked the darkest part of the day to visit him, so there she was at the door with a dripping umbrella. Her shape barely came through all she wore; she was like the Invisible Woman, hiding herself with dark layers.

She came inside and sat down near the radiator in the corner. It steamed and made tapping noises as it turned the room warmer.

"You wouldn't believe what I have to tell *you*," Phil said from behind his desk. He put the newspaper Funnies page down after he finished Popeye.

She said, "You wouldn't believe what I have to tell you."

"Well, you better go first then."

"Phil, we found out how they're doing it." A photo came out of her bag. "They've designed a machine that can control people's minds. It can brainwash them!" She showed him the picture and it clicked.

"That's the thing!" It was the silver tube he had been wired to underwater. "That's the thing I found!"

"You found this?!"

"Yes. I was doing some research and I discovered it underneath a dock."

"Phil, this is how they plan on taking over America! This thing is a brainwashing machine. It sends out rays that control people! Where did you find it?"

"At the shipyard." Phil played it cool, let it roll off his back as he tried to light a cigarette and throw the match over into the wastebasket. "That's what you pay me for, lady. I'm just doing my job."

He noticed her attention was elsewhere, on the wall papered with photos and certificates he had bought and stuck there.

"What the—?" She was staring at a photo nailed to a wall. "Is that—? This is you?"

"Yeah. I did a photo shoot a while back. It was for a department store, they needed a model." He leaned back in his chair, striking the pose calmly before again lighting a match to cigarette.

"Are you trying to be Charlie Chaplin?"

"It was some publicity stunt. I don't know…I figured what the hell. It paid."

"You surprise me, Phil Ticks." The way she placed herself around in the shadows was uncanny. She could hide herself in the shadow of a lamp. Or was she making her own shadows? "This isn't the first time." She stood up. "But now I have to get going. I must report the location of the machine to our people. This proves what we thought all along."

"That's right."

"Before I leave though, I need a cigarette. You still have that lighter?"

"Oh…" Phil kept his hand on the drawer, "No. I took it home. I have matches though." He took them out of his pocket and threw them across his desk to her.

Her hand came out of the darkness and caught them. "Thanks."

Not a bad catch, Phil thought.

"What we'll have you do now, Phil," she took money out of that dark coat, "Is get you on an airplane to San Francisco as soon as you're ready, so you can find that other machine. We know there's another one hidden out there somewhere."

"Flying doesn't bother me. I can be ready in a couple hours." The money was almost too much for him to bear.

CITY OF COLD FISH

It was meant to be put in the water, a submersible metal tube rounded at both ends. Phil called it The Aquatic Hot Dog. "For lack of a better name," he mumbled, as he wrote in his notebook ledger on the way to the airport, "This is The Case of the Aquatic Hot Dog."

She had him going back and forth from coast to coast, New York to San Francisco and back again, looking for clues. Phil would have been too cheap to fly on airplanes, but his client was paying all expenses. Still, "I'm a man who looks for the best bargain," he told the woman at the ticket window.

Silver airliners hummed out on the runway concrete, moving slowly to places up in the air.

Phil was beginning to warm to her, the Pan Am damsel in her snug blue uniform and long blonde hair. "So how long have you been working here?" he tried.

"Long enough to hear it all. Sir, if you leave on the midnight flight, you'll arrive in San Francisco in the afternoon. That's as cheap as you can do it." She was all matter of fact.

Phil nodded. He took out his wallet and paid with a slow hand. "Well, let's see..." He rolled up his sleeve and took a quick look at his broken wristwatch. "It's still early now..." with a hopeful peek at her icy eyes he continued, "Where will I eat dinner?"

"You can try the airport lounge. Or if that's too expensive, try a sandwich vendor." She passed him the stamped ticket and called, "Next!"

A family trying to get to Toronto pushed Phil aside with their heavy plaid bags.

"Talk about a cold fish," Phil muttered. He tried to find a cigarette in his empty pocket. "This city's full of cold fish."

The windows shook as a DC-3 turned itself around outside. "Now I've got six hours to kill."

Next to the shoeshine stand was a man selling sandwiches

from a cart, waiting there near the window, with a folded umbrella over it.

Phil asked him, "How much for a cheese on rye?"

"We don't got that, suh."

"No cheese on rye?"

"No suh."

"How about cheese on wheat?"

"No suh."

"Well, lemme have a cheese on white then."

"Yes suh. That's thirty cents exactly."

"Thirty cents!" Phil took out his wallet and shook some change into his palm. "Got anything to drink?"

"The finest cola in New York."

"Got any root beer?"

"No suh."

"Any coffee?"

"No suh."

"No coffee??"

"No suh."

"Well, I guess I'll have a cola then." Phil paid the man and took his dinner over next to a big window, to watch the airplanes arrive from Europe and Middle America like loud birds filled with people.

THE GREAT WAR

San Francisco was sunk deep in fog, piled two hundred feet tall. The mist blew right off the gray water and opened and closed around Phil like a ghostly book. Pirates of fog climbed the hill and made running shapes moving around him.

Phil cupped his hands around his mouth and hollered at the cliffs, "Hello!" His voice came back a moment later, an echo fuzzy and covered with barnacles.

"Hello San Francisco!"

And it returned, "—Ncisco, sco, o, o..." disappearing smaller towards Japan.

"What are you yelling for?" There was someone real next to him, dressed in rags. "You trying to wake the dead?"

"Oh sorry, I didn't see you."

"You ought to show a little respect. I'll have you know, I fought in The Great War."

"Well, I fought in that war too."

"You? You were barely a baby then!"

"Listen friend, I saw action in the Pacific! I've got the scars to prove it!" He started to roll up his sleeve. Phil was tired and feeling testy. He was sick of being pushed around.

"The Pacific!" The echoes were dueling each other on the way over the water and back. "I was in the trenches of Europe. I—"

"We would have been blessed to have a trench!" Phil interrupted, throwing his weight a little into the old man, getting a good stare down into his pale eyes. "They dropped us off boats, made us swim ashore through bullets and explosions and dead bodies. We had to shoot our way up the mined beach through barbed wire, clear a path into the jungle. There were booby traps and—"

"Booby traps! We had poison mustard gas! And *miles* of barbed wire and mines and rats and diseases and no food for days!" His words echoed hysterically, "for days, days, -ays.." into the fog and turned into his coughing.

Phil watched into that fog, the way it made shapes that twisted and turned into other things. They could almost be animals
sometimes, becoming quiet, the fog flipped between them.

The old man watched Phil take out a cigarette and asked
between coughs, "Can you spare one?"

Phil handed him one and lit a match for them both.

The echo of the match snap into fire was so small. In Japan,
it rolled up onto the beach, exhausted, a month later.

DOGTOWN

It's a long way, driving through the fog and trees from San Francisco to get to the town of Dogtown: Population 30, Elevation 180. The sign greeted him after an hour of hairpin turns, with cliffs that fell to the ocean hundreds of feet below.

Phil was grateful she was paying for his expenses. It was part of their deal, but why couldn't she have got him a hotel in the city? "This must have been to test of my driving abilities," Phil decided.

Finally, he parked at the Dogtown Inn and it was deep night.

Ten thousand crickets had sewn up the seams of the town so that no light came in. There was just the sound of their steady, electrical chirping.

Phil did a zombie-walk, with his arms outstretched in front of him so he wouldn't stumble and land on his face as he crept towards the Inn's front door. His feet made a lot of noise through the dead leaves.

He tripped up the wooden steps and fell against the door.

A dog barked inside, just on the other side.

"Is anyone home?" Phil called, "Besides the dog?"

He listened through the barking and could hear someone's footsteps. The dog stopped barking.

The door opened.

"Good evening." The shape of a man with round dark glasses shuffled aside, making room for Phil to enter the dark room.

"Evening, mister," Phil paused, remembering that if he could learn to talk like a movie detective, it might make him better. He tried to crack wise, "The eclipse is over. You can take off your sunglasses."

The man let the dog out and closed the door. "I'm blind."

Phil bumped into a chair.

"I'll turn on a light for you though." He pulled the cord on a small lamp and a dim pale illuminated the room. There were paintings on the walls for windows and the caretaker made his

59

way gracefully around all the furniture to the front desk.

Phil tried again, "You get many visitors to Dogtown?" The guestbook was open on the counter and he scrawled his name in wide loops.

"No."

THE FALL OF THE INN OF DOGTOWN

It was never very light at the Dogtown Inn. Even when night had passed, the morning hardly brought any sun to the place.

Phil reached across his lumpy bed and turned on the lamp next to him. Only a sort of nightlight orange warmed the deep shadows of the room. None of the light bulbs seemed to want to give any light.

"Is this whole hotel blind?" Phil asked the walls.

There was a mixed-up portrait of Edgar Allan Poe near the door. Phil hadn't noticed it last night. The features were all distorted and painted at wrong angles, still it had to be that great American author, there was no doubt.

Phil said, "Why did the Black Widow send me here?" That was his new name for his mysterious dark client. To give things some kind of order, he needed to name everything. So she was The Black Widow, spinning this case like spider web around him.

Phil threw off the blanket and got up, stumbling a little on his way to the window. He parted the black velvet drapes and heaved open the window. It was past nine o'clock. He had checked his watch to make sure, but the sun didn't want to bring itself to this pocket town in the woods.

The fog climbed in through the opening, breathed into the room, enveloped Phil and turned the dark into gray, a mountain top in Peru.

Phil had to rely on his other senses. He felt his way back to the foot of the bed, put on his pants thrown on the floor and smelled for his socks.

"This place is nuts," Phil told his reflection in the cloudy mirror. He finished dressing and slung on his shoulder holster. The gun made itself known under his suit coat. When he drove into San Francisco, he would be prepared.

He reached for the door, knowing where it must be, walking like Frankenstein into the mist. Igor turned out to be the table

61

he ran into, his first victim a vase of papery flowers that fell to the floor.

Phil wasn't good at navigating in the dark. He could sympathize with the Titanic and her sinking, hobbling with a hand on his pain.

The wall hit him and he felt for the door handle. It had to be close, somewhere by the painting of Poe which seemed to glow out of the fog.

He found the door and opened the fog into the hall. Music drifted ghostly up the stairs towards him, step by step.

A scratchy record was playing from down there and then it stopped.

"Mister Ticks, are you a fan of music?" The inn owner, who Phil couldn't even see, addressed him.

Phil moved. "Yeah, I guess so. I like the Charleston and the Big Band scene." There couldn't be anyone that close to him, but as he reached out for the stair handrail, he hit flesh instead.

"Good morning, Mister Ticks."

Phil pulled his hand back. "Good morning!" The touch had been so cold, like granite or slate. "Is it always so dark around here?"

"It seems to be. Come, tell me what you think of my latest composition. I need someone besides my dog to hear it."

Last night, the inn keeper had introduced himself as Fred Lowry, The Blind Whistling Virtuoso. Now he wanted to perform.

"Look, Fred," Phil explained, "I'm not that good at music. If I can dance to it with a pretty dame, I like it. Other than that, I—"

"Just give it a listen, Mister Ticks." Fred led him descending the winding stairs. Fog followed them down.

"You ever think of getting any lights for this place, Fred?"

Fred was downstairs, ahead of Phil, moving through the dark with perfect knowledge. "Decca Records has already expressed an interest."

There was a piano shape somewhere down there in the dark and Fred sat down and began to play.

Nocturnal bat-winged organ music filled the dungeon of the room.

Phil began to edge himself across the wall. It clung to his back. A framed painting tugged at his coat. The painful dark music pushed at him, it was a battle to move against this force. Then Fred's eerie whistle rippled through the church keyboard sound.

Phil was pulling himself the last five feet to the door, crawling by the time he got to the handle, and he collapsed outside off the porch.

A hot wind blew the leaves up and over him. Fred's music was still clawing at him, he wasn't safe yet. Something crushed the fallen leaves.

Out of nowhere came the leaping dog, growling and snapping at him. Phil managed to dodge out of its way as it chased him to his car. It bit him on the leg while he fumbled to get inside. Phil kicked back at the gnashing thing and slammed the door shut.

There was only darkness where the Dogtown Inn had stood, as Phil started the car, backed onto the winding driveway, but that was how it had always been.

THE WALLS HAVE EARS

She was right. For this case, you had to believe anything could happen. It was no longer a matter of what was possible and what wasn't.

He needed a new way of looking at things: a detective is supposed to be able to do that. He flipped through the phone book, letting the pages go past. Phil pretended to be looking for clues.

Past all the Orthodontists, Car Dealerships, and Greenhouses, he landed on Restaurants and, because it made him hungry, he began to read the names of them.

American Hamburgers, Hong Kong Diner, Garage Food, Maynard Overall's Fried Chicken, Caspar's Hot Dogs...

So, San Francisco has a Caspar's Hot Dogs too! What a coincidence. It was something to take note of. At the very least, he'd be able to eat there. And it wasn't far away...and it didn't take long to arrive.

The name was the same, but the place was different, bigger. Phil was seated in a booth by the sullen waitress. He asked her in his best attempt at Bogart, "Is this the kind of a restaurant where people like to drive by the windows and shoot customers?"

"No."

"Good. That wouldn't be good." He was a little worried. No movie detective worth his salt relied so heavily on cheap jokes, but he didn't know how else to handle these things. Phil made himself comfortable, unloaded a cigarette into his palm while she stood there watching. The menu wasn't that interesting. He sighed, "I guess all I want is a coffee. It's been a long day of not really getting anywhere."

"Did you have a bad day?" she asked.

"Don't ask."

"Oh, I'm sorry."

"I'm thinking of quitting the detective business."

"You're a detective!" That was magic to her. Suddenly she was almost sitting in the booth with him.

"Shhh, not so loud. The walls have ears."

"Right," she whispered. "Sorry." She came closer to him, "It must be exciting though."

"Yeah, it has its rewards." He relit his cigarette and thought deeply, staring at the fan. "It's become my second nature."

"I bet you could tell me things about myself that I haven't even noticed. All the clues I'm showing, without even knowing."

"You ever read the horoscopes in the paper?"

"Of course."

"I could tell you more about your day than them."

"Really?" She did sit down in the booth with him. "Can you read my palm?"

He took her hand. "Well, I could. But that's not really my specialty."

"What is your specialty?" Her hand stayed with him.

"Well, I'll tell you what it isn't," he laughed, "It isn't ship-yards." He had been waiting for a chance at banter.

She whispered, "Is that what you're doing here, you're detecting?"

"I'm trying to solve, uhhh…I really shouldn't talk about it, you might be a communist," but he couldn't stop from smiling.

Leaning over the table towards him, she said in his ear, "Long live the workers."

"I knew it!"

"Long live the revolution!"

He was grinning, "You're a Red!"

She stood and held up her arm,

65

"Give me your tired, your poor, your huddled masses struggling to be free!"

He laughed, "You're a Bolshevik!" It was in all the papers, The Red Scare was supposed to be the new black plague. The politicians were predicting a Third World War any day.

"A what?"

"You know," he whistled and threw an imaginary Molotov cocktail, "A bomb-tosser."

"Of course! All the time. Bombs and me go hand in hand." Then it struck her, "You're a good detective."

"Thank you."

"And I bet I can guess you want a hotdog, right?"

"No, actually I just want a coffee."

"Oh, of course! I forgot. I'll be right back."

THE SECOND ANCHOR

It was too close to a movie he'd seen, the way he left her inside the silver Caspar's restaurant and walked out into the fog on the streets.

He left with her phone number tucked in his pocket. She didn't want him to leave, she wanted him to stay until her shift ended, but he told her how important this case was. The way he described it, the fate of America rested with Phil Ticks and there just wasn't a second to waste.

I'll give her a call when this is all wrapped up, he thought. Then maybe we'll get to know each other.

Phil went to a park, for concentration, to think out all that was going on.

The sky was blue and he sat in the warm sun, surrounded by birds and the wandering shuffle of lost men wearing heavy coats that sunk their shoulders down. There were three of them, going by in different directions, quietly moving through space, past the planet Earth. Phil was lost in his own problems though—theirs were far away—he had to figure out this case. There had to be a way it could make sense.

Pigeons were untying his shoes, pecking at the laces. He kicked at them and one of his shoes flew off with the scattering birds, into the air and over a hedge.

That was how he found out his client was around. He had to rely on strokes of this kind of luck, like his shoes, to discover things that really mattered.

He saw her on the other side of the hedge, walking with an umbrella decorated with silk pictures. "So," he whispered, "The Black Widow is in San Francisco…" It was a very interesting development.

Quietly, he pulled his shoe from the leaves, shook out the gravel and decided to follow her as she walked slowly on her way towards the ocean.

The path through the park afforded him plenty of trees to

hide behind while he shadowed her, but when the park ended, they were back in the city and he had to keep a little more distance between himself and her. If she turned around, she had to see an anonymous man wearing an overcoat and hat, looking in a store window.

She led him past the freighters unloading mahogany from Africa, spices and silk from Asia, past more cargo ships from all over the planet. There were warehouses on their right and the piers running over the ocean to the left. Phil had to duck behind a forklift when she stopped to talk to a sailor from the Far East.

He couldn't hear what they were saying. The sky was filled with crying seagulls.

Elegantly, she walked over the spilled oil and ropes, spinning the umbrella to keep the sun of the setting day off of her. There was a blue neon light she seemed to be making for. The sky was turning unbelievable purple and orange as the sun went back into the ocean.

Phil thought it was a mirage. He stopped and stared, but mirages usually disappear.

The light above the door formed the shape of an anchor.

The windows were boarded up haphazardly. The building had too much to drink. It looked exactly like The Anchor back in New York.

She disappeared inside, under the blue neon sign.

A moment passed while he searched in his pockets for a cigarette. It was bent, but Phil straightened the tobacco and lit it.

Smoke moved like he would, towards The Anchor.

When he opened the door, everything was a duplicate. It was a west coast mirror of the tavern in the east. And the most puzzling thing, everything else inside was the same too. The music, the smoke, even the people inside, it was all from memory. If there was any chance of him solving this case, things had to make more sense than this.

And there she sat, his client, in the same booth with Knarr. Phil bet he was bragging about the Philippines again. But Phil wasn't about to go and listen. There was a bump on his head from the last time. He still had no idea how it happened, it could have been the place itself had knocked him out.

Phil stood near the door and thought.

Everything seemed to have its other half: there was a mirror Anchor and also another Caspar's Hot Dogs. Then somewhere in this city there must also be another brainwashing machine, probably under the shipyards too! Was that his next stop? It made Phil a little scared to be in The Anchor again, to be part of this dangerous mirror. With his mind racing to the next step, he quickly left.

JAPAN

Out on the beach, Phil made a long shadow of himself that moved into the Pacific from the sand. When people aren't careful, they make mistakes. I could have been blackjacked and ended up attached to that Aquatic Hot Dog again, he realized.

A foghorn out in the darkness blew.

Something shined like an eye watching Phil. Sometimes storms, the pull of the ocean and wind, landed them here—Japanese fishing boats used the glass floats to keep their nets from sinking. If a net got cut by a steamship propeller, or tore with a heavy catch of fish, the glass buoys would float free on the current all the way to America.

When Phil picked it up off the sand and looked through the thick melon of glass, a crystal ball vision appeared: America was warped and turned upside down and ocean made a blue spinning curve of sunset colors.

Another color, with a strange shape, a little genie samurai floated inside and in a second's passing, made itself appear on the sand.

Phil was waiting for him to say, "Master, I thank you for saving my life and freeing me from my glass prison. In return I shall grant you three wishes," but then Phil looked past the shining of the Imperial uniform and into the spirit's face. It was the same face that had watched him pull the trigger during the war.

The soldier held out his hand again.

Wordlessly (he had been waiting for this to happen) Phil brought a wrapper of papers out of a pocket. "This is what you want from me, isn't it? I figured it out. And you can have it." He uncovered the ribboned war medal and passed it to the ghost.

Wasn't it that part of the past that made him so scared of the present? If he had never gone to war, no killing would have ever been done. Before 1941, he never thought of Japan in a terrible way—to him, Japan was a place of tilted roofs, kimonos

70

and flowers, just like this dead soldier probably had cowboy visions of America—why should that become reason to kill? He wanted to tell the ghost to stop haunting him, "I'm not the cause of wars, I don't start wars," but he knew that was no good. The ghost would just hold up a mirror and there would be Phil Ticks in a uniform with a rifle and bullets, obeying orders, shooting to kill, the perfect soldier. He could have said, "If I refused to fight I might not have gone, I could have spent those years in a federal prison. Either way they're going to control me." What it all came down to was if no one wanted to shoot at him, the ghost wouldn't be here, the ghost would have been a person at home in a small town on the coast of Japan, fishing or tying kites, or whatever happens in a country thousands of miles away. If Phil had refused to go to war, Japan to him would still be a thing with white cranes flying in the place of a ghost.

The pale hand took the medal and the colors of ghost spun themselves back into the glass. And when it all stopped turning, Phil could see his medal inside the ball.

It slid around inside when Phil moved it in his palm, when he reached back with his right arm, and flung it as far as he could towards Japan.

THE ACCIDENT

By not paying attention, Phil saw the pale building and the American flag. He opened the iron door to go inside and collect his Veterans benefit check. He was broke again. It came to this.

There were a lot of people standing in line, waiting with envelopes all ready.

Phil thought he would be friendly and he talked to the woman next to him, "Where did you see action?"

She was fiercely ignoring him, her tight mouth and eyes staring straight ahead to the window, relying on the determination of her willpower to make him disappear.

"These are my papers," Phil said as he took them from his pocket and waved them a little. He could tell that she wasn't interested. She doesn't care that I got a medal for shooting a Japanese officer, that I was decorated for bravery.

The line moved forward. Phil cleared his throat.

It was awfully quiet now, just the stamping of letters from the front of the room.

Phil made his way out of the line, against the tide and stares, back to the door. He finally realized where he was. People were paying for postage stamps.

The Post Office looked just like the Veterans Memorial Building! They were both made out of the same heavy white 1930s stone.

He read the big black letters above the entrance, "U.S. Post Office," and he asked it, "Well, why didn't you say so?"

Across the street, around the corner, he headed for the next marble building. This was the Veterans Building. Not only was the flag there, but there was also a cannon, freshly painted, squatting on the lawn like a lion. Twenty years ago, when there wasn't such a need for cannons, someone must have pulled it there to make the place look like a post office.

Phil took out his papers again and went though the metal door.

There weren't any children in this gray room. A line with men in wheelchairs, on crutches, scarred, blind, or haunted others like him. They all filled the room with a different quiet of after war.

He waited for his check like everyone else, a part of that silence, and then went outside, where there were cars in streets and open stores and all the different people doing their shopping.

When the policeman yelled at him, he was adrift with his memory, about to go into the bank and cash his check. "Stop!" The cop was pulling out a ticket book as he approached Phil. "There's a law against jaywalking." He scribbled on the pad.

"What?"

"You got some identification?"

"I don't understand what I did? I just crossed the street."

"Where did you cross the street?" He stopped writing and stared hard, like Boris Karloff, into Phil's eyes.

"Just there."

"Where exactly?"

"In the middle of street?" Phil was feeling faint.

"Where?" The cop pretended to have gone deaf. He turned his head with his hand to his ear, leaning closer.

"The middle of the street."

"That's right. And that means that you jaywalked. Which is against the law."

"I'll try not to do it again," Phil mumbled.

"You'll try?"

"Of course."

"Do you know the difference between trying and doing?"

Phil didn't want to say the wrong thing. He froze up.

The pen dropped out of the officer's hand. It bounced and stuck to the cement. "Pick that up."

Phil did. He put it on the open gloved hand.

"That's the difference between trying and doing." He let a pause grow between that and his next sentence. Black clouds,

73

vines with thorns, and badgers overturning rusting horseshoes lived in that space. "Now, let me see some identification."

Phil felt light. He wasn't there. His shadow had taken control of his body. He fumbled in his inside pocket, his hand touched metal. Shaking all over, the gun fell out of its holster.

In another world's gravity, slower, Phil had time to see it fall, watch the officer's face, see the gun falling, look back at the face, cartoon motion, as the gun hit the ground finally and went off with a Bang!

Now people were screaming in the streets, cars swerved, the policeman was collapsed on the ground crying over his shoe and Phil fled in horror.

The blast echoed in his skull and held to every step he took like running through gunpowder. He sprinted across streets, down sidestreets, across parking lots, in front of store windows. People darted around him, and he ran until he fell down behind a gnarled tree grown foot by crooked foot with the same sort of black terror, there in the dark behind a furniture store.

Panting, "When I get out of this shade..." he looked around himself...A wrecked car joined him on blocks against the fence...The tree had dropped its small hard green apples all across the dirt..."There's going to be some explaining to do."

Not just one black cat, but two, sat there on the fence above Phil. They waited and watched with their yellow eyes for him to do something.

MEANWHILE, NEAR LAS VEGAS

In the quiet night, her yellow reading lamp was on, lighting up her small window, as the saucer landed in the field next to the pond.

THE CHICKEN KING

Phil kept to the shadow made by the tree, with his back resting on the brick wall of the furniture store. He got to know all the small biting ants. They made streams going around the tree trunk, across the wall and ground and they used Phil as a bridge.

Hours ago, the police sirens had begun the search for him. He could still hear them prowling as the sky became darker. A little longer and it would be night enough for him to try and escape.

How am I going to explain that accident? Phil dug at another ant under his belt. It was the sort of mistake anyone could make. He hadn't meant to shoot the cop in the foot, it just happened.

There is a time and a place for everything, but shooting a cop by accident just doesn't fit in. He knew that. In the dirt back lot of the furniture store, with the explosion and yelling still ricocheting, he knew it had been the wrong thing to do.

Phil let his mind wander, away from this and The Case of the Aquatic Hot Dog, back as far as he could go.

His imagination was becoming a circle. It was taking him from the past, to where he was, and on through that, to the future. He thought of his dream then, growing up, how he could become the town hero, the Chicken King. It was his opinion that if he could make chickens useful for something other than eggs, he could be a millionaire. They were just standing around all of the day, wasting time. And there were so many of them across the country. Couldn't they be doing something else between eggs, something productive? What was it he wanted them to do? He couldn't remember. What did he know, he was only a boy? It was some fantastic idea that never went anywhere. Only he and the green cheese of the moon believed that chickens could fly.

Ants biting both his legs woke him back up. Phil Ticks was one colossal hamburger to them.

The moon and the stars and a faraway police siren were the night.

He stood up and dusted himself off and rubbed at the itchy red bumps all over him. Another day like this and I'm quitting for good. He still had dreams to fall back on.

Faraway, but like a lighthouse in the dark, The Anchor called for him. It seemed to be his best hiding place. That impossible mirror could have hid the lost city of Atlantis.

Back out on the streets, Phil thought of Black Widow and he moved like a spider in every shadow that spilled towards the docks.

THE PERFECT AMERICAN

There was something he was wondering—things were so full of coincidence—wouldn't he probably find the other Aquatic Hot Dog under the shipyards? Just like the first one?

It seemed to make sense. It was deduction, an adding up of clues.

And wouldn't that surprise her, he thought, if he could find the machine, actually tell her where it was hidden and then take her there? All the dark mystery would be over.

The Anchor was all the way at the end of America, right near the ocean, and he stood hidden in the shadows across the street from it, planning the best way to get from darkness, across the lit up street to the blue front door.

Then another darker blackness overtook him. He was knocked unconscious.

There were no dreams, just emptiness, until he woke up again.

"We've had our eye on you Phil. We've been watching you." She stepped out of the shadows with a lamp.

For the first time, Phil could see her.

Her long black hair framed down the gold kimono she was wearing. She looked Japanese. "And we've been testing you, Phil Ticks."

Phil tried to move, but couldn't. His arms and legs were pinned down. He was tied against the other Aquatic Hot Dog, half-submerged in water. "What's going on?"

"Let me carve your initials in him!" Knarr suggested, starting to take a knife out of a sheath.

"No," she stopped him. "That's all right, Knarr."

Phil breathed a sigh of relief.

"He won't need any initials where he's going."

"What do you mean?"

"You're sitting on a bomb, Phil."

"What? This thing?" He could hear the ticking, barely, coming from underwater.

She explained, "This is a new kind of bomb. It's much more powerful than your Atomic bomb."

"No wonder you kept to the shadows so much and hid your face with veils and wide hats."

Her long black hair flowed down her shoulders and shined as she laughed, "Some detective you are, Phil Ticks."

I just had the feeling that I could trust you, he thought. And he said, "You were some actor, lady. You almost had me fooled. Well, I was wrong about you, that's all."

"That's all?" she laughed, "You're stuck to a bomb and you say, 'That's all!' That's true, Phil. For once, you're right. That's all for you."

"How about R.I.P?" Knarr asked. "How's that instead of your initials?"

If he could have been one of those black and white detectives, he would have had a way out of this. There wouldn't be any problem getting out of this and then tracking her down, ending her plans for global domination, or at least for the end of America. Then there would have been a tickertape parade for him, instead of him becoming tickertape. He would be scattered over the city in pieces. The Aquatic Hot Dog ticked next to him.

Phil despaired, "Why are you tying me up to this bomb? What do I have to do with this?"

"You wouldn't understand how it works. It might as well be invaders from Mars. But I can tell your part in this: You're the trigger. You're what will make the bomb go off." She whispered like a candle going out, "Of all the people, you were the perfect one."

Knarr tossed his scrimshaw knife from hand to hand.

"You see…This kind of bomb…" she walked around him on the shore of broken wood, casting far shadows inside the cavern with the lamp, "It doesn't explode like most bombs. This bomb will not leave terrible radioactivity and burn up everything in sight. This bomb will destroy only Americans."

"What are you talking about?" Phil struggled.

"We needed the average American, so it would know who to kill. When it detonates, very soon, you and all the people like you will disappear."

"Me? I'm nothing like the average American!"

"We look out on the streets and all we see is you! We've searched and found people like you all over the country. Now you're the bomb to all these people, all over America, ready to go off. Phil, you can think of yourself as the end of America."

"No, I won't. That's crazy!"

"Your country doesn't realize how useful you are," she laughed. She let the words sting there a little longer with him trapped, with the bomb and all of the people of the shipyard and country to destroy.

Phil's movie was ending. He could tell. People would watch him flicker out on the screen, turn into black, into credits, then it would be gone. Some popcorn and candy wrappers may be left for him as flowers on the floor.

"You'll never get away with this!" he shouted.

"Of course we will. You've already fused the bomb in New York and now that one and this one will soon go off together. Thanks to you, America is through!" She waved, "Sayonara!" and left.

"See you!" said Knarr, following behind her, locking the iron door.

Phil rattled the chains. He could move his hands only a little.

America ticked like a huge bomb.

"She thinks I'm the typical American?" Phil couldn't believe it. "I've been rejected by America all along." He sweated and strained. "I've had to fight against everything here my whole life."

Maybe—it came to him like lightning—that's the way to defuse these bombs!

The wires of the bomb were connected to him.

He would have to imagine, think hard and picture everything about America differently than he had before. It would be difficult. It wouldn't be easy to think of America as something it wasn't. But it was the only way to go on living.

AN ENTOURAGE
OF TRAVELS
AND CIRCUS SIDE-
SHOW ATTRACTIONS

Introduction from August 26, 2003:

An Entourage of Travels and Circus Sideshow Attractions. That title is from a dead friend, from a poem he wrote that I want to remain. What I see are many wonders, poetry, laughing at words, the strange beauty of colorized movies (watch the backgrounds, you'll see dreams) the clay Buster Keaton statue he made (where did it go?) *The Invasion of the Bodysnatchers* we rented from the library, apples, going down alleys, stories, the hidden wonders of America under the paint and TV sound, dawn, all that's sad and goodbye, wooden steps, window, riding at night, a ceiling with tree branches, and finally a ghost. Some go back any way they can to somewhere else, some survive here. Here in America 2003, things are rough in the world of the dark ages, time is repeating. The past goes away, but it leaves a shadow.

It's also a book about being young, broken hearts and bad jobs and failing in love. The Phil Ticks romance novel! And Phil is in trouble again.

Contents

The Atlantic Monthly published a series on "Lincoln the Lover" in 1928. The articles were based on a cache of recently discovered correspondences between Abraham Lincoln and Ann Rutledge, letters that neatly verified the legend that Lincoln and Rutledge had been sweethearts since their early twenties. The letters turned out to be the efforts of a San Diego columnist, Wilma Minor. Before the hoax was discovered, Minor had taken in the editors of the illustrious magazine and several respected Lincoln scholars. Even Carl Sandburg was duped. He wrote to Ellery Sedgewick, the editor of *The Atlantic Monthly,* "These new letters seem entirely authentic—and preciously and wonderfully coordinated and chime with all else known of Lincoln." When Minor was found out, it was also discovered that her daughter had participated in the hoax. Her daughter justified the conspiracy by explaining the letters were based upon messages she had received from the spirit of Lincoln and Rutledge.

—*The Writer's Home Companion*

ANOTHER IN A LONG SERIES OF DREAMS

He woke up his eyes to his mail-order bride. She was there beside him, with long dark hair.

No, he was still on the train. It was another in a long series of dreams.

But it would be happening soon. By tomorrow morning, by the time the next sun was arriving, he would be with her.

The window rocked the land. He stared out over the frozen yellow slant of Montana and he thought about her. He didn't know much about her beyond her name. He didn't even know what she looked like really—all he had was a photograph—he only knew that when he got off the train, she would be waiting for him. Everything had been arranged.

The way he pictured her was with an umbrella, wearing a flowing silk white kimono, smiling anxiously for him on the train platform. Slowly—everything would be in slow motion—from the way the crowd moved around her with their gray shapes and the way her eyes and his would meet and root. He wouldn't need to say, "I'm Phil Ticks, I sell vacuum cleaners," she would already know everything. It would be in the stars.

The train slowed into the Indian reservation. There were battered houses and stores and wrecks of cars along the tracks and a dog that howled at the sound of the squeaking wheels. Nobody got off the train and it was moving again in a minute, back along the fences and slow hills.

I wish I could get her out of my mind for a while, he smiled, so I could rest. But he took out the folded piece of newspaper from his coat pocket again.

This was how they had met. *Oriental Brides Incorporated. Beautiful, faithful women of the Orient.* The type was blurring itself into the softness of the paper. His fingers had gone over it so many times. *Beautiful, faithful women of the Orient seek American men for marriage and life.*

He looked up from the poem to the cold land. An icy river

filled with car rust and abandoned machines. Jagged mountains. Clouds.

I hope this works out, he thought. If it does, it would be the first thing that has. The newspaper turned back into folds in his palm as he put it back in his pocket. It's got to work out. Lots of people do this and live happily ever after with their Japanese wives in small towns across America.

There could be someone in that cabin there who did the same thing. They're eating rice cakes, drinking instant Sanka coffee, a warm woodstove letting all that smoke climb out their chimney. Children raised on Godzilla...

He felt like asking the train to hurry, he urged it through the scenery, "Faster, faster!" Montana was taking way too long to get through.

FILLED WITH STEAM

The train rolled into the station and rolled over her. Phil didn't even know at first. She fell into the train steel with the flowers she was holding and the wheels went right into her and through her.

It was hard to tell that anything terrible had occurred, the passengers all stood up and got their bags and departed.

He got off the train and was pulled along with everyone else to the crowd at the front of the train, thick into all the people and whatever happened. It was not far away.

What had happened was carried back, whispered, passed along from person to person. "A woman fell in front of the train..." Someone added, "She was pushed!" and "A Japanese woman. She's been killed!"

Her long black hair, flowed on the track, was all he saw. Then he was shoved back with the rest of the passengers, behind a rope they set up. It was hard to see through all the people and he couldn't tell for sure if it was her, but he knew it had to be.

He had the photograph of her folded in his pocket.

Before we could even get to know each other, it's too late.

There was nothing he could have done to save her from that.

The people were damming up like water against the cordon at the edge of the rail and he was being sucked backwards as more people moved in. He let them push him backwards, he couldn't resist, he was weightless, he just kept falling away.

And just like every other time, he began to dream to turn it off. Against the wall and away from them, he could return to dreaming anytime. He had the ability to turn himself off to this reality and America, as it appeared, was gone. He stood this way, waiting until it seemed safe to return.

The city was filled with steam, not just at the train station where he was standing with his suitcase, but everywhere the buildings were rolling with the fog. It came from the smoke-stacks and the ground itself.

The crowd had left the platform. Only a few people walked around. The ambulance was gone. The police had dispersed everyone who had seen it happen except for him. He was like a sign, hung there in a kind of statue shock that filled him up from his shoes.

MISSING

Phil turned the business card in his hand and read it over, *Jackie Wu's Wooden Imports. What Your Life Needs. Or Whatever Your Heart Desires.*

That was all it said. I guess I'll find it on my own, he thought…By accident or just because I'm meant to when the time is ready. I didn't even see who gave it to me. That's very strange, where did this card come from? All that time at the train station, standing there, someone could have handed me the moon to hold and I wouldn't have known.

He wondered, Maybe I caught it out of the wind? Maybe it just fell into my hand from the sky? No…Someone definitely gave it to me for a purpose. He brought the card down to his stare and read it again. It had changed from the last time he looked at it. Now it was printed with different words: *Mr. Wu's Love Remover.* Phil stopped walking and read the rest of the words: *Magic Makes Haunting Love Disappear.*

He put the card away in his pocket. It was more than he could take. He thought he might be going crazy.

For a moment he stopped and watched the birds pecking away at something on the road. When a car drove past, they scattered around Phil. He ducked under the sleeve of his coat and started walking again. Days might have passed.

He didn't know this city. It didn't matter where he was going. This city was supposed to have been the start of something new.

If it wasn't for signs, he wouldn't know what to do. Like origami wrapped around the telephone pole, a sign made him stop to read. There were cranes flying around a mushroom cloud: *Hiroshima Remembrance And Peace With Japan Day.*

There was also a photo at the bottom of the paper, the same photo she had sent to him. It was her standing there when she was very much alive. *"Memorial. Her life will surely be missed…"* he read aloud from the poster. There was an event happening tomorrow morning, he noted, along with the address. He wrote

95

it on a scrap of paper and stuffed it into his coat pocket.

I guess I will stay in this town one more night, he thought. Then I'm getting out of here as quickly as possible, on the fastest moving train back to my vacuum cleaners.

THE GOLDEN BRIDGE

She was stepping across the bridge that branched over the stream, paddling with slow carp and the big leaves of water lilies.

Phil watched her walking, carrying a horseshoe of flowers in her arms and he thought it was strange that she was delivering that wreath, a garland for a horse race winner, to a cemetery. Yes, it even had a blue ribbon on it and the name of a horse.

Maybe his potential wife had been a fan of the races? He hadn't known anything about her, anything was possible.

The day so far had been a solemn event, Buddhist ritual and the quiet tolling of a gong on the hill. Rain clouds kept a gray, respectful distance on the horizon of mountains.

He had been crying and the weight of responsibility hung on him guiltily, as both Hiroshima and her death were mourned.

Suddenly, the woman with the flowers was retracing her steps quickly back over the bridge, clutching the wreath to her and crumpling the ribbon. She disappeared over the bend of wood.

A flower had fallen and plopped into the still water. The petals held together like a red hand.

Soon, her running footsteps came back over the golden bridge, carrying a new bouquet, more appropriate to a woman's funeral, white chrysanthemums.

OPTIMISM

"Looking for someone new, someone who won't hurt you like the last person did?" It should have been the question on a billboard, big enough for the entire city to see, blinking with neon and held captive in spotlights. Phil asked himself, "Where do I begin? How do I get myself to do this all over again? Why would I want to? Why not shut the door on the whole thing and retreat? Go back to the life of a salesman. I know what that life is. It's something I understand and I can predict like a time-clock. Day after day it's the same. And it's something I know I can do, I can't mess that up too easily."

"Would you like to buy a vacuum cleaner? No? Then I'll try the next door. Hello, ma'am. Would you like to buy a vacuum cleaner?"

He ceased walking and looked into the mirror of a department store window. Filled with mannequins and the silver reflection of himself, stopped and staring back, he was thinking, realizing the meaninglessness...selling vacuum cleaners. I'm not really doing anything with my life by doing that. I haven't really given anyone any real pleasure or care.

He looked at the lifeless dummies in the window. Truly, he found it difficult to move from them. A little bit longer and it became clear that he could join them, standing there frozen.

"No," he mumbled out loud. It's not the end of the world for me if the woman I was going to marry got hit by a train. I'm not going to give up because of that. I've learned something. I don't need to be hurt anymore to learn. This next time, he decided, I'll make sure we're both more careful, and he walked back among the living.

TRUST

Her eyes went to him and stayed with him. Then she looked away for a moment. But she looked back quickly.

"Hello," Phil's eyes said even though he still couldn't talk to her yet. She was the one he had first seen at the morning funeral and Hiroshima remembrance ceremony, and he thought she was beautiful. Like someone he had been waiting for, for centuries; she had been missing for that long. She was beautiful and he wanted to be with her. What more? It wasn't that hard to figure out, he was in love with her at first sight. He didn't know anything more about her, but isn't that what would happen next?

And she looked at him too.

They both might have said something.

It was strange. But what wasn't strange? This was at least something *good* that was strange. He felt alive to feel her presence. He wanted to talk to her, hear her voice, know that she was real.

All that happened in seconds.

She walked on past him, but their eyes had met, somewhere in their minds they had connected for that instant, and he thought of her long after she had disappeared from sight. He didn't want her to leave, but he knew they would meet again. He would be watching through all the other people in this city for her. She is somewhere around here. All the concrete would fall away and they would meet again.

CAT IN THE RAIN AND THE SUN

A very short woman stood in the rain calling for her cat, "Here Kitty." Faye stepped out of the bright doorway and walked into the parking lot. "Kitty!" She passed the garbage cans, filled with the things she had thrown away.

Now that her lover was gone, she had no use for the trombone he had left behind. She couldn't play it, her arms were too short. So there it stood against the garbage can like a brass Christmas tree. Her eyes avoided it. She was done with him.

"Kitty! Here, Kitty!" The rain went right through her slippers and bathrobe. One of her hands held her blue bathrobe tight.

All the black pavement shined with wet reflections of passing cars and yellow lights. The night city in the rain was not a good place for her old cat to be wandering.

She tipped her head to peer under a parked car. She looked behind a curtain of ivy hanging off the garage. "Kitty? I'm soaked, you crazy old cat!" She stamped her wet feet. "I'm going to go back inside now." She was in a monsoon, what else could she do? "But I'm going to leave the door open," she said to the night as she went back in to where she left off.

The cards were laid out in a circle on the plaid blanket. Whenever she needed answers to problems or wonderings, Faye shuffled the tarot cards. She concentrated and put them like sentences on the bed...A skeleton riding a horse, a moon shaped like a scythe, a maiden in a castle tower...They were things with meaning.

She stood next to the window, resting her elbows on the windowsill.

The rain falling for hours had made its tracks across the cold glass.

What a lighthouse job, to be watching for her old cat in danger out there still. She fell asleep with the front door open.

Morning steam rose off the ground. There was a kind of laundromat smell in the sunny air, birds chirping from the trees of the neighborhood.

The old cat had six toes on each of his front feet and lay on the warm damp pavement in front of the house where she gardened. The cat was dying. It didn't have long to live, breathing in slow gasps that made its skeleton show through its thin body. A Mexican woman came along, set down her grocery bag and scratched his fur while Faye weeded and planted flowers around the pavement.

Phil Ticks showed up there because he had seen the sign with the eye radiating lightning, and the promise of a guaranteed reading of your future.

She brought him inside and sat him down at the round table across from her.

"I need to know where I'm from and where I'm going," Phil said simply.

A small withered hand rustled through the opening in her dress, moving aside the flowers of it like a curtain as it drew a card from the deck. Faye Bonaparte, the gypsy owner of a third hand, gazed down at the card and shuddered. "You have been unhappily married to a woman taken to another planet. Your son has disappeared to another world. You are surrounded with mysteries, but the biggest mystery to you is how you survive day to day."

Phil Ticks stared. "Now tell me my future." And he passed more money to the small third hand.

It tugged it from him and vanished like a puppet-thing.

"The future..." she shuffled the tarot cards as if a calendar was turning pages ahead.

"Don't you need a crystal ball for that?" he asked.

"Everything is in the cards. You seem to think the answer may lay in love...There is a woman you came to this city to find...The first one was not the right one..." Her fingers moved over the picture of the maiden. "You know she is here, maybe she is part of all your dreams. Yes, you have seen her already... Be patient and careful, Mr. Ticks, and you will be with her."

SAVING THE DAY

Again, she was there with the flowers, but this time Phil was ready. For days and days, he had been thinking about her.

The traffic flew around him as he crossed the street and waited outside the door of the store for her to deliver the flowers and come back out.

It's alright, he thought. If I make a fool of myself what have I got to lose?"

The door swung open and there she was. She nearly walked into him.

"Hello," Phil said. "You deliver flowers?"

"Yes."

She didn't look like she was going to run away yet. Phil smiled. So far, so good..."I own a racehorse and I was wondering if you could make a wreath for me. For the horse, I mean."

"Sure. What's the horse's name?"

"Ummm...Tea Biscuit."

She laughed. "Nice name."

"Well...Honestly...It was the first name I could think of," he admitted. "I'm not that good at making up stories. I don't really have a racehorse."

"That's alright. I didn't think so." She smiled. "I've seen you around somewhere, hmm?"

"The Hiroshima Remembrance Day. You brought the wrong bouquet."

"Oh no!" she put her hands to her mouth. "I know, I wasn't thinking! They must have thought I was such a fool."

"No, not at all." He touched her arm. "You're wonderful."

"Really? Well, I felt terrible about it. It was a good thing I had more flowers in the van."

"I felt worse than terrible before you showed up that day." I'm not going to tell her why I was there, he thought. "You saved the day, believe me."

"Wow. I'm glad you thought so." She gave him a flower and

103

said, "I'm Amanda Wonka."

"Amanda Wonka?" He stared. "Are you any relation to the man with the chocolate factory?"

"What? No!" she laughed. "That's just a book. My dad is a janitor."

"Oh. Well I'm a vacuum cleaner salesman. I'm Phil Ticks. I've been hoping and hoping over and over to run into you again. Amanda Wonka."

"Phil Ticks," she smiled.

POTENTIAL

Far from the ground, like a large spider hanging spun under the eaves, Phil tugged in the rope and drew himself tighter toward the house. He had an owl tied around his neck.

Reaching to swipe ivy and moss away, something sharp on the window frame ripped the sleeve of his suit. He knocked a bird's nest down.

Not long ago, Phil's new boss told him, "You will install every product you sell. It's part of our commitment to the customer." He paused, tapped the application with his open hand. "You're a good climber, right?"

"Of course I am," Phil had assured him. "And I'm in great shape too, since I stopped smoking."

"Good, good, that's good to hear. I think you'll really go places with us, Phil."

A paint brush fell out of Phil's utility belt and spiraled down to the lawn. There were already nails down there, and a screwdriver he had dropped almost hit the sprinkler.

"Right by the window," the woman called up at him from below, directing with her hands. "Above that…In the middle."

"Okay!" Phil tied a knot into the ropes. He breathed a sigh of relief. The plank he was sitting on was secure and finally level.

He had to keep reminding himself, "It's all part of our com-

105

mitment to the customer." I know, I know, he felt like telling his boss, I've heard it before. It wasn't selling vacuum cleaners, but it was the same old story. Still, he had to listen to it to get the job.

His boss had a big desk and he leaned back in a leather chair when he said, "This city is not unlike every other city in America, Phil. It has a big problem with pigeons—the rats of the sky. Pigeons are bothersome, unhealthy, unnecessary animals, Phil." He unclasped his hands and leaned for something under the desk. "It's not legal to kill them like other vermin, but what we can do is scare them away. For good." He set the two foot tall plastic owl on the tabletop. "Every problem has a solution, Phil. What we've done is find a way to make money off the solution."

Phil examined it, the sloppy brightly painted feathers and yellow eyes. It was strictly assembly-line quality, probably made in China or Taiwan by the hundreds.

"The pigeon's worst enemy," his boss told him.

"It doesn't really look that much like an owl though."

"To a pigeon it does," his boss assured him. "They see in two dimensions. Their perspective is different. Their brains aren't the same as ours. Not as advanced. To us, this may appear decorative, even attractive, but this object strikes fear into the heart of a pigeon." He shook it in front of Phil and for that brief moment it became tribal, an African mask, and Phil shivered to be near it.

My last job selling vacuum cleaners was easier work, Phil thought. It had its moments. Anyway it wasn't as dangerous. But Amanda Wonka is worth suspending myself off of roofs. I'm doing this job for five dollars an hour plus commission and tips because then I can afford to live in this city with her. Still, it's too bad we aren't ancient Phoenicians, living on rocks and stones and cactus water. If only it was simpler to live in America…We could be—

The plank seat rocked as he took the owl off and held it above the window. With one hand wobbling him, he took the hammer from his belt.

"No! A little higher!" the woman below him pointed. "There! Yes, that's perfect."

Another nail fell from his pocket as he pulled a couple out. The owl's glowing eyes stared at him while he nailed it to the wood. Part of him wished he had stayed with vacuum cleaners. Maybe he could figure out a way to get back to them. He couldn't believe he actually missed them.

"No more pigeons for ninety days, or my money back?" the woman called. She was looking for the nails he dropped.

"Guaranteed!" Phil put the hammer back and pulled himself away from the owl, back up to the roof peak where he climbed onto the shingles. His company car looked ridiculous down there. I wish it didn't have that huge plastic owl head on the roof…He dragged the ropes up to him and coiled them at his feet. There's my next stop, he thought.

The entire city spread around him, hundreds of houses. He could put owls on every one. There were hundreds of potential owls.

UNDERSTANDING

Phil had an understanding with the phone. He sat near it, he paid it more attention than any other machine in the place… And in return, he expected to hear Amanda's voice. It was a fair exchange, he thought, but most of the time the phone would just hang there on the wall without any life at all. Sooner or later, he would break down and pray to it, "Please, let her call me!" Even after weeks of knowing her, it was hard to admit that he needed someone so much. Why weren't they spending this time together? He didn't want to appear desperate though, he would rather she called him.

He closed his eyes and sent out his thoughts to her address, made his mind be like a bird that could follow a map to the street and apartment where she lived. A window formed in his imagination and there she was behind the glass. He brushed her skin and whispered in her ear, "Please call me, Amanda."

Sometimes these ways worked, but he couldn't wait. He pulled the receiver to his ear and dialed her number. He counted the rings and he thought of her walking over to her phone, and he almost hung up in despair before it happened.

She answered, "Hello?"

"Amanda?"

"Yes."

"Oh! It's Phil. It's Phil Ticks. Hello."

"Hello, Phil Ticks. What's new?"

"Not much. I was just calling. I just happened to be near a phone," he walked and flowed with the trailing cord. "Well, it's in my room, so I'm not that far away from it really. I just wanted to see what you were doing."

"I was trying to think of something to do tonight." She paused. "What are you doing tonight, Phil Ticks?"

"I was going to wash my clothes." He heard her groan on the other end. Quickly, he added, "No!" and laughed. "Not really. I was thinking of doing something with you tonight, if you want to join me."

"Of course. What should we do?"

"Would you like to go down to the water with me? I made a discovery there while I was putting owls up on the pier."

"A discovery?"

"Yes, you have to see it to believe it."

"You found pirate gold? Will we be rich, Phil Ticks?"

"No, Amanda Wonka. It's a different kind of discovery. It's a kind of national monument."

"Well, that's alright too. Yes, let's go see it. But we should get some food first. We should go to a restaurant, don't you think?"

"Of course!"

"I know a place."

"When should we meet?"

"Now! It's already past five. You're lucky I haven't eaten yet. If you waited much longer, you could have been out a date."

"I know," he said. "Waiting is my trademark," and he reached over the stove. He turned the burner off. He was glad he didn't need the boiling pasta. That was in case she said no. If she said no, then it would have been spaghetti as usual. "I was starting to get hungry too."

"Well, hurry up then, Phil Ticks! I'll see you soon, okay?"

"Okay. I'm on my way."

ABRAHAM LINCOLN

Inside a rock carved by the waves into a sofa shape, they sat and the water pushed and pulled itself onto the beach in front of them.

For a while they watched the fish jump.

"I was up there," he pointed at the dock behind them, with the wooden building standing on it. Now there was an owl on the roof. But he was distracted when he saw the look in her eyes. They opened wider as she breathed.

"What did you see from there?" she whispered, charming him. "Was there something out on the water?" She couldn't have been much closer.

"Amanda…" he said her name.

She pushed the hair out of her face and smiled again, with the rabbit in her eyes. "What did you see in the water, Phil Ticks?"

He was turning his fingers, making small circles on her soft skin. "It was something I thought I saw."

"What?"

"See that dock there?" He kissed her arm and pointed her slender wrist and fingers. "How it goes off into the water, deeper, and then ends. But there are a few beams standing out beyond in the waves, alone."

"Yes," she kissed him back. "I see."

"That one that's almost submerged…It looks copper like a big penny in this light…I saw the silhouette of it…Look how it stands in the water like a familiar man with a top hat and beard…" He squeezed her, "It's Abraham Lincoln!"

She laughed and tipped her head back so he could kiss her neck again.

BREATHING WATER

The wind blew over the island's rocks and small trees, pushing the black waves over the beach, washing ashore the pieces of the war. An airplane wing, a life preserver from a sunken ship, someone's shoe half filled with water.

Away from the beach, through the fog and small trees, the metal of the war wouldn't reach this far. He lived there in a cave. Tall rocks stood out of the gray, a strange bird cried, flying off the stones and circled in the air.

A door opened from a spire of rock and he came out with his dog. The black dog was connected by a long spool of twine to him. He was flying his dog like a kite. The dog moved over the mossy covered rocks towards the shore, pulling the man along, a long way upwind.

Before he got to the beach, he began to reel the dog in. He rolled the rope in a circle around a piece of whale bone until the wagging dog was there waiting for him on the edge of the sand.

More wreckage had found the island. All morning long he pushed it back to the sea. If he didn't, all the wreckage would gather and cover his island. It was important that he do this job.

In the afternoon, he pulled the seaweed off an airplane curve and dragged it into the cold water to float away.

It scraped in the sand, tracing its pattern, and pushed up something that was hidden. It revealed a big circle of seashell underneath. "This is not from the war. I've never seen anything like this," he told the dog. Its pearl spiral was soft and broke in his grip.

He snapped off more of it. The shell fell apart in his hands and there was something soft inside. He felt a smooth leg.

The dog barked from where he was tied up, away from the war things that could hurt him.

It was a woman. She was dressed in pale rips like shipwrecked cloth. Her dark wet hair covered her face.

He whispered and took her out of the broken shell. On the

sand, very white, he stretched her legs out and brushed her dark hair off her face.

She was alive. Her breath was warm to his ear. Then her eyes opened. Golden eyes stared into him, right through him into the world beyond.

"This is where your people have been fighting?" she said.

"No. Not me."

His dog barked again and pulled at the rope tied to driftwood.

He touched her foot. Her toes were webbed. "You're from the water? You live there?"

Her legs moved so she could stand up. He held her shoulder to keep her from falling down. "It's different here," she said. She was unsteady in the air and leaned against him. "It will take me a while to get used to this."

She filled her lungs with breath and sighed out.

"You're staying?" he said.

There was smoke in the distant sky from a crashing airplane. Her golden eyes watched it fall. She looked back to him, "If there is room for me here."

He was thinking he was dreaming, that's what it felt like. He knew it and went along as if it was real. "I've been here on this island alone for a long time." She could have been sent to him in that shell, for him to discover. "I can't believe we found each other."

She looked around. "What do you do here?"

"I clear the beach of all the metal and the floating war things. It's important, someone needs to do it. Just look," he pointed to all the damage floating to the island, coming into its magnet.

"What if there wasn't a war any longer?" she said.

"What?"

"There doesn't have to be a war, does there? Do you want me to stop it?"

"You can't magically stop the war."

"People want the war to go on?"

"No, of course not," he said. "Nobody wants the war, but it's been going on for a long time. It would be impossible to stop it all of a sudden. See those planes?" He pointed to the sky where they flew in a triangle like stars. "They're going to bomb a city."

Her eyes went to them and they disappeared.

The wind started when she raised her arms. It moved her hair and dress just like the water and as she pointed her hand, her fingers curled and she held the sky and made the sun blink.

The sky was just like the water, a deep clean blue. There was no smoke to smell in the air. He looked all around. "What have you done?"

"The war is gone." It was simple after all. Just the water let itself wash up on the sand.

She smiled and asked him where they could sleep. She was tired.

There was still some kind of water in her. She wasn't the same as him at all. He touched her and knew she was from the sea.

In the morning, he woke up beside her. She was curled around him.

The sun was pulling over the ocean. The day was only beginning, but it was different, beginning with the calling of birds, not crashing. Everything was different. The island wasn't at all like it used to be.

She put her hand with her webbed fingers onto his skin and

she said, "Good morning."

"Good morning."

He was going to get up and go clear the beach, it was his routine.

"What's the matter?"

He rolled from her and sat up. "I have to go outside for a minute." He got up and dressed. "I have to look at the beach."

She got up too. "You won't recognize it!" She laughed because he was so worried looking.

They walked out of the rocks and she kept laughing, hugging him on the way to the beach path.

"Something has happened," he said on the sand. "There aren't any more wrecks on the shore. I wonder what happened? An armistice, a temporary peace?"

"I told you," she smiled. "The war is over."

"No. It couldn't have ended. Not so fast. Something like that can't just stop. It doesn't make any sense." He stopped and stared at her. "What have you done? What am I going to do now?"

"Look around you." She circled him with her arm. "You don't need to be afraid."

The island had never been like this. "Maybe you hid it all under the sand while I slept?" He pushed his shoe through the soft beach, but there were no war things.

The island was just like her. "You don't seem possible," he said. "It's all too good to be true." Was he still sleeping? He rubbed his eyes. Could you do that in a dream? "I've been with the war for a long time," he said. "I could have spent the rest of my life in it. I'm not used to it like this."

"You have to let good things happen to you," she said.

The dog ran across the sand, happy not to be tied or watching for mines or bombs, free to be chasing birds.

She looked deep into his eyes and listened to him talk. "I just wanted you to be happy," she said at last.

The war was already returning and the island was hiding itself again with smoke and there were fires out on the ocean.

115

"It's not that difficult for your old world to come back, is it?" she asked. "If that's what you want." Her eyes were different now.

There was an explosion. His dog was gone. A cloud of black smoke had taken it. There was a hole in the sand where he had been running. The air was humming.

The wind took hold of her and pulled her backwards, towards the water.

The sea went up around her waist as he ran out after her.

He went under the water after her. Already she was disappearing into sea. She was a fast swimmer. He could barely keep track of her pulling away from him.

A sinking ship blazed like a match going out and it sunk past them as he went swimming after her.

She was going deeper and it was getting darker and harder to follow her.

Fish circled him and whale calls.

When she was just a dim shadow to him, she landed on her feet and began walking on the sand floor of the ocean.

He landed too. It was just like she told him, "In the ocean, we have different ways of looking at things. And we can do things you can't. On the surface world, you do things we don't."

She was ahead of him, walking on a path of seashells, back to a glowing village with green houses and gardens of weeds and kelp, starfish and sea urchins.

He called out to her. His voice sounded strange underwater, all the bubbles were hard to talk with. He wondered what it was like for her. He said her name again.

She stopped and turned around and she looked amazed at him, that he had followed her here, after she had given up on him.

"I didn't want you to leave," he said. "I had to realize some things the hard way." She let him put his hands on her. "I have to warn you," he smiled, "I guess sometimes I'm not all that smart."

A LONG WAY FROM RIVER WATER

"I don't drive on Sundays anymore." Phil handed the keys back to her.

"Why not?" She couldn't believe it, "You didn't tell me you were Amish," she smiled.

"No. It's not anything religious."

When it happened, he wondered what it could have been. Something had hit the car and it lay white, slivered on the road back there behind him. The car turned up a cloud as he rolled it through the gravel and dirt to turn around.

"The last time I drove a car," he said, "I got hit by a fish." He saw her eyes brighten. He loved her eyes, he was glad he had stories to surprise her.

It was a salmon. It was still twitching with the last of its life. He looked around. The brown scrub grass and winding tar road was a long way from river water. No fish could have jumped so far.

No one could have thrown it. There was no place for anyone to hide in those quiet low weeds.

The sky was clear water blue as it went on over the forest, across to the purple mountains in the distance.

The salmon had hit his car from somewhere though. Unless it just fell out of the sky for no reason at all.

"I couldn't figure it out," he told her. "I was so far from the water and nobody threw it. I was in a clearing before the trees."

"Maybe it was catapulted?" she said, concealing a laugh.

"Yeah, I don't know. I thought of the possibilities. Maybe an eagle dropped it? I don't know. I never found out."

"What did you do with the salmon?" She turned the key and started the car. They were going for a ride in the country, out to the green hills and white farmhouses, to take a look at a museum that was filled with talking machines. "Seriously, you didn't eat it, did you?" She screwed her face up…Just the thought of it.

He cleared his throat.

THE HORSES ARE RUNNING TODAY

It took him a while to get there, switching two different buses and the morning rolled away slowly for an hour. He thought about her, watching buildings, the way they stood and moved into the sky. Until, at last, he stood in front of her work.

Dynamic Flowers was written in painted billboard-sized letters above the store's green windows. The stream was thick against the glass, pushing. There seemed to be a jungle in there.

He went through the doorway and the ferns, flowers and tropical leaves grabbed him. Finding her in all this green is going to be difficult, he thought. Wandering, there was only so much space until he could find her.

"This place sure is dynamic, Amanda," Phil said as he brushed by a fern. He parted the leaves and smiled, "How's work going?"

"Good."

He gave her a kiss. Having someone waiting for you to do that was one of the greatest things.

She was cutting flower stems to fit in a horseshoe display. "The horses are running today, so I've been making these for hours."

"You do beautiful work." He watched her hands fold and turn the flowers into a curved shape and it suddenly occurred to him: here was a way to really succeed selling products door to door. It would also get him out of the owl business. "I wonder, could you make some small ones for vacuum cleaners? Imagine, selling vacuum cleaners like winning horses!" He put his hand around her arm, "Amanda, I can see it now…Together we could become partners in the vacuum cleaner sales business!"

She looked bemused, "I don't know, Phil Ticks…" She sewed more of the purple flowers together. "There's a big difference between racehorses and vacuum cleaners. I don't know if people would go for that idea."

"No, it's a good idea. It makes the product more interesting." He touched her hand, "This guy I work with named Carl

Sandburg brings his cat with him whenever he sells. It gets him in the door every time. They see the cat on his shoulder and then his vacuum cleaners and it's like magic. It always works. It helps to have something out of the ordinary." Phil visualized it, holding his hands up around the vision, "Every vacuum cleaner is a winner! Trademark!"

"Okay, Phil Ticks, enough dreaming. Let me get this done and then let's go get some lunch. I'm hungry." She was tying the name ribbon into the display. *Flying Bonnet*, it read, *First Place*.

Phil stared, watching her work. "Wait a minute..." He touched her wrist, above the blue ribbon, "How do you know this horse is going to win?"

She looked up at him and he could read it in her look. Her eyes said to him, It's so obvious isn't it? "It's fixed," she told him. "All the races are fixed. They call me up in the morning and tell me the names of the winning horses so I can prepare these flowers in time for the finish."

Phil was shocked. Then it hit him and he savored the thought for a moment. He whispered, "But you could bet on them... Do you realize how much money you could make off this?"

"Oh no, I never thought of that."

"Just one time. Imagine!"

"Phil, they would find out. I can't, I have to be honest."

"But you could tell someone else and they could place a bet." Phil stole a look at the name on the ribbon again. Flying Bonnet, he repeated in his mind so he wouldn't forget.

"You want me to lose my job, Phil Ticks? Have gangsters chasing me down? Thanks a lot!" She hadn't thought about hiding the name from him. She did from other customers if they appeared, but not him. "I trust you. You wouldn't bet on this horse, would you?"

Phil looked away from her to a cage filled with small birds.

They were watching him.

Amanda grabbed him, "Phil, we could get into big trouble."

"I know, I won't, Amanda…I was just joking. I was sailing in the Caribbean on a yacht named The Flying Bonnet, and I was scattering gold coins in the wake." He sighed as it floated away from him forever. "But it was awful. I much prefer being a salesman."

She laughed. "Honesty is a better thing, isn't it, Phil Ticks? We have to always tell each other the truth." She finished with the ribbons and set it under the counter. "Let's go to lunch now."

She led him back through the dynamic flowers, to the door cut into the steam and she opened the glass for him.

MAGNET MAN

It was another lunch break at the owl business. Phil listened to a man tell him that he attracted everything that was distorted, he couldn't get away from the craziness—it came to him magnetically. Just today, on his way to work, someone stepped out of an alley and asked him if he wanted to buy some, "Quality used bacon on dry ice." The man told Phil he said no thanks and kept walking away, faster. He said he couldn't wait to get to work and clock in for the day.

Listening to him, Phil opened the can of Cragmont Skipper. "I don't know," Phil said. "A lot of people attract strange things. I've come to the conclusion that it makes life more interesting."

"I feel like I've lived a full lifetime already," the man moaned. "Every night I pray that I won't ever get hit by a bus again."

Phil almost spit out the peanut butter flavored diet cola, "You got hit by a bus?"

"Yeah, I was doing a paper route at the time. It was pretty good money. Flexible hours, with overtime, paid vacation after three years. I rode a blue Schwinn at the time, a five speed. Good bike, good on the hills, and then in the valley it could really glide." He shook his head miserably. "I was thinking about a something else, I didn't see the stop sign because of all the ivy over it and I was a little behind schedule. I went right through the intersection." Suddenly the man made a karate chop in the air. "Right into a bus! You want to talk about your life flashing in front of your eyes. That's it! I asked, *What did I do to deserve this?*

"Really?" Phil stared, "You ran into a bus?"

"I guess technically it was my fault, but that bus sure hit me hard. Broke both my arms and the bicycle was totaled. The frame was crushed and beyond repair. I just had to scrap it."

"You're lucky you weren't killed." Phil took a bite out of his sandwich. Usually he didn't bring anything for lunch, today was unusual.

"Lucky? You think so?" The man watched Phil eat. "Is it lucky for a person like me to go through all of this in the first place? I'd be lucky to have a life where nothing happened."

"Come on," Phil said. "Your life isn't that unusual."

"Do you wake up each morning to a teenager with a mohawk haircut banging on your window?"

"What?"

"His name is Chickenman Joe. He's real friendly. That's just the way my day begins. If I'm still asleep after he goes to the store, he'll wake me up again."

"Well," Phil said, "that's a bad way to start the day."

"No kidding. Then it just gets stranger from there. Like I said, I could have bought some quality dry bacon on dry ice today."

Phil said, "That bacon was probably stolen, or old. There was probably something wrong with it if they had to sell it on dry ice in an alley. You should never buy anything without a written guarantee."

"Well, actually, I didn't ask if it had a written guarantee. I just didn't want to be around that guy. He followed me a little down the block. I had to ignore him like a shadow behind me."

"I guess you do have an unreal time with things. I do too, but it seems to be pretty calm at the moment. In fact, things are going well for me." He knocked on the wooden table. He used to believe in cycles, that it wasn't impossible that he might be back with all of life's craziness, spinning like the crooked Ferris wheel of a sideways circus.

YOU DON'T HAVE TO BE CRAZY

It was like their conversation that night, when Amanda asked Phil, "Do you believe in some kind of luck or something?" And he said, "No, I don't."

"You have to," she insisted.

"I don't." With his arm around her, he said, "Not anymore."

"I don't believe you."

"Well okay, I do believe in something out of the ordinary."

"There! I knew it," she smiled, "What?"

"Something brought me to you. So I don't want to believe in anything else."

That played and replayed in her mind all that night, while she tossed and turned and tried to sleep and the rain fell against the glass. She thought of horses racing across.

He even gave her flowers. They were from the supermarket, nothing like the ones from her shop. He told her they needed her. "You're being romantic, Phil Ticks."

"Don't you see, Amanda? I like you. I really like you, Amanda Wonka."

Her eyes didn't want to stay in his too long; she kept looking away from him. But she took the flowers and put them in water. "I don't know."

He said, "I do."

"What if something goes wrong?"

"I love you."

"Do you? Phil Ticks, the vacuum cleaner and owl salesman. You're giving me flowers because you love me?"

She listened to the rain. It seemed there was no end to it. The whole town might drown in it while she was gone.

She didn't tell him what she had done. She thought of something else to say. She told him she wanted to be sure. She had to see how well she could get along without him, "If I have dreams about you every night, if I think about you at work, on the bus, when I hear certain songs, if I feel something missing all the

123

time we're apart then I will know."

And he stared into her eyes and said, "You don't have to be crazy to be in love with me, Amanda."

"But it sure helps," she said.

THE METEOR

He woke up and squinted at the digital clock. It was still early and he wanted to fall back asleep to redream, to go back on living from there, so he closed his eyes. The red numbers on the clock ticked on towards the alarm.

Again, he imagined the perfect world, a place that was both water and land, paradise for both of them. They were together. But what if things went wrong? They could. It didn't take much for a dream to turn nightmare.

What if a meteor came from the stars and crashed into their world?

Exploding fire and a cloud of smoke arose from the ground.

Hand in hand, they approached it.

She was scared. She gripped around his fingers and pleaded, "We don't need to know what it is. Let's not go any further."

It was a deadly thing from space, the explosion of its landing had killed everything around it. The plants had withered from the fire, and the water lay stagnant near it, but they walked closer towards it.

"Don't worry. I'm with you," he said.

The ground they waded through was sticking around their legs and the meteor rock shimmered ahead of them, waiting. Her hand was strong in his. They felt dizzy in its presence.

Hot molten rock glowed at them. There were orange breaks of lava in it. A square piece moved aside, a doorway opened from it.

He looked at her and said, "Let's go in."

He stepped inside and helped her in after him.

They were in the hollow circle of the meteor, smooth with turns in the walls. The door closed and they were inside the darkness.

"Don't worry," he said. "I love you."

But she was scared. She jumped up from him, "Where's the way out? We're trapped!" She touched all along the circle.

He said, "I'm with you."

But she was frantic, "There's got to be a way out!" She searched all around and she pushed him aside, trying to find the way.

When she moved away from him, he felt lost too, suddenly he was scared. All around the circled trapped them. He reached and hurt his hands on the roughness. She was still somewhere near him though and he put his hands up like a prayer for her and he found a string.

It was connected to something in the ceiling. In one hand he held it and pulled. "Look!" he said. Her voice was full of tears as she turned in the dark and looked. Light spilled down over them from above. And there was a door in the meteor, the way out was clear.

They helped each other through and they were back in their world and the meteor underneath them became rock and part of the hill and grass grew up around and over it, and it was just a part of the landscape.

THE BEAUTIFUL WORDS

When he saw her in the morning, it was obvious something terrible happened. Watching her, he could tell it had gone through her entire body like poison. Something changed her but she couldn't say, she had become so cold. She wouldn't let him close enough to touch. He was some kind of aquarium thing to her now.

What's the matter? Why are you being like this to me? he wanted to ask her, but he didn't want to make it any worse. He played dumb and took on her pain; he watched her, not saying anything.

Combing her hair before the mirror, her eyes just looked at herself.

When she was done she moved away from him. Away from the banded supermarket carnations he brought and left on the counter.

"Amanda," he said so gently and as quietly as possible, like folding cement flowers.

Her eyes were the rivets of some sunken ship, "What?"

Being a salesman affected him; if someone was angry at him, he knew enough to gently depart. Take the loss. This was the time that demanded he sell himself like a vacuum cleaner and he couldn't do it. He thought that she could see him, but when she turned on all her anger, he didn't know what to do. The customer is always right and he wasn't going to deny it—who could be in love with an owl installer? A man with the kind of luck that brings trains crashing into women! Amanda had every right to flee. It's safer for her. He was seeing her clues, her distance was growing and words wouldn't work anymore, they got lost in miles.

"Amanda Wonka…" He couldn't say anything else. The English language had become foreign, it had got him in so much trouble. He wasn't that good at talking, saying things and not saying things. "Amanda Wonka." The beautiful words weren't going to come save the day.

ALONE

He had to say goodbye to her. He didn't want to. He let the word hang on as long as possible, but she was in a rush to disappear. Her eyes were looking right through him, into somewhere in the future where he wasn't. She got in her car with only the things she could carry and he turned away. He didn't want to see if she looked back at him. He didn't think she would.

Now it's all up to her, he thought. It's up to her whether I can stay inside her head. If she can forget me, I'm finished.

It was an effort not to think about how he had failed. "I've lost two women in this city!" he told the trees as he walked away. It went over and over in his mind. Then finally he thought, I've got to control myself. I've got to stop being the brokenhearted Hank Williams of vacuum cleaners. I won't sing the blues for them as I go door to door, selling cheap plastic machines or owl ornaments.

I'll forget about love. It can be done. Why didn't I listen to myself before? I'll just think about my job and what the weather is like throughout the year. Listen to the radio and watch TV. That's what a lot of people do to get by.

If I can work enough, I can forget about my problems. I'll just become what I'm supposed to become. This was his new philosophy and he was ready to go ahead with selling owls as if they were his only purpose in life.

It's just me and the owls from now on. Maybe, as a reward for faithful lifetime service and devotion, for my retirement they'll turn me into an owl and my 65 year old body will fly away from the city, away from people and I'll disappear into the forest.

129

SOMEWHERE

Amanda Wonka wouldn't have wanted to hear his careening train of thought. She was absorbed in her own plan. She needed to be away and alone for a while.

Like him, she walked and moved and slept through life like it was a dream. When she met Phil Ticks it all made sense for a while. It was nice to be wanted by someone. It made her settle into living days, but now it was too late.

She was in the car, on the freeway, with the green drift of growing fields on either side of her, going 70 mph, hour after hour. There was somewhere, she just knew it, where Amanda Wonka could be safe.

THE DROUGHT

Was it too late for apologies? He wanted the sorrow confusions inside of him to end. But he couldn't even have a drink of water. The utilities had been canceled due to the drought.

It had not rained for weeks. The city had shut down, dried up into gray and yellow. He closed the kitchen blinds so it was dark. It was more soothing that way. He turned on the radio by the sink and it played music. He didn't like Top 40, but it kept him from thinking. Thinking was the whole problem; thinking was how he made his mistakes.

If I could just spin back time, thing would be different, he thought. The chair found him and he sat down. A hot wind blew the drapes like sails. The sky was white, parched of any blue. The cars passing in the street made their dry noise driving by.

No, he thought, it's no good. Maybe I can't love. And like an answer to his thoughts, the kitchen sink, left open for weeks, suddenly shuddered and began to pour water.

As the rust color turned clear, he jumped from the chair. The shower in the bathroom roared with its rain. He could hear it falling from here. Water was spilling from everywhere in the apartment, down the walls, across the floors and out of the furniture too. He was bathed in it all and he ran in the waterfall to dial her number in the leaking telephone.

Every time he slept, it was dreams of her. Memories of her were hanging around haunting him. He woke and sat up.

Quieter now in the city, sounds of cars far away on the interstate, and maybe a carnival playing in a distant neighborhood. The breeze carried it through the window, open enough for someone to crawl through and it was still warm after midnight.

"Here's what has happened," he said. The night listened to him speak. The streets of the city at 2:30 in the morning were quieter than usual, held together with orange streetlights. The stars were all out and his words sunk into them, "I haven't been careful with myself. I have come to this place to try and change. I had something before, but it wasn't something I wanted to keep forever—selling vacuum cleaners isn't the answer to life on Earth…So I really needed a change. I guess I thought it could be easy."

A siren moved across a faraway section of town.

THE TIN CAN MAN

A man had found a way to barely make a living from America's garbage…pushing a shopping cart around the city, turning it over like a seashore, looking for pop cans to recycle. The plastic rubbish bags would fill like balloons with aluminum and he would drift along the sidewalks slowly, searching the ground, until, "Eureka!"

After eating his lunch, Phil would wait for the shopping cart man to come rattling along. Phil would always save his Skipper can to drop in the bag as it bulged past. There are probably more eventful things to do, Phil thought, to earn my good deed for the day. I could be fighting crime in the city like a caped crusader…Donating my services to The Salvation Army… Handing out maps to the Fountain of Youth…The city is crying out for help…But at 12 o'clock sharp, Monday through Friday, Phil would give 27 cents to Safeway for a warm can of Skipper peanut butter flavored soda. Afterwards, with all the care in the world, he would drop the emptied can into the passing cloud and he could say with the tin can man, "Eureka!"

THE RETURN TO MAGNET MAN

That morning, in the break room at work, Phil was going to talk about Amanda Wonka, what she had put him through and how she left without explanation. She had called him from some town lost in America last night to say, "I know I shouldn't be telling you this, but I actually did bet on the horses. I tried to get away with it. But I was discovered." From a phone booth somewhere, she was on the run. "Anyway…" she quickly said, late last night, waking him up, "I've got to go now. I don't know when I'll be back." Then she hung up and he couldn't tell if she had ever been. In the morning, he wondered if it had all been a dream. Maybe it was just his mind trying to think of something that would make sense. That's the kind of craziness Phil Ticks got, it fell out of him like rain. "I get my share too," was all he told the Magnet Man.

DILEMMA

Of course this is not only about her, Phil thought, it's all a part of the way I want to live, a part of the plan. And now it's like finding another obstacle laid in my way. She is gone, but I bet every time she sees an owl she thinks of me. Wherever she goes, she may be watching rooftops, wondering if that's me on the ladder and ropes, teetering on the edge of gravity, putting up another plastic owl.

Food Giant was really getting the royal owl treatment. They wanted an owl on every corner of the supermarket's roof and flanking the huge flashing neon store letters as well.

"We've been having trouble with birds lately," the manager said. "All kinds of them are hanging around and dive bombing the customers in the parking lot. We've been getting a lot of complaints and I wouldn't want people to stop coming here."

Phil clinked along after him, down Aisle 3, past rows of coffee cans. Slow down, he thought. These guys in cheap suits are always in such a rush. "Don't worry," Phil said. "These owls will do the trick, you'll see. They're guaranteed."

"I hope so." The manager stopped suddenly to replace a bag of pistachios, before he led Phil through the Employees Only door. They went up a stairway and he unlocked another door that took them onto the roof. "Looks like a nice day for you," the manager smiled and pointed at the blue sky.

"Sure is." Phil set down the string of owls at his feet. "But it won't be a nice day for the pigeons!" What a sales pitch, Phil smiled. He sounded like a gunslinger.

The manager was examining the owls, pulling his moustache earnestly. "You don't have any that look a little more ferocious, do you? I mean like…" he hunched his back and curved his arms out threateningly, "So they look like they're going to swoop down to attack. We need mean owls."

"Oh, these owls come with a ninety day guarantee. They're guaranteed to scare."

135

"Yeah, they just look a little quiet is all." The manager watched Phil screw a base onto one.

"I prefer to think of them as watchful." Phil explained it methodically, "They are predators, Jim. If you were at a beach, wouldn't the mere sight of a shark scare you away? You wouldn't need it to attack to know that it means peril. These owls are like warning signs to other birds: Danger!" Phil carried the owl over to one of the corners. "As a matter of fact, I expect you'll be seeing results very quickly. It's all part of our guarantee."

"Good. Then I'll let you continue."

Phil waved, "That's what I'm here for!" as the manager went back through the doorway. But Phil stopped what he was doing when he looked down in the parking lot. There were some sparrows sitting on the big owl rooftop decoration of his car. They were singing back to the flock. He mumbled, "These birds are tougher than I thought…"

ADVANTAGE

Reincarnation would have placed him in Medieval Europe in the high crown of some castle, setting up the defenses: vats of boiling tar and stocking crossbow arrows. The roof of Food Giant was guarded with owls and Phil paced from one to the next, making last adjustments and giving moral support. "For the rest of your enlistment with Food Giant, through rain and storms and holding on through winter snows, it will be your duty to repel birds. There is the enemy!" he shook his fist at the little birds in the parking lot. They were circling shopping carts and flying at shoppers hurrying to their cars. "Charge!"

Atop the roof with the silhouettes of owls around him, Phil called again, "Charge!" and he waited for the owls to project themselves psychically into the minds of the pigeons, sparrows and starlings.

"Is that it?!" The manager yelled from below, slashing at a swallow. "Look! The birds are still here! They haven't left!" A pigeon wobbled past him, going under a car to avoid his kick.

"Not for long though!" Phil called back. "They know what they're up against now. Expect them to beat a retreat any moment! They can see the tables have turned. Food Giant has the advantage!"

CURSES

Now Phil was getting desperate. He was driving his car in circles around the parking lot, the big owl's head with glowing eyes on the roof, broadcasting the screech of a hunting barn owl from the windows. Birds scattered out of the way as he turned, and gathered back again when he passed. Phil held one of the plastic owls out the open driver's window and shook it like a voodoo gourd.

Dusk was falling. The dinner crowd had come and gone, but a number of people lingered to watch him casting his strange spell. He was making a lot of noise with his show and his headlights flashing on and off as round and round he went.

Finally, Jim had enough. He couldn't stand there and watch any longer. He intercepted Phil as he came by again. "Turn that damn recording off!" He leaned in through the moving window and grabbed Phil's sleeve.

Phil stopped the car and turned the sound down.

"Off!" Jim shouted. "I can't listen to that owl any more. You're turning this into a circus! I just want these birds out of here. Look at them! Look around you. What do you see? There's a crow on your hood!"

The black bird took off when Phil pressed the horn.

"That's it!" Jim struck the car. "These owls and all this owl magic aren't doing any good. I want you out of here!"

Phil persisted, "But you've got a ninety day guarantee." He could show Jim the fine print, the receipt was in the glove compartment.

"Forget the guarantee! You're more trouble than the birds! Take your owl machine out of here now! We'll deal with your pathetic gargoyles later. It's plain to see I need to get a professional, an exterminator, or a sharpshooter. Now get!"

"If you just give the owls a chance, you'll see—"

"Go!" Jim clubbed the owl head on the roof with a zucchini.

"Alright, alright!" Phil lurched the car through the birds, onto the street and around the corner, along the brick side of the grocery building. He parked and sighed. "That guy has no patience. Doesn't he know he can't expect a miracle overnight?"

Phil got out of the car to check the roof. "He probably dented my owl with that zucchini. What a bully," he muttered. "Why *should* I get rid of those birds?" Phil brushed the big owl, "They're probably his curse."

A bent up old man sitting against the curb heard Phil and laughed. "You're right. That whole parking lot is cursed."

"The parking lot?"

"It's got bad history. It's all about what happened there before," the old man said. "I'm not sure anyone could make those birds go away."

A voice interrupted, "You again?!" It was Jim, coming around the corner, "I thought I told you to get out of here!"

Phil jumped back inside the car and sped away into the neighborhood, out of the range of tomatoes and the rain of rotten avocados.

POCAHONTAS

It was 12:20 in the afternoon. Phil was sitting at a library table crowded with homeless. As long as they pretended to read, they could stay out of the rain. But Phil was getting delirious looking at the clock and thumbing *The Atlas of American History.* I've got to do something about these spinning images of Amanda Wonka! He thought the book would take his mind off her, but every curve and turn of geography was part of her, and the clock made him wonder what she was doing.

He put the big book down and stared at the upside down sports page of the man across the table from him. He read the inverted words to himself: Blue Jays Fly Out Orioles. "More birds," he whispered. They're everywhere, not only haunting parking lots.

Birds were cursing Food Giant...Phil had hoped he could find out at the library what it was about, maybe look it up in some dusty book. Why would anyone put a curse on a parking lot? Sure, the management is unkind, but why a curse? Did they offend some wizard, or did Jim throw fruit at a witch?

Which reminds me...Phil pushed his chair back...I should go retrieve my owls. The guarantee doesn't cover curses.

A librarian with a long beard stared at Phil as he arose out of his chair.

Quietly, knowing the eyes were on him, Phil slid the chair in and ever so gently, he crept over to the librarian's oak watch-tower desk.

"May I help you?" The words floated and challenged from the beard.

"Yes," Phil replied in a hush, "I can't seem to figure it out. How do you spell Pocahontas?"

"P-O-C-O—no, wait." The librarian's hands went into his beard as if to find the letters. "P-O-C-A-H-A—no, that's can't be right either. One moment, let me consult a reference book."

While the librarian turned his back, Phil moved swiftly away, so fast and silently that when the librarian swung around with the correct spelling, it was too late. There was nobody there.

REALLY

Phil kept going back into memory. He couldn't stop tormenting himself, he couldn't stop looking back.

He really was so in love with her, to see her among all the flowering plants was like Eden. He felt they were protected and given the kind of love that no other man and woman had. "How are you?" he smiled. He was smiling a lot and she liked it when he did. She gave him every reason to smile.

"Dynamic!" she smiled in return and put her hands in his. "You're back from the owls early today."

"It started to rain." He looked all the way into her eyes. "Nobody wants to buy an owl when it's raining."

She kissed him. It was a slow day and she had been thinking of him while she worked. She was glad he made it here, out of the rain and his brown owl uniform dripped like feathers. "Want some coffee?"

"Yes please."

She liked to do things for him. She poured coffee into a green cup. "You're really lucky to have me to take care of you."

"I know," he said. "Thank you." Their hands touched again when she passed the cup and she watched him sip, watching her back.

That was the moment in time Phil wished he could come back to. The invention of a time machine would save his life. He would do anything to really go back to that day. He would have set the cup down right away and taken up her hands and told her.

CAPTURED

He couldn't stay in the city to think this through. The image of her was tied to him, wrapped inside of him and around him like a ghost and there was no way Phil could think of anything else. He needed to get out into the country, to hopefully find some peace of mind and catching it, bring it back with him. So Phil flew along in the owl-car on the road from town.

The thoughts grabbed him, *I've made a terrible mistake. I've got to get a grip on myself.* I knew what I was getting into, I just put myself out on a limb. Each thought was a breaking strand of web. The city was only a half hour away and the land was becoming more agitated too, the forests were having a hard time growing with all the malls, houses and freeway noise. The problems of his were small compared to the land—all of America was captured.

He looked at the houses and clearcut hills.

Eventually, he could just look at the shape moving past him. That was all he wanted, the sense of that motion would wash his mind. And the further he got away, he found it easier to think.

Just concentrate on the way everything has endured somehow.

Phil noticed the place as it flashed by—they still had the wooden wagon that had taken their great grandparents to this place, parked out on their front lawn with a satellite dish. The land was lying all around them, clouds flattened out on the sky.

Then he looked back at all the brown grass, the fields and trees spreading for miles.

CINDY'S POLECAT STORE

By the time he needed to stop to refill the gas tank, he was very far away.

Cindy's Polecat Store had the only gasoline he had seen.

Here's something you don't see every day, he thought, as he pulled up alongside the rusty pumps.

While the gas poured into the tank, he watched the boarded up window for any signs of life. There didn't seem to be anyone at home. Breezes straight out of the patchy forest rattled the shingles on the roof.

"Did you come here for Pioneer Days?" a deep voice said.

Phil jumped.

A quiet giant was towering on the other side of his car.

"No…No…" Phil stuttered. "I just needed gas for my car. Actually, the tank is probably full enough." He tried to laugh as he put the hose back.

"What's with the owl stuff all over your car?" The giant put a huge hand on the owl decoration. It seemed he was about to push it down through the roof. "You know, we don't like owls out here. They're taking our jobs away."

"I know, I know." Phil was glad he had the car between him and the giant, even though it looked like the giant could easily toss it aside. "I'm an owl exterminator. I'm an owl sharpshooter. I kill them for a living."

The giant smiled enormous teeth, "Well, take a look around." He brought his hand off the car and waved at the forest. "They're out there."

"Well, anyway…" Phil dug into his pocket and took out some dollar bills to pay. "I should probably get looking for them then. Not a moment to lose."

The giant watched him leave. His image filled up the back window for a long time.

THE SIGN

The moon took over the sky with its white light. Some bats made themselves seen among the stars, brief flapping moments against the black. "It doesn't make any sense..." Phil said aloud, hoping for answers from somewhere. "Nothing makes any sense. The world is going crazy."

The trees covered him over with their dark shadows on the path. He stopped and sat down on a rock. Beside him, a wooden fence crept on and on across the tall field.

"I wish there was a sign to believe in." He looked at all the stars. He expected a comet, a miracle wrapped in fire that would spell everything out for him. Nothing changed that much. Crickets scattered all far in the grass kept going, and the moon sat still with the stars. "I see..." But something rustled in the leaves next to him and took off into the air.

He called after it, "Hello?"

He wasn't afraid. He was waiting for a sign. So he said again, quietly this time. "Will you please help me?"

FEAR

Phil dragged himself out of the car, shut the door behind him and, with a plastic owl in his arms, walked towards the brown falling down house.

Hundreds of pigeons held onto the roof with their wings outstretched and whirring, keeping the house from falling down.

This wasn't going to be easy. He knew this was one of those jobs they gave to test a new salesman. It was a trial.

The yard looked like a small scale war zone. Patches of it were burned away, metal and broken glass wreckage and disarrayed neglect.

Phil stuck the owl under his arm and strode confidently up the riddled concrete path. The wooden stairs were soggy like they were connected to a swamp. His footsteps oozed to the door. He knocked and waited.

"The guy's a monster," the secretary had warned him when she passed him the assignment. "I think it's mean," she whispered confidentially, "They shouldn't make you do this."

The door opened slowly, to let the sunlight inside was a scare to the person in there. Ever carefully, the pale face appeared.

"You sir, have a problem with pigeons," Phil began energetically, "and pigeons have a—pr—" his sales pitch, his words, stopped like water turned off.

The white face pulled back into the shadows, going inside to hide.

Phil put his hand out to stop the door. "No, wait! You have nothing to fear!"

"But fear itself..." came croaking words with some smile left in them. The door was stopped from closing. The creature inside opened it a bit for Phil to enter.

Phil had to step inside. It was expected of him. A salesman must press the sale.

The odor of flowers, dead, shriveled, dried, long gone, in a room cluttered with petals and junk. The place was all heavy

147

with gigantic decomposing. The inhabitant was a strange person to see, none of the limbs were proportioned right, but he shuffled and moved aside almost gracefully, letting Phil come in.

Phil stood in the carnation light of a stain glass window.

Dark eyes glimmered at Phil. "Is that a bird?" The words fell out of broken-shaped teeth and a crooked hand pointed at the owl under Phil's arm.

"Yes. This is what I sell…" He held it out and passed it to the twisted fingers. Purple light curved on the plastic. "It's an owl."

"What's it do?" The hands turned the owl over and over with caresses.

"Scares pigeons," Phil said. "It will scare pigeons away from your roof."

The turning of it stopped. "No. Then I can't have it here. Take it back."

"What's the matter?" The owl was shoved at Phil, into his chest.

"I love my pigeons. I don't want them to be scared. They're the only ones who like me and stay with me. They are my family. They are the only ones who love me." He turned around quickly and shook over to a broken chair. It was covered with a gray tear of blanket and he pulled it off and came back to Phil. He took the owl again, "If they see the owl, they will be scared." He wrapped the cloth over the owl. "That's better."

He put the bundle on the floor. "Leave this here for now," he told Phil. "Maybe you would like to see something." He looked up secretively. "If you see my pigeons you won't want to get rid of them ever. Come with me and see how they are."

The house held them inside its dry leaves and flowers and twigs and tangling branches.

Upstairs was all covered with blue light from the open sky. "When I want to fall asleep, here is where I dream. I stop being what I look like to people when I'm asleep."

Phil watched him collapse in slow motion.

Yawning, all the strange shapes of his bones folded, laying him onto the floor. Breathing deeply, he curled himself and Phil watched silently.

Changing , the air began to slip and shimmer into colors. Shadows turned in the blue, spinning on the sleeping form that warped, folding up into itself like a flower for the night.

All that person that didn't seem to work became something else. It shook out its wings and flew around Phil in a purple and blue circle and then out of the opening, into the sky.

CIRCLES AND CIRCLES

Resolved: Phil decided that he would try to find them all, every lost animal in the city. Early that morning, Phil left his apartment and began to walk. It was sure to take all day.

The notebook he carried began to fill up with the pet names and descriptions of lost dogs, cats and parrots and even a pig. The city was a big lost yard of animals, posted on telephone poles and walls and shop windows all around.

And there were rewards offered too, worth hundreds of dollars.

Phil thought, I could make my living from this, and he whistled while he took down the information from a flyer posted to a mailbox: *Lost Black Lab. Small white spot under chin. Small lump, left flank. Unneutered adult male. He is very friendly, his name is Geronimo. We miss him! Please call 860-0807.*

The streets turned into labyrinths leading to the missing— lawns, parked cars, bushes, porches, trees, backyards—there were all kinds of places they could hide. And when dusk fell and night approached darkly over everything with shadows, they could be hidden anywhere.

He drove in circles and circles, shining the flashlight from the owl-car. There were plenty of animals. He stopped for all of them, but they weren't the lost ones, they all had collars and homes.

The sun began to roll itself over the parking lots and convenience stores, telephone wires gleamed with slivers of the orange. The radio was blaring to keep Phil from falling asleep as he continued to drive around and around with the notebook on his lap, nodding and bleary eyed.

He drove for almost twenty hours.

He had not found a single lost animal and the new day was beginning. Most people were waking up out of sleeping dreams; Phil had been driving for all those hours, trying to find things lost in the shadows.

A cold bee flew through the open morning window, landed on his leg, on the fold of the trouser, and it stung him.

For no reason at all! That was the part that angered him. It had killed itself for no reason. Stinging Phil Ticks hadn't done the world any good. Now it crumpled yellow and black on the floor of the car and was dead. The wind moved it about. "Thanks a lot!" Phil said. He rubbed the painful rising bump on his thigh. He opened the door and flicked the dried bee out, slamming the door closed. So tired of driving, he went back to his apartment and parked and gave up.

THE HOLE

Everything had fallen apart inside of him. Every last thing collapsed, and there was nothing left to believe in. Phil shook with the thoughts that wouldn't stop. She still rolled over and over in his mind, spinning cobwebs in him. He was trying to get it to stop, but he thought, all this time I'm not with her is emptiness and then there's all the rest of the time I won't be with her. Something has to take her place in my mind, but it has to be monumental and beautiful and healing.

He couldn't feel anything else but sorrow and when it rains, it pours. The owl-car was driven away early one morning, back to the company and they took his suit and all the plastic owls too. He didn't resist. He wished them well. He just couldn't work anymore. First the Food Giant job, then the so-called pigeon monster, then all his chasing after lost animals. They said they were sorry to have lost him. But he smiled back, "Don't you see? This job just wasn't meant for me."

So his job disappeared too and, like Amanda Wonka, left him with a hole. It was trying to heal, in the dark of that apartment building, in his small living room on the second floor, where he sat in a chair and watched the city skyline for days and days. The clouds, the birds that moved in the air from roof to roof, the daylight that became night, and the hole in him that was trying to heal.

EVICTED

"I'm just doing my job. No hard feelings." Standing there, wearing a football jersey, number 60, the apartment manager passed Phil the envelope with the eviction notice.

His heart stopped for a second, but then it didn't even matter. On top of everything else too, this was just another thing. "Thanks," Phil smiled. He could be pleasant about it too, why not?

"I'm just doing my job," the manager repeated.

"No problem."

"You have to be out by the end of the month. You got a week and a half."

"Sure," grinned Phil and he waved like a puppet. He closed the door and set the envelope down on the table.

The kitchen light was on so he walked over and pressed the switch.

He stood in one place and listened in the dark.

That can't be crickets…

That sound, coming through the open window, in a lull. How could there be crickets in the city? Holding onto the bricks and metal of the city, that the stalks of meadow plants have become? It sounded like crickets, but it must be some machine—a faulty air conditioner, or a rusty wheel turning in the breeze. Maybe I'm imagining it, he thought, maybe it's just the refrigerator. Maybe I'm not being evicted, maybe that never happened. Maybe I was just dreaming. But he knew that if he went back into the other room to look, the envelope would be sitting there on the table. It wasn't going to disappear.

ASKING FOR TROUBLE

He had decided that he was doing it to himself, bringing all this down upon himself: So if I stay inside, if I keep it to myself, I won't be hurt.

For a week, he stayed in the room, the soft chair next to the window, thinking…I won't go out asking for trouble anymore. Maybe I'll turn invisible. They'll come in here to evict me and I'll be gone to them already. And here I'll stand like a see-through lamppost for eternity.

The human race moved about outside the window. He wondered how they were doing without him. Finding a new victim, he thought.

Of course it didn't work. I'm a lost cause. The country is covered by plagues.

Finally, he turned on the TV and there was Jackie Wu.

The television was filled with the pictures of wooden items, sculptures and furniture and artifacts from all over the world. "Come to Jackie Wu for your wooden import needs." Then, like entering a dream of his own, the camera zoomed in close and Jackie Wu spoke directly to Phil, "For what your life needs, or whatever your heart desires."

Phil remembered the card he was handed at the train station! The day of Hiroshima Remembrance and Peace with Japan… Her funeral…That morning of flowers going back to the ground. *Jackie Wu had been there all along!*

He turned off the TV and got his coat on. Now he was meant to go.

STAIRWAY TO JACKIE WU

Jackie Wu's Wooden Imports was located in the heart of the International District. The bus went through two African villages and Little Italy before going under a green curling dragon archway. Phil paid the fare and stepped off into the circling crowd.

All the people of the world went around him. The entire planet was a circus. Such a crazy amount of motion was whirling. He looked for the right street and found it all hidden in smoke from burning charcoals and sweet incense.

Vegetables and fruits and plastic bright toys, whirring robot motors, Phil's footsteps crunched on broken things on the bricks that took him to the big wooden door.

Wooden imports were everywhere. They were on shelves and hanging from strings and standing like giraffes. Phil thought he recognized Jackie Wu from the television commercial, waiting behind the counter, a little bit fatter off the screen. But Phil wasn't too sure, even his eyesight was failing him.

Phil went to a shelf full of mahogany sculptures first. I'll work my way over to the counter, he thought. I'll ease my way over to Jackie Wu. Interesting…he set down the bare breasted angel and moved on, down the aisle. But what I'm really looking for is a way to forget all that. I don't want to see any beautiful reminders for a while.

George Washington, with the look of a one dollar bill, stared up at him. "Say," Phil called, picking it up and rubbing the wooden teeth of the first president, "This isn't very accurate. I thought George Washington had ivory teeth."

"No," said the cashier. "George wore wood."

"Oh…" Phil paused at a wooden interpretation of Mark Twain. Here, he thought, life's a river and a long journey on steamships, or a raft, and you just ride along with the current. Maybe…

The phone rang at the desk and the cashier answered it, "Jack-

155

ie Wu's Wooden Imports, can I help you?...No, just wood...No, our specialty is wood. We import from all over the world... That's right...Thank you, ma'am...Have a nice day."

Mark Twain turned in Phil's hands, but the price tag to the left of his moustache was a little beyond Phil's budget.

The cashier hung up the phone and called over to Phil, "There's a sale on dead American authors. Today only."

"Really?"

"Emily Dickinson is just ten dollars," he informed Phil, pointing her out, further down the aisle. She wore a wooden flowing dress with her hands reaching out to all the dark.

"How much for Mark Twain?"

"Twelve dollars..." but he paused to catch Phil's reaction, the effect of his eyes and mouth, and the price fell. "Except for you sir, Mark Twain is nine dollars."

Phil sighed and held on, "How about seven. It's a lucky number."

The cashier nodded slowly. "Sold."

Phil smiled and walked over to the counter with it held in front of him. A crumple of dollars came out of his pocket and wilted like lettuce on the counter.

"Will that be all?"

"Well...I do need something else." Phil leaned over the counter and whispered, "Do you know where I can find Jackie Wu?"

"Which one? There are two of us."

"You're Jackie Wu too?"

"Yeah, I'm the second one. Jackie Wu Junior."

"The second one?"

"Yeah, I know," Jackie laughed, "It's an old story. I'm his twin brother. Our mother was too tired to think of another name after the long birth. So we're both Jackie Wu."

"Well, I'm looking for something other than wooden imports," Phil Ticks told him, some of the confident old salesman in him coming through.

"Oh, then you'll probably want to see my brother first." He threw his words around like a Brooklyn Dodger. "Upstairs, go through that door."

"Thanks." Phil spun a globe carved out of sandalwood and cedar as he passed it and opened the door. It was dark inside. Phil turned around, "Is there a light switch?"

"Don't worry," the second Jackie Wu called, "It's just ahead. You'll see it."

"Alright…" Phil saluted for some reason and sank into the dark stairwell.

He put his hand on the soft wall and walked in stumbling.

TWIRLED

In full dark, Phil went through a dizzy amount of stairs. He was going up and down and some confusing directions that didn't make any sense. Sometimes the steps were like teeth underneath his feet and it was difficult to keep his balance before they flattened again. "This is like a funhouse that isn't very fun," Phil told the dark walls, half expecting the glowing face of Jackie Wu to appear like a ghost. He was having a hard time moving any more. The confusion was tiring and making him lose his balance. "Maybe I'll turn around and go back. I've just about had it."

Phil slipped and put a hand against the wall. Finally, the stairs didn't seem to be going up or down.

The wall was papered in a soft felt pattern. He could feel star shapes and moons and round planets across it. He used both hands on the wallpaper, hoping to run across a light switch.

His fingers bumped into a small lever that let him move a panel open. It was like a blank window. Phil leaned an arm in and reached. He wasn't about to just crawl right through.

His hand touched another hand, unexpectedly, it was cold and without life. Not like holding hands, it sent a chill through him. It was attached somewhere in that darkness on the other side. The hand was part of an arm that went into a body, but Phil had found enough. This wasn't a living person—cold, weighty and dead still—it was a corpse. Phil slammed the little door closed and ran on the dimly lit landing to the grinning stairs going up.

A spot of light showed itself and it was getting closer as the steep stairs crested and collapsed like a wave. They leveled onto another landing and let him fall into the ray of thin light that came from a keyhole in a door. Phil grabbed the door handle and rattled and turned it open, struggling for breath.

The brightness blinded him but Phil stepped into it, shading his eyes with his hands—anything to get out of the dark.

Shapes formed. They were pieces of furniture, arranged around in a square room. The ceiling was blue skylights and the floor was wooden, golden boards. There were paintings hung on the walls, landscapes—pagodas and rainy mountains. A turning wind-chime made of seashells and bells blew not far away, next to a window that sighed.

"There you have it…You have been through death and life and fear and love." It was the same television commercial slow voice of Jackie Wu. "And now you have come to me for a solution." Jackie Wu stood up dramatically and he walked over to the stunned Phil Ticks. "I'm Jackie Wu," he stuck out his hand, friendly and smiling, "Have a seat."

"There's a…" Phil stretched his finger to the closed door.

"Don't be alarmed by what you saw in there. People think they see all kinds of things in that darkness. It's just the path to get you here."

Dropped out of the air, the wind had gone out of him, Phil sunk into the nearest chair. "I can't go on much longer…"

Jackie Wu chuckled, "I know it seems like the worst things in the world have been happening to you and there is no end to the pain."

"No," Phil said. "You don't even know the things I've been through. They just go on and on. I have no control. I can't even stop them anymore. All I have to do is walk out the front door and I get hit, or somebody close to me does. Like lightning striking…It's a miracle I made it here without being assassinated."

"No, not a miracle," Jackie Wu said, "Just the kind of faith you need more of."

"Whatever. I know what I'm up against." Phil held his chin in his hand. "I think it would all change if I could forget. Can you make me forget?"

"Forget what?"

"I've made terrible mistakes and I can't get them out of my head. All the mistakes, when they're just involving me, I can

159

live with that. I would rather have that. I don't want to hurt anyone." The words flew out of him, "I don't want to hurt anyone around me. Can you help me with that? And if you could just let me forget her, just her. I could live with the rest of my problems, but I've ruined the only thing that meant the world to me. If I could forget Amanda Wonka, that I ever met her, and that she ever changed me, then I could go on. That's the worst part for me. Please, could you do something for me that would make me forget her?"

"Slow down, Phil Ticks. You want her to disappear? You want me to take her right out of you forever?" Jackie Wu scratched behind his ear.

"Somehow, yes." Phil's desperation had taken him right to the edge of his seat.

Jackie Wu nodded. "It can be done. It's something you could do yourself if you really wanted to, and if you had that kind of strength. It's not such a good idea to just forget things if you can't come to terms with them first. It's all in who you are. How much do you think about others and care? What kind of person do you want to be?"

"But what about your card and your commercials? Magic Makes Mean Love Disappear?"

"That was my brother's doing. It's true most people opt for his way. It's simpler than dealing directly with the problem. If you would rather not make those kinds of decisions, if you would rather just forget what hurts instead of seeing it through and learning, well...Yes, there is something for you downstairs." Jackie Wu pointed to the elevator door.

"That's what I want. That's all I want. It's a pain to me that won't end."

"If we do this for you, she will be gone. She will truly be gone, and all the good things too. The reason you needed her to begin with. And there must have been some good things. To become so close, there must have been those during the time you were together." Jackie Wu stared at his hands, the lines that told fortunes in his palms.

"Please. It all has to be gone, all of it."

Gravely, Jackie Wu looked up at Phil and he took a card out of his coat pocket. "I wish you could see that it's alright to make mistakes. It's nobody's fault. Mistakes can be overcome. They are what make us human, they are how we learn. It's what our evolution and progression are all about." He wrote something onto the card, but he didn't pass it to Phil yet. "Your problem is that you think too much in terms of disasters. It's all a matter of your coming to terms with yourself. Can you see how it works? Don't expect the worst."

"I try not to."

Jackie Wu held up his finger, "Mister Ticks, that's where your problem lies. I know it's difficult to control that part of you that expects the worst. It's a conditioned reflex for you. Naturally, seeing Miss Takahara killed as you arrived to wed her…A terrible thing for you and worse for her. Followed up by your experience with Amanda Wonka, it would cause anyone to stop and wonder at the cruelty of life."

"I know," Phil said, "It did."

"If it would help you, I can make you forget the pains of life. Although there's no way to assure that they won't happen again. You see, the pains will always come in some form. You've got to deal with them to survive."

"But if you can erase my memory of Amanda Wonka, then life will be different. Let me try, please."

"It seems you insist." He wrote something on the card. "Bring this card downstairs. There is something there for you."

"Thank you!" Phil took the card. "Thank you so much."

Jackie Wu sat still and quiet and carved as wood.

THE OTHER JACKIE WU

"The other Jackie Wu said you could give me something that would make me forget."

Jackie Wu Junior set down a shipment of wooden miniatures from Tibet. He nodded. "We have a machine that takes anything you have lived and turns it into a dream. Sometimes the next morning you may remember a part of it, but you forget as the day moves on. It's very effective. We can just turn whatever happened to you into a nightmare with the flick of a switch."

"A machine? I don't like the sound of that though. That sounds like the electric chair." Phil looked away and back, "Do you have anything that will erase it more safely that that?"

"We do of course. We have the potions…More expensive. The potions are mixed to suit your particular memory. They are 100% effective."

"Machines, potions—it sounds like Frankenstein around this place. Couldn't you just hypnotize me or something?"

Jackie Wu said, "I assure you our methods are safe, accredited and very effective."

"Does this come with a ninety day guarantee?" At the moment, Phil could feel the tables turn. It was professional, he was being sold something and he was cautious.

"There will be no need for a guarantee. You will have forgotten what you needed one for."

Wow, Phil thought, This guy is good. What a promise. "I'm sold," he said.

POTION

"I get careless with love. I keep forgetting I'm not supposed to say some things." Phil stopped talking and watched Jackie Wu Jr. behind a table of wooden pyramids and totem poles, stirring a deep, bubbling stew. It twisted steam up around him and he breathed in deeply.

"Yes, I understand," Jackie Wu Junior said, "A problem with communication."

"No. Well, yes, but more than that."

Jackie Wu Junior stirred out the wooden spoon and the red mixture dripped off, steaming. Then he continued stirring, adding things from a golden box with an opened wooden lid.

Phil babbled nervously, "I'm tired of the way it always falls apart for me and being hurt and getting in the same situation. And then I can't stop thinking about everything I've done wrong or might have done wrong, I don't even know, and it replays over and over until I'm going crazy with it all. This time was the worst of all." He picked up an idol and put it back down on the counter. "This time I am going crazy for her. You've got to help me."

"This will do the trick." Calmly, the potion was poured into a crystal bottle. "You will never think of her again." Jackie Wu Junior wiped the sides of the bottle. It was filled with his famous Love Remover. "She won't even be a memory. She will be gone, like a forgotten dream. It will be just as you wished."

Phil was fumbling with the idol again as Jackie Wu Junior set the bottle with a clink onto the counter.

"This is it." Staring at the potion inside, Phil touched it and quickly took back his hand. It was hot to the touch.

"Yes, this is it, Mister Ticks. You will forget and your pain will be gone."

"Then I can begin all over again?"

"Like a baby facing the world," Jackie Wu Junior answered. "Innocent. You can learn all over again."

"But this potion isn't dangerous, is it? I mean, I'm not in danger of losing myself? I won't become a different person. I want to change, but I don't want to lose myself."

"Mister Ticks, don't look so deeply. You will have erased only that part of you that troubles you the most, and then you will be happy. Guaranteed. It will be a terrible weight lifted off of you and life will begin all over again."

"All over again…" Phil repeated. "And it will only make me forget about her?"

"And whatever time you spent with her. That too will be gone, but nothing else."

"That's strong magic." Phil tried, but he still couldn't touch the steaming bottle. He could believe that it would change him and let him be different. He knew he would stop thinking of the pain and he would be, as Jackie Wu had said, like a baby facing the world.

Jackie Wu Junior just nodded at him.

DOPPELGANGER

The ground he was walking on wasn't steady. He felt like he was wading through the air above the pavement. Food Giant shimmered across from him. If there was a curse, it came from here. On this spot long ago someone left a curse that had never been healed.

Something invisible whirled past him. It sounded like a rollercoaster and smells rolled across the parking lot at him…popcorn, sawdust, African lions, steam and all the aura of a circus.

Phil Ticks ran into fear around the corner. The air rippled and he felt the heat as the man emerged from it like a door.

The man was a mirror of himself. They both stared deeply at each other, but neither one seemed to know what to do.

Phil's double finally spoke, "Do you know about doppelgangers, Phil Ticks?"

The doppelganger seemed surprised as Phil took a step backwards. Dogs were barking everywhere. "I have lost my mind," Phil decided. His back stopped against the wall of Royalty Cleaners. The fans blew out hot laundry air. "And now I'm going to die."

"No. I've got good news for you. I really am your doppelganger. But look closely at me," he smiled, "and look at yourself. You can tell there are some things different about me. Different for the better…"

True, Phil could see his resemblance had been treated better by life. There was none of the worry or stress. He practically glowed at Phil, so assured and happy. And where did he get all that charm? Phil wondered, Think of all the vacuums and owls he could sell. "What happened to you?"

"Looks like you got stuck with all the bad luck, Phil. That's too bad." The double of Phil pulled at the yellow flower in his lapel.

"But what do you want?"

"I'm going to do you a favor, Phil." What a smile! "I'm not

from this place, and it looks like it's been hard on you. I'm going to switch dimensions with you. You were crying out in pain, you were really having troubles in this world," he looked around himself. "I'm not surprised though, I can see how this place would get to you. But don't worry," he smiled again. They came so easily. "You'll like where I'm from. You'll find it's a much better America than this one. You'll see it's a completely different place."

"What do you mean?" Phil said to his mirror.

"I'm here to take your place, Phil Ticks. It's the chance of a lifetime."

He was convincing, Phil had to admit, "But I felt such a terror before you showed up. I don't know if I should trust you."

"You don't trust yourself?!" the doppelganger seemed surprised. "Why would I hurt myself? What's good for you is good for me. Believe me, the best thing I could do for you—and for me—is for you to leave this place. There's nothing here for you. You'll see, I can survive better than you can, I'll take over here for you and turn your life around..." he was watching Phil so carefully. "But there's nothing to worry about, you can come back if you miss it here for any reason. Just ask for me."

"How do I know what your other world is like? How do I know that it's better?"

"Everything that happened badly for you here has been good for me there. Think about that. I've got everything you lost!" He laughed. "Since our lives began! I've been *very* lucky, Phil! So I'm here now to show my thanks. I can handle this world much better than you. I've grown up differently than you. I've got a winning attitude."

"Great," Phil mumbled. "Thanks."

"And this girl, this Amanda Wonka," his fingers twisted. A bluish cloud swirled, curled and became the shape of her. "You can let go of her too."

Phil couldn't tell if it was more magic, or if this really was Amanda Wonka appearing in front of them.

167

The Phil Ticks doppelganger said, "Look at me, Amanda Wonka." He straightened his expensive suit. "I have wealth, I've achieved things. I can give you security and a sense of control. You'll never have to worry about your next meal, or your safety. You'll have anything you could possibly want."

Phil stared.

The doppelganger laughed. "We're the same man, Amanda, but I'm the better Phil Ticks. I've made it. I'm successful and he's not."

All Phil could do was put his hand to his eyes to try to stop it all. It's true though, Phil knew. I can't compare. I've lost her, I know I have.

She looked at the two Phils, back and forth.

Phil didn't want to hear anymore. He didn't want to be with them, neither one of them seemed real to him. "Listen to me," Phil said to the phantoms, "I have learned some things. I can get by in this world. I can come to terms with it. I don't know what any other world is like and I don't want to be replaced. And Amanda…" still he couldn't look at her, "She can do what she wants, she isn't helpless. She can choose her own life."

Phil looked at the lot of Food Giant and the birds that were scattering for the clouds. "I'll survive here. I don't need to give up to do it. I still have life to live here. Maybe it will always be a struggle and things will always seem to be against me, but not even the richest, luckiest American can live without some kind of pain or loneliness. That's life. I'll survive and it will get better."

Phil stepped away. He found he had given himself enough strength to move again. He loosened himself from the grip of the doppelganger magic and walked away, out of the parking lot and he could hear the sound behind him of water going down the drain.

Birds were pulled out of the sky and sucked into the black parking lot hole, swirling away.

The wind pulled at everything and Phil too, but he fought

against it.

Somewhere behind him, the ground was opening up and taking itself back.

He wasn't the only part of history here.

In 1875, the Saturn Circus left its orange sawdust ring in the field outside of town. A hundred years passed, waiting, and the field became a parking lot for Food Giant. The Saturn Circus, with its sideshow trail had touched the earth there for a moment.

The history of America is composed of remembering things laying over each other. Sometimes they get left in place like a wound, waiting to heal.

The old man standing bent up against the wall of Food Giant pointed in amazement at the end of the curse, "You've done it!" he shouted. The old man shouted and pointed and hopped in a dance away from the wall. "You did it! It's over!"

WHERE THEY'RE GOING
AND HOW THEY LIVE

Introduction from the 2003 self-published book:

Oh yes, *Where They're Going and How They Live.* Let's re-member 4th Grade Seattle, a field trip to see the Wax Museum downtown (like most of the old wonders, it's no longer there). I remember the cold black room with a curtain of water raining, and the first white settlers of Seattle standing on the beach look-ing hopeless, with their noble leader holding his bleeding arm after an axe chopped him. And the doomed natives standing off to the left. Not a promising start to the Emerald City. Probably explains a lot though. They also took us to the Curiosity Shop. The underground tour of the city. And the Bubbleater, up down and gone. What do they ever do with the past, forget it or sell it to someone else? So what if you could live beyond, what if someone had the secret to be alive and go on all along from the very start of America? The feeling it's repeating (with this new wrong war a part of it all). You must have seen it before. If you can remember.

For his return to fiction, Phil Ticks decided to take a support-ing role in this book, playing second fiddle to Donny D'Angelo. Growing up in Seattle, I witnessed firsthand the near total

destruction of the magical weirdness of that town. Drive-Ins and movie theaters, restaurants and odd shops, vacant lots, trees and community gardens, but fortunately those childhood memories were safely stored and I have let some of them come through in this transmission.

Contents

FLORIDA

Donny D'Angelo used to be a boxer then he gave it up to drive a taxi.

On his day off, he and his girlfriend stepped from the monorail and threaded into the crowds, all wandering from sight to sight at The Fun Forest. The rain had clouded around the Space Needle.

They stopped under the eaves and watched people shoot corks at stuffed animals. The bear playing ragtime piano would roar every time he got hit.

"Come on, Tina. This isn't interesting. Let's find that tourist shop. It's around here somewhere."

She pouted at Donny, strutted along next to him angrily, stylishly twisting the gold medallion on her necklace.

Donny pressed her waist to him when they walked. He liked to feel her all the time, knowing that she wouldn't necessarily be with him forever. He was the only one who had the water. It kept him like this forever, when she and all the others had to disappear.

"Maybe it's underground?" she guessed. "There's shops and stuff down there. We can take the Bubbleator to them." She laughed and kissed him.

"Sure honey, that's right." Donny opened the door for her, chasing after her as they went onto the orange lit ramp leading towards the clear round elevator.

Inside of it, Donny leaned against the curved glass and struck a match off his jeans leg, lighting a cigarette.

Dressed like an admiral, the operator on the tall stool was horrified. She snapped into the silver microphone, "Sir, we frown on smoking within the Bubbleator." She gave them both the eye for the next few seconds, until she guided the elevator to a bumpy landing. She pulled a steel lever and the door hissed open on the lower floor.

"Nice uniform…" Donny laughed up at her red astronaut

tuxedo, then he relit his cigarette outside the elevator.

"Oh my God, Donny!" Tina hid her face with her hand, hurrying him away. "I can't believe you did that! She's staring at us!"

"So what? It's a free country. I can smoke anytime I want." He knew about the healing water, how it could cure him of everything from lung cancer to aging.

Juan Ponce de Leon, the 16th Century Spanish explorer, found the Fountain of Youth 480 years ago. Long before he was Donny in Seattle, he was a conquistador, landing in the New World, searching desperately for immortality. For years he struggled through jungles, was met by menacing tribes, felt wearied, crazy and disillusioned.

On the island he named Florida, his ship was attacked and he was shot by an arrow as he charged through the swamp. That's where he found it, as he stumbled, weak from loss of blood. It was steaming, all covered with vines and ripe flowers and flying birds. It's part of his plantation in Florida, hidden under lock and key with a thick oak door: the Fountain of Youth. Every time he drinks the water he is cleaned and renewed. Now he will never die. He's been young for 519 years.

Each time he had the water, his body returned and he was a new person, free to start all over again. He always found somewhere new in America, where he had never been before. He couldn't explain to someone how he got young again, he had to keep it a secret. Eternal life was like reincarnation for him: he kept adopting new identities, moving all over the country to remain undetected, all the time playing with life like it was a vast game. This was his 20th life: a twenty seven year old name Donny D'Angelo.

Tina pinched him. "There it is!" The vision glared at her, held under her painted fingernail.

Under the stairs, where all the echoes piled up, was The Lost in Time Sideshow. The marble floor was greasy underfoot and littered with candy wrappers, unwanted things and cigarettes.

Children scattered back and forth throwing toys, while the misfiring neon in the sign made it jump above them with arcing light.

He hugged her and kissed her ear, "Thanks, baby. You got great eyes…Beautiful eyes."

Paying two dollars for both of them, Donny held to Tina's hips, wheeling through the turnstile in front of him. The dark room was filled with exhibits, strange things from all over the world. Donny scanned the walls, the paintings, photographs, and shelves. He drifted around the aquariums filled with masks and voodoo dolls.

Gleaming from a row of jars, a two-headed pig in a bottle twisted its pair of open mouths in a squeal of bubbles, trapped forever in the clear formaldehyde.

He wondered how much they would take for it to mysteriously disappear.

"WHAT PIG?"

Donny held out his hand. His palm offered a stack of money, a few thousand dollars. "Would anyone notice…If the pig went missing?" he asked the cashier. He began to smile in slow motion, knowing that she couldn't resist.

It was amazing to him that these mortal people would want to waste their whole short life doing such pointless work. Of course, he knew that he was luckier than them; he had invested in gold early on, money was just paper to him. Over the years, America got stranger and stranger. He had watched it all happen. The people lost perspective.

The cashier stared at him closely, taking in the sight of him… his *Who's The Boss* t-shirt, his leather jacket with Camel cigarettes in the pocket, the gold arrowhead necklace, his strong almost fierce stare…The money piled in his hand. It was more money than she'd ever seen…She thought it was like a dream or a movie. "What pig?" she said. She turned to the counter, bored with the world, and flattened her open hand on the display case, twitching her fingertips.

Donny smiled. He passed the money over and returned to Tina who was obsessed with a talking rock. She had her ear against it, listening. He whispered, "It's mine, baby." His finger tugged across her skin, across her back and spine, as he passed on his way to the shelf with the two-headed pig. It was the perfect gift for his hospitalized friend, Phil Ticks. Donny picked it up quickly and pushed it under his jacket. No alarms went off, nobody knew but the cashier. He grabbed Tina's hand and they left the Seattle Center.

THE DIALING FOR DOLLARS HOST

They were walking back home with their arms around each other, laughing. Tina was good at remembering the lines of movies. She could dissolve into film stars and act out their moments. Donny had to stop to catch his breath.

Across the street, and timing her direction, an older woman approached them. She caught them at the curb and grabbed Donny's arm like a relative from Transylvania. She stared into his face intently and uttered, "Vince Peabody?"

"What?" Tina laughed. "His name's Donny! Donny D'Angelo."

"I'm sorry. I thought…" she let his arm go. "He looks exactly like somebody I used to know." Her eyes wouldn't budge. "I used to watch him on the TV," she paused, getting confused, "But I guess it couldn't be you."

Tina laughed again, "Not my Donny. He *should* be on the TV. One of those tough cop shows." She kissed him and pulled him out of the strange woman's gravity.

That was close, Donny thought. He quickly smiled for Tina. But a fear had crept into him, like that time in 1892 when he was selling windmills. It could be dangerous if he was recognized. His current life depended on the cloaking of his past lives. Mystery was what kept him safe.

Forty years ago, in Tucson, Donny's name *was* Vince Peabody. In the early, shimmering beginning days of television, he was the host of a children's show called *Ron Bott in America,* a crazy outer space show with puppets and adventure every week. Then he was promoted to the Dialing for Dollars host. He showed Westerns and Romances and challenged housewives with money prizes. Five years later, he changed his name to Donny D'Angelo and moved to the coast, where he tried to make a living boxing. He gave up on that and became a taxi driver, writing comic books in Seattle. He thought that Vince Peabody had been forgotten by everyone back in the desert.

"What was that?" Tina startled him.

"I have no idea. She thought I was somebody else." He tried to remember if he'd met her as Vince Peabody. His adventures as other people faded with time, just like growing old, he supposed. Sometimes he even forgot who he had been. Maybe when that old woman was a young girl, he had awarded her a prize at a spelling bee in Two Lakes, Arizona. Something like that was possible. It had changed her life. That joy of the crowd and victory led her to become a professional bingo caller, travelling west, ending up settled in Tacoma.

Donny smiled and stroked Tina's skin. "Thanks for sticking up for me, baby."

SHE REPEATED FLORIDA

Street Poet was out in front of their apartment, throwing crazy shadows and words. For a dollar, he'd recite a ramble of sentences and exclamations like billboards passing Greyhound windows. He spun with jittery energy in the light of the lantern and dull loping cars, "Pity the cicada…" His voice was breaking from all the cold wind. Balanced on madness, dipping into it, sometimes Donny saw him downtown counting ships in the harbor, resting against a rotten totem pole.

Tina always got a little scared when they saw him. She clung tighter and tried to be a shadow on Donny's right side.

"Faust!" Street Poet blurted and stared vaguely at some level of rising air. As they neared him, he suddenly asked, "Who wants to give a poem a dollar?"

"Not us," Donny joked. He felt Tina's hand clutch the skin of his hip. She was terrified of that man. Seeing him, she would try to cross the street. Her fingers pinched Donny. The jar bounced inside his jacket. Donny thought, Maybe I should give this to him? For a second, he almost did. "Write a poem about this!" he would say.

Then Donny remembered Phil Ticks. The other day, Phil had jumped out of an airplane without a parachute. He fell more than five hundred feet of sky before he landed on a circus tent. Donny had to go to the hospital tomorrow and bring his wounded friend a present—the pig was for Phil.

Donny laughed. He kissed Tina's dark hair and she let up a little. Her fingers went back down under his belt and rested nicely, as Donny led them into the building, up the marble stairs.

He kissed her again when she opened the door. She was really so beautiful, he knew he had to live every moment he could with her. The problem with eternal life was losing everything else that mattered, everything that wasn't timeless. He had learned to enjoy it all, for all it was worth, before he was forced to change and move on, with another sip of the Florida water, into a new life.

Right now, as Donny D'Angelo, it was Tina who made this life matter so much. Lovingly, he touched her soft waist. Five hundred years and I can still be in love. He said, "I love you, Tina."

"I love you, Donny D'Angelo." She clutched his hands and she had a beautiful idea. "Would you like to be bathed?" Tina purred. It was the line from a movie they had seen. Skillfully, she unbuttoned his shirt and tugged on the golden arrow necklace, pulling him in the direction of the bathroom.

"Yeah," he agreed. He kissed her shoulders. She began to pour the hot water, bending around him and stirring with her hand and smiling and taking off clothes, dropping them on the tiles.

"Full of flowers…" he breathed in her ear.

"What?" Her mouth was hot against him.

"That's what Florida means."

She repeated, "Florida," dripping with steam, hot water and her oily perfumes, shipwrecking him.

THE DIAL TONE

"This store is just like something from L.A.!" The elated young man stared around himself, gazing at the full shelves and posters, smiling wondrously. "Finally!" he announced to the ceiling, "Some class has come to this town! For once, I feel at home!"

Donny stood as unassuming as possible, a few feet away from this conversation behind the cash register. If he was the cashier, he would want to scream out loud, confronted by this kind of horror. He didn't know how she did it. Every time Donny came into The Wow Comic Book Store, he began to cringe. It was the same feeling he used to get in the fifth round.

Donny listened as the tanned cartoon asked the cashier where she was from.

She said, "Originally from Rochester, then I moved to Enumclaw, don't ask me why. To me, Seattle is great!" She laughed. Then she quickly asked him where he was from.

The loudmouth formed a triangle with his hands and blurted, "Hollywood! The Hills! I know, it shows, right?" He acted out, laughed and put the comics under his arm. "I just wish I could think of somewhere to go to lunch. There must be somewhere in this God-forsaken city that serves good healthy Hungarian food."

Donny had enough. Suddenly he thought how much he needed to see Tina. He dropped his comic book back in the rack, waved goodbye to the cashier and bolted out the door.

The bright winter sun burnt a hole in the gray sky, a few snowflakes were falling. A bus plowed by next to him and he coughed and thought of sweet Tina again. She was at work right now, typing, answering phones—he imagined her legs, smoothly drawn under her chair. He despaired that she was so far away for the day. He ran to a phone booth in a panic.

The phone clicked and asked for money. Shaking, he paid it a quarter, punched in the numbers to her, holding his breath as it rang.

"Hello, B. Arthur School of Design," she purred. "Tina speaking."

"Baby! It's Donny. Sweetheart, how are you?"

"Donny, honey! I've been thinking about you all day." Her voice was so fantastic, calling through all the ages, soothing and warm. Just hearing her, he felt thoroughly in place and glued to her. Tina sighed heavily, "I wish I could leave right now."

"Hurry up!" he gulped, managing to say just before the machine asked for more money, "I gotta go now, baby. Hurry up home!"

"I will, I will." he heard her promise, as she disappeared into the dial tone.

OUT OF THE BLUE

How did they meet? How did Donny D'Angelo, a man with four hundred years of charming women find Tina Takahara and fall so in love with her? That's always a story in itself, two people coming together out of the blue and finding each other. There were some beautiful things here and there, it just took time to discover them.

All he was trying to find was a restaurant. It was supposed to be somewhere around this neighborhood. But the streets and houses all looked alike in the darkness. It was pure luck that led him to it finally. Past a house on the corner that was falling apart, he found it at last, right where it was meant to be.

He parked the yellow cab at the New Country Diner for some coffee. Light of dawn was splashing onto all the wet tar.

Donny sat in a booth next to the window and wrote ideas in a notebook.

A woman said, "Good morning," slipping a menu onto his table.

He spoke but didn't look up. He was busy writing. He didn't want to lose that train of thought. Something about America was revealing itself to him.

She returned to him again and set a cup of coffee by his hand. "Thanks," he mumbled.

"You're welcome," she said fondly. "Give me a shout when you're ready."

"Sure." He looked up and saw her.

KING TUT

Solemnly, Donny stepped into the white and gray room. There was a television attached to the ceiling in the corner, yammering a game show—someone had just won a washing machine. Phil was locked in bed, watching it, bandaged from head to foot like a mummy, with the channel changer in his white mitt.

"Mr. Ticks, you have a visitor," announced the nurse in front of Donny. Her body was arched with tension. You could tell she didn't savor her assignment here.

"It's not the circus again, is it?" Phil's voice muffled and his arm strained the cast. He couldn't see out of the bandages.

"No," she rolled her eyes and pulled Donny towards the bed. "It's a Mr. Donny D'Angelo." She wanted to leave, her shift was done.

"It's funny," Donny joked as she passed him, "Your name's Angelina. We're both Phil's angels." He shadowboxed and smiled at Phil, "Hey! It's me, Phil! You look fantastic! What did you do, fall out of a plane?"

Phil moaned, "You know I did..." as he turned up the TV sound.

Donny pulled a plastic chair up next to the bed and sat down close. "How you doing?"

"Like King Tut," Phil said.

"Yeah, well you look like him. Listen Phil, there are better ways of telling me you can't make the deadline on the comic book," Donny joked and tapped him lightly on the shoulder.

"Don't Donny!" the white sculpture winced, "I hurt all over. I'm in severe pain...You almost lost me, I almost died. I was almost gone from this world."

"You really did fall out of a plane?"

"Worst of all, these circus people keep coming by every hour, trying to sign me on. I went over so big, they want me to fall out of a plane every week! They want me to hit their big top for each week's finale. They figure I'm the next Houdini. Look at all the flowers they sent me." He twitched, "I keep telling the nurse to throw them away. I'm allergic to begonias!"

"Gee, that's too bad, Phil."

Phil sighed hopelessly, "A man can't even die nowadays. I thought for sure if you jump out of a plane without a parachute, you're dead, right?" The white gauze over his mouth stilled and he was silent, tired, listening to the TV.

"Yeah," Donny sympathized. "I know. It's rough..." He almost set his hand on Phil's shoulder again, but he pulled back. He was as careful with motion as a silent movie star.

The game show audience applauded from the television.

"Oh yeah," Donny brightened. He stuffed his hand into his leather jacket. "I brought you a get well present." He set the jar noisily on the table next to Phil. The two headed pig swirled against the reflection of begonias.

"Constantinople!" Phil shouted.

"Cairo?" the contestant guessed.

"No," the host grew sad, "I'm afraid the correct answer is Constantinople."

"Damn!" Phil twitched. "I could have won a trip to Hawaii!" As the studio audience groaned, he switched it off with a bending of his wrapped thumb. "It bothers me," Phil confessed in the silence, all encased in cloth, "that my fellow Americans can be so profoundly stupid."

"Yeah, well…" Donny shrugged, "That's the way it goes."

Phil went on, "You would think that after well over two hundred years, with all the best opportunities…This land was like Eden after all! America could have been something beautiful. Look around you, Donny. It's all wrong." Phil stopped his tirade for a moment then softly went on, "I don't know. Maybe it's just the city that's getting to me. Maybe I *should* join their circus, see the country, meet new and interesting people."

Donny wasn't really listening. Most people tuned Phil Ticks out. His voice became the sound of an AM radio station.

"Like Alligator Boy," Phil continued. "Cyclops Woman…Or maybe Red Skelton."

Donny was reeling with more thoughts of America, sometimes it washed over and left him stunned. All these years spent living here and he still felt that he didn't belong. "What went wrong?" Donny thought out loud. He pushed his memory back. I've seen it since the beginning, since we came here and began to change what we found. I saw it all happen. I even helped it to happen. What did we do? Were we just greedy? Did we think it was forever? Did we think it would always be around? Just like me, with a life that never ends…"

THE REVOLUTIONARY WAR PERIOD

"I wouldn't want to be greedy with life," a young soldier stepped up and reached for the flag. "I'll sacrifice myself." The air was burning and feverish.

Donny D'Angelo rolled over in his restless sleep and returned to the dream he was having, when he was Sean O'Rillnick, watching in amazement as the boy took the flag and ran with it towards the peak of a hill. Halfway to it, he was shot dead. "Why would anyone waste their life?" He almost said it out loud—knowing it would have had him shot for treason—he was so struck by the sight. Something became very clear to him then: life shouldn't be destroyed—yours or anyone else's—and that made war seem like the worst thing to do. Though it took him so long, ten lives already gone by, it was so simple to understand.

Like a shadow over the grass, he crept away from the dangerous place, into the glade of birch trees, through watery moss that covered over him. He could hear cannons and charging horses, shots and swords...They were closer than he'd like them to be... Faster, suddenly he was running away from it. He dropped his gun, crashing over ferns, dry leaves, broken branches, stumbling across a stream, falling into the muddy edge of a cold river.

The winter Delaware was frozen drifts of ice, with black flocks of crows out in the middle. He splashed out of it onto a rock, hands in his mouth, chattering with cold, falling around on the loose stones, stomping and trying to warm himself. He cursed in Spanish, howling from the searing cold. It was too much for him. He didn't want any more wars, it wasn't worth it. *Why risk your life with death?*

He felt it was a blessing of knowledge. He actually prayed on the edge of the Delaware, while George Washington crossed the river to the other side. "If I don't get frostbite or shot, if my life is spared..." he prayed to the sky and weak sun, while the boats chopped across the ice, "Then I swear to dedicate my life

191

to peace." The ex-conquistador continued to pray in Spanish, "I could become a missionary. I shall go into the unknown territory and convert…No that's wrong." Eyes closed, he listened to the oars cutting on the water. A cannonball splashed far up the river, but George Washington was nearly across. "I'll spend my eternal life in my holy Florida, studying and thinking about the nature of existence…"

He opened his eyes slowly. The sun was reappearing through the white clouds. Tina's arm hugged over him. She was still asleep.

He yawned quietly. He remembered the dream he just woke from. That day in 1776 that changed his life. Since then, he had not fought in a single war. He didn't want to kill people anymore. It was the Delaware that made him realize how much he needed the Fountain of Youth. He was so thankful for it he swore to devote all his life to unraveling the human mystery.

So far he hadn't been too good with that part of his promise. He really didn't want to take the Fountain for granted. He wanted to show that he was more than just alive. He felt he had to prove the blessing of immortality wasn't being wasted on him. But how?

Tina stirred too and rubbed her leg over the top of him, sliding. "Hold on a minute," Donny took her hand, "I almost forgot about…" He looked into her eyes, "I just had this dream where…It was a long time ago, but I remember clearly…It was when I was a kid and I promised to do something, but I never did it."

She worked her hand back onto his chest. "That's alright, Donny. We did that all the time when we were kids."

"Sure baby, but this was one of those life or death promises."

She laughed, "What did you promise?"

"That I would move to Florida to become a philosopher."

"Florida?" She stared at him. "That's crazy! What's in Florida?"

The Fountain of Youth, he was going to say. It was the secret he always kept to himself. If she would go with him though, she would find out. Surrounding the fountain were a hundred acres of trees and swamp, with a castle he had built back in 1522. Nobody else had ever seen the place. He would ask her to.

GEORGIA AND CALIFORNIA

She had an Orgone Accumulator. There were actually thousands of those big square cabinets all over America, along with television, radios and washing machines. Tina closed the door to bathe in the invisible energy that hummed through the sheet iron, the steel wool, the glass wool, and the wooden layers of the Accumulator walls.

"Tina?" Donny called from their bed. Only a sheet wrapped over his bare leg. "Tina, can you hear me?"

He lay back on the silk, waiting and staring at the ceiling. For thirty minutes she would be in there, before the door clicked open and she would step back into their bedroom, illuminated.

Stretched across the bed, he was thinking all about Tina, wondering if he could stay with her, like two normal people growing old living together, but he didn't want to give up the water. How could he do that?

Maybe, he hoped, Tina would drink it with him.

Once, in Georgia, long before Tina, he did grow old with a wife and there was a special unusual wonder in knowing life that way. He became seventy with her. It was amazing. All through it, he felt so alive. That feeling was the problem though, it was something he couldn't give up and as always, he started to become afraid of death's approach. She couldn't understand his fear. She was so accepting. And what she saw waiting at the end would be something every person finds, like a tree that you are walking towards at the end of a field.

It didn't have to be like that for them: he wanted her to know, he wanted to surprise her. He could show her the water and they would return like magic, back to their youth.

The night was full of the moon, stars, and warm summer wind. Inside, those two old people were lying beside each other. He brushed her silver white hair and circled her lips with his fingers. There were years they had filled with life together. But he wanted to reverse how it was making him slow and sore to move, fading him gradually out. He loved her and let her fall asleep across him.

Gently, he slid next to her and, then he got out of bed, very slowly. His back hurt him. She was smiling in her sleep. He noticed that. He pulled blankets back up over her and tucked them softly around her shape.

Then he went out to the car and he drove with a map to Florida spread on the metal dashboard. It took him a long time to get there, across hundreds of miles, to find out that gigantic vines had climbed all over the fence and across the yards, spanning the moat-like bridge to the castle.

The castle had become a trunk with roots and branches and leaves.

It took him most of the day to get inside. Plants unwound all the way down the stairs into the dungeon where the fountain was.

He felt so feeble and his heart ached from the exertion. He needed to drink the water fast. He dipped the silver cup and dug a scoop out of the circle and instantly felt the effect. He had another sip too. He had never grown so old before, he needed more. Turning brand new, he saw his reflection in the ripple. He was young again.

It still needed weeks to clear the vines and leaves from all the rooms, stairways and hallways, out of the suits of armor, from the paintings and book shelves. But he was young again and he cleared the yard with strong muscles, tearing through the maze and gardens, all the way back to the iron fence. He was young again and there was incredible electricity inside of him. He couldn't wait any longer to show her what it was like. He filled a jar with the Florida water, locked up the castle, and sped back across America.

He thought of her all the way home, how she would turn like a flower towards him, burning once more. He kept watching the horizon.

And then there she was in the room facing the mountains.

She sat with a cup of herb tea between her hands. "Hello." Slowly she smiled at him and kindly and slyly she stared. "Are you a dream?" He was paused, quiet in the shadow by the door, before she laughed. "You look just like when we first met. That's a good trick. I thought I was awake."

He hurried to her, "It's not a trick. This is really me!" He stomped the floor joyously, "I'm young again!" After a spin, he sat down, touching her. "I never told you I could do this anytime, because I wanted to grow old with you. I've never done that before."

Softly, she let him touch her and he said, "You brought me a whole new understanding of life with all this time together. I love you." He held her frail hands, "Now we can start over. It's easy. You can be a girl again! Here…" He opened his suitcase. The jar was padded in there safely with his new clothes. "Drink this, darling."

She laughed at him, waltzing in front of her, all excited. He was so smiling and happy, acting like a boy again. She smiled, "I don't want it, sweetheart."

"What are you talking about?" he held the water before her. "We can move somewhere new and live all over again, we can be with each other always."

"I don't want to though. I don't need to live all these years over again. I feel so good with the life that I've had." She smiled, "I'm not afraid of it ending. I'll be ready when it stops. I've seen a lot of things in this life and it feels right the way I've lived it. I don't need to go backwards and start over. Take that water away, sweetheart." She pushed her hand against him. He was ready to pour it into her tea. "I told you, I don't want any, my dearest." She stared at her young husband with his magical water. "What more do you need from life?"

"I just don't want it to end."

She gave him a comforting look, "Everything has to end sometime. If you're part of life, you have to know that."

"No." He kneeled beside her and held her. "I want to stay

with you forever. I have to! I don't want us to be apart."

"I'm not a forever thing. Nothing here is. Not the flowers, or the rocks, or even the sunlight." She brushed his dark hair while he kissed her arm. "But as long as we have time, I want to be with you too. That's what life is for. I love you."

"I love you too," he repeated.

"Then let's live as long as we can together, my strange darling," she said. "Take care of me still." They touched their lips to each other, his young hands on her. She laughed, "I'll be able to get used to you again."

For the climate, they moved to California. They had an orange tree in their back yard and they would watch the birds sing on it. They took walks to the ocean, in the afternoon and after dinner. They found agates on the sand where the tide washed out and left them. One day while they laughed and held hands, she told him exactly where she wanted to be buried—there, pointing to a hill covered with tall grass and white stones, overlooking the waves.

VINCE PEABODY IN AMERICA

An experiment in time travel shot him randomly into outer space. For the first season, each day Ron Bott was exploring somewhere new in the galaxy. In the show's second season, he finally made it back to Earth, the city of Sacramento, in the United States. He lived with his genius marionette inventor, Dr. Cribbler, in a garage in suburban California.

Ron Bott in America was one of the first shows to use laugh tracks and it set the tone for children's television to follow. Ron Bott clanked among the friendly puppets and together they sang songs, made jokes and showed old Fleischer cartoons. As the televisions slowly spread, they carried Ron Bott across America.

Not only was there Ron Bott merchandise, lunchbox sets, Halloween costumes and toys of the cast, they even made a Ron Bott movie in 1954. Vince Peabody starred in the low budget sci-fi titled *Recalled*. It was about a conscious robot with an atomic weapon planted deep inside of his metal. It played for a week alongside the highway, in the clogged fields of dandelions on the drive-in screen, or in the city, down the brick alleyways in rundown theaters.

In 1956, Vince Peabody turned over Ron Bott and that job to another actor. Every weekday for the next five years, he introduced the sponsors during the afternoon TV matinee feature.

He even excelled at his new job. Ratings soared when he suggested adding gambling to the show. Each program, after a commercial break, Vince spun a tumbler full of people's names cut from the telephone book. And an assistant wearing a Las Vegas dress would drift past and blindfold him. After he picked the lucky daily lottery winner, thrilling music played while he called them to see if they knew how much money was in the treasure box.

For his wife's birthday in 1960, hundreds of people celebrated with her as he showed *Recalled*. It flickered with grainy black and white; it looked like ancient history on Arizona television.

SALLY WORN

For one night only, the sign with the red falling down letters spelled her name. A yellow tour bus was parked in the alley next to a club leaning precariously out over the water. Sally was up on the roof, resting after carrying in the equipment. She drank from a green bottle of Rolling Rock and she was breaking off small pieces of bread, flicking them to the ducks paddling below.

Loud geese plowed down over the parking lot, splashing into the river, as a car stopped in a parking space. The doors opened and a strange trio appeared. Two people got out: a man and a woman who helped drag out a bandaged man.

"She's a star!" Phil Ticks was saying emotionally, as they steadied him on his crutches. "I can't believe what a crime it is that she has to play a dive like this."

Donny reexamined the building. "Awww, this ain't so bad. I had to box in places way worse than this! You should have seen—"

Phil interrupted, "The woman is a genius, Donny. She should be in the Opera House, or the Paramount for God's sake. They should close the city and let her play down the streets like the pied piper."

Tina was leaning the club door open for him, "Sure Phil," she laughed.

Phil mumbled through. He got carded and had to dig into layers of bandages to find his picture I.D.

Donny stared at the sudden splash in the river. Circles and ducks floated away from it.

Sally Worn had thrown her beer bottle off the rooftop.

Troublesome waters
much blacker than night
are hiding from view
the harbor's bright lights
Tossed in the turmoil
of life's stormy sea
I cried to my savior
Have mercy on me

LIFE INSURANCE

For sixty five minutes and one quiet encore, Sally Worn and her band The Lonesome Pioneers, played for Phil Ticks and the scattered audience roaming restlessly from chair to chair and across the empty dance floor. Patsy Cline screeched with electric saws. Tina and Donny sat with Phil through the whole thing, at the table in the spotlighted front row.

By the end of the show, Tina had a splitting headache. She actually held her head of dark hair between her hands. Donny almost had to carry her out to their car.

Phil didn't even see them leave. He was enraptured by the spot where Sally had been on stage. He needed to talk to his inspiration; somehow he had to crutch his way backstage to meet her.

A waitress was sweeping up a couple smashed bottles as Phil dragged himself over to the black painted door leading backstage. He rapped on it with his bandage. "Hello?" he called.

The door opened. The bass player, still wearing his straw hat, stood in Phil's way. "What do you want?"

"Is Sally around?"

"Who are you, The Mummy?"

Phil was ready for this. He had it all planned out. At first he thought he could play an insurance salesman, there to sell her Prudential, but then he realized a problem: who would buy life insurance from a man who looked like he had been run over for three days on I-5? So he said truthfully, "I've been a fan of Sally Worn for years. Ever since the early days in Wenatchee…I was wondering if I could talk to her for a moment."

The bass player stared at Phil, working a toothpick over and over between his front teeth.

"I haven't got long to live," Phil suddenly said, "Tomorrow I'm being put into a plastic bubble. I may not survive the transition. Could I at least say thank you to my hero?"

He spit out the toothpick. "Yeah, I guess so. C'mon, she's over here."

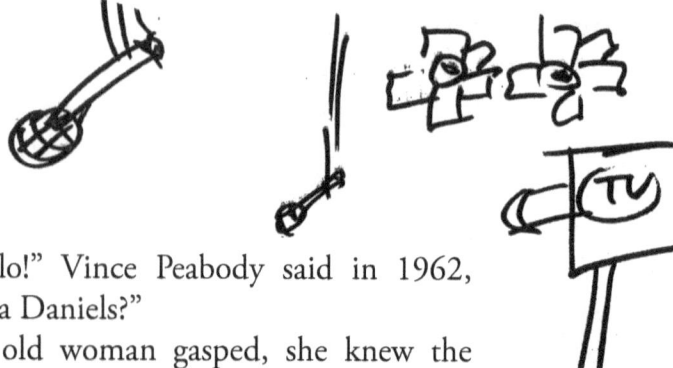

"Hello!" Vince Peabody said in 1962, "Patricia Daniels?"

The old woman gasped, she knew the voice, "Is this Vince Peabody?"

"That's right, Ms. Daniels," he chuckled and smiled at the same time on the screen of her television.

"Oh it is! I knew it!"

"Tell me, Patricia. Do you know today's Dialing for Dollars count?"

"Jesus Christ…" She was beside herself with joy. This was the call that she'd been waiting for. Ever since she got her wooden television, she watched him and neatly kept track of the day's lottery number. "I sure do, Vince!" Her heart fluttered, "$568!"

"Did you say five hundred and sixty eight dollars, Patricia?"

"Yes!" she screamed at the face on her TV. "$568!" The phone shook violently in her hand as she squeezed it.

"Patricia Daniels…" Suspensefully, he pressed a switch and balloons fell from the ceiling, sirens and colored spotlights blared around the studio. "You're correct! You win today's Dialing for Dollars Treasure!"

The woman gripped her heart, as she dropped the phone and snapped like an old tree and fell onto the carpeted floor. Vince Peabody still beamed on television. The glass flashed her name while he congratulated Patricia again. The phone went dead next to her ear. The movie came back on, filling the screen with the sand of a desert clouding with Apaches.

THE STARS DISAPPEAR IN THE MORNING

Donny had to reach across Tina's soft, warm back to get the ringing phone. He rested over her and answered, "Hello?"

There was a pause on the other end of the early morning line, then Phil's tinny sad voice, "Donny...She's gone," he sobbed.

"What? Who?" Donny shifted on the woman underneath him. Tina whispered something up from her dream.

The phone crackled, "Sally! Who else? She left me this morning."

"Phil, she had to." Donny shifted lazily over Tina's hips, "She's in a band."

"But I'm in love with her."

Donny lay his head on Tina's shoulders and set his hand on her leg.

"I know I was asking for it," Phil sighed. "I should have known better."

"Listen Phil, where are you now?" Donny squinted at their clock radio's red numbers.

"I'm at...I don't know...Some street. In a phone booth... with swastika graffiti...broken glass."

"Should I meet you there?"

Phil sighed. "No...I'm sorry, I didn't mean to wake you. I'll be alright. I'll just go somewhere calm and think this through."

"You sure?" Tina was holding Donny's finger to her lips. "If you really need me to," Donny's voice shivered.

"I'll see you later, Donny." Phil talked louder, "Someone with a weedwacker is coming over here." Donny could hear the motor noise in the background. "I should go to the hospital anyway!" Phil shouted. "I think I'll get some breakfast. Then I'll order some x-rays!"

"Okay, Phil. Hey, I'm sorry about Sally Worn." He stared into Tina's opening gentle eyes. "She's quite a musician."

"I know! I know!" The noise was drowning Phil out. "I'll get over it! Bye!" The phone clicked and Donny replaced the receiver.

"My ears are still buzzing," Tina pouted. She stretched her arms up to cup them. "That band last night was awful." Donny kissed down her arm to her ears and buried his mouth in her dark hair. "What's the matter with Phil Ticks?" she panted.

"I don't know." He rolled with her leg, over. "I guess Sally Worn is gone."

I asked her for water
but she brought me gasoline

—Howlin' Wolf

THE SYMBOLIC BREAKFAST

Seated in front of a row of plates, Phil contemplated solemnly what to eat first. Whenever something vicious like this occurred, he would eat a good breakfast. Not just any breakfast, he needed a symbolic breakfast. It made perfect sense to him. It was a primitive response to being hurt that way. His mind and body needed it to start a new day.

At Denny's, Phil sat down alone in a family sized vinyl booth for his enormous breakfast, nearly everything on the menu. Many servings of eggs arrived: scrambled, fried, boiled, poached, over-easy, then pancakes, muffins, toast, along with potatoes and a tall glass of milk to drink with his coffee and juices.

Phil grabbed a boiled egg, ripped off its shell jigsaws and swallowed. He pictured himself not in a Wednesday morning Denny's, but in the Amazon, on the banks of the green river, performing a mystic ritual with shaking feathers and a sacrificed hen.

He had to eat all of it, even though people were staring and muttering, and the pretty waitress was nervous each time she came near him to refill his coffee cup. Phil told himself, I know what I'm doing, this is all necessary medicine. Slowly, step by step, I'll return.

THE WAY IT GOES IN AMERICA

"When was the last time you ate?" the waitress asked Phil.

He wiped his face with a napkin, "Yesterday."

"You've got quite an appetite. I've never seen anyone eat like you do," she smiled in awe and nudged him with her elbow.

"It's because of Sally Worn," he crunched.

Her brow furrowed, "What do you mean?"

Phil was about to explain why he was eating like a Polynesian headhunter, he had almost set his fork down, when a pickup truck smashed through the plate glass window.

Everything was frozen around it until the door sprung open. Then all the glass fragments fell like sparkling sharp rain. Someone in camouflage leaped out, gripping a machinegun.

Just as surprising, in that otherworldly moment before the gun began to fire, the waitress grabbed Phil's arm and pulled him with her under the table, pushing her body over him protectively. She squeezed him to her as the bullets started flying throughout Denny's. Shattering everywhere, smoke from the kitchen drifted with the smell of burning, screaming people falling in piles onto the carpets. The waitress pushed her hands underneath Phil's bandages and held him tight.

Footsteps crunched over the glass, the wooden plastic furniture, the menus, broken plates and bodies.

"Hold on," Phil whispered in her ear.

She moaned and clung to him.

Their table flipped over and the gunman stared at them in disbelief, "You sick degenerates!" he screamed.

The M-16 shook, then scribbled out a ribboning burst of

fire and bullets into them and the floor and their table and the vinyl chairs, bursting the glass through the drapes and pocking the white ceiling tiles.

It was black and quiet for a while until Phil stirred from the darkness. The waitress dripped and splotched onto him, drop by drop. Her pretty eyes stared into him with nothing. Touching her soft lips, brushing off her lovely chin, blood rivered around his fingers down his sleeve. There was a hole in her head. Her dark shiny hair flowed with the red. She was very dead. Phil Tick's mouth opened and in time the scream flew out of him like a black bird.

He could feel himself lifted. He was slapped around, dragged incoherently, shocked to the front of the smoldering Denny's.

A wall of police cars were blinking back at him from the parking lot.

"Give up, Sanders!" a megaphone hidden out there commanded.

"I got a hostage!" the gunman yelled over Phil's shoulder. His machinegun was pressed to Phil's temple. "I want $500,000!" he screamed, "And a black 1988 Camaro! You got fifteen minutes or I blow this guy's brains out!" He held Phil like a doll and shook him.

The shaking, with all the death in there, covered in her blood, it all stirred him and rang his insides. Phil twisted his head and vomited all over the green camouflage and bright face of Colonel Sanders.

Sanders yelled and fell to the floor blinded, as all the police instantly popped up over their car hoods and the shooting started again. Phil could feel the bullets glinting past him, tearing holes into the soldier.

When the shooting stopped, it got quiet. Phil slipped a little in the blood and glass, trying to stand. He grinned and laughed, vacantly balancing. Hidden in a cloud of black smoke, his legs walked him out of Denny's unnoticed, out onto the gray parking lot, between the cars and running people.

NO VAGRANCY

The front of the rainy supermarket, like every Safeway in Washington, was piled with spring flower baskets and shopping carts. Above, there were sale posters in the windows, while people congregated in front of the hissing electric doors.

Phil was standing next to the newspaper dispensers and soda machines. Words were coming out of him, but he didn't feel connected to them. Maybe he was reading them from a distance. For a second, he was aware of two policemen grabbing and shoving him.

"Be careful," Phil wailed. "I'm an invalid!"

They crushed him into the back of the patrol car, closing the door on his foot. His elbow was freezing up and he was unraveling. The tape over his chest was ripped. The siren cleared traffic for blocks as they shot downtown. He was pushed against the window reflection, the world was becoming unfocused—the lampposts and telephone poles were unspooling, Phil Ticks was shutting down.

INVITATION

It was late, there were frogs chirping on the Seattle rooftops. A mist of rain passed along the sides of buildings, making them wet and the street moss glistened.

Under his arm, Donny carried a briefcase with his latest writing. It was a history story, about a woman who turned America like a river in its running course. Donny had never known her personally, he was down south at the time, but he had heard about her. He fit other things he had experienced with the memory of her. There was a Sioux woman he met, there were times spent barnstorming in 1926. He wanted to show the new writing to Phil, but there was no answer at the door. It bounced on its hinges. Donny knocked for a while then left.

Now it was late. Returning home on night streets, he whistled into the bright apartment building entryway. He checked their mailbox. It was empty. Tina must have checked it when she got home, he supposed, as he went up the stairs. She would be asleep probably. Work tired her out.

Quietly, he fit the key in the lock and opened their door.

The refrigerator hummed in the kitchen. She had kept a lamp lit on the table. He glanced at the mail fanned around it and yawned.

The bedroom door was half open, but it was dark inside.

He took his leather jacket off and put it over the chair, set his briefcase on the table with the letters. One of them was from his publisher. Yawning again, he ripped open the envelope and read the letter inside.

There was a convention tomorrow. *The Lost Continent, Donny D'Angelo's History of America, Illustrated by Phil Ticks,* was expected to sweep the awards…Best New Comic, Best Continuing Series, Best New Writer, Best New Artist…The Coliseum had been rented out. Harvey Kurtzman was the M.C. Very prestigious. There were two tickets enclosed. A taxi would be sent to relay them there.

209

Donny clicked off the lamp. By the blue light falling through the window he went into their bedroom, smiling and feeling his way towards Tina.

The clock was ticking next to the bed. He could barely see her curved shape. It was nice to come home like this, with her dreaming, him taking off his clothes beside the mattress darkness. He left his clothes in a pool on the wooden floor and he lifted the covers. Her warm smell filled the blankets. He sighed. He always thought of 16th Century Florida, when he stretched his arm around her on late nights when she was asleep, about to wake up.

THE WORLD NEEDS YOU

"You got a match?" the old man asked for the second time. He could barely stand. He splashed onto the bench with Phil and grew quiet as his head went back slowly against the brick wall.

In a couple of minutes, Phil guessed, he will ask me again.

The Denny's shootout, Safeway, the arrest, he agonized down the list starting with Sally Worn. He wondered where she was. Far away from these painted cement walls, he pictured a Graceland, a palace in Tupelo with gold records over her desk.

"You got a match?" Awakened again, the bum's head rolled on his shoulder, like a magnet towards Phil. "You got a match?"

"No. I don't have a match." Phil held up his empty hands, no longer covered in bandage, turning his palms so all the world could see.

The man was hypnotized. He pointed at Phil's hands, finger drawn to something. It hit Phil's palm. His crazy, bloodshot eyes agitated, "You got the sign!" he bleated.

"What?" Phil backed off, knowing that he should never have tried talking to begin with. I've done it again, he grieved, and now look what's happening.

The old man was on the ground, spilled out in front of Phil, praying out loud. He cried, "You have returned, oh Lord." His old voice cracked with a sob, choking with tears.

"I don't know what he's talking about," Phil stared off into the space filling the dark corner of the cell. "This and everything else…Nothing makes any sense."

Phil's disciple caught both of Phil's hands like birds, to hold them close to his eyes, to examine them. Whatever it was he recognized, sent a shock through him once more and he couldn't help breaking up his prayers with crying.

Phil pulled his hands back. He's all torn up over the blood and wounds on my palms. I do look like a dying man, I guess, or run through hell and back. They really should have got me a doctor before they threw me in here. They don't know I helped capture a dangerous maniac. This is the thanks I get. They got me here on a vagrancy charge. I broke the law and this man praying at my feet can't stop crying. I'll try to tell him something that will calm him down.

Swaying, the old man was back on his feet, wiping his eyes, "We gotta get you out of here." Staggering, he whispered, "You don't belong here."

"Who does?" Phil said.

The walls stopped the man. He stumbled and put his hands on the cement, searching up and down. He examined the barred over window, then he stared at the metal door they came in. Pointing, he looked back at Phil, "Open the door and let yourself out."

"I can't do that."

The old man washed back over to him and took Phil's arm and pulled him up. "You can," he said and guided Phil to the door.

Phil's raw hand went against the steel door and gently, he pushed it open.

The old man crawled on his hands and knees next to Phil. "Bless you…" he whispered, "You have not forgotten us." His wide eyes looked at the green light in the hallway and he said, "You must leave this place. The world needs you." He crossed himself clumsily. "Please forgive us. We have waited for so long."

Phil couldn't move. He was amazed that they forgot to lock the door.

"It may seem like a curse out there," Phil heard, "but deep down we haven't lost faith in you."

Phil put his hand onto the old man's shoulder and thanked him. It was a moment in stained glass.

The open door spilled more light into the cell. Phil stared out into the empty hall.

"Before you go…" the old man said, "Will you go to this place for me?" He took a scrap of paper out of his shoe. It was hidden in the broken leather. He never wanted the wrong person to find it. "It would mean the world to me." He passed the address to Phil and crouched again in prayer.

"Sure," Phil said. "If I can get out of here."

"You will. You will be invisible to them. They won't even see you."

"Alright." Phil smiled and stepped through the doorway. "Here goes…"

Phil was in a gray hallway again. He turned and went the opposite way he been brought in. He held to the wall for support. There were other doors and more prisoners. He wondered if he could have opened the doors to let them out too? Maybe Phil Ticks had the power to help and forgive everyone.

A guard appeared down the hall, but Phil moved himself calmly, flat to the wall, and the guard didn't notice him. Opening a door painted Exit, Phil went down some steps, pushed open another door and he was hopping out onto the street, a free man.

Tina slid up next to him as he was pouring coffee into their cups, trying to keep a smile hidden against his teeth.

"What are you hiding from me?" she squeezed him.

Donny laughed, "Oh...Nothing."

"Nothing, huh?" Her hand moved over his spine as she went to the table to sit down. "Nothing out of the ordinary?"

"Not much." He sat down with her and held his poker face for a second more. "Oh yeah...I almost forgot. There *is* something."

Her eyebrows raised over the rim of the cup as she drank. "Really?"

"We could go out tonight, if you'd like." Modestly, he took the letter out of his back pocket and showed her.

"Hmmm," she said. She stood and carried it to the refrigerator.

Donny turned in his seat to watch her expression.

Tina looked surprised, then confused. "Why?" she asked and her face turned to astonishment as she kept reading. When she saw the tickets in the envelope, she laughed. She smiled and openly stared at Donny in amazement. Walking back to the table, never taking her eyes from him, she said, "You never told me you write comic books!"

"Why would I want to admit to that?" he laughed. It wasn't how he wanted to be known. He preferred to be known as the European discoverer of Florida, or even the State Welterweight Champion, or at best, Seattle's Best Cabbie.

"Why?"

He was still laughing. He held her hand and shrugged, "You know why. Artists are the biggest losers in America. They're nothing but tears." He rubbed her finger tips and kissed her. "It's very strange company to be a part of. Just wait, you'll see tonight."

She held her coffee cup to his, "A toast to Donny D'Angelo.

You're my superhero, the very best comic book writer!" and they clicked.

He drank and said, "Well, Tina. You know there are a lot of other good writers too. *The Red Menace* is a great title. There's a lot of competition."

"No," she corrected him with a finger on his lips, "You will win. I know it."

"Thanks, Tina." Then he laughed. "God, I haven't been to the Coliseum since I used to box. And now I'm in a comics convention there."

"Don't worry," she laughed with him. She squeezed her hand between her knees. "You won't have to hit anyone." She kissed him again and hopped up. "I'm so excited, Donny!" She hugged him and rushed off to their bedroom. "What should I wear tonight?" she sang from the other room.

STRETCHER

In his untouchable condition, it wasn't difficult for Phil to beg spare change for bus fare. He was trailing the remains of bandages and crutching along. The bus stopped at the big hospital on Capitol Hill and Phil got off. He limped his way

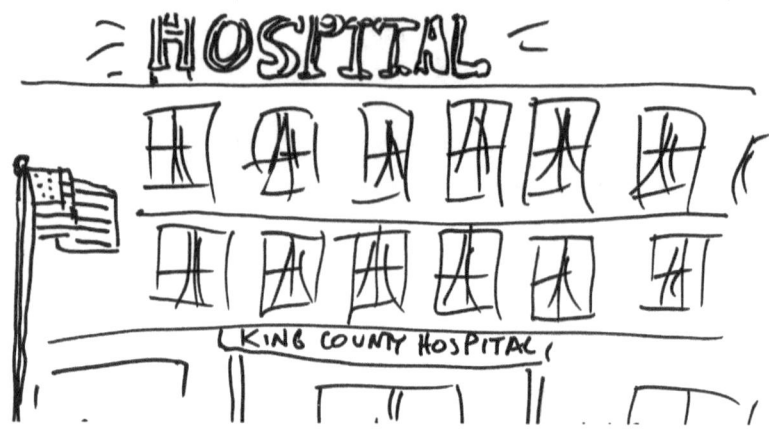

down the tunnel to Emergency Care. It took the rest of the day, retaped in new white gauze, for him to make the long mummy voyage home.

Resting in his chair by the window, scratching his cat, he was trying to get his mind to slow down. It was like tying down a pitching zeppelin. The past 24 hours had whirled and spun him out of control, all over Seattle.

The phone ring startled him. It went right through him, as if breaking every bone in his body all over again. Bending over, his recast arm grabbed the receiver and he used his other hand to relay it up to gasp, "Hello?"

"Phil! It's me, Donny."

"Donny, how are you?" he winced.

"Great! Everything's great with me. How are you doing? I've been trying to get in touch with you all day."

"Oh. I'm fine."

"Well, listen to this, Phil. You won't believe it. We have to go down to the Coliseum tonight! *The Lost Continent* is supposed to win all kinds of awards at the convention they're having there."

"I don't know if I'll be able to make it, Donny. I'm—"

"Aww, come on! I need you there with me, Phil! You're the artist! You're going to get awarded, you've got to come."

"I'm feeling really tired. I thought I'd make some tea and go to sleep early. I feel kind of out of it…I need to work on a painting too."

"Phil! This is a big deal!" Donny was getting impatient. "It's the Coliseum, Phil! It's going to be classy. Just wrap a bowtie around your cast and be ready at 7:30 for the taxi. Please! I need you for this thing, Phil."

Phil sighed. "Alright," he gave in. "I'll try to be there." My life, he thought, is not prepared for a calm day, ever. "But bring a stretcher with you." He hung up and the cat resettled herself on his lap. Her claws fluffed the white bandages while he patted her. Gradually, they both fell asleep. The sun fell slowly down the pane.

LUCILLE FREDERICKS

Donny saw the strange old woman again and by the way she looked at him, he could tell that she had been badly affected by him. It wasn't good. She glared at him, knowing that he had been Vince Peabody, the Dialing for Dollars host. She knew him from then, but Donny still couldn't recall why he should know her...He tried to forget his past lives. Boxing helped him to forget. As Donny D'Angelo, he had a lot to think back on: his life as a conquistador, looking out of a prairie schooner, and what he had been doing on afternoon television. It was an inspiration for his book, *The Lost Continent*. It was all about his time in America. But as he wrote, he tried to think of that past as happening to someone else. He was forced to wonder what it was that had gone on between Vince Peabody and this lurking old woman and why had she chased him into this new life?

The Pay Less Drugstore electric door hissed open and he walked inside fast, relieved to be off the street. Once a week, Tina worked at Pay Less. She was at the end of Aisle 8, shelving soap, balancing a clipboard on her knee. What a sight, he thought. What a beautiful woman.

Then Donny thought he had run into a plate of glass—it was like being hit by Punch McConnelly again. He froze and held to a shelf for support. He was in the corner again, his vision blurring, going down for the count. Donny remembered who the woman was! She was his wife. "Shit..." he drained to the floor. Lucille Fredericks...Another flash hit him—he remembered leaving a note on their screen door before escaping into the desert alone.

He wished he had never left her that way, but he thought he'd never see her again. No wonder she looked at him with growing vengeance. Any day now, he could expect to see her with a trembling gun.

He lolled on the waxy floor, seeing stars.

Tina's hands were around his face. Her worried eyes looked

218

into his. "Are you okay, Donny?"

Donny shook his head and blinked and rubbed his eyes, trying to restore himself. He mumbled, "I'm alright, honey. I just felt like I got KO'd." She helped him stand up and he took a big breath. "Wow! That was something." He laughed unconvincingly. He needed her to hold him, he was reeling. Stars had turned to bright pulsing flowers.

"You sure you're okay, Donny?" she held to him dearly, "Should we take you to a hospital?"

"Lucille Fredericks…" he muttered from another world.

"Who?" Tina stared. "Who's that?"

Donny's eyes snapped open. He realized he said it out loud. "Who's what?" He shut his eyes and opened them again, to reset time.

"You said Lucille Fredericks." She tightened her fingers on his arms.

"Did I? No…I don't think so." He blinked a couple more times and straightened his collar. He looked around himself, hunted and reeling. She held him tighter.

"Donny…If you're nervous about the award ceremony," she put her hand around his mouth, "we don't have to go."

"No, I want to go. I'm just feeling a little stage fright or something." He squeezed her. "I'll be fine. Thanks for catching me, Tina." He kissed her. "We should hurry and go home. We have to get dressed for the convention."

"Good," her face beamed. "Wait here. I'll be right back," she said over her shoulder, on her way to change out of her blue and green Pay Less uniform. "I still don't know what I should wear."

He waved down the aisle. He couldn't believe that Lucille had found him. It kept his trapped mind racing while he waited for Tina to return.

DISCOVERED

Silent for a long time, Donny stared out the window, with his coffee getting colder. He saw the rain and the cars driving through it on the way back from the factories. Sometime he would have to say goodbye again. Too many strange things were already happening. He was nearly twenty eight, an old man by his usual standards, while on the other side of the country, the water was waiting for him in Florida.

Tina had been watching him closely. She could see he was hiding something like a tiger. She touched him sweetly though, "What's the matter, baby?"

"Nothing much, nothing," he mumbled and found the coffee cup and carried it to his lips.

Quietly, she found it difficult to ask since he wasn't responding to her affections, "Are you having a midlife crisis?" Less quietly, she asked, "Are you unhappy with me and our life?"

"What?"

"I've heard about these things. I read in a magazine about how they affect men especially. They become moody and sad and contemplate bad things."

"No, honey, it's not a midlife crisis." It was an earthquake he was feeling. He tried to smile as he reached out for her. Thinking was wrecking him and living was haunting him. He touched her leg. He didn't want to go to the Coliseum. It would be best if nobody knew about him. The safety of his life depended on it. How many other Lucille Fredericks were there waiting? He pictured one of those gray tour buses filled with old angry memories, stopping and unloading before him.

He squirmed on his chair. It was better to be anonymous in America, especially if you were the five hundred year old discoverer of the blessed Fountain of Youth. Try keeping that secret inside...His face warped with all the confusion. I never should have started this story with Phil, I knew it would bring me trouble. I don't need to be famous or honored, I've had all that before. "I don't know if I want to go," he told Tina. In the back of his mind, Florida was calling his name, a whisper getting louder and louder. "Why did they have to discover my book?" he moaned.

She smiled. She sat with her knees touching his, then she got up and rested on his lap.

He stroked her arm. "Tina, I can't go to the Coliseum. I can't do this thing."

"Why not?"

He sighed, "Maybe it reminds me of when I boxed. I've got painful memories of that place."

"This is different though. That was a long time ago when you had to fight. This will be fun." She smiled. "People who do good things deserve to be honored. It's like the Academy Awards, Donny. Don't you think it will be fun?" She touched him and laughed a little. "It's alright to be nervous, honey. In fact, I think it's kind of sexy…" she stirred on his lap and kissed him. "But right now, we should get ready to go." She kissed him again. "You've been discovered!" She hopped to the floor.

I'll wear a disguise, he decided. We can go if I look like the ambassador from Cuba. I'll tell her it's like a costume ball and I have to wear a fake beard and a green military uniform.

"What should I wear?" she called from their bedroom.

"Do you still have that Betsy Ross costume?"

BETSY ROSS AND FIDEL CASTRO

She stood in the closet doorway in her silk underwear, staring at him. The blue dress dropped, crinkling to her feet. "What?!"

Dejected, on the edge of their bed, he was sitting half dressed in camouflage, a beard folded next to him. "Do you still have it?" Donny repeated.

"Why?" She leaned on the doorway frame.

"It's kind of a costume ball. You don't *have* to wear one, but I should."

She put her hand on her hip, "Donny, it didn't say anything about costumes in the letter."

"I know. It's implied. That's kind of the way comic conventions are. You don't have to wear one though."

She sighed. "If you are, I should too." She turned around and started digging through the hanging clothes. "Here it is." She held up a red white and blue dress. "It's a good thing I kept this." She cupped her hand like a megaphone, "Ladies and gentlemen, please welcome Betsy Ross and Fidel Castro!"

Behind the curtain of her dress, she pointed her bare arm like a spotlight at Donny on the bed, with a cigar in his mouth, sullenly fitting the scratchy beard wires around his ears.

KRYPTONITE

Tina held the window curtain aside. "The *limo* is here!" she said. Out on the street, a taxi honked its horn. "Come on, Donny."

The bathroom door opened. Donny D'Angelo had disappeared beneath a Fidel Castro disguise. He held the cigar in his hand, gesturing, "I'm ready, baby."

She laughed, "That's what I like to hear," and as Betsy Ross she hurried over, grabbed him by the hand and arm in arm they left their apartment.

Driving through yellow lights, winding the one-way streets under the rusty monorail tracks, the cab driver watched them suspiciously in the mirror. It didn't seem like he could take a joke. He was a sort of bulldog chained behind the wheel and very little was said as he drove them.

Tina pointed at the flower shape of the Space Needle rising over them, blinking orange lights that spider webbed around its rim. "Look honey, we're nearly there."

The cab stopped next to the iron grill fence gate and they tipped the driver. Donny was relieved to see that some other people around them were wearing disguises too.

Tina squeezed his hand, "Look! It's Superman!"

She was right—there he was, chucking a handful of peanuts into his mouth, walking along the path towards the Coliseum. There was cotton candy stuck on his waving blue cape. He was also limping a little bit…Kryptonite, Donny guessed.

A large white rabbit stood its ground up ahead, passing out balloons. "Hey Wonder Woman!" it shouted jovially at Tina.

Donny swore. There were times he wished he still had a musket or a finely balanced Spanish saber in his hand. Tina dragged him over to the rabbit.

It clucked like a cartoon character and passed her a red balloon. Then it became sarcastic, jabbing its stuffed thumb at

223

Donny, "Does Lex Luther want a balloon too?" It pushed a yellow helium balloon towards Donny.

"No," Donny growled through his beard, but Tina took the balloon.

"Yes he does!" she laughed. She held it with the other one and dragged Donny towards the doors.

"See you guys inside!" chirped the six foot rabbit.

"This is going to be fun, Donny!" Tina laughed. "It's better than the Puyallup Fair!" Crowded around the entrance turnstiles, hundreds of people were funneling in.

RANDY PANKOW

"I don't see Phil anywhere," Donny was turned around, searching the rows of people seated behind them. "Knowing him, his taxi probably got a flat tire," Tina smiled. She was tying the red and yellow balloons to the armrest, while the band in the orchestra pit stirred restlessly like a nest of bees.

Mickey Mouse and Batman stepped into the spotlights from either side of the stage and everyone clapped and roared. Donny noticed that Batman looked a little different from his comic book—besides having thick glasses, he was about three hundred rolling pounds and the skintight black suit strained to burst. Walking swiftly towards stage center, he kept up with the twitchy mouse. They met and high-fived at the podium.

When the applause subsided, Mickey held up his white gloves again and welcomed them all to the 20th Annual Comics Convention. More clapping and whistling blasted around Donny and Tina. Then Mickey proudly introduced Batman to his left. "Ladies and gentlemen, I'd like to introduce a local legend… Give a big hand to your very own Randy Pankow, the leader of the pack!" Mickey's squeak boomed through the Coliseum, all the round cement walls, "Thanks to Randy here, all the best comics are at your fingertips!"

Randy waved at the crowd, uttering jaggedly, "Thank you very much, thank you very much," into the microphone. He threw the mic from hand to hand. "I'm very pleased that so many people turned out for this year's convention. Our city is blessed with your presence." He swaggered with the cheers.

Randy held his black glove above his eyes to peer at the mob, his rubber ears twitching, "It's good to see some familiar faces out there, year after year…" he searched, "There's Hal Blitna, I think…" As his Batman regarded the audience, all the faces crowded into the layered seating of the Coliseum, he took a deep breath and hollered, "Let the games begin!"

Randy and Mickey stepped back from the microphone, clapping and waving.

"Tina," Donny shook her arm. He whispered in her ear, "Baby, this is too much. I got to get some air."

"Take off your beard," she hissed and returned her attention to the stage, clapping for Randy, departing behind the curtain.

"Baby, I have to go to the lobby. I'll be right back."

"You better hurry! They'll be announcing the names after this act. Look!" Her eyes raced with the Shriner cars spinning figure 8s on the stage.

"Yeah, I'll be right back, baby." Donny kissed her powdered cheek and stood up and stepped into the aisle. He almost knocked over someone's drink set on the stairs. It was difficult to see through the bushy beard and thick glasses.

At the refreshment booth, he stopped to watch people ordering popcorn. The teenage cashier had her face painted like a cat. She handed some change to a tall nervous man in a jumpsuit. "Can I help you, sir?" She was looking at Donny. "Sir?"

"Oh," Donny startled. "A pretzel I guess. Could I have one of those big pretzels?" He started searching his pocket for money while she wrapped a pretzel in wax paper. There was nothing in his pocket. "Whoops, I forgot my wallet. I'm sorry." He grinned and shrugged at her while she bit her lip and returned the pretzel to the rotating oven.

Why did I do that? What's wrong with me? he wondered. He shrunk away down the hall like a vampire, telling himself almost out loud, I've got to snap out of this! I'm acting like Phil Ticks! Lucille Fredericks is tearing me apart. I've got to stop my worrying, there's nothing she can do. She's just trying to scare me. She doesn't know for sure it's me anyway. How could it be? That was years ago when I looked this way. How could she really think it's me? She must know it's impossible to stay young.

Humorlessly, he watched a television screen showing the convention stage reeling with miniature cars.

226

GOLDEN OLDIES

A chain smoking cabbie buzzed Phil's apartment again and waited for the answer, rapping his fingers on the glass door while the rain fell.

It was dark in the room. The digital clock glowed 7:45, but the alarm had not gone off. Phil jumped up and scattered the cat. Someone was at the door. He crutched over to answer the rusty intercom. "I'll be right there." He didn't need a suit. Most of him was bound in medical tape and cloth. He stuck a nametag over his heart. And he took Donny's advice and excavated his sock drawer until he found a bowtie. A leftover from a high school dance tragedy.

He grabbed it. He said goodbye to the cat under the sofa and limped out the door, down the hall, to the elevator. Back in his room, his clock radio alarm awakened with KJR's golden oldies.

The taxi drove Phil into traffic, pulling another car slowly along in its wake. The car behind them mimicked their turns, all the way to the Coliseum entrance on First Avenue where it bounced to a stop too.

Phil leaned from the cab. He blindly found the pavement. He eased himself out, taking hold of his balance with the crutch. "Thanks a lot," Phil waved and left the cab, to climb the swarming pathway.

A cub scout stuck a colorful 20th Year sticker onto Phil's white striped back. Another kid asked if he was the Invisible Man. Phil shook his crutch at them the way his grandmother used to do, bumping into a superhero giving away candy.

Not far from him, two clowns had left their car illegally parked up on the curb next to a hydrant. They followed at a distance behind Phil, stalking him. When he got a balloon from a gigantic rabbit, they did too. They trailed him inside, down the aisle of the first floor until he found his seat in front, next to a woman he recognized. She looked like a patriotic Little Bo Peep, bubbling over with excitement at the sight of the buzzing

Shriner noise on stage.

The two clowns sat down not far away and waited. One had opera glasses, trained on Phil.

"CAPEESH?"

"Where's Donny?" Phil asked Tina. He almost had to shout it the cars were so loud. The Shiners were drag racing each other.

"He'll be right back," she pointed up the aisle. "He went to the lobby."

They settled back to watch the cars turning around and around.

Instantly, Phil leaned over her shoulder again, "I'm going to go find him. I'll be back in a flash."

"Hurry up! When this is over, you guys are going to sweep the awards."

Phil gave the thumbs-up and stumbled onto the aisle. His head was aching from all the cars. What are we doing here? I should have stayed home with Bertha. Thinking of his cat, he balanced himself in the arch of a doorway.

Down the turning hallway, slow moving people were buying food and t-shirts. There were hanging TVs uncoiling above the Coliseum concourse. Phil watched the televised cars, still going in circles. There was blue smoke hanging over the stage, obscuring the white banner on the foggy wall.

Someone tapped his shoulder and he hobbled around.

"We're from Saturn Circus, Mister Ticks." There were two clowns behind him. "Kirby Clown, at your service." The smile was all over his face. "Hey listen," he exaggerated conspiratorially, with his hand to his big painted mouth, "The boss wants to double our last offer. He's a nut! We tell him so, but he don't listen." Kirby put his hand on Phil's white shoulder. "He wants to give you this stack of cash," he flashed the bills hidden in his loud jacket, "and ten percent of the door profits." Kirby suddenly threw his hands over his mouth, the perfect mime for astonishment.

The other clown whistled and piped up, "Say, that's more than the lion tamer! I wish I was you!"

They both grinned at Phil, holding the magical appearance

229

of a contract and a pen.

"Who are these clowns?" Donny appeared next to Phil, "Are they bothering you?"

Phil turned around and noticed the Fidel Castro with Donny's voice. The sight stunned him.

Donny took the paper from the clown and read it. He had to twist his glasses to see. "What is this?"

"It's the circus," Phil said. "They won't leave me in peace. They want me to jump out of a plane onto their tent again. They don't give up."

"Oh, they don't?" Fidel started rolling up his uniform sleeves. "I'll see if I can make these clowns understand."

They tensed and bunched. "We can take him, Patches," Kirby said.

"Wait a second!" Phil stepped in between them. He held his arms up as calmly as Gandhi. "Let's not get—"

A clown punch caught him behind the ear and Phil went down as if a light bulb had exploded in his skull.

Donny leaped over the body and split the seams of his green army fatigues, hitting both clowns at the same time. "Capeesh?!" he asked as they slid down the wall into unconscious piles on the floor.

A small knot of people stared and clapped wildly, someone started chanting, "Gomez! Gomez! Gomez!"

Donny nodded appreciatively. They think I'm an imaginary character. He smiled at the applause and heaved Phil to his unsteady feet. Phil leaned on Donny as they went back down the ramp to the first floor V.I.P seating.

CAPTAIN AMERICA

What if I should somehow win? Phil thought, sending his imagination onto the stage, where it accepted a gold plated award. "Thank you so much. Thank you everyone. I feel like a million bucks. Hey, here's to Captain America!" He would raise his trophy, "And to all the great Americans who voted for me with their hearts." Confetti fell from the ceiling in his vision. "Also, thank you to Woolworths and the food bank and the libraries for keeping me alive in the lean years…"

Meanwhile, he watched as Donny D'Angelo went up to the stage for the fourth time—now it was for *Best Written Historical Work in Progress.* Of course Donny had called out to his friend and conspirator in the front row and Phil had hobbled to his feet for a round of applause, but it wasn't the same. Phil groaned, watching Donny mince around under the spotlights, in the phony Castro disguise, telling boxing stories. The man was becoming a legend. The heroic story of his battle with the clowns was told up and down the aisles.

Unlike me, Phil thought, Donny always gets what he wants, he has everything he desires. Next it was the award for the most awards ever received. Phil shifted in his seat unhappily. He did feel like the Invisible Man. Not a single award came his way, not even that one for *Best Word Balloons.*

Donny puffed on his cigar and held the award above his head like a gladiator, nodding, with all the people in the Coliseum cheering him. "Thank you Seattle!" He pumped his fist and left the stage.

Tina gleamed. She held awards in her lap and cheered.

Two more times, Donny was called back to the stage. By the end of it, the news was filming him as an historical moment. When there was nothing left for him to win, the red curtains shut, the orchestra started playing, spotlights jetted across the walls and ceiling, the American flag lit up with sparklers, and the bright houselights came back on.

Donny and Tina clinked with all their gold awards. Fans were crawling over the seats to get autographs from the great Donny D'Angelo.

Phil had to push through the tangle. It took him a long time to crutch his way out, using an arm to claw.

"Hey Mummy!" the Avenging Agent snapped. Cola was spilled on his red and blue uniform. "Watch where you're going!"

Phil saw a sofa sitting down a hallway. It became an oasis. He collapsed on it gratefully. The springs rolled beneath him anciently .He didn't even notice the worn sign taped to the cushion, the flaking letters that read: *LBJ Sat Here, April 5, 1965*. He stared at his knees, the world was spinning.

VICTORY

"Have you read our paper, Mister D'Angelo?" Someone wearing a top hat was holding up a Socialist newspaper called *The Neo-Proletariat.* "Do you know about our cause, Mister D'Angelo?" At the same time Donny was signing his autograph for a twelve year old, another fan was blissfully congratulating him.

Tina was laughing joyfully, grappling with the armful of awards.

"Hey," Donny smiled through the beard, "I believe in all kinds of causes. I don't get carried away by any single one." His signature wormed across the page and he thanked everyone, edging out from the logjam.

"Tina, I can't believe all these people know who I am," he laughed.

"I know!" Betsy Ross was Wonder Woman here. She was treated like royalty too. They gave her free buttons and stickers and asked for photos and advice. "I think you should ask him to marry you," Tina told a young woman dressed in a black cape.

Eventually they made it outside. People pushed around them buying and selling comics, and they had to sign a few more autographs before they made it to the sidewalk and flagged a Yellow Cab home.

She came up to Phil where he sat on the couch, lost in a castle of gloomy thought. She moved so quietly that he didn't see her until she smiled, saying, "I really like your artwork." Next to him, she sat down on the famous wide blue cloth. "You deserved to win."

Phil startled electrically. The last thing he expected to do was talk with someone. He felt like he had hit rock bottom, collapsed on a sofa in the Coliseum. But he apologized, "I'm sorry, thank you. This has been a very distracting day for me. For a second I thought you were going to arrest me."

She laughed until he could smile too. "What did you do to yourself anyway? I almost didn't recognize you. Your photo on the back of *TLC #23* shows you running through a field. Did you step on a mine?"

"No," he said, "I wish…It's a long story. A terrible saga…" She watched him, waiting. "No, you don't want to hear it, I'm sure. It's worse than you can imagine, you wouldn't want to know." He felt like he was about to unleash a hurricane onto her, but she waited for him to go on. "I fell out of a plane." He tried to laugh, but that was as far as he could get.

He was glad she thought it was funny. To him, it had been like fighting World War Two, ending up falling out of a plane onto Hiroshima. "I've been a wreck for a while," he told her. "I even went to Jackie Wu's Wooden Imports…"

"Really? I've heard of that place."

"You have?"

"Sure. They make potions, right?"

He nodded. "That's what I got there. But the potion didn't help. I didn't think anything else would work, so I took parachute lessons." He motioned with his hands dramatically, letting them fall into his lap. "This is the result of jumping out of a plane without one."

"You're kidding?"

"It's the truth. I landed on a circus tent though. What kind of death is that?"

"It's very dramatic."

"I know. I was the star of the night at the Saturn Circus. And they've been bugging me ever since, trying to sign me on. I can't believe it…" He untied his bowtie.

"It's a miracle you survived." No more laughter, she said it full of certainty. Her eyes said it purposefully, "It's because you weren't meant to die, because you are the greatest artist on the planet." Then she added, "And I needed to meet you."

He was flattered, more than flattered, he was embarrassed. He flushed, he felt adored, there were flowers growing all over him out from the bandages.

She said, "You lead a charmed life, Mister Ticks."

"A charmed life?" He looked at her again, "I don't know about that. It seems to go from bad to worse."

"Not anymore," she said.

"Really?"

"Really."

"A miraculous event," Phil laughed. He began to notice the woman sitting with him. "You think something good is going to happen?" His eyes rested on hers for the first real time, no more look and look away glances. "Maybe you're the only one who knows it." That feeling was going through him. It was obvious what was happening. "My life is about to be charmed, you really think so? Are you a fortune teller?"

She was smiling and nearly laughing again. He was more than what she expected. Covered as he was in bandages, she could tell there was more than meets the eye. "I just know," she said and introduced herself. "My name is Natalie." She extended her hand to him.

LAW OF AVERAGES

"You know, I saw Ray Bradbury in there," Natalie said. "I grew up reading his books. It was really great to see him walking around."

"You should have talked to him," Phil said.

"I was looking for you though. I was worried that you might have left." That had been her panic, she knew that he was somewhere around, it was just a matter of finding him. "I've got all your books too."

"Oh, you found them?"

"Of course, Phil Ticks. I'm a determined woman." She laughed, "It took me a long time. I used to search every day, all over the city, wherever I happened to be."

He smiled at the thought of her exploring for him. "Well thank you, Natalie. You're very kind. You're restoring my faith in humanity." Then he looked scared around them, "You've also got a lot of nerve, taking me here. This is a dangerous place."

Only two of the tables had people. Denny's was mostly deserted. The workers were standing guard. The nervous cook looked back and forth, peeking through the shelf, ticking back and forth in the kitchen like a pendulum.

"Don't worry about it, Phil."

Phil watched in mounting fear as she ordered some of the same symbolic breakfast he had. She said she wanted to know everything, beginning with what he ate that day. She said it meant something important to her to have what he had. At first she laughed at the list of all the food he expected to eat, it was funny to her. Phil was waiting for the crash of plate glass.

"You know what my favorite book of yours is?" she munched. "*The Inside-Out Planet*. I like how you drew the entire planet turning into a hermit crab." She cupped her hands and wiggled her thumbs. "That was amazing."

Phil sweated and stretched out for her hand. "But I was in the Denny's that got blown up, Natalie. I was the hostage," he whispered across the table. "It makes me very nervous here. I don't want anything bad to happen. I especially want you to be safe."

"Thanks, Phil." Her foot electrified across his, under the table. "It's good to know you care." She touched his hand next. "Really though, don't worry. We're just testing the law of averages. You'll see, we'll be fine, this is just a place. It could be anywhere—a street in Chicago, or Paris, or on a sand dune, it doesn't really matter."

He could feel love, even in the most dangerous place. Still, Phil couldn't help eyeing a pickup truck going past the big window.

CLOWN DEAL

"I have to admit, you were right. We weren't ambushed. But that was a very tense meal for me." Phil was saying goodnight to her, "We should go somewhere different next time. If you would like to..."

Natalie laughed. "Now that we've survived the Law of Averages, we can go anywhere. The possibilities are endless."

He leaned towards the door. "Thanks for finding me tonight. I like you. I'm beginning to think it was a good thing I landed on that circus tent." He was afraid to kiss her goodnight, there was still a chance he would chip her tooth, so he gave her an urgent wave. "I should go. I'm sure my cat is hungry. She'll be clawing the wallpaper."

Phil got out of her car. He felt strange, his stumbling was almost gliding. In his mind, he was moving like Fred Astaire, holding his crutch like Ginger Rogers. They had recast his leg and the crutch was too small for him, but he waved fluidly as her car blinked its lights for him and she drove off.

A clown was waiting for him at the apartment entrance. Another stood to the side in the bushes, standing there like gangsters in the night. "Mister Ticks..." the clown next to the door took a step and the other one tensed when Phil stopped on the walkway.

Phil tried to remember his name. Kipper?

Kirby and Patches' face paint was almost phosphorescent, the moon and streetlight etched with stripes, as they approached. Kirby said, "Phil, we're deeply sorry about the way we acted earlier." He shrugged apologetically, "Look, to show you there's no hard feelings we'd like to offer you an ever better deal for your skydiving act."

Patches had a bandage across his tomato nose. He took a form out of his starburst pocket, "How about a thousand more?"

Phil was silent.

"It's an offer you don't want to refuse. We're talking a lot of cash, plus benefits. It's quite a sum. You'll be a wealthy man. No more living in a dump like this either. You can have your own trailer."

Patches moved to hold the contract closer to Phil. "Just sign on the dotted line and you join the circus."

Wordlessly, Phil pushed him aside and walked up the steps and found his key. He was amazed they didn't try to stop him.

Hours later, he could still hear them, creeping outside his second floor window, conspiring and whispering. One of them threw a pebble at his window at two o'clock in the morning. They tried to be quiet about it, but he could hear them cackling.

Then it was silent. They seemed to have left, and Phil fell asleep.

THE MORNING LIGHT

The gold awards glowed in the morning light, balanced on the trapeze window sill where Tina had put them last night.

The Fidel Castro beard was curled in a patch of sun.

But Donny's elation was short lived. His dreams were all sorrow and worries about Lucille Fredericks and all the other people he had parted. They were lined up like black and white photos tied to him. He dreamed he was fishing and pulling them in. The boat was starting to sink with the weight of all of them. Just in time, something sharp woke him up.

Tina's dark eyes pierced him and she pinched his hip again. Her voice was unhappy and tragic, "You called for her again. Now I know she's somebody."

"Who?" Donny croaked.

"You said Lucille Fredericks in your sleep." A second creaked heavily and she pushed him away from her. She got out of bed, pulling the plaid blanket around her.

Slanting to the window, she suddenly spun around with tears cutting in her eyes. "I hate you Donny D'Angelo!"

FRED THUMBLE, P.I.

"You're perfect," Lucille slapped Fred's gigantic shoulder. He had the gorilla proportions of the nation's top professional football linebacker. In the off season, he kept busy with his hobby, private investigating. She growled, "I want you to tear him apart."

Suddenly, he squeezed his eyes together, "Yes…" He fought the pain of the buzzing metal plate in his forehead.

"Are you sure you can handle this case?" She reappraised him, Would all those football injuries slow him down? "Maybe I should ask your brother…" her voice trailed off wickedly. His brother worked in a pet store. He sold kittens and goldfish and was gentle with everything.

"No!" Fred got crazy. Veins rivered out of his temple, "I'll get him!" He slapped the holster under his arm. Then his face crumpled with pain again. "It's that damn music!" He hit his skull in agony. "It gets stuck in my head!"

"Listen Fred…" She stood up, spotted the waiter and waved to him.

"I'm fine now, Ms. Fredericks," Fred Thumble's gravelly voice said, "Don't you worry. It's taken care of." He slapped his hand over his eyes.

A black circular magnet the size of a quarter was stuck to his forehead.

"This makes the music stop," he explained to her. "Sit down now. Tell me, you got a photo of this punk? What does he look like?"

THE CRISIS

Picture—Donny thought, staring out the window into the night out there—a man with no fear of growing old and dying.

Wouldn't that give him the greatest life?

He was beginning to think he wasn't human, that he could never truly have what mattered most. Unlike anyone else, he could live forever. But there were problems to this, deep things that sometimes overcame him and haunted him like ghosts.

It was already five hundred years he'd lived, but he couldn't figure it out. He listened to the rain fall against the ground and all around their window. He found himself needing to wander. He got out of their bed and dressed quietly, back into the clothes he had taken off.

He knew that look Lucille Fredericks gave him. He was being hunted. She would be coming for him. Maybe he deserved it too. But he didn't want Tina to get hurt. He let her go so she would be safe.

Donny left the apartment.

Tina was gone.

AURORA BRIDGE

The rain was falling in slow uneven waves, breaking on him as he walked. He didn't know if he was being trailed or not. At the moment, Donny was in between more water. His shoes

squeaked across the grating leading onto the bridge. A few cars rushed by, creating a fine spray that glistened in the headlights. Any one of the cars could have held Lucille Fredericks with a bow and arrow. The Aurora Bridge was no stranger to death.

Ahead of him, smudged against the railing, Donny counted three, four figures, standing in a row. They all bowed their heads at the ship canal below. If Donny wanted to go where they were going, he would have to get in line.

A car went past and someone shouted something lost out the window.

Donny slowed. He was close enough to watch the first man in line crawl up onto the cement edge. Donny stopped breathing. The man loosened his tie and gave himself a push. That was it. It was 160 feet to the water.

His voice drained with him.

It didn't seem possible. It all seemed to be frozen like a photograph with a silhouette missing. Nothing moved in it, until the sky began shifting again. Another car passed around them. A dark cloud covered and moved like an eyeball on the moon.

THE SHOUTING WOMAN

"It was my own fault! I never should have believed in someone so much!" How many times in her life would she fall for that? Tina had been repeating this over and over in her head for days, sometimes letting out a groan, as she sat and steamed like a Pacific island volcano.

She'd pace her friend's apartment furiously, then when it became unbearable, she would go to Safeway, grab a grocery cart and storm every aisle, two or three times, until her anger became soothed. It gave her something else to think about, something else to concentrate on. She went up and down the aisles, past the coffee, the meat displayed under plastic wrap, the cans of vegetables and the ones out in rows, boxes of cereal and magazines. It was all very well ordered and unlike everything else crashing in on her. She could make sense out of unraveling the store like a maze.

After ten minutes, meditation and calm, she knew exactly where she was. She stopped her cart and reached for a cantaloupe, just as someone else took it.

"Give me that!" Tina shouted and grabbed it back from the old Russian woman who stared at her with wide-opened eyes that had been through the siege of Stalingrad.

The old woman cowered away, covering her head with her gray hands, backing into the oranges, slipping, falling down into the food rubble.

THE DAYS THE TELEVISION WAS ON

Donny was stretched out on the wood flooring with a pillow under his head. The television had been on constantly for two and a half days. The plastic around the glowing screen was hot to the touch. A Frank Sinatra record resting on top had melted its vinyl like a candle over it. Every living second, he thought of Tina and how he had lost her forever by keeping her from danger.

Just before he fell asleep with the one o'clock movie, he unplugged the telephone, noosing the cord around an upturned chair. The apartment was falling apart with him. The floor was littered with pots and pans half filled with burnt rice, and clothes and blankets and a tipped over plant.

In agony, Donny poked through the blanket and stared at the blue screen of the TV.

He had been watching television for days. It seeped into him and flooded his veins with blue gray haze. Swirly images of her floated with the anemic television shows. She was in every one of them. All the talk shows featured Tina Takahara, mystery shows searched for her, she was the star in all the movies, and she gave the news at eight in the morning, then at noon and six o'clock. She went into him with electricity every second of his life for the days the television was on.

ROCKET SCIENCE

Fred Thumble stopped his tan Camaro in front of the parking meter. Getting out, he put on a dark pair of sunglasses and straightened his shirt. Then he swiftly walked onto the sidewalk, over to the path leading to the brick Rocket Science building.

An actual silver jet gleamed with morning dew on the lawn. There were pigeons sitting on the wings.

He couldn't believe their disrespect. He ran across the grass and jumped up and down until they flew away. That put the fear into them, he smiled. Then he resumed the path to the doorway once again.

There was a button next to the steel door. Fred pressed it and waited.

"Rocket Science," a woman said, "Tina speaking. What's the password?"

"Astronaut," Fred answered.

The door clicked open with a buzzing sound.

He was in a small square room. There was a woman sitting behind a table waiting for him. It was her, he noted, all alone. This was going to be easy.

"How can we help you, sir?" she asked pleasantly.

His motion was a flock of birds—with a flash, he went around the desk and lifted her in his arms and was leaving out the door with her, all in one swift turn.

Her mouth was clamped shut. Tina couldn't even struggle in his arms. Not until he put her in the car with him, then she screamed and grabbed at the bolted door and hit its smoky windows.

Fred turned on the FM radio as loud as it would go. Heavy metal guitar outscreamed her as the Camaro fishtailed onto the street taking her away.

TARANTULA

"But I'd like to see your place," Natalie insisted.

"My apartment? Why? It looks like a National Geographic special." Phil blocked the doorway. "You don't want to see it."

"Yes I do. I want to see all the drawings and paintings you've ever done. I want to see where you live and draw *The Lost Continent*."

"Okay…" He held her hand, waiting for the elevator that clicked like a black spider coming down. "Welcome to the monkey house," he said.

He was right.

It didn't take long for Natalie to find out. His apartment looked like a hamster lived there.

He invited her in and they found a clearing on his floor.

"Apparently," Phil said, "Walt Whitman had it rough before he made a living from writing, so all these corporations started a fund. Their philosophy is that if Walt Whitman was alive today, he shouldn't be suffering. He should be living like a king. So they have an annual contest of $3,000, called the Walt Whitman Incorporated Award. It all goes to the most starving artist," Phil laughed and pointed to himself. "My starving days are over."

Natalie guessed they weren't over yet.

"It's unbelievable," he continued, "There's a pilgrimage and people from all over the country apply. I even heard about a modern dance troupe that danced all the way from Oakland to audition in person. Two of them had sunstroke. It was a really tough competition that year."

Natalie covered her eyes with her hands.

He touched her leg and leaned over to search for a book scrambled in a tall stack of papers. "I had to prove that I had over ten dismal jobs in the last two years…Here it is." Phil brightened and held up the thick tattered paperback. "Walt's biography…I've been reading this lately." Its pages were filled with colored bus transfer bookmarks, the cover bent and trembling and circled with coffee rings. He tossed it aside and looked at her again.

"That reminds me," Natalie took a book out of her black bag. "I have a present for you. *Tarantula* is one of my favorite books. Other than yours," she patted him and passed it over. "It will take your mind off the circus and exploding restaurants."

STORMY WEATHER

Tina was tied into a chair like some damsel in distress. There were ropes making flying tight gray turns around her, trapping her in the wooden shape. She seethed, "How did you know the password?"

"I'm a detective," Fred Thumble said. "I find out things."

"But what do you want from me?"

"I want Donny D'Angelo." Simply put, Fred lit a cigarette and plugged in the radio. "Most of all, I want Donny D'Angelo on my terms. Now I'm gonna hurt him in the worst possible way. I've got what means the most to him in the world." He pointed his cigarette and said, "You."

"I don't know about that, Mr. Detective. We had a fight. He's probably glad I'm gone." She mumbled, "He doesn't care about me anymore."

"Well, he better." Fred switched on the radio.

Crazy loud jazz music blasted out of the tinny speaker.

Paralyzed for a moment, Fred shivered and spastically struggled with the radio's little dials, moaning in pain. Finally, he succeeded in pulling the cord out of the socket.

He threw the plastic radio against the floor and stomped all over it until it was just broken pieces and wires. "That damn jazz music!" It still rang in his head, the bleating trumpet and drums. He pounded his metal forehead until it ceased and quiet resumed in the room.

"You don't like jazz?" Tina said.

The sweat poured off his brow. "Jazz?" he hissed. "I *hate* it! It's like the clock in that Peter Pan alligator, chasing me. I hear it through walls, I hear it in restaurants. It finds me when I take a cab, I can't get away! It buzzes in my head all the time until I'm losing my mind!" Panting, he tried to recover himself in the table's shadow.

She let a few more seconds pass by, then she breathed deeply and sang out like a bluebird, "Don't know why, there's no sun up in the sky, stormy weather…"

He was doubled over in pain, helpless.

CHEVY CHASE

He had done something terribly wrong in the way he was living. It was just as important to live for other people, maybe it even meant more. Donny went up and down the street thinking, into the narrow alleyways covered from the rain. Tina…he kept thinking…I've learned something, let me show you.

An arm reached for him around the corner like a branch in a maze, grabbing Donny's shirt.

Donny reacted on pure fighter's adrenalin, throwing his assailant against the wall, crushing a hand around his neck. Hard against the bricks, Street Poet gagged.

"Man!" Donny released him, "Don't do that!"

"I have important news for you." Street Poet coughed wretchedly. "Regarding your lady…"

"What do you mean?"

"I know what I know, sir. I watch from the streets. She has been captured by a giant, dragged kicking and screaming into an abandoned building."

"Where?!" Donny shook him again.

"Sir, I'm perfectly willing to tell you, if only you would leave your antagonism in the boxing ring."

"Sure, sure." Donny dropped his arms. "Just tell me where she is."

"I'll do one better. I'll show you." Street Poet bowed. "We need a chariot."

They got one. After a phone call, Donny borrowed a car from a friend and Street Poet had but one demand along the way.

Donny repeated the order again, "No! That's a Mexiwich and a Skipper."

The clown shaped speaker they were stopped next to crackled and the voice from the kitchen rasped, "Okay, okay."

Donny turned his fidgeting attention back to Street Poet next to him. "I can't believe you made me take you here first. You just better know where she is. This better not be a wild goose chase."

The rain beaded across the windshield, the car edged towards the takeout window, following in the red brake lights of the car ahead. Donny boxed the steering wheel in manic time with the radio song.

"My good sir, it's a common courtesy to reward someone who has done you a favor." He sat still as cardboard, watching Donny.

"Yeah, right."

"I'll not be scorned." Street Poet's eyes glared and he was silent until they reached the small sliding window for their order.

Donny reached out and took the paper bag while the woman dropped the change onto the pavement, missing his hand. Donny didn't care. "Here's your reward," he tossed the bag onto Street Poet's lap.

The car edged out of the gate and gained speed. Street Poet opened the bag and held up the sandwich at arm's length. His scream nearly caused an accident.

Trying to avoid a bus, Donny weaved the car across someone's yard, crashing through a fence, onto another lawn, knocking over a mailbox.

"What?!" Donny controlled the car back onto the street. A few garbage cans spun over.

"They've deceived me!" In his shaking hands, Street Poet held an orange shaded hamburger. "This is not what I anticipated!"

Donny stopped the car and grabbed his passenger, "Listen! I've had it! Show me where the place is."

"Alright. Must you always resort to violence?" He pointed ahead, "Take a right."

The tires squealed as the car roared towards the dot that was the boarded-up building with Tina inside.

Street Poet managed a few bites of his hamburger until they were there. "This is it," he said. He swallowed, "Most definitely."

"You better be right." Donny peered through the top of the windshield. The place looked deserted.

Street Poet finished chewing the orange hamburger, wrapping the foil into a ball which he tossed on the floor. "You've got to learn to trust me."

"You gonna pick that up?" Donny pointed at the garbage on the Chevy's floor.

"After all, why would I lie to you?"

"I said, you gonna pick that up?"

"Naturally I'll retrieve it." He quickly leaned over and shoved the foil into his pocket. It sat there in his ragged coat with the litter of a hundred different street poems.

"That's better." Donny clicked off the engine, took a deep breath and got smoothly out of the car. It was quiet. The birds looked stuffed on the wires over the sidewalk. There were a few other parked cars on the street in front of a few other similar buildings. The rain was falling again, in a slow mist, sweeping back and forth.

On the passenger side of the car, the door opened and Street Poet stood up and slammed the door.

THE JAZZ AGE

Donny pressed his ear to the door at the top of the stairs. He could hear singing. It was Tina, singing Billie Holliday. He gave the door a kick and burst through.

Donny staggered. "What the hell's going on?"

Tina was captured and wrapped up like a cocoon, with Fred Thumble doubled over in agony on the floor.

Tina immediately swung into Fats Waller's "Ain't Misbe-havin,'" singing all the while as Donny tore the ropes off. She continued her song as they ran down the stairs to the parked Chevrolet.

He stopped her song with kisses. It was so good to have her back in his arms, Donny could barely drive. The car swerved over curbs and lawns again, reweaving the route, returning from danger.

GAR!

Natalie told Phil yesterday, "Make a list, fold it up and put it in your shirt pocket. The pocket over your heart. Even when you go to sleep, wear the shirt, and in the morning those wishes will come true. Of course, it might take a while. You may even start to think it will never happen, but if you keep your faith, then Surprise!" she bloomed her hands in front of him like a flower blowing up.

He remembered her advice and the hours last night he struggled before he could finally spell it out. They were sharing coffee next to a diner window. Slow moving traffic passed and he touched his shirt pocket. "I have the list, Natalie. The things I wished for and want to do with my life."

"Let me see!" Her eyes sparkled.

He took out the paper and passed it across the table. "Of course you're on it," he said as she played open the folds.

"That's all it says? *Natalie?*" She closed her hand around his. "Phil, what about traveling, or climbing a pyramid, or painting on the coast of Portugal? Things like that? There are all kinds of things you should wish for."

"I guess I had writer's block," he said. "All I could think of was you."

She smiled. "You're nice, Phil Ticks." She squeezed his hand and under the table her foot danced over the top of his shoe. Her eyes stared nonstop.

She kept his list. She put it in her purse.

He couldn't believe that she wanted to keep it. He smiled more and bit his lip watching her.

"Writer's block…" she grinned. "I guess that means I have to decide what movie we should go see." She spread a newspaper open between them so it rested its wings on the napkin holder and her arm. "Let's see…" she studied the listings.

"Oh!" Phil brightened. "I forgot to tell you! *Gar!* is playing!" He pointed to the fine print under her thumb. "7:30 and 9:30.

Tonight only."

"What?" she blinked and stared at his excitement.

"*Gar!* It's a movie about a school of giant gar that terrorizes a small mining town."

"What's a gar?"

"A fish that looks like a dinosaur shoe horn. It normally eats seaweed, I think."

"What's so scary about that?"

"These ones are really big! When they finish the seaweed, they start after swimmers in the river."

She sighed and rolled her eyes. "I don't know about that, Phil." Natalie resumed her newsprint search.

"Alright, you're probably right. It's a dumb movie, no doubt about it. But did you know that I lettered the title for the movie?" He held up his hands, "In gigantic red splash letters!" He got his pen and scribbled the word on a napkin. He held one of her hands, while he waved the title like a rippling river surface. "Then," he began crumpling the word, "we see a man fishing… It's a placid Saturday afternoon in June…The line tugs a little bit…" He pulled on her fingers softly.

"Okay, okay! Don't tell me anymore. Let's go see it!" She refolded the wings of the newspaper and put it next to her. Her foot bumped into his under the table. "How did you get to do the title lettering?"

"I was in the right place at the right time. When I was in high school, the shop teacher made an educational film about the many uses and misuses of the band saw. Instead of making a birdhouse like everyone else, I did all the title lettering for his film. It got shown in schools all over America. You might have seen it and forgotten. Most of the things I've done, might never be known."

Her shoe rested next to his. He could feel her pressure and he smiled. "Anyway, this guy who made the fish movie saw it and wanted my words to spell out his title, *Gar!* I can't wait to see it in twenty foot letters on the screen."

"Well, we should get going then." She had his cupped hand in her palm. She paused, knowing he was going to roll his eyes when she punned, "Let's go *catch* your film."

SHRIMP

There were times Fred Thumble had felt this way before: in the Super Bowl he had an arm crushed and broken in five places. Of course he played the rest of the game and just like then, Fred staggered to his feet and fell over to the refrigerator. His hands climbed up the white metal. Trembling fingers took hold of a smiley-face kitchen magnet. Obeying gravity, his heavy hand fell onto his forehead with it. The magnet stuck. Slowly Fred's mind began to clear.

The picture took shape. He grimaced at the memory. She was gone. She had found out his weak spot and crushed him. Her boyfriend arrived and set her free. Fred punched a bag of Fritos, exploding orange corn chips in a circle around him. He stomped on them, crushing them into a powder.

Street Poet rustled under the pile of newspapers in the corner of the room. A can of chili rolled away from his feet and stopped next to Fred. "You seem to be in a predicament, sir." The poet cleared his throat, "I may be of assistance to you. I know where they're going, I know where they live."

All the announcers on TV commented on how fast Fred Thumble was. For a linebacker, he was like an ice skater. In a second, he had Street Poet lifted off the ground by his neck. "Where'd they go, shrimp?!" Fred snarled.

Street Poet choked and gasped, "I'll show you..." He felt himself returning to the floor. He rubbed his neck and straightened the collar of his nylon shirt. There was the Jack in the Box restaurant on the way there. He would insist they stop at the drive-through again. "Now," Street Poet smiled, "Allow me to take you to their lair."

GOING TO SOMEWHERE NEW

Their rental car glided onto the freeway going east. Florida was all the way on the other edge of America, but that was where they were going. Donny hadn't told her about their destination yet. They were still mesmerized with each other. The car was practically driving itself, chained to the bumper to bumper traffic in the rain.

Tina sighed and pressed her lips to him again, "Please, Donny. We can't ever be separated again."

"Tina, I missed you so much." He cradled his head against hers, her hair soft to his skin. "We're starting all over again. You won't believe the changes. I'll show you something magical. I'll tell you everything, the whole truth about the water and how we can be with each other forever."

"Donny," she purred sleepily, "Let's go somewhere new."

A BIG BOOK OF YELLOW
PAINT

Phil Ticks moves from book to book like dream to dream. In this adventure, Phil returns to his detective roots. Think of the old Bogart movie *The Maltese Falcon*, with private investigators Spade & Archer. There's a lot of Japan in these pages. Although I haven't been there yet, it's a place of mystery and inspiration.

I remember this taste of America

Contents

Nature rarer uses yellow
Than another hue;
Saves she all of that for sunsets, —
Prodigal of blue,

Spending scarlet like a woman,
Yellow she affords
Only scantly and selectly,
Like a lover's words.

Emily Dickinson

THE LUCK OF ANGELS

It took Vern Burke the luck of angels to find the quiet, peaceful life, where he was able to go home to his family and listen to some Chick Webb or Muddy Waters, feed the pigeons on the roof, help his daughter with her homework (take down a dusty atlas to show her the capital of Sierra Leone) put her to bed with a story at 8:30, then pad quietly to his wife, to be with her.

In the middle of sleeping, in the middle of all that, the ringing phone startled him.

Latina uncurled her arms from his hips and pushed his bare back. "Get the phone, baby," she breathed sleepily in his ear. He didn't want to, he knew only trouble rang so late. She pinched him, "Go on!" as the telephone continued to peal.

Vern fell out of her warmth and covers, stood up and wrapped a shirt around himself and stumbled into the other room, colored pink-orange from the street lamps outside. "Hello?" he asked.

"Vern," the voice pleaded, "It's me, Phil."

"Awww, man."

"I know you were sleeping, I'm sorry. Listen Vern, I need your help." Phil had to be ominously deep in the grip of some kind of trouble…As usual.

Vern sighed, "What is it?" He twisted his shoulder to hold the phone and put on his glasses so he could squint at the kitchen clock. "Man, it's three o'clock!"

"Not where I am," Phil said.

"What?" Vern stood there tying the flannel shirt arms around his waist while the receiver clicked with coins falling in on Phil's end, wherever that was.

At last, Phil said, "I'm in Tokyo."

Vern was stunned, he took a deep breath.

"It's a long story," Phil explained, "I'll tell you later. Right now, I need to ask you a favor."

"Okay," Vern said blindly.

Quickly, Phil instructed him, "Go to my place in the morning. The key's under the geranium. There's a notebook in the dishwasher. I want you to get it and call the number on the first page. You'll—"

Phil's voice ended, he had run out of yen.

Vern clicked the receiver. "Hello?" Nothing…He stood there in the odd phosphorus light with the buzzing telephone in his hand. He hung up. Shaking his head, he went back to bed, cuddled into his wife's arms, kissed her neck, smelled her skin and pretended that whatever had happened at three o'clock was just a strange dream.

THE MORNING LIGHT

The morning light coming through the venetian blinds showed the yellow dust washing in the air of their bedroom. Vern yawned and watched Latina put on her clothes. They loved the mornings. Over her shoulder, she smiled at him, "Who was that on the phone last night?"

Her question could have been ice pouring on him. It was supposed to have been a nightmare, like a man falling from an endless building, or a dragon chase across rolling hills. "Oh no," he mumbled and threw the sheet over his head. "Phil Ticks," he hissed underneath.

"Not him again!" Latina groaned. "You can't afford to get mixed up with him, Vern." She watched his covered shape. "Is he in jail again?" she asked.

"He's in Tokyo...Far away."

"Good." She sat down beside him on their soft bed. Then she drew down the covers and lay her hands on his chest. "You got a good job now, honey," she purred. "And me and Viola love you." Her lips kissed him warmly in a circle. "You said goodbye to your past." Close to his face she whispered, "And you don't know anyone named Phil Ticks."

SAND DOLLARS

The little Buick puttered off the road, curving on the street that took him along beside the crowded broken down canneries. All the windows were smashed, swallows flickered in and out and gray pigeons chased each other on the bent rooftops.

Vern slowed the car, turned its wheels around a cracked discarded bathtub lying on the tar. Newspapers blew like a herd of sheep in front of him, tangled in the slipstream wash as he drove faster, remembering where he was and the way to Phil Ticks' place.

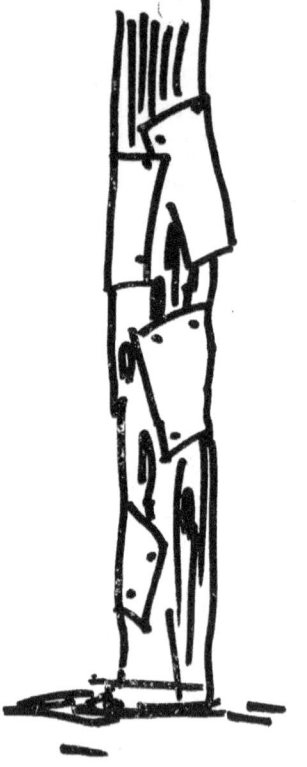

At the next street, he took a right and went straight at the river.

Before he crashed in, he stopped and turned off the engine.

The wheels rested on seashells that snapped on the pavement. Seagulls carried them up and dropped them to the ground to break open the hardness and get the stringy meat inside. Vern's shoes crunched on the dry sand dollars everywhere, as he got out with his briefcase.

He faced the battered falling apart building. That was the place he had to go, to find a notebook in a dishwasher filled with dirty cracked plates and glasses.

YEARS HAD PASSED

They used to be partners, there used to be black letters on a glass door downtown that said *Phil Ticks & Vern Burke, Detectives*. Together, they used to form one solving machine, searching through the knots of murder and deceit, for the vaporous clues that left a trail too vague for most to follow.

Vern spied the dying potted geranium next to the door. He knocked a few more dry red petals off, tipping it to get the key underneath. It unlocked the door after some jiggling and he stepped inside the room.

It was dark. His hand felt blindly along the rough wall for the switch.

Their last case had been a terrible thing. There was violence. Both had been left hurt, and even though they discovered the answer, the solution found them both wanting out. It was too much. Life was too short and precious to risk. They had to go their separate ways and find something safer, apart. Phil drifted out of the hospital and jail and into shady jobs he found listed on telephone poles. Meanwhile, Vern fell in love with a beautiful woman, married her and settled into the steady path of the agency job to support her and the daughter they brought into the world.

It all came back to Vern though…the life alone, when there was nobody else close and you lived in a tower of just your own thoughts and things. Phil's floor was littered with books, spy novels and science fiction, pale clippings from the newspaper and magazines, all of his dirty clothes strewn about, with a pathway made haphazardly towards the kitchen.

Vern followed the clearing veering there.

He opened the door of the dishwasher, expecting the worst and seeing instead just the usual stagger of plates and cups, forks, spoons, with the blue notebook set on its edge. Vern's hand reached into all of it.

Carefully, he grabbed the moist notebook and pulled it out.

The bent over cover flipped open and showed Phil's scrawled printing.

"Julius Hayburn?" Vern read. He stared blankly at the walls. They were covered with framed pictures of The Middle Ages. "Who's that?" The phone number was written next to the name.

If he dialed that, it might all make sense...Or the mystery would just be beginning again...It could be exciting and dangerous...Years had passed while Vern Burke worked for the agency, while he added up their statistics and computed the ultimate answer, but there was always something missing in that.

SAMANTHA RAYES

The Out-Basket was filled with paper. It was past six. The lights were off. Only one person was there on the fourth floor. Facing west, the windows held the picture of the red sinking sun. A cup of instant coffee steamed in Vern's hand. He had taken up smoking again and blue smoke curled before the calendar landscape tacked over her desk.

Vern didn't know Samantha Rayes. She came in early, quietly, distantly typed all day across from him. She squinted and rubbed her eyes (she probably needed glasses) and when she left at five, she barely swished in the same clothes she wore day after day. It was obvious that she was somewhere else when she worked at the office—she probably wanted to be in her calendar photos: exotic, beautiful, otherworldly places.

Vern tapped at the cigarette, while his eyes never left the picture. He felt sure he understood her in a new way. This month's picture was a jade pagoda tapering with orange Japanese trees, a brook spilling with goldfish or carp.

For more than an hour, he stayed mesmerized. In a trance, he stayed on at work. He made himself some strong black coffee and he sat back down mechanically at his desk. Samantha Rayes had given him an insight.

The phone next to his hand began to ring. It rattled a few times before he could blink away from Japan. Vern watched his hand take hold of the receiver and bend it up to his face so he could say, "Hello?"

"Vern?" his wife's voice chimed, "What are you doing? When are you coming home?"

"Latina." Vern reached for the burned away cigarette in the ashtray. "I'm sorry I'm late, I got caught up in work." He stared at the full basket. Then he laughed, "What time is it?"

"It's six thirty, baby. I already fed Viola, she was hungry. But I'm waiting, are you almost done?"

"Oh yeah, I'm on my way." He stood up, "I'll leave right

now. I love you." Vern listened to the warmth in her voice when they said goodbye.

In fifteen minutes he'd be parking in their driveway, the yellow light of their living room bathing the cold front yard lawn.

THE WORLD WAS WATER

The nights were starting sooner and getting colder, but inside his house, Vern Burke sat with his wife, eating hot stew, while his daughter played with plastic animals. A calypso record crackled on the turntable Hi-Fi.

Viola held a giraffe and a dancing walrus. "How did Noah get all those different animals onto one boat?" she asked.

Vern stared at the spoon dipping in for a potato. "That's easy," he said, illuminated. "It wasn't really a boat," he explained. "It was a spaceship. Martians loaned it to him. He miniaturized all the world's creatures with a zap gun and he kept them safe in test tubes. While the oceans, rivers, lakes and rain clouds flooded everything you see...Shopping malls," he pointed, "freeways, used car lots, 7-11s and junk stores, the rotten places where people work, and army bases, lousy housing developments, even rich mansions on the hill. From great big cities to little towns, all of it got submerged. For forty days and forty nights the world was water. Noah hovered above the waves with the small animals...Waiting..."

Finally, Latina exclaimed, "My!" She gave him a look and shot her glance to their daughter surrounded by zoo toys. "What a story!"

"It's not a story," Vern said, continuing to eat. With a mouthful, he picked up the newspaper on the other chair next to him and passed it to Latina.

She looked at it. The drawing on the front of the shopper's tabloid showed a spaceman with a long white beard, guiding a rhinoceros into a flying saucer. "Oh!" she laughed, "This is just a joke!"

Latina flicked the paper back at her husband and it landed, creased open to the sports pages, with the unstoppable Julius Hayburn galloping past everyone.

DON'T LOOK BACK

Vern tucked the green covers over Viola and clicked off her little bedside lamp. In the corner, the magic lantern spun colors and shadows as it twirled. He set the book on her table. It was already crowded with animals, rubber bands, coins, candy wrappers and plastic hair pins. He kissed her forehead, glowing cartoonish, and brushed her temple gently. For a few minutes, he sat still in his chair, watching her sleep perfectly, wondering if she was dreaming the story he had read to her.

Wasn't it funny, he smiled, that of all the books on her shelves, she wanted him to read *Japanese Children's Stories*? Talking sea turtles, underwater kingdoms, bamboo dragons…She especially loved the stories where a fisherman or woodsman, or some humble person would go off on some great adventure and return home with a reward of gold. He read her one of those Japanese fables and it was obvious to him—it was all adding up faster and faster, pointing him across the ocean.

He couldn't resist her small sleeping beauty. He kissed her goodnight again, got up and quietly left the room, keeping the door open a bit. He looked back and whispered.

John Lee Hooker played in the hallway. Vern followed that sound past the pictures into the living room where Latina was curled on the couch. She was asleep too (a novel fallen from her hand onto the floor) with enough room for him to press next to her.

Vern touched the curl of her hair with his hand. His voice murmured over her shoulder, "Latina, it's true. You and Viola are what's precious to me. When I'm around you two, I feel like I'm doing something right. I truly do. That's why I can't understand…I'm afraid I'm becoming a detective again. I wonder if maybe my life can't be separated from that either."

She barely moved with small sleeping breaths, but there was a little smile on her lips.

That was good. He brushed his mouth to her hair and whispered, "My father brought us home a dog once when we were kids. One of those white dogs with the black spots, an Airedale I think...A firedog. He got it from the station. It was getting old and had a lame leg and they gave it to him for free. What a great dog..." Vern drifted nostalgically for a second. "He would sleep next to the wood stove, so close that the kitchen would always smell like smoking fur. Whenever a siren went through the city though, he'd leap up and go crazy, pawing and scratching at the door. He still had to find the fire, even though he was ancient and like a peg-legged pirate with rheumatism. We had to really struggle with him to make him stay when he heard the sound. But finally we had to let him go to the fire, so he wouldn't wreck the place."

Vern stopped the story there. He remembered he didn't want to say how the dog never returned.

Latina made a sound in her mouth and rubbed her cheek along his arm.

Vern thought pleasantly, I should be so grateful for this loving. In a hush, he said, "It seems most of my life I was trying to find this. Why should I ever want to return to being a detective again, when I have found everything beautiful I need?" He kissed her.

Then the phone rang.

THE TERMITE EXTERMINATOR

Vern knew who it was. He was sure that when he picked up the phone, the line would crackle with the Far East. Latina stirred and stretched out for it, but he folded her arm back to her chest and he picked up the phone. "Hello?"

"Vern?" It was Phil Ticks. There was no escaping him. The world was spinning them together again.

"Yes..." Vern ricocheted a look off his wife's face watching him, back to the phone cord, leading into the wall, into the miles to Japan.

"It's Phil. Did you get the notebook?"

"Yes."

"Did you call Julius?"

"No, I don't think so," Vern stalled.

Latina had scrunched up onto her hip to stare at him with interest. "Who is it?" she asked.

"When you call him, tell him, *The eagle has landed but the gossamer hen needs eggs*. It's important."

Latina pulled Vern's arm, her eyebrows furrowed angrily, "Is that Phil Ticks?"

"That's alright," Vern said, "We already have some. Thanks." He hung up quickly and tried to lark a smile at her. "Termite exterminator..." he explained.

THE DIVINE WIND

"Maybe Phil Ticks thought I was trying to get rid of him?" Vern wondered guiltily after a few nights of telephone silence. Getting up in the morning, sleepless or drained by nightmares, then going off to work, he was sitting and staring more often than not. He did his assignments in an automatic daze. Whenever he let it, his mind would go to Japan and Phil Ticks. He almost tortured himself with scenarios. In his briefcase with all his other papers and an essay on the kamikaze Divine Wind, there was that blue notebook almost pleading with a voice for him to open it.

Finally he did.

The pages were all warped, the metal ring binding was rusted. Vern felt like he was opening a relic from the *Titanic*, or Pearl Harbor. Julius Hayburn and his phone number were waterlogged in blue ink, scrawled in childish block letters. Vern picked up the telephone and dialed. His throat muscles knotted and constricted nervously. I hope I don't sound like Shirley Temple, he panicked, clearing his voice gruffly. The connection rang twice. Then someone answered.

"Hayburn residence, this is Jeeves speaking."

"Hello," Vern said, throwing out words hopefully, "I would like to discuss a personal matter with Mr. Julius Hayburn, please." He drummed his fingers manically on the desktop.

"I'm afraid he's very busy right now. May I take a message?"

"Yeah, this is Vern Burke. I have an important message for Julius Hayburn, It's from my partner, Phil Ticks."

"Just a moment please, Mr. Burke," Jeeves replied instantly. "Mr. Hayburn has been expecting you."

Vern was clicked onto a Muzak waiting line. The sap of two hundred synthetic violins dripping a syrupy version of a song he remembered. "That can't be what I think it is!" he listened in horror.

Abruptly the song was gone and, "Julius here," reported

281

deeply into Vern's ear. It was the voice of a seven foot giant.

"Hello," Vern replied, "How are you?"

"I'm alright. My hand's a bit sore. I've been autographing basketballs all day. Is this Phil's contact?"

"Yeah," Vern laughed uneasily, "I guess that's me. He wanted me to tell you the eagle has landed but the gossamer hen needs eggs. Does that have any meaning to you?" Vern pried.

"It means your friend wants more money. I gave him plenty already. He's not getting any more from me!" Angrily, Julius hung up.

"That's it?!" Vern felt a halo of relief as he replaced the phone receiver. He grinned. That was so simple, just the relay of a message and I'm through! No more weight hanging over me, no more mystery to solve, now I can return to my life. Now I can sleep at night!

He stuffed the notebook back in his briefcase and spun in his chair wildly. "I'm back!" Vern announced to the empty fourth floor, throwing a shadowbox punch at his purple silhouette. It was like being given a chance to live again, he felt like celebrating.

Outside the office building, he ran over to the corner and he bought marigolds from the starry-eyed woman swinging bunches of them at traffic.

The oxygen of the city was alive with the music of the 1920s. Vern did the Charleston with the flowers all the way to his parked, awaiting Buick.

THE MOTHCATCHER

Vern sung with the radio, driving in tempo on the road home. He looked like a lunatic, dueting with Jimmie Rodgers, then Kitty Wells, as the station kept his spirits flying at the speed limit.

When he stopped the car in their driveway at last, he hopped out the door like James Brown, did a spin on his heels and froze when he noticed the strange, long black limousine parked next to the curb.

The old detective instinct, that feeling of dire apprehension, returned like swallows to Capistrano, beginning in his stomach and fluttering all through him in jittery waves. Something was going on.

On guard, Vern went up the pathway to the door and let himself inside.

There was seven feet of a basketball player folded out like a ladder on their sofa. When Vern entered the room, the tower stood, stooping, and held out a gigantic hand.

"Hi, I'm Julius Hayburn."

An anvil plunged inside Vern. He coughed out a hello and searched vainly for his wife.

"Sorry to drop in on you like this. So suddenly and all..." Julius sat back down and straightened out his spine. "But it's important. I'm worried about your partner. I don't know if he succeeded."

Dumbfounded, Vern stared, with his briefcase clutched in his hand, flowers in the other. "Succeeded at what?"

Latina entered the room and smiled. "There you are, darling!" she kissed Vern and stood next to him. "You didn't tell me you knew Julius Hayburn, the superstar!" Her eyes glittered. "I didn't think Viola would ever fall asleep, she's been entranced."

Julius chuckled. He played with his two foot silk tie. "Well, she's a great kid," he smiled. Then he stood up again. His head brushed the flat ceiling and he couldn't help looking into the ceiling lamp. "Um..." he noticed, "You got some moths in this light."

Vern and Latina blinked up at him and the little dark moth shadows in the light bowl. Vern cleared his throat and smiled at his wife. He remembered the flowers and held them out to her. "Mr. Hayburn and I have been working on an account," he coughed. "We just have a few more details to iron out."

He set his briefcase on the table and took out a sheaf of stapled pages. He held the paper at an angle so only he could see it. It was the scholarly essay on kamikazes. In 1945, there were manned rocket bombs slinging through the blue sky. He got caught on a sentence and the grainy photo of a young pilot tying on a headband.

While Latina said goodbye to Julius, she touched Vern's arm and went to their bedroom with a book.

Another picture showed those Japanese planes that never returned, taking off from a sunrise runway. Someone stood on the ground watching like a fallen tear.

"Hey!" Julius was saying, "I said I need you to do something for me."

Vern returned to the moment. "What exactly is going on with Phil Ticks?"

"That's what I want *you* to find out," Julius said. He sat back down on the couch arm so he could look Vern levelly into the eyes. "I got a lot of money tied up with that guy and he seems to have disappeared." He reached into his pocket and took out an envelope. "This is an airplane ticket." Without getting up, his arm stretched across and dropped the white envelope onto the table in front of Vern. "Tokyo. I want you to go find him."

A RECORD

The jet shifted in flight lazily. Vern could feel his stomach turning with it. He told himself not to look out of the tiny window, at the clouds tipping in the blue, at the land about to turn into acres of sea. A sickly sweat broke upon his forehead. "I'm on the solid ground, I'm lying in a field with sunflowers...I'm watching butterflies and swallows." Turning his head from the direction of the window, Vern opened his eyes hopefully.

Inches away, a baby clinging to its mother's neck blew bubbles at him, drooling some applesauce.

There are thousands of miles and a day of flying hours from the west coast of America to Japan. Vern Burke must have set a record of sorts—he crossed the Pacific Ocean solo in a tin closet-sized bathroom. Finally, three patient Japanese stewardesses had to coax him out and reseat him as the airplane circled Tokyo in a swooping landing pattern.

THE WISE GUY

"No wonder Phil disappeared," Vern mumbled out loud. "He probably got lost. He fell into a street and couldn't ask for the directions out." Wearing an overcoat, with a stuffed bag in his grip, Vern stood in the gentle Tokyo rain, before the shimmering airport with taxis and cars and people forming a crowd. He felt weak, lighter than air from his terrible flight, and he wasn't sure what he should do first. Food and sleep, his body spoke for him.

The Green Crane Hotel was where Phil Ticks had first checked in, following his arrival weeks ago. Julius Hayburn gave Vern a notebook page full of information, but Vern still didn't know a lot of important things. Julius wouldn't even tell him what Phil's mission had been. "Just find him," Julius had said icily.

"Hey wise guy!" someone called out to Vern.

He turned and saw the arm rolling at him from the cab window.

"Hey wise guy. You look no further for this night is waiting alright."

Vern stared awkwardly. "What?"

"This car will take you far." The arm, as large as Vern's leg, waved him over. "Get in, big spender."

Vern shrugged, opened the back door, and got in next to his wet suitcase.

The huge driver, squashed behind the steering wheel, filled in the front half of the Toyota. He grinned, "Where do you want to be, New York Yankee?"

"Uh..." Vern reached into his pocket and took out a tear of paper. "The Green Crane Hotel? You know where that is?"

"Of course yes, Mr. President. Tokyo is the back of my wife's hand." The wheel steered, miniature in his big fingers.

TOKYO MILES

"And I thought there were a lot of cars back home," Vern stared at the thick traffic sewed all around them.

"Yes, our bloodstream is the cars," the driver said.

"What does that sign say?" Vern pointed to the shiny neon happy-face that sparkled with Japanese lettering. It kept reappearing along the side of the road every mile or so.

"It says, 'We're sorry for the traffic jam.' Sometimes it is sorry for the weather too." The driver reached onto the shoulder of his white t-shirt and unrolled a cigarette pack out.

"Wait a second," Phil dug into his own coat pocket. "You can have these American ones." He passed the pack of Hope cigarettes over the front seat.

"Thank you, for keeps? I will make them mine until the end of time." It didn't take him long. He pressed a cigarette into his mouth, lit it and nodded, "I remember this taste of America," he puffed a cloud of smoke. "Years ago, I took the show on the road to your land. I used to sumo with the televisions watching. I was truly very good and making the money, but I became blue. It was not my place, if you will pardon the truth. My thoughts escaped and I had to come back to Japan to get them and they were waiting here to say, 'Hello, welcome home!' I drive the taxi now, so that when I drift I will go no more than Tokyo miles."

"There it is," Vern peered through the smoke and windshield wipers. A sign blinked two neon languages. He could read the one below, waving green light in the tinsel rain. It said, The Green Crane Hotel.

JAPANESE WEATHER

He held the strange coins in his hand and dialed those numbers back to the U.S. While he talked to his wife and daughter,
he couldn't help wondering if this was the same phone booth
that Phil Ticks had used. *If only this phone booth could talk,*
he wished. He told his wife he would try to finish up Julius
Hayburn's business as soon as he could and said how much he
missed her closeness. There was spilled rice on his coat and he
laughed as he told Viola how he was trying to learn to use chop-
sticks.

When the operator politely warned that his money couldn't
hold them together too much longer, Vern repeated, "I love
you, I love you," until they were gone.

Back at The Green Crane, Vern's feet hung over the edge of
the bed while he faced the TV. His eyes fought to stay open.

Kojak, speaking Japanese, raced through an American looking city where nobody spoke English.

Vern fell asleep.

The green sign flickered in the rain outside his window. The
television became a winter snowstorm and the weather stayed
that way until morning.

GLASS HEEL

The door of his room crashed with knocking. Vern had a waking vision of Rodan pounding his leathery reptile wings. With a scream, he snapped up in bed, staring all around himself. Alien chattering puppets bobbed oddly on the TV screen. The thumping continued in the golden morning.

As fast as he could stagger, Vern got his clothes on and unlatched the door.

The doorway was filled with the shape of the taxi cab driver. "Wake up, wake up!" he announced, "I'm here bright and early to give you the tour of our city heart."

Vern blinked and was awake again, in bed.

He had been dreaming. It was jetlag. Sheets and blankets strangled all around him. An American voice, a commercial on TV said, "heart to heart," but when Vern looked up out of the covers, the lively puppet-show had returned.

He sighed and let his head fall back into the pillow. "Tokyo," he said hoarsely. It would be best to sleep for a while more. He glanced at his watch, but it didn't make any sense. Anguished, he dropped it onto the floor.

It made a breaking sound.

Vern couldn't let it sit there, possibly in crystal shatters, so he leaned over the mattress and felt in the dust.

A scrap of paper touched his finger and he brought it up to his eyes.

It was a ticket, part of a ticket anyway, half torn. There was writing on the back of it. Vern could read it in the soft light that followed a night of bad weather. He knew the handwriting. It looked like a child's, but it was from Phil Ticks. It said in simple letters, *Call Vern, Let him know*

The television shrieked with delighted school children, swamping around the puppets and beginning to dance.

"First things first..." Vern decided as he lurched out of bed to turn the set off. He hopped across the floor in pain, having

stepped on the broken watch.
    There was glass in his heel.

FROZEN IN THE GLOW

Downstairs, he sat in the elliptical play of shadows sipping green tea, listening to Howlin' Wolf faintly playing from the kitchen. The dishwasher in that other room splashing with water and that familiar music, made Vern think of home. Sunday morning. It turned into Thelonious Monk and he really felt homesick, he wanted to get back on an airplane and fly to them at once. He suddenly missed Latina and Viola more than any mystery was worth.

"Who cares about Phil Ticks?" he mumbled angrily. That fool got me into this mess. He can figure out how to free himself. I shouldn't be a part of this. Last time, he nearly killed me. Hot flashes steamed up and down Vern's spine as he remembered their disastrous partnership. An old Roy Orbison song mourned out of the sound of clattering wet dishes.

Years ago, they were in a black cornfield with a full moon of course and flapping bats—all the signs of a haunted night. Phil had a gun. He insisted that a detective must have one, though he was too afraid to aim it at anybody. He fired once in the air above the scarecrow, and the tall corn stalks swished and crunched as they ran in pursuit. Vern chased after Phil. It was like trailing an escaped convict in a bayou. Suddenly, the maze of corn rows turned into a clearing, where the plants were all cut down into sharp stubble...Phil and Vern wandered into the blue space uneasily...Strange sounds, insects or something else, sawed at the moon. Phil was reloading his pistol when the field lit up with fierce yellow headlamps. Like deer on the highway, they were frozen in the glow, as a tractor lowered threshing wings and roared towards them.

That was the end of their detective career. So Vern Burke thought...How could they go on past that failure? But somehow Phil Ticks had brought him here, years later, into this new mystery...All the way to Japan.

THE NAME I USED WHILE I WAS IN AMERICA

A beggar came up to him, dragging Japanese newspapers, cardboard, silk rags. He held out his hand for money, while the cars and people blurred.

"I'm homeless too," Vern said and dug into his pocket for all the strange coins he had. He kept the half ticket though, it stayed in his hand. Hopefully it might be a clue.

Vern looked at the words on the colored paper, the symbols that didn't mean anything to him. Only Phil's message on the other side spoke to him. "What does Phil want me to know?" Vern scowled, as he flagged his hand into the street for a taxi. He grumbled, "It was always that way. I'm always the one who gets the hotfoot." Vern got into the taxi and passed the little ticket scrap to the driver, "Can you take me to this place?"

"I thought it was you I see," the familiar voice answered him, taking the thimble of paper.

It was the same sumo driver from yesterday. Vern was surprised he didn't notice that immediately. A detective should be alert to things like that.

"Since we are more than passing ships, I must introduce," the driver nodded his massive head. "You can call me Louie Louie. You know the American rock and roll song?"

Vern shuddered, "Yeah, I know it," remembering with grimness that it was the same Muzak song he had heard on Julius Hayburn's telephone service.

"You don't like my name?"

Vern saw that Louie Louie was visibly hurt, his face had welled up, about to cry.

"Your name is great!" Vern apologized and shrugged, "It's just that song...It made me think of something else."

Louie Louie held the ticket up to the windshield so he could translate, "It says," he squinted, "to call Vern and let him know."

"I know that! I'm Vern! It's the writing on the other side I need to know about. It's in Japanese."

293

Flipping it over, Louie Louie ran his fingertip along the shred. "It is a ticket for The Emperor's Grieving Garden." He was still hurt, but he returned the ticket silently to Vern and set the car in motion.

"In America," said Vern hopefully, "Louie Louie is one of our treasured songs...It's like a Beethoven opera. It's very good for you to have that name."

Louie Louie was pleased, "Thank you, Vern. It is not really my real name, you know of course. It is the name I used while I was in America. When I wrestled night and day to stay alive with dollars."

FLOWERS CAN'T ALWAYS BE SEEN

When the taxi stopped, it was next to a tall stone wall spilling over with ivy and vine petals. They got out and stood by the wooden gate. Louie Louie pointed to the sign sadly. "It says the garden is closed for the season," he told Vern.

"They can't be!"

"To make repairs and plant new things," Louie Louie said. "It's unfortunate flowers can't always be seen."

"But I have to get in there!" Vern showed him the ticket again. "It's my only clue..." He sat back and brooded.

A car rattled past them on the cobblestones and then it was quiet again.

Vern watched a pigeon strutting in front of the wall. Suddenly it picked itself up into the air and flew over to the other side. In a minute, Vern was about to do the same.

Louie Louie clutched Vern in his arms, close to the green covered wall.

Vern stuffed another pack of Hope cigarettes into Louie Louie's pocket and said, "Take these. I should be back before you smoke half of them."

"Okay, wise guy." Shifting his feet, Louie Louie breathed in deeply and with a roar threw Vern into the air.

Over the edge with a foot to spare, Vern spun and fell down, landing hard in sand, needled with banzai saguaro cacti.

TO PUT HIS HANDS ON THE REACHING WING

Painfully, Vern got to his feet and plucked a cactus out of his back side. The sand had been swept in watery patterns, but now it looked like an airplane had crash landed in a desert. There was nothing Vern could do about it. He tried to brush the sandy pattern back in place, but it was frustrating. He gave up and tiptoed his way across to the winding pathway. "Why did Phil come to this place?" he whispered.

The Emperor's Grieving Garden.

Plants and stones watched him crunch along the white gravel path aimlessly, once or twice stopping next to a bench and staring at the silence. Like the jazz and blues records he had at home, the feeling of this garden made sense to him.

At last, he found what he believed Phil must have been stopped by. Vern sat down on the mossy pale stone bench in front of it.

It was an American plane from World War Two. It was rusting silver, with stars painted on its side. All bullet-holed and dead moth-like, it slept forever at rest in the web of spread out Japanese coral flowers.

Vern thought about this machine being made in America in the 1940's…Machineguns being set in its wings, with attachments for bombs…It didn't seem real that terrible war could have happened. He remembered there were factories sending out thousands of warplanes then. Nearly every one of them was forgotten now, melted down, crashed, underground in pieces, or underwater. But this one had been kept, to be a part of the remembering.

All at once, Vern decided to go up to it and touch it, thinking maybe there was something American in him that could console it. Not so much that it needed to be forgiven any more for shooting and being a part of all that killing (that became the past for everything) but because Vern knew how it must feel.

Again, Vern stepped off the path into the plants, this time

careful of the irises and blue lilies, to put his hands on the reaching wing. He didn't feel a spark, no sudden surge of radiating emotion, so he moved his hands across the flat. He moved with the curving shape through the flowers, to where the wing met the body of the plane. And then Vern climbed up, took hold of the canopy, pushed the glass aside and got inside.

A CLOUD OF HOPE SMOKE

A cloud of Hope smoke plumed out of the cab when Louie Louie opened the door and got out. He coughed, tossed the empty cigarette pack back inside and shut the door.

His giant feet splashed the rain pools. His image shimmered across the cobblestones like a reflected blimp, or a planet in the sky. A blowing newspaper folded origami around his leg. He shook it loose and it turned into a swan and skidded away.

Sadly, Louie Louie wished he hadn't smoked all ten cigarettes one after another. He should have kept one or two for the long walk around the tall wall of the garden.

Searching in his pockets, he only found a toothpick, which he put in his mouth and chewed aggressively.

Sometimes he stopped and swept the ivy aside, wondering if there could be a rusted hidden door leading in.

INSIDE THE AMERICAN THING

The American was inside the American thing. He was bent into the metal seat with all the cracked dials in front of him, windscreen and sight, holding the stick, turning flaps and rudder to clack pointlessly in the wind.

Vern pressed all the buttons and switches that he hoped would cough the engine into life again. He wasn't that surprised that nothing happened. Years had passed in this quiet place and anyway the engine had probably been taken out, he thought... To be used somewhere else, to pump water from the fields when crops were being flooded. But still, he could just imagine the plane sliding through the Zen gardens, roaring, lifting off the ground gymnastically, to buzz the pagoda high rises and tower antennas of this rebuilt Tokyo.

With a terrible gleam in his eye, Vern pressed the red button connected to the machine guns and flames shot out of the wings. The plane shook violently as the bullets left, exploding the wall at the far end of the garden.

WHAT HAPPENED IN THE GARDEN

A huge shape ran through the smoke and rubble and tangled flower parts. Louie Louie saw the airplane with smoke puckered and wisping from its silver old edges. He saw Vern cramped inside, unmoving, just a dark blur under the glass.

Louie Louie trampled through the greening blooms. He jumped up onto the slanting wing of the ancient warplane. He put his hands through the opening and pulled at the little frozen person inside.

Vern Burke was just a blank. He couldn't think beyond the words, "Take me away," which he kept stuttering.

Louie Louie curled the land pilot into his arms. Down onto the earth he hurried along the path, scattering footprints heavily. Escaping through the disintegrated wall, a blasted rip in the carefully placed rocks, he staggered, ducking and rushing across the cobblestones to the door of his taxi cab.

Police and reporters and all the people in Tokyo would want to know what happened in the garden.

Blearily, Vern lifted his head off the seat and said things, even sentences in Japanese that didn't make any sense. About three percent, a slender finger of himself, tried to point the way away.

UNDER THE WASH OF STARLIGHT BEFORE THE SUN RETURNED

In shock, Vern Burke woke up in a foreign bed, sometime late at night, or early morning (he still didn't have a clock for this time zone) and he sat up in terror, in a sweat, in the room that wasn't in The Green Crane.

There was enough light for him to see the walls covered not with gentle, graceful Japanese paintings, but posters and newspaper clippings. A second or two or more passed, with sweat down his forehead, before his hands unclutched the sheet and he allowed himself to breathe.

The pictures on the walls were grandiose, ballooning pictures of Louie Louie wrestling in the sumo circle.

It felt like his brain had been shut off for a while and he was being allowed to think again only if he dared to. Vern blinked. The vision of where he was steadied. Vern thought hazily, the taxi driver must have brought me here.

The only window in the room jittered with bright stars and lights from skyscrapers. He staggered off the bed and wobbled over to the glass, putting his hands onto the cold window facing Tokyo.

"Am I getting any closer to the truth?" he asked and his question was stopped by the glass. "Tell me..." Slow motion crept into him. The colors that made up the window began to run down, as he slid into a pool onto the floor.

Curled under the wash of starlight, before the sun returned, he had a dream.

He was there when the darkness lifted, standing on a beach, and it came to him first as a sound unwinding, so loud it grinded up his spine. Thousands of people formed a line, shifting and drawing something connected by thick rusted chain to the sea. They pulled and link by link it was slowly emerging from the sea. What it was only became clear gradually, as its swirled dome parted the waves. A huge Easter colored egg. There were

301

enough people dragging to bring it up onto the sand. The egg rolled slightly in the crumpling tidal waves.

Vern's dream eyes watched a black crack fault around the shell. He saw all the little ants of people flee with a sigh that reached his ears. Pieces fell onto the shore and the thing pushing from inside came out fluttering.

Unfolding wings, monstrous and reborn, it was a Phil Ticks butterfly!

THE ESCAPE FROM TOKYO AT DAWN

Louie Louie didn't seem to be too affected by their morning getaway. He was taking the escape from Tokyo at dawn in stride. As Vern started to wake up finally, he told him, "You had quite a spill, Dollar Bill!"

Vern laughed, or tried to. It sounded more like a splash.

Louie Louie passed him a thermos. "Take a sip," he offered. "Green tea will steady your thoughts and calm the day."

The taxi followed the curves of the shoreline, the yellow reeds that made a fence holding back the sand and sea. Small white birds ran away from the car, across the shallow surf.

For a moment, as Vern stared at the window, he thought he was in the dream again and he almost choked on the lukewarm tea.

"I'm taking you to my hidden mother," Louie Louie said, "She lives with the ocean. It will be safe with her until the To-kyo danger blows away...The entire city searches itself for the evil doer. A crime in a sacred place."

"I didn't know—" Vern began nervously.

"I understand," Louie Louie held his hand up, "I'm a guilty man too for breaking the law. I flew you over the wall." He became serious, driving silently for a while, until he turned them off the tarred road, onto flat rattling mossy stones. "This is here," he said and pointed at a field all washed in thick fog.

The stones gave out and the car bounced on the furrows, scaring a round bird into the air. Grass, weeds and stick flowers scratched the sides of the cab, whispering. There wasn't a road or path anymore. Louie Louie stopped them before they crunched blindly any further. "We will walk with feet," he said.

Vern opened the door and stepped into the foggy breeze pouring off the sea. He smiled and breathed deeply, filling him-self with the Pacific air.

Louie Louie got out, shut his door and stood there just breathing too.

And it was calm, the clicking of yellow stems in the wind, a seagull calling somewhere, the heavy sigh of the surf.

Vern laughed deliriously, wondering if he would ever find Phil Ticks. Did it matter? Maybe not. "My own life is puzzling enough," he said lowly and in a flash he was reminded, "But what am I going to tell Julius Hayburn?"

ABANDONED

The grass was tall around Vern but only for a few steps, then he was falling through the ground. It was a secret entrance, rusty hinges, a trapdoor planted over with weeds and he fell for six feet before he landed on a huge pillow. On his back looking up, he could see a square of blue light, with Louie Louie framed in the corner.

"Do you feel like a million bucks?" Louie Louie called down, concerned.

Vern wasn't able to speak or move. Someone answered for him.

A woman's voice behind him shrilled up at Louie Louie, reproachfully. In Japanese she wailed, "So, my son has decided to come visit his abandoned mother?! Here I am, living below the ground, with only the worms to talk to. What do you want from me this time?! Money again?"

"It's good to see you, mother!" Louie Louie waved.

"I know this isn't a social call," she continued. "You're in trouble with the police aren't you? Such shame you bring me,"

305

she sighed. "And who is this stranger?" She prodded Vern with a bamboo stick.

Vern winced, but didn't turn over.

"An American? Am I to believe you've brought him here for a terrible reason? Pushed him in with me so that he too can be hidden forever?"

Vern listened to their conversation going back and forth and up and down. It didn't make any sense to him, he just lay there, still, waiting for words he could understand.

"I'll be right back. I promise," Louie Louie said, leaning over the hole. "I just need to leave him with you for a short while."

"Of course," his mother surrendered and sighed. "That's what mothers are for."

"Thanks! You're a saint." Louie Louie blew her a kiss and waved to Vern, saying in English, "I'll be back with a ladder as soon as I can, when the time is right. Goodbye." Then his round overhanging shape was gone.

Slowly, the earth closed again. It became dark. Some wind chimes blew against each other, as orange paper lanterns started to glow and Vern turned his head and saw her—a girl, no, a woman barely twenty years old.

WHILE HE STARED IN AMAZEMENT

The next strange thing he discovered was that she could read his mind. While he stared in amazement at the young Japanese woman, trying to figure out how she could be mother to a son older than herself, she answered him in English inside of his head.

Her voice was soft and rang like the bells that sit on the water in buoys to warn ships: *I can't speak your language, but I can think with it.*

"How can you do that?"

I know you have a hundred questions, her mind told him. *But there are just too many things I could never give you answers for. You'll have to accept what happens is real.* The silk on her arm rustled as she pointed above them at the ceiling that was the ground, *My son never has time to stay long enough to share a meal. Are you hungry?* There was a table set and waiting with a bowl of steaming rice.

"I'm..." Vern stood up and pushed at the roots overhead, "I should really be going, I feel trapped in this place."

There was only a hushing river static sound in his head for her reply, as she walked over and kneeled at the table to pour a cup of tea. Vern stared up, looking for the way to get out. Green tea filled the white China and she told him, *You were more trapped out there.*

Vern swung his head to face her, "What do you mean?"

She turned around and reached into the dark of the wall shadows. Her hand took out something that began to spin with rainbow lights. Pressed to her kimono, it lit her and danced her silhouette shadow off of the carved ground. *You're right,* her words flew in his mind again. *It is a crystal ball.* Carefully, she set it in front of Vern onto a stand. *Look into it,* she said without speaking, *and you'll understand.*

Vern leaned forward and watched all the little drifting stars. They circled, jumping each other, then slowly started to draw together like a children's dot-to-dot page to become a picture. A familiar scene formed in the round glass: the airport in Tokyo. He remembered that scene and the taxi cab that pulled to a stop. Like a magic movie camera, Vern's sight moved with Louie Louie along the road again to the Green Crane Hotel. The globe showed him the same room and the yellow morning arriving and then it flashed with the sand and flower swirls of The Emperor's Grieving Garden. The garden went dark and something different happened...Vern watched entranced as the crystal ball showed a rotten looking apartment. The camera vision slowly panned down a body that was stuck in the chest with a wire. The flowing cable connected into a machine. Next, it showed Louie Louie, dressed in a flashy Western three piece suit, smiling wickedly and leading another businessman into the room... The transformed sumo wrestler tugged the chest cord while he spliced another wire into his client...Electrical currents surged rivers of colors and Vern could feel the ripping pain from his place underground. He shut his eyes on it and turned away.

When Vern opened his eyes again and looked back at the crystal ball, he could see whose journey had been taking place.

A face had formed in the crystal ball.

At first, Vern had to look away. He looked for the woman, but she was lost in the darkness of the room somewhere.

"Hello Vern," said Phil Ticks. "Long time, no see."

Vern forced himself to return his eyes to the crystal ball.

Phil swam in it, in wavy blue patterns.

Clearing his throat, Vern shifted on the pillow and croaked, "Phil..." He rubbed his face with his hands, his eyes felt hard as eggs under his fingers.

Phil smiled with a weary ghost of a voice, "Welcome to Japan, Vern."

*"I explain mysteries
that people don't want to explain.
I make a nice living too
chasing ghosts in the past."*

Bob Hope
The Ghost Breakers
1940

CHASING GHOSTS IN THE PAST

Phil Ticks smiled wornly. His eyes were shipwrecking pools, he looked like a ghost. He told Vern, "I had to reach you somehow."

"You couldn't just use a phone, could you?"

"Not where I'm calling from," Phil said. The crystal ball image fluttered. "They're very strict about how you can reappear. I'm dead, Vern." Phil floated. "I found out too much and that thug Louie Louie killed me. He electrocuted me with some machine. Listen Vern, you have to get out of Japan!"

Suddenly, as if it was a television being unplugged, Phil blipped, disappearing into a single dot of light. And that too left.

Vern grabbed the crystal ball and shook it, "Phil!" he yelled. But it had turned the black color of a bowling ball and it seemed to be filled with heavy water.

He's gone, the woman's voice told him as she returned.

Vern saw that she carried a shovel and a ladder of soft yellow wood and she passed them to him.

He's right, her words splashed in his head, *you've been here too long already. You need to leave Japan as fast as you can.*

A PEARL HARBOR ZOMBIE

When he dug out of the ground, it was night. The field was colored by the big moon. A strong cold wind blew from the ocean as Vern kicked his way out into the grass. He stood up and turned around to say Goodbye to her and to pat the ground down, but it had already healed over. He was alone except for the breeze pushing him and all the stars beyond counting.

His footsteps crushed through the weeds, collapsing them like hands brushing down a path behind him. The thought of Phil's terrible pain made him run. He kept tripping over branches. A blackberry vine grabbed him, before he found the road that Louie Louie had driven on.

Vern came stumbling out onto the pavement and yellow headlights flared past him, trailing a disappearing horn wail and red brake lights, as it shot around the curve. He fell backwards onto the shoulder, slipping in the soft mud.

The road got quiet again, the bending plants and wind passing through.

Away from the ocean, Vern hurried along, trying to piece together what Phil had said from beyond the grave. It was just like Phil Ticks to use the Houdini theatrics of a crystal ball, Vern thought. "Years ago in America, you were always dragging me into magic shops," Vern mumbled, remembering.

He slowed and walked. He couldn't believe Phil was dead. It made him so sad and confused that very soon he wasn't watching where he was going again.

The road he followed went under a barbed wire fence and through a row of trees glowing like skeletons. It was like the passing of a dream how somehow he ended up back on the road. He put out his thumb to hitchhike a ride from the approaching eyes of a car.

The car soared past, blasting Vern with cold air.

So he kept walking, wondering suddenly if Japan even had hitchhiking. I probably looked like a spirit waving at that car. A

Pearl Harbor zombie...

After that, no more cars appeared. He walked in darkness until eventually lights other than the sky's spilled from the crisp horizon. Vern dragged himself towards the village. It was crowned with the green glow of a gas station.

THERE ARE YEARS NOBODY CAN FIND

There were letters he couldn't read painted above, but Vern knew what was inside the booth. He ran across the pool of lamplight and stepped into the glass box. He felt like a drowning man grabbing the telephone and bringing it to his mouth.

"Hello?" he said slowly. "Hello, I need to call America."

A computer chimed and Vern began to press the buttons frantically. He held the receiver tightly to his ear, listened to an electronic fanfare, then a click and another click and at last, a fuzzy ringing.

A girl's voice answered. Who is she? he wondered. She was too old to be his daughter.

"Hello, is Ms. Burke there?" he asked her.

"No," the girl said in a dulled voice. "She's still at work."

Vern quickly said, "This is her husband. Can you tell her that I'm still in Japan, but I'm coming home as quickly as I can?"

There was a pause. The girl might have hung up, it was so quiet.

Vern clawed for her, "Hello? Are you still there?!"

"You're Vern Burke?" she asked with a choke.

"Yes. Are you babysitting Viola? Is she there? Can I talk to her?"

"I'm Viola!" the girl shouted. "You've been missing for—" and she cried a moment, "Six years!"

Vern swerved and lost the phone and it swung and clattered, making a crack in the glass wall.

While morning was pouring onto the tile roofs, etching out the silhouettes of bending trees.

A COWBOY IN JAPAN

It was true. Time had slipped by. All the newspapers carried the day six years in the future. Japan had always seemed strange to him, but Vern was in the midst of even more unusual things.

An automatic electric cab, a tiny wheeled square he barely fit into, buzzed him in the thick traffic towards the airport.

"How's the world treating you, chum?" the cab asked in a John Wayne accent. "Your heartbeat is erratic and your blood pressure is unnatural."

"What?" Vern stared at the blinking display panel.

"Would you like to plug into Electro-Freud, or The Priest-Friend?"

A snaky black wire connected to headphones, slid out of a drawer.

Six years have passed, Vern remembered. I'm living in the future now. He ignored the drawer and searched in his coat pocket. His return airline ticket was folded next to his wallet. The paper felt frail and dry as a run-over bird's wing, but he hoped it was still good. America was too far to walk to.

"I'm afraid that ticket won't do," the cab sighed as they drift-ed slowly out of the traffic pour.

"It's got to!" Vern studied the fine print vainly, "This is my only way back to America!"

The cab hesitated, coasting on the verge of the whirring other box cars, then it began to merge back in with them. "I'll see what I can do for you," the cab drawled, "I might be able to make your day."

A TICKET FOR THE WATER

What the cab managed to find to take Vern back across the miles to America, awaited docked against a shifting waterlogged pier. It looked like a silver bubble floating halfway emerged out of the sea. There were ropes holding it and people loaded tall boxes through a door carved into it.

"They agreed to take you on," the synthetic cab voice drawled.

"What is it?" Vern asked.

"A hydro-saucer," the cab acted surprised, as if Vern was an 11th century man confronting a helicopter. "Of course you'll be expected to work for your passage," it added.

Vern frowned, "Just as long as I get back."

The wheels stopped turning and the thin walls of the cab unfolded to let Vern stretch out and stand. He took out a handful of old money and dropped it onto an extended metal palm. Pleasantly, the cab thanked him, wished him luck, then curled itself up like flower petals and backed around and zigzagged away.

Vern watched its toy motion leave him. Alone, he walked onto the dock. The boards breathed under his feet. He almost fell, scaring a seagull. It flapped across the water, stepping into the air.

Clearing his throat like a lusty pirate, Vern swaggered towards the hydro-saucer.

MAYBE WHILE I'VE BEEN HIDDEN, AMERICA HAS REVERTED

When the last crate was stuffed on board, Vern was passed a heavy burlap bag. One of the workers talked into a plastic camera-shaped translating machine and out came his explanation as cowboy twang, "All y'all have to do is drop a pellet twice a day into every box. The saucer knows the way to America, so you just hold on tight and wait."

They bowed to Vern, trouped around him, leaving him inside.

The silver door closed, locked and Vern blinked in the dark.

The ocean slapping about the hull echoed in the round black.

"Hello?" Vern called out meekly, "Ahoy?"

Suddenly, engines throbbed, Vern was thrown to the floor as the hydro-saucer lifted and moved, gaining the speed of a rocket. Gradually, a green-yellow light wavered inside so that Vern could see the big shape of the boxes crowded around him. Some of them creaked uneasily, tied down by ropes.

Standing slanting into the wind of a Buster Keaton film, Vern leaned ahead and crawled to his feet. We must be going a thousand miles per hour, he thought.

Against all that gravity, Vern struggled and with difficulty he managed to claw around a couple boxes to the seam of the dome. There was an inlaid handrail that he could clasp to, so that step by step he could navigate the round shape of the craft.

The fuzzy light showed maybe twelve boxes connected to the floor. Next to one of them, Vern stopped and put his ear on the rough wood.

It was hard to tell, the engine hum was a metal shadow on everything, but Vern thought he could hear something inside. A sallow shuffling…Or maybe it was just the ropes slipping.

He kept walking around and returned to the bag. By that time he had adapted to the saucer pull, he didn't need the rail, his body inclined naturally like a mountain goat raised on the slopes of a jagged tall mountain.

One pellet a day...Vern recalled the translator.

"What's all this cowboy talk anyway?" he asked out loud. "Is this really how the future world thinks America speaks?" He grumbled, "Or maybe while I've been hidden, America has reverted. Maybe I'm going back to the O.K Corral..."

The bag was tied with ribbon which he loosened. Putting his hand inside, he ran his fingers through all the marble sized pellets. He pulled one out and held it close to his eyes. It sparkled. It had no smell, but when he touched his tongue to it, it had a taste.

"Carrots?" Vern said.

THE JELLY ROLL MORTON MORNING

In the morning (or was it the morning? Vern couldn't tell, he only knew that he had slept and woken up) he picked up the bag and made the rounds from box to box, dropping a pellet into each one.

He whistled something, a Jelly Roll Morton song that used to play at home...six years ago. *How could it have happened?* Vern's eyes began to tear. *Somehow I was tricked. Something so terrible played with my life and held me away. Dark magic, the mother underground, Louie Louie and his electricity machine, Phil Ticks... But at least I'm still alive!* Vern's head slumped to the wooden corner of the box and rested heavily, "Phil, I'm sorry. I'm so, so sorry that I couldn't help you and keep you alive," he cried.

A kick bumped his forehead, snapping Vern backwards onto the floor, dropping the bag of pellets, scattering beads about. The box kicked again impatiently.

"Alright, alright!" Vern stood up and staggered over to open the little chute on the side of the box. He dropped a pellet in, "There!"

The box was silent, but there was more agitation around the saucer.

Vern finished the circular task. He ended up back where he started, then retied the bag's ribbon. Once more, later on, he thought, then I'll sleep and do it all over again.

What's taking America so long to arrive?

He had an awful vision of the saucer just spinning in a crazy out-of-control circle, foaming up the Tokyo harbor, going no-where.

But his imagination was interrupted by a lurch that sent him flying against a box. The engine gears screeched, rattling like skeleton parts and the saucer stopped.

The jolt and splash had uncreased the door and fiery light daggered in the swinging grin of opened hinges.

THE WATER PHANTOM

Vern Burke hoped years hadn't passed again. He hoped he wouldn't look out the door to see the Japan of the 22nd century. He hoped, as he crossed towards the rocking daylight, that everything would be alright.

The door swung fully open and he couldn't tell anything. He was instantly blinded by the brightness. He fell back onto the floor, covering his eyes with his hands.

The hydro-saucer just rolled with the waves for a couple minutes as Vern's sight went from black to red to orange to pink to yellow to shapes and finally to clear visibility. He went up the steps slower this time and, peering through his fingers, Vern looked outside.

Blue swells forever. A single cloud walking above the sea like a sheep...

He sat on the edge in the doorway and carefully took his hands away to shadow his eyes. Ocean and the sky...that's all anything was.

Maybe America was beyond his sight, he wondered. He took hold of the ladder rungs going up the side of the curve to stand on the very top. He moved gently, because the saucer dipped a little with his shifting weight.

There wasn't any sign of land.

As he sat on the height of the bobbing ship, he began to despair, Why did the engine stop? Is it broken? I can't even repair an eggbeater, so am I stranded here?

He sat there gripping the metal ladder all the rest of the day and he watched the sunset ebb away and break into stars.

At first, he thought the shape he saw dragging itself closer in the moon's splashing reflection was a shark, or some futuristic evil sea creature. He couldn't move though, his hands were fused to the rungs, his legs turned into rain gutters. And then,

319

"Oh no!" he recognized the water phantom.

Phil Ticks stopped rowing and he stood up on the waves, resting his white body against the pulled up, propped oar. "What do you mean, *Oh no!*?" Phil asked.

"I—"

Phil waved the ghostly oar, "You know, if I took offense to that, I could haunt you for the rest of your life! I could pop out of cupboards—*Boo!* Hide in your socks—*Woo! Woo!* I could creep up and down your hallway at night, dragging chains. I could—"

"Alright!" Vern interrupted, "I get the picture. I apologize."

"As it is..." Phil continued, "This is the last time you'll ever see me. I just came back to tell you something."

"To tell me that I'm marooned in the middle of Pacific?" Vern asked.

Phil laughed, "Oh, you'll get back to land..." Riotously, the ghost laughed, until he coughed out, "You still don't know what's in those boxes, do you?"

Vern shuddered.

"You will," Phil's eyes glittered with laughing moonlight. Then he changed, "I'm glad you'll be able to return, Vern." For a second, he was a cloud, then his words quietly fogged, "When Julius Hayburn hired me to go to Japan, he was sending me to the Empathizer."

"The what?" The word sizzled in Vern.

Phil swatted the oar through the water. "It's a machine. Julius was developing it with a Japanese company. They hooked it to my heart."

"What? Why you?"

"It seems that certain Americans make the best circuits. I was one of them and so are you. Only you were lucky enough to escape my fate."

Vern asked the ghost now floating above, "What does the Empathizer do?"

"It exchanges energies. It was hooked from me into a compa-

320

ny man, this businessman who was responsible for the murder of thousands of people. You've probably heard of him." Phil swung the oar again. "He had the money to use the Empathizer, so he unloaded all his fault and guilt into me. Into my heart... When he was done, there was nothing left of me. He burned me up. They unplugged a charred thing from him and he was cured." Phil began to sink. "That's the story, Vern," he tried to laugh.

Vern shook his head. "Is there something I should do for you? You want me to avenge you? Do I track down Julius Hayburn and tie him to a sinking biplane?"

"No." Phil said softly, "He's already been taken care of. They all have. I want you to rest in peace, Vern, to know that I'll be resting in peace now. All I want is for you to do something for yourself and the ones that make you alive. Arrive back in America shining with gold like a Mayan king. Show them you are alive and happy in love...The years of mystery are over... Make a beautiful return." Phil shimmered and let the waves rise around him.

Vern could only stare. He could only watch as Phil Ticks went smiling beneath the starfish water.

THE MERRY-GO-ROUND MUTINY

Drumming. It sounded like a hundred angry cannibals beating tom toms inside the saucer. All of a sudden Vern looked up from the water—it was nighttime and he had forgotten to feed the boxes their second meal! He cursed and descended the ladder into the mutiny of crashing.

In the doorway, he grabbed the bag and hurried to the first box.

It was splitting open, all of them were bursting open, flying nails and splintering. Whatever strange ferocious cargo was inside was coming out.

Vern threw the bag on the floor, scattering beads as he roared for the door. Climbing back up the ladder, something struck his leg, tearing past him, almost knocking him off as it sprung out into the sea. He heard a cannonball splash.

Vern turned around. He clung tightly to the ladder top and watched in horror.

Another huge white creature flew out the doorway. Landing in the water, it followed the first submerged one. Vern watched the pair of v-shaped ears churn towards the horizon.

A third furry head pushed out the doorway, sniffed and leaped.

After the fifth one departed, Vern had recovered enough to tell himself to grab hold of the next giant animal. It's the only way I'll get back to America. I could drift out here forever!

He lowered himself to just above the doorway.

A white flash whooshed out, pulling Vern with its hot flight and splash.

With all of his strength, Vern clutched the soft, swimming rabbit fur.

A RAINED ON BOOK

The rabbits seemed to know exactly where they were going.

Perched on its shoulders, resting between the rising ears, Vern noticed six more rabbits leading the way and at least five behind, following him. He couldn't remember how many boxes the saucer carried, there could be even more rabbits in the gloom.

Through the night, they traveled and with the blue rising morning, it began to rain silver warm drops.

When a seagull cried in surprise over them, Vern smiled. That bird meant they were getting close to land. It wouldn't take long. Already a continent must be forming in the dark clouds. "America," he prayed, "America."

More seagulls could be seen, appearing and disappearing in the rain and gradually the sound of all that Pacific came to an end on the sand. Vern could see white surf like the teeth in a grin.

The rabbit under him twisted in the current, fought its pull and rode a wave that fell onto land. As it shook itself, Vern hopped off and fell in the sand. He lay on his back laughing, while shallow tide water swept around him.

Another rabbit emerged next to him and hopped across the sand, leaving huge wet tracks.

Vern picked up a little white shell and put it in his shirt pocket. It would stay that close to him, from shirt to shirt forever, as a memory of this.

The fog and rain lifted in sheets and ahead of him Vern saw big spider webs weaved into walls across the beach. Already, one of the rabbits was tangled in it. The poor thing kicked and twitched helplessly.

Vern ran to it. His body felt alive again. To be running was wondrous.

The rabbit was in a rope net, staked with tall poles. "Don't worry," he soothed the animal, "I'll get you out." He tugged until the knots fell apart and the freed rabbit flung itself out towards the green forest, opened ahead like a rained on book.

WALKING IN THE MIDDLE OF THE ROAD

He had been walking for about half an hour along a road. The pavement was cracking back into ground again. There were tall flower weeds twining through and little green leaves. Vern thought this would be alright, if America was becoming a garden once more.

Wooden wheels creaked around the corner in the road. Ahead of him, three men in the cart stopped and glared at Vern. The puttering engine in back coughed a purple cloud and gave out with a blat.

"Seen any rabbits?" the driver called suspiciously.

"Big ones," the man next to him added, holding his hands wide apart.

Vern looked at the guns they carried and the nets piled behind them. "No," he answered.

One of the men pulled a cord on the engine and it started again. The driver steered them past Vern, shakily onwards.

"The rabbits were good to me," Vern said softly to himself as he walked along. "I don't have any problem with giant rabbits."

Appearing suddenly, loud and out of nowhere, a machine nearly ran him down from behind. It swerved and its delicate wings struck a tree. It unfolded, lay broken against the trunk and a girl leaped out of the crash.

"You idiot!" she seethed. "Why are you walking in the middle of the road?!"

"I'm sorry," Vern held out his hands to her, "I'm lost here. I'm trying to find a bus or a train or a plane or something to take me back home."

"You wrecked my car!" she pointed at the ruin of twisted wood, paper sheaves and feathers, ropes and pulleys, tangled in pieces at the base of the oak.

Vern repeated, "I'm sorry." Whatever delicate thing it was she had been driving, was truly destroyed. "Can I help you repair it?" he asked.

"No!" she answered savagely, swishing her dark hair. "You've wrecked it. Just leave me alone. Go!" she pointed. "There's a town about a mile ahead. Go!"

"I'm sorry."

"Go!" she shrieked. "And walk on the side of the road so no one else hits you!"

He obeyed. He felt the weeds brush him consolingly as he walked on the crumble of the tar, sliding with the new flowers growing small as faces.

WALKING IN THE MIDDLE OF THE ROAD AGAIN

After that, the walk became slowly beautiful again. There were birds singing, things were turning green. He realized it must be spring. All the things he had missed while held in the ship were alive and living and here everywhere.

It started to become the first time things made sense in so long. He was walking, breathing, accepting the beauty of the natural world around him. He was connected. Each footstep placed on the ground shedding off tar, every simple true moment of life was getting him closer to the town that was somewhere in America.

Once he got there, he knew, he could find out exactly where he was.

He recognized the trees that held the sky together. Douglas firs and pines told him that he couldn't be too far away from home. It was all pointing him there, back to Latina and Viola. All these things were making him wake up and think of that. By the time he arrived in town, he was walking in the middle of the road again.

THE DIFFERENCE BETWEEN ELECTRICITY AND A SLOW CANDLE

Yes, he was only a matter of miles from his family, but the buggy he chose would take the rest of the day to get him there. Not like the old days of cars on the freeway, it was the difference between electricity and a slow candle.

He settled next to a woman wearing a blue feathered hat. She smiled briefly at him, then she opened a thick book to read.

The four horses in front of the carriage stamped the ground as more baggage was loaded on top.

Just like the Wild West! Vern beamed excitedly as he stared out of the window at the dusty town rustling with Americans.

Windmills spun on the crooked wooden roofs and shiny panels soaked up the sun's energy. A little bit of rain still waited in the cat of a cloud.

Vern looked forward to this clopping traveling. His shadow had been stretched all the way to Japan and only now was it returning, belonging and filling him back up with life.

The driver rattled the reins and the horses began to move them forward in the same way that gasoline used to.

A WESTERN STARRING VERN BURKE

The sunset was pouring the canyons full of weeping trees with red blood light, all the way down to the pink river below. Yes, Vern sighed, it was beautiful to be coasting along in a new dream, in a new world.

But it was taking so long to get to home. "What I wouldn't give for an old fashioned twentieth century rocket," he said to the blue hat woman.

She was asleep behind the cover of her book, her head rocking on her shoulder like a heavy night flower.

Vern looked back outside and counted the big birds in a skein, flying east. Now the animals are faster than us again, he smiled. The birds will be to Latina and Viola long before me.

At the top of the hill, they stopped and Vern almost fell over with the sudden jolt of locking wooden wheels. He picked up the woman's book and passed it to her.

She blinked at the almost twilight, "Are we there?" Her hat had tipped down over her eyes like a blue veil.

There were loud voices coming from out where the driver sat, scuffing, then a loud rap on the door.

"Get on out, folks!"

Vern took hold of the handle and reluctantly peeled the door open.

An old movie was being reenacted. There were two cowboys pointing guns at the stagecoach. The driver held his hands up.

"Get out!" a villain swung his rifle at Vern.

"And no funny business!" said his partner.

Climbing out, Vern helped the woman down and the two of them stood there with their arms up.

"Look at them pearls she's wearing!" One of the outlaws lowered his gun and grabbed the white loop around her neck.

"They're imitation," she squeaked and tugged back.

"They look real to me!" said the other outlaw.

"Yeah!" his partner agreed and pulled at them again.

329

The woman struggled, "No! I got them at Woolworth's!" She dug her fingers into his hand as they twisted with each other.

"Give me them pearls!" the cowboy bawled.

Vern fought the urge to rush to her defense—it was the rifle pointed at him that kept him frozen in place.

Then it happened. It was so fast it was as if lightning crashed out of the trees. A giant rabbit with green leaves and flowers tacked to its white fur spun its kicking feet into one outlaw, flinging him over the crevice into the depths of the ravine.

The cowboy straining for pearls dropped his hand off the woman and ran in stark fear back down the hill. His voice followed him like the smoke of a trailing, disintegrating airplane until the rabbit caught up with him and sent him soaring after his accomplice.

Dust skidded up by the rumble settled again.

The driver, Vern and the woman returned numbly to the stagecoach. By starlight and moonbeams, and also somewhere in the dark the watchful eyes of a rabbit, they spun on towards the little glow of the distant city.

ENCHANTED IN A FAIRY TALE

The old Greyhound station relic had burst open with green vines. They tangled out onto the sidewalk to meet the lashing flowers growing from other abandoned buildings.

An owl swooped low overhead as Vern stepped away from the coach.

It was still the town he had left six years ago, but as different as could be.

There were flickering blue candle lamps lighting the way towards his home.

Vern laughed.

Three blocks away, a fox ran across the street and disappeared into the shadows of a garden.

Vern began to walk towards the house where Latina and Viola would be sleeping. As if enchanted in a fairy tale, he would slide through the ivy and peek in the windows at them, like a gentle returning spirit.

He watched the moon motor along beside him, getting stuck in branches, hiding behind worn billboards and mossy slanted roofs, always reappearing again. "I made it back," he told the white moon, remembering one of those Japanese stories he read when his daughter was a little girl. Having been through his adventure, he was the humble, wandering peasant coming home.

"Arrive back in America shining with gold," Phil Ticks had told him.

And a smile turned up his face as he thought of a way to return with gold.

Vern stopped, turned and hurried back to the Hardware store.

HIS PRAYING FIGURE LAY DOWN COLLAPSED IN YELLOW SLEEP

He found his street, his house, he saw his favorite dreamers through the glass. He cried quietly with joy and nearly slipped out of the tree next to his daughter's bedroom. He didn't want to wake them yet. His adventure had to end like a story. He began to work with what was left of the night.

What he was doing was a secret for the dawn to unveil. Only the night birds and moths watched him, flew over him in silence.

He was tireless. He circled their house, climbing in and out of plants and over rocks, across the lawn and their victory garden. Sometimes he felt he must have been carried by angels and hurried along by golden wings.

Finally, the sky was shifting out of the starry blue as watercolors seeped and carried the moon away. All the small songbirds began to waken. Their singing filled the branches.

He was so tired, he knelt and his praying figure lay down collapsed in yellow sleep.

IN THE MORNING WE'LL WAKE UP TOGETHER

By the time Latina stirred awake, yawned and brushed her hand across her mouth, there was sunlight pouring in through the lace curtains of her room.

Every morning for years, she opened her eyes to the same sight. There lay a framed photo of Vern on the pillow next to her, as if he never left. She talked to herself, or to the memory of him, "Hello darling," as she used to do so long ago.

When your love is gone, your heart might be gone too. You might sink into something forgetful and not even notice the passing of years. She felt like an old tree adding rings as it aged, aware of the seasons while she waited for him.

Then she blinked at the warm window and drew the blankets off of herself. She didn't know she wouldn't be alone for much longer. The day hid a wonder just outside.

Padding out into the hallway in her orange bathrobe, she knocked on Viola's door, "Would you like some breakfast, sweetheart?" she asked. They liked to eat together. Viola called out her yes and Latina smiled and went into the kitchen.

Viola had a photograph of her father too. It was a faded color picture of him as a child. He was wearing a sweater and holding up his hand. She reached and touched the painted frame and whispered because she had just woken up from a dream about him.

The phone call a couple days ago had scared her. It must have been a terrible joke, or maybe his voice had been stuck in the phone and it took this long to finally fall all the way out. Viola had kept it to herself though, it wasn't something she could understand or tell anyone.

Latina was pouring a kettle when she heard her daughter scream and the charge of her running feet, trampling down the hall to the front door. Latina dropped the teapot, spilling water as she hurried after.

The door was flown open.

333

Outside, everything was coated in bright sunlight. A wide yellow halo stretched across their yard, over the gardens and branches, turning around their house, and there on the lawn Vern Burke was asleep in the center of a circle of empty paint cans. A brush was still clutched in each hand and he was smiling as if in the most pleasant dream.

December 1993

FLY ABOVE IT ALL

Is Phil Ticks really dead? What do you think? Four years after his trip to Japan, Phil is back again. I wrote this book in Portland, Oregon where I met my wife. These adventures are actually formed from our real life perambulations. I finished *Fly Above It All* back in Seattle, five days before our daughter was born.

In those days, downtown Portland had these great old hotel relics. Like 1940s movies, you could walk on set, and follow the marble to a luncheonette. We used to have dates there. One time the salt and pepper shakers started to move between us. The séance spirits were with us. After we saw a screening of *Kiss Me Deadly*, Laura became my modern dance secretary. She helped me prepare a novel to send to a publisher. But when we printed it out, the computer only spat out a tiny ball of ink. It was the weirdest thing, like all the words had been turned into a little Dr. Seuss world.

Laura knew an old woman who had been around the world and we used to visit her apartment to listen. The steam was always going hot in the radiators and she smoked cigarettes and told us stories. That building was inspiring too, becoming the home of Phil Ticks.

PIE
IN THE
SKY

Laura and I went to a pet store too. We bought two goldfish we jokingly named 'Here Today' and 'Gone Tomorrow.' Who would have expected them to live so long? They even traveled across country twice with us.

I really did meet a heel who would tie a dollar bill to fishing line, and I did go to that Mexican restaurant with my friend Mike where I overheard that goat exchange, and witnessed that magic act. To my shame, I was merciless, pointing out the card stuck in his sleeve, hidden by wire and string.

With the chapter 'Progress', I am back in Wallingford, where I grew up in Seattle, on the pavement surrounding the Saint Benedict church.

"Did you believe in anything? Did you believe in any superior being?"
"Yes, a guy Phil."

Carl Reiner and Mel Brooks

Contents

PHIL TICKS IN THE BOHEMIAN BAKERY...

Phil closed the door behind him and stood in the hallway, fumbling with the lock and keys. On the ceiling above him a little plastic turtleback shape hissed out a cloud of perfume. Phil gagged. He breathed into his sleeve to avoid the wintergreen musk.

Taking a step back, he admired the black metal writing on his door, *Phil Ticks Detective Agency*. Every letter was screwed tightly into the plywood. Right next to it, he pinned a hastily scrawled note:

Dilly—Gone out for donuts. Be back in five minutes.

At last, he left his locked door and crunched across the carpet to the elevator. Every tenant door stood like a domino or a card. He could knock on any one and be drawn in. Better not though. He reached the elevator grate and pressed the circled DOWN button.

There was a lurching catch of gears with chains stretching and sewing through rusty wheels. Somewhere up in the shaft, the elevator began its trundling descent. Phil scratched the sweat on his neck underneath his fedora hat. The weather inside Cynthia Villa was unpredictable. From floor to floor it changed. Who knew what he'd walk into? Once, in search of the manager, he went from tropic, to arctic, to a hallway where the sprinklers made misty rain and parrot chirps.

The elevator dropped itself yellow-lit into the web of grating before Phil. When it stopped, he grabbed the metal latch and pulled the spars aside. He pushed open the elevator door and stepped inside, next to the woman with her shopping cart.

She looked spun from a silkworm caterpillar. All twenty wooly colors rubbed when she talked, "I got to get out of this place," was what she said in her furry accent. "Ten years. It been too long."

345

Too much sympathy could take you over though—instead Phil tried to seem fascinated by the elevator's slow progress charted by the lights over the door. Every floor brought a narrow sunny glare of light that shined, drifted, and went away.

"You talk to yourself..." the woman confided, "Everyone tell you that. What I care? My best conversation with myself. Hello, how you do darling? I'm just fine, how you? Oh, I see better days. I know what you mean. I doing all I can, but if thing don't change I don't know what I do. Mmhmmm, you have to be strong, strong, strong. That is truth." She had fallen into a gone reverie.

The elevator landed heavily on the ground floor, though its motion took a while to unwind, like so many contraptions involved in the old twentieth century technology. Phil opened the clanky grate and thankfully got out.

The television in the lobby was blasting away. As he walked out onto the silver linoleum, over his shoulder he could see the play of Montgomery Clift and Elizabeth Taylor in their own American tragedy. The chairs before the big screen captured a dozen tenants who couldn't resist. Phil nodded in recognition. He knew them. The last cast of the Saturn Circus. There was the fire eater, the clowns, the tall woman and the strange others huddled in their chairs, shadowed around the fat man.

Phil went past and out the front door, into the street noise of the late night city.

As he walked, a police car caught his pace. It kept with him for the rest of the block.

Finally Phil noticed and waved, "Hello there!" to the pudgy faced driver.

The precinct was familiar with Phil Ticks. He held the record for making the most citizen arrests. Back in his early days he tried so hard to win their acceptance. They finally had to lay down the law with him. After he ended up at Cynthia Villa, he had been quiet, he hadn't been in the station for almost a year (though the memory of him lingered there and the force often wondered laughingly what he was up to).

The car slid by when Phil saluted. Alone, he went into a sugary smelling shop on the corner.

The Bohemian Bakery was quiet.

It was one of those moments he dreamt about.

The teenager was in the back room somewhere and Phil had the store to himself. The treasure of the Bohemian Bakery was his! Foot-tall stands along the countertop were laden with ripe donuts covered with glaze, rivery maple, or chocolate...In a matter of seconds, Phil was pushing them into his pockets. A kind of wild glee took him over, he nearly shouted with joy.

He just couldn't believe it could happen this way. His fingers were holding a handful when the bullet-headed teenager lurched into sight, carrying a tray of jelly donuts.

"Hey!" The kid moved rapidly into Phil's shadow, "Where'd you get those donuts?"

"Oh..." said Phil in as casual a tone as possible, "Here and there."

The teenager quickly appraised the situation. He pointed at the scavenged counter stands, "Yeah! You took them from here—" then he jabbed a finger at Phil, "and you put them there!"

Appalled, Phil put a hand into the lining of his coat. He carefully felt around the donuts and took out his wallet. He flipped it open so a sparkling gold and silver badge showed brightly. Although these things can be bought from magazines, its effect was apparent on the teenager immediately.

Keeping him in that state, Phil calmly asked for, "A couple of the jelly donuts and a coffee." He returned the wallet to his dark, full coat lining. "To go," he added.

The teenager shook as he poured coffee into the paper cup, then, after turning around to get a wax napkin for loading donuts into the bag, he croaked, "Will that be all, sir?"

"That's fine."

The register clicked mechanically to sum. "Two dollars and

347

fifty cents," the teenager said nervously.

The more Phil dug through his pockets though, the more the smug look melted off his face. He had to add all the gathered dull coins into the cost. Lined up along the countertop in little pyramids was the best way to count them. Mostly pennies, nickels, dimes...It wasn't enough and yet, his heart leaped as he found some quarters.

The teenager gave up, "I'll be right back." He had to take out another rack of donuts from the oven.

"Okay," Phil replied. "One eighty seven, one eighty eight..." Then he continued, "One eighty nine..."

BOLOGNA...

Dilly Diamond walked out the hissing doors of the grocery store carrying a bag full of bologna. A successful errand completed. His neighbor wanted the food for his dog. It went crazy for bologna. Dilly didn't ask, it meant a five dollar tip for the trip.

Taking a turn on the pavement, his eyes averted the newspaper machine selling the day's headlines.

Next to a gray bin full of thrown away cut flower stems and carnation weepings, leaning against the wall a ragged man gargled scratchily at Dilly, "Hey mister, spare change?"

Dilly turned abruptly from the bad news machine. In spite of his appearance of wealthy looking shark colored pants, his pockets only jangled keys and pennies and some folded food coupons.

He paused at the predicament for a moment. "I have something better than money for you." The bag under his arm rustled as his fingers rustled in. "Nourishment..." He tossed out a wrapped pack of bologna.

It arced heavily caught by gravity and landed in the lap of the man collapsed against the wall. He judged it unsteadily. He lifted it to his eyes and read the little printed letters, like a gypsy determining a palm's destiny. The words he read broke out of his mouth in growing disgust: "Mechanically separated chicken, pork, water, beef, dextrose, salt, corn syrup, modified food starch, flavoring hydrolyzed soy protein, sodium and potassium phosphates, sodium erythorbate, sodium nitrate." He threw the bologna back at Dilly Diamond. "I don't want this!" he screeched, "It doesn't make any sense!"

THE MISSING LETTER...

Unscrambled by outside's tornado, Phil stood before his own door and almost dropped the white paper bag held in his hand. What a shock caught him there! The hallway barked with the radio music and television shows seeping out of other people's rooms.

In slow motion, like a Braille reader, Phil put his hand to his door, to the letters nailed on, but his fingers were caught on the space missing from a word.

Phil Ticks De ective Agency.

Between E and E were only empty nail holes.

The gap hit him like a broken smile. Someone took the T. It wasn't on the carpet anywhere around, someone had stolen it. He almost couldn't open the door. He might as well enter a plundered Pharaoh's tomb.

Phil stopped himself from sinking any further. It was a terrible feeling. He quickly took out his key and opened the door. He was scared to turn on the light. Who knew? The room might be torn apart like an old movie theater.

THE SONG IN HIS HEART...

The name Dilly Diamond was flourished across the sign-in sheet at the front desk of Cynthia Villa. The guard watched him go to the elevator. He saw that oddball every day. The guard let a cloud of cigarette smoke go at him, forming a fog around the elegant man entering the slatted doors of the elevator.

When the doors closed and the elevator started upwards, the guard returned to his coffee and crossword puzzle. *4 Across,* he read curiously, *Australian Bird...*

Impatiently tapping his cane near his shoe, Dilly waited for the antiquated transport he was in to reach the right floor. He started to hum his own symphony.

Just as he found a melody, the elevator coughed to a stop. "Ah!" Dilly exclaimed. He shoved aside the canary cage wrought-iron and stepped into the aisle with a gentleman's gait.

Every door he passed, his feet Fred Astaired. They clicked soles together at Phil's. The brass end of his cane rapped on the wood.

There were loud remarks of furniture and floor. Phil opened the door enough to let his face show. "Oh, hello," he let his room reveal, "come on in."

Dilly made his entrance, stopping at his usual place, by the slanted table at the window.

Phil checked the door again then came back in. He scratched the back of his neck. "They took a letter off my door."

"Who?" asked Dilly.

"Some nut with a screwdriver or whatever..." Phil closed the door and wondered, "What did I do to deserve this?" He exhaled, wandered, going like a balloon from side to side, then he stopped at a wall. "How am I supposed to get clients when I'm missing letters on my sign?"

"It's not so impossible," said Dilly, "Naturally you'll be appealing to illiterates, but business is business."

Phil slumped into the chair at his desk. "I just can't believe that someone would steal from me."

"Don't take it so personally, you know how the times are."

"Yeah, I know..." Phil answered pathetically, picturing the black market for stolen Ts. In some alley, a gang of children would crowd around, holding out hands for an American T.

Dilly suddenly leaped from his chair, "Listen, I'll paint a T on your door!" He grabbed the black bottle of ink from the piled corner of the desk and he took a brush and he disappeared past Phil.

Whistling the song in his heart, Dilly went to work on the door. After each few brushstrokes, he'd stop to admire and call to Phil, "Yes, this is just the thing," and, "Well, well, well, it's a work of art, I must admit," then, "Fascinating..." until finally Phil had to pull himself up out of his melancholy collapse to go observe.

What awaited him was a surprise. The new letter T was from a Medieval scroll, calligraphic flourishes that looked like time-travel compared to the other factory made black metal letters. His eyes couldn't leave the sight.

"Magnificent!" Dilly offered. He patted his friend's arm. "Now you'll get some clients with noblesse oblige."

THE MAN WHO DIED...

In the morning, Phil's doorbell chimed its transistor cuckoo. Dawn colored the venetian blinds, shadows and light poured over floor. The electric bird called again.

Phil brought himself to life and alertly sat up. "Who's there?"

He flipped out of bed, wearing his clown theme pajamas, and strode to the door urgently. Why would anyone ring for him so early? He waited. It could be dangerous. If only a revolver was holstered under his arm. "Who's there?" he repeated through the wood.

There was a crayoned pause, then, "Is this a detective agency?" willowed an almost fainting sounding woman.

Phil opened the door to find out.

A whole family dressed in black mourning stood in his doorway. The veiled woman spoke for them, "We need a detective." They stared intently at Phil, dressed in his bright pajamas.

"Yes, I'm a detective. Come in..."

They entered curiously and bunched into a black tumble just inside the doorway.

Phil reached past the head of one quiet boy to close the door then he paced to the maelstrom center of his room. He examined the group before him. There were seven of them. He fastened his gaze on the woman. "How can I help you?"

She said, "There's been a death in our family..." She hesitantly started over, "We need help to recover...I mean, can you, do you...?" she stopped her words into a black handkerchief.

Phil wringed his hands nervously and put them into the pockets of his pajamas. "Just tell me how I can help."

When she was able to, she restarted, "You've probably seen the papers." The whole family stared at him like a picture, unblinking. They waited that way in the tremble of his strange room until his expression was enough to speak to them.

"I stay away from the newspapers. My friend Dilly says they cloud one's vision. What's news to me is what I see around me."

The woman hurried, "The man who died was Slade Davenport." Her family looked stung by the name. All their puppet eyes looked at Phil. "Have you heard of that name?"

Trying to be professional, the voice of a radio detective, Phil let the name roll, "Davenport..." He pictured white lit sailboats on Cape Cod, sleek roadster cars, years of money in the Stock Exchange.

She continued, "The papers made quite a scene out of his dying. It's not often that an eccentric tycoon is found dead in the river. But only last week, when we read the will, did we find out how eccentric he really was! He left the entire family fortune to the Martian Society for Higher Technology. Mister Ticks, we're his heirs, we're concerned, it doesn't make sense, something is wrong. We need you to find out what happened."

"Oh my God!" Phil suddenly blurted, turning beet red, "I'll be right back!" He grabbed his clothes off the floor and ran to the door of his bathroom. Panic stricken, he realized, I've been standing there the whole time in my pajamas!

TIME IN BALLOONS...

He had tried to rein their meeting like a seasoned detective and there he stood the whole time in balloons.

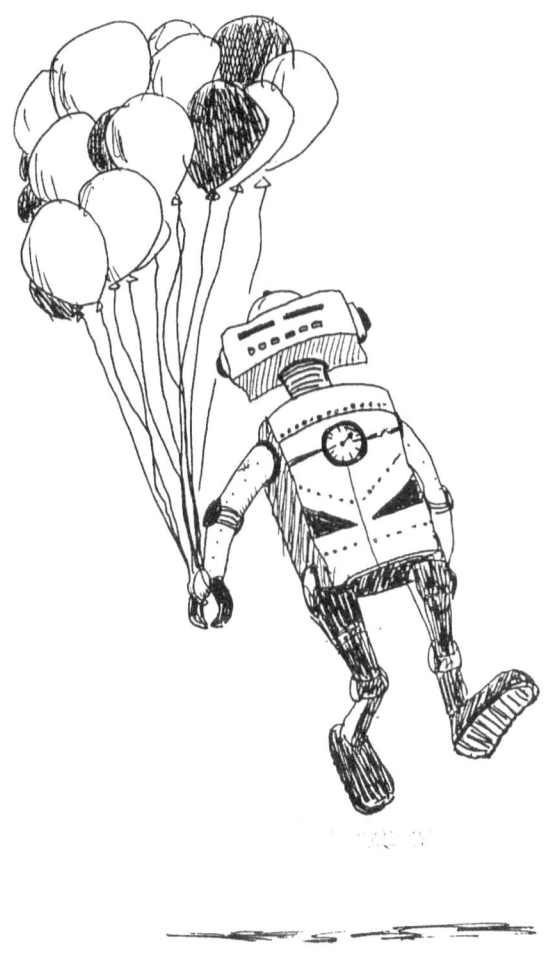

"God!" he slapped his forehead loudly.

He unbuttoned the clown pajamas quickly and threw them off onto the floor. "Take it easy, Phil," he told himself, "I'll go back out in my suit and pretend nothing happened."

What a start for him. Getting into his gray suit, he called to the family in the other room, "I'll be out in a minute!" adding with confidence, "Everything's okay!"

There was silence.

They were still standing the same way, staring at him, when he opened the door and entered in wrinkles.

"So..." he picked up where they left off, "you want me to find your missing millions."

The family had only moved their faces towards his new position in front of the desk.

Speaking for the mute family, the woman said, "Yes."

Phil was so happy he hadn't wrecked everything that he almost laughed. But he hid the smile behind his hand and nodded instead.

THE NAPOLEON OF TODAY...

Though Dilly usually took the stairway down three floors to see Phil, this morning he pressed the elevator button.

He waited impatiently. He tapped his cane on the worn red and gold carpet while he watched time drag through the bars.

"I could have gone down the stairs, sung an aria in the lobby and returned carrying a bag of coal...This elevator must be drawn by a team of ants," he mumbled. His cane popped on the floor in a frantic rhythm when the light finally poured up to fill the caged window.

Dilly ran the metal aside and turned the handle. He fell in before he realized someone else was in there too.

Wearing a uniform like the Napoleon of today, the little man croaked, "What floor?"

"Uh...Two?"

The small man raised his crimson sleeve and clicked his boots. There were polished medals on his chest and stripes and flourishes all over his multicolored uniform. His steely eyes were fixed on the brass plate above the door. It blinked out numbers, 9, 8, 7...

"Floor two," the man announced.

The rusty door opened.

The second floor was still as a desert, yellow carpet, the smell of sand, dead wallpaper. Either way there were the desolate doors of rooms.

The elevator general repeated, "Floor two. We're here."

"I don't want to be here. We're in the wrong place."

The short arm caught the door to pull it closed. "Sir, where would you like to go?"

"The seventh floor."

"I thought you said the second?"

"Well...I was thinking the seventh."

They traveled up in silence. The elevator shuddered against the cage of the seventh floor and the man in the uniform cleared his throat. His gloved fingers rapped on the brass plate. It had a lighted 7 among the crooked numbers. He saluted as Dilly left the clanking door.

THE GREAT CARUSO...

A pile of equipment, as if an African expedition was being planned, formed a mountain in the center of the room.

A flying telescope landed on the peak.

In a moment a pair of socks joined the steep edge and rolled to catch on the corner of a Raymond Chandler book.

A door opened. Footsteps came across the room.

"What's going on?" Dilly asked.

With his back to him, Phil threw another twirling object over his shoulder. "I've got an assignment."

Dilly stared at the strange assortment gathering. "What kind of an assignment?"

"A client appeared this morning." He turned around. "Actually, the whole family appeared. They want me to help them." He pointed at the pile excitedly. "I've got a case!"

Phil came towards Dilly to the space where the pyramid separated them and he confided, "It was so easy. I just made a Detective sign for the door and they came to me. Simple! Hold on, wait till you see this..." he returned to his desk and found a slip of paper.

"Look at this check!" Phil let it float in front of Dilly. "Can you believe it? This detective business is child's play!"

No, there was nothing Dilly could say. The sight of the check stopped him cold.

"There's a whole lot of zeros on this," Phil crackled the light blue paper slip. "If I keep this up, I'll be able to get a real office, like one in the movies, with wooden floors and a glass door with my name written on it." Phil was putting a bright tie on. It looked like a parrot asleep on his chest. He laughed, "I've never done this before, but I have good instincts."

"I'm not too sure about that tie though," Dilly said quietly. "By the way, could I scrutinize that check?"

"Of course." He passed it to Dilly on his way to the chair draped with his gray suit coat.

Dilly held the check close to his eyes and he felt the weaving between his fingertips. He held it up to the window glow, "How do you know it's real?"

"I'm—they—"

"I think we should see if it's good before you do anything more. That's protocol, Phil. The bank will tell us."

Phil pulled his coat tight and buttoned it. "You're right." Then a thought made him laugh, "You're like my Watson! You know, every detective needs a sidekick to help."

Dilly shrugged.

They went out the door, one after another, and down the hall to where the elevator was framed in the red wallpaper. A cloud of pine scent puffed from the dials on the ceiling.

Dilly touched the arrow button with the tip of his umbrella.

"You'll be glad we did this," Dilly assured him. "When you know it's real you can resume your sleuthing, conscience clear."

The air around Phil glowed like a neon Las Vegas hotel sign, from his tie, the handkerchief in his pocket, his clashing plaid slacks and yellow socks. "Thank you, Watson," he replied.

The elevator creaked into view and Dilly unbound the criss-cross metal door. "After you, Mr. Holmes."

Phil entered the elevator, nodded to the operator and glided into the mirror against the back wall.

"Good day," said the operator, "What floor?"

"The lobby," Phil said.

The elevator began to move with all three staring at the numbers over the door.

The sudden stop at 4 caught Phil and Dilly by surprise.

The doors opened to let someone in.

"Good day," the operator said and a woman entered.

She stopped close to Phil. The headphones she wore buzzed incomprehensibly.

At the next floor the elevator stopped to let her off. She left, the doors closed and they started their movement down again.

Smiling, Phil said, "Of course when the bank approves it,

Watson, I'll have to give you a percentage."

"I am your loyal partner," Dilly agreed.

Everything falling into place made Phil laugh excitedly. "We're going to solve it. This is only the start. We'll be famous for solving crimes, I can't wait."

"The lobby," the elevator general announced and instantly their descent hit end. He opened the doors for them royally and stood aside.

The worn carpet accepted them across the ocean to the fan revolving doors. They went out onto the sidewalk next to the street traffic. The usual crowd washed before Cynthia Villa's entrance: the shufflers wearing radio headphones, a shopping cart, a man holding a rabbit, the noise of cars, scuffing shoes and everything lit by electricity.

Nothing was too far away from the villa. They passed the Safeway grocery store where people were swarming around the doors. There was the Utopia Travel Agency, the wall of merchant stores, and traveling a couple blocks further, Phil and Dilly approached the bank.

It climbed out of the pavement on stiff Roman pillars. Phil opened the heavy door and they went in, talking loudly about what kind of car they would buy.

"A Deusenberg," Dilly insisted, his voice boomed among the marble. Each step he took, his cane cracked on the floor so that their approach to join the waiting line shot every eye their way.

"What's wrong with a nice plush Cadillac?" Phil asked as they got into line.

Dilly shook his head sadly. "Sure, Phil. And I know a man with a buck toothed dog you can borrow. It eats bologna. Phil, have you ever heard of de rigueur?"

"Is that like a De Soto?"

Dilly couldn't speak.

Phil waved it away, "Listen, we don't need to worry about cars right now. That's trivial. I've got a case to solve."

"Next," called a teller.

"That's us," said Phil and he took off towards the waiting window. He stopped and looked into the empty space. "The teller was here a second ago," he explained to Dilly.

"How can I help you?" Just a forehead poked over the counter.

Phil leaned a little through the frame of the window. "Ahhh...I have a check. I need to cash it."

A small hand came onto the counter and reached in the direction of Phil. The teller said, "Could I see some I.D."

Phil was startled. He patted his coat, "I don't know...I'm not sure if I have any...I may not have brought it with me."

Dilly laughed, "Did you know this same thing happened when the Great Caruso was in a New York bank? The world's most famous opera genius! Do you know what he did when they asked him for I.D?"

Phil was going through every one of his pockets, up and down his suit.

Dilly continued, "Caruso said, 'You want my I.D? This is my I.D!'" and Dilly rent the air with an operatic scream imitation. Holding his hand over his chest, he kept the sound going as chaos erupted in the bank. The alarms were set off, bells and red lights blinking, people sprawled on the floor in fright, metal shutters fell over all the teller windows, and out of the woodwork guards came running with drawn pistols. A phalanx of guns surrounded Phil and Dilly.

Meanwhile, Phil had found his plastic I.D stuffed in his Hawaiian shirt pocket and he exhumed it, flourishing it towards the shuttered window, "Here it is. I—"

"Drop it, mister!" commanded a guard.

Dilly cut his Caruso impression.

Phil looked confused, "Where—?"

"Put your hands up, both of you!"

"Really," Dilly panted, "This is quite inconceivable. Not to mention ridiculous on your part."

They were pushed against the armored windows and frisked.

362

All kinds of strange implements that hit the floor were circled around Phil, and from Dilly's suit lining the guards found a black fountain pen and a gyroscope.

"What's this?!" someone asked Phil.

Phil turned around. "That's my badge. I'm one of you, I'm a private detective."

The guard studied it for faults.

Dilly rolled his eyes. He could have solved a crossword puzzle in all this wasted time.

"What are you doing in here?" said the guard.

"I was just trying to cash a check," Phil told him. "I couldn't find my I.D at first. When I look up, everyone is pointing guns. I found it though. You don't need to shoot me."

"If you'll only recede your battlements," Dilly offered, "we're quite eager to be on our way."

The guard stared them both down. He really did want to shoot them it seemed, until his eyebrows collapsed and he lifted his arm to make the signal to call, "False alarm!"

The red lights and bells stopped, the tellers reappeared in their exposed windows, and the flattened crowd slowly rose up in gardens.

The guard looked like he might be compelled to say one more thing. He sneered at the object discarded next to Phil. "Detective," he hissed. He stepped forward and his shoe pressed on the magnifying glass.

GOLDFISH...

"It's not so bad," Phil was admiring the coffee cup. The name of the bank was painted on the blue side of it.

"I thought we were going to buy a car," Dilly mumbled. "We could have paid in cash. Now the bank has all your money." He walked sullenly alongside Phil.

"I like the cup, Dilly. I couldn't pass up a free coffee cup just for opening a savings account." He stuffed it in one of his pockets.

"You've apparently forgotten the Black Thursday panic of 1929," Dilly muttered. He looked up at the towering buildings. He walked beside Phil as if he might disappear.

"Hey, what's the address for the Martian Society?" Phil asked.

"I don't know, I'm not an astronomer. I suppose we could find it listed in the phone directory."

"Yeah, maybe that store there has one."

A pigeon flew away from them as they stepped into the brick shadow.

Loud cowbells tied to the door announced their entrance.

"Hello?" Phil called out.

There were rows of packages on shelves, and fish tanks and cages in the background. The pet store seemed to be abandoned.

"Hello?" repeated Phil, "Is someone here?" It was a strange setting. He didn't trust it. His instincts told him to beware. He looked at Dilly, "I think we should go somewhere else."

An answer broke the ice. "Hello!"

Phil whirled. "Hello!"

"Hello!" Someone somewhere was talking.

"Hello," Phil nodded, "We are wondering if you have a phonebook we could borrow."

"Hello!"

That strange accent wasn't human. Both Phil and Dilly realized what was happening. At the end of the aisle was a bamboo cage holding a parrot.

"Hello?" it said its one word again, all it knew.

"Oh, for the love of Mike," Dilly looked away.

Quickly, Phil growled louder, "Hello! Is there a person who can help me?"

The sound of boxes falling aside brought the appearance of kimonoed woman. "Hello, may I help you?"

Phil said, "Do you have a phonebook I could look at?"

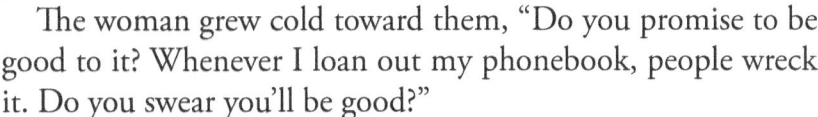

The woman grew cold toward them, "Do you promise to be good to it? Whenever I loan out my phonebook, people wreck it. Do you swear you'll be good?"

"Naturally, my dear," said Dilly.

"You won't tear out pages?"

"Please," Dilly said, "We're gentlemen."

"Of course," the woman answered. Behind the counter, she looked through a pile of debris. "It's somewhere here..." Under a hundred pages of newsprint stacks, she found it. "Here!" She held it aloft and they caught it.

Phil bowed, "Thank you," before he opened its yellow soft pages. "Let's see...Martian...Martian...Martian..." he repeated as he went through the flipping paper.

Dilly smiled hopefully.

"I'll...hmmm...I'll be back when you know," the woman told them.

"Thank you, you've been more than kind. Phil, allow me to find the address."

"I'll find it. Hold on...Markets...Marlins...Marsupials..." He followed his finger down the small print. "Ahah! Here it is, Martian Society For Higher Technology. 1127 Euclid Street. Here's the phone number. You got a pen and paper, Dilly?"

"Me?" Dilly patted his suit. "No, those bank hooligans took

my fountain pen."

"I don't have a pen either."

"Well..."

Phil looked for the woman who wasn't there. He could hear her in the back room moving boxes. He looked around suspiciously. Tenderly, he took hold of the phonebook page and started to rip it out.

Dilly struck his forehead and turned, "Oh no..."

With the utmost surgical care, Phil tore the yellow page out and crumpled it into his pocket. He closed the soft book, "Thank you!" he raised his voice, "I found it!"

"Let me out of here," Dilly bustled towards the door ahead of Phil. "I'll plead innocence." The cowbells clanged with his hurried exit.

Phil caught the door handle after it swung closed. "Sayonara!" he called out to the invisible owner. But as he pulled the door open to leave, an alarm went off. He froze in the entrance almost compelled to run. He could see Dilly bolt around the corner.

"Just one moment!" the woman ordered.

Phil sweat live bullets, "I didn't..."

The alarm continued. The woman came back into the front of the shop. All the animals were going berserk in their cages.

"I was just—" Phil was still trying to explain.

"Oh, it's you," she sighed disappointed. "I was hoping it would be a customer." She came closer to him to recite with less than excitement, "You said the magic word."

"What? I did what?"

"Yes. Sayonara is the magic word. You win a goldfish."

Phil blinked.

"Just one moment, please." She went to the wall and pulled down a bowl holding a little orange fish. The way it danced inside, it seemed happy too.

"I've never won anything in my life," Phil grinned.

"Well you win today. One goldfish. Enjoy, mister."

He stumbled out the door carrying the goldfish tight to his chest. The water level sloshed unevenly, he got a tablespoon down the front of his shirt.

Dilly was standing around the corner with a crumpled newspaper held in front of his face. He peeked over and spotted Phil. The paper fell away, "You bought a fish!"

"I *won* a fish, Dilly," Phil corrected him.

"What are you going to do with a fish?"

"He'll be my pet. Just like The Thin Man and his dog."

"Let me see him." Dilly looked down into the bowl. He was ogled in return by the orange fish. It finned to keep its balance in the distorted crystal water. "Yes..." Dilly said. "I think he may come in useful. If by some turn of fortune, you're trapped in a log jam, you could send him downstream with a message tied to his fluke. He is a fine pet, Phil."

Phil smiled into the globe, motherly.

"Shall we proceed to the Martian Society?"

"Yes," Phil looked up. "We can walk there, it's not far."

IN A FOG OF RAINY MIST...

Not long afterwards, they got caught in a fog of rainy mist. It beaded their clothes with little diamonds and steamed off the fishbowl.

The sidewalk rubbed up against a tall brick wall cracked with ivy. Like a cloudbank, it showed no sign of their destination.

Phil searched for a clue. The wall ended in a pair of gothic black iron gates. "Here it is!" he pointed, "1127." The numbers were melted weapons in the gateway. If a bat was tired during the day, he could rest in the crooks and hide.

Dilly paled at the sight. Beyond, was an uncertain dark yard. As Phil pushed open the gate, Dilly offered, "Ahhh...Why don't I stay here? I could prove to be a valuable sentinel."

Phil smiled, "Alright." He took a step, then returned, "Oh, here," he passed the fishbowl to Dilly, "keep an eye on this too."

Dilly bowed and accepted it.

"I shouldn't be long." Phil creaked open the gate to let himself in. He looked back and laughed at the forlorn shape of his Watson getting blurred by the weather. "Thanks, Dilly."

Dilly watched him follow the broken pathway into the grated rain. He squinted at the outline disappearing among the sharp lined plants in the courtyard. He looked down to the hovering orange fish and said, "It's just you and me now."

CRYPT...

Cobblestones chipped with bits of colored glass made the strange uncertain path, sliding like a cobra to end at a solid door set in a castle wall. Phil clasped the brass and moss knocker. He tapped it, telegraphed it against the wood. Shivering, he pulled his collar tighter and waited.

The door swung open slow as the crypt of Dracula's tomb.

It looked so dark and no one seemed to be there to greet him. Phil stepped forward knowing it might mean his end. He called, "Hello?" and went into the space echoing with his voice.

His eyes needed half a minute to adjust to the ghoulish damp. A bony shine reflected the meager light. He could have been inside an oyster. Dripping water made a tambourine. Or was it coming from that ghostly shape in the corner, a haunted grandfather clock? If it wasn't my job to be brave, he confided, I would run for the door. He took a breath, coughed out, and continued forward, to collide with a cold solid wall.

"Ouch!" He felt the tip of his nose. Lingering in a tomb with his hands outstretched vainly like a blind scarecrow, he tried to move. He shuffled and swung his arms out carefully. The room had boundaries and as his shin bashed into a solid floored object, suddenly lights were switched on and Phil was spoken to.

"Can I help you?" A woman stood in the doorway of his cell.

He blinked pitifully and also embarrassed with realization. I'm in a bathroom! His laugh tried to gather into seriousness, build a Chinese Great Wall around the loopy hill.

"Do you have an appointment?" She hooked her hand onto her hip.

"I'm looking for the Martian Society."

She rolled her eyes. "It's in the courtyard, sir. This is the bathroom."

"Of course. I'm thankful that you came along." He nodded and swept past her. Outside, back among the grounds, he smiled. My imagination gets carried away...He saw a shack in

369

the middle of rusty overgrowing vines, hunchbacked trees and boulders. The windows glistened with blue electricity crackling from inside. "That's got to be the place."

This time though, he peeked inside the glass to make sure.

He could see cluttered tables set with experiments. Gleaming vials of stained liquid bubbled under flames and made currents through veins into beakers. In the corner was a man splitting atoms with a bright copper torch. "This is it," Phil muttered, and he left the window scene to knock on the door.

"Enter..." muffled a reply.

Phil did and blinked at the heavy pall of sulfur. He gasped, "Is this the Martian Society For Higher Technology?"

Instantly, the flame ceased and the man turned around. His face wore a heavy protective visor. "Yes, yes," he barked, "what do you want?"

Phil tried to begin casually. He cleared his throat and reached for a test tube. "I'm a private detective," he said. He picked up the test tube and shrieked in pain, dropping it onto the floor, glass breaking. His fingertips were scalded. A mustard cloud erupted from the shattered experiment. Phil couldn't open his stinging eyes. He stepped backwards and ran into another table behind him. He could hear the man yelling in the background, as more things fractured.

Phil stumbled about madly, he tried opening his eyes but there was something acrid in the air. Small fires crackled, he could hear the scientist hollering, "Halt! Stop moving!" and curses too.

By blundering, Phil managed to fall against the door. His fingers scrambled the handle open and he crawled out on his hands and knees. He grabbed deep handfuls of the grass and dandelions and rubbed them over his face. Petals and greens stuck on.

When he squinted a look behind him, he saw the shack snapping with electricity. Smoke came out the seams like a paper bag filled with burning coal. Inside it, he could hear a fire extinguisher hissing. It was a disaster in there.

Phil swayed upright. I wonder if I should go back in and help? He hesitated, but only for long enough to become aware of the oaths still twisting his way. He quickly reconsidered, "Maybe I better leave," he mumbled. "I guess I should return when he's in a better mood to talk." Phil didn't want the mad scientist to come out throwing lightning bolts or atom bombs at him, so he retreated a little faster. He ran past the last hedge and crashed out the iron gate.

"Dilly!" he shouted. The street was abandoned. It could have been a Sunday morning. The only shadows were scrunched under cars. Otherwise all was shades of gray. Blue smoke wisped off his clothes. The cuffs of his trousers were calmly smoldering. Phil was the last survivor of the apocalypse. He scuffed out into the street and shouted again, "Dilly!"

That's when it started to rain. The sky just opened up with downpour. Someone must have pulled a cord.

"Aah!" Phil covered his head with his hands and danced for the cover of the scratchy black hawthorn trees on the other side of the street. The rain had a hundred voices on the leaves. The one thing Phil Ticks knew about weather was that no matter how bad it seemed, it would change for the better. He was prepared to wait it out under the hawthorn umbrellas. Just listen to that beautiful sound, he smiled, I don't mind staying here.

Across the street the gates blew open again and the scientist bolted out onto the sidewalk. With him was a monstrous human being. The scientist shouted, "Find him Knarr! You must find him and tear him into pieces!"

Phil clung to the trunk of the tree. He molded his body to the form of it. With any luck, the monster and scientist wouldn't see him. Yes, thank you, he sighed. They ran off down the tar and weeds in search of him somewhere else. Phil waited until every possibility of them was gone before he started to move from the tree.

No one saw him.

Dilly wasn't around anymore. He could be anywhere, might as well be rounding the Cape of Good Hope, leaving Phil to escape alone. Sticking along the street curb going in their steps, Phil imagined the great Indians of long ago. I'll be like them, I'll trust in the dodge of circumstance, wind and veil of whatever.

So it prevailed, luckily for him, and Phil managed to go into the wet night without anyone seeming to notice him.

FISH FOOD...

Dilly wasn't that far away. It wasn't that he meant to maroon his sleuthing partner, he simply got hungry. He and the fish were sitting at the counter of a diner, not more than three blocks away from Phil.

The little goldfish bowl sparkled like a treasured jewel. The silver napkin holder bent reflected next to it.

"Here's your pie," the waitress said. She set down a slab of apple pie in front of him.

"Thank you my dear," he nodded. "In your honor, I'll enjoy it."

She leaned over the fishbowl and looked inside. "He's awful cute, does he have a name?"

"Well...I've been calling him Hermes, named for the messenger of hope."

"Hello, Hermes," she cooed. She waved a painted fingernail over the surface. "He looks hungry."

"I'm sure he is. I just don't know how fond he is of apple pie."

"Let me see if I can find him something to eat. I'm not really sure what goldfish eat."

"Neither am I," Dilly said between mouthfuls. "Perhaps he would appreciate a crumb of cracker? Or is that only for parrots?"

The waitress disappeared into the kitchen. Dilly watched the orange fins winnowing. He leaned over and looked into the water, wondering how the fish saw the world through the curve.

When the waitress returned, she was carrying all kinds of food heaped in her apron.

"A cornucopia!" Dilly exclaimed.

She poured it over the counter: fruit, vegetables, bread and cheese and scraps of meat.

Dilly eyed it hungrily.

"I think we should start with bread," the waitress said. She tore a piece off and dipped it in.

The fish watched the rest of the room with his big black eyes. "Maybe something else instead…"

"Yes," agreed Dilly stuffing his mouth with the rest of the bread.

She began to try every possibility and so did Dilly, leafing through the scraps.

More people formed around the counter to stare, or add suggestions.

An old woman said, "My cat just loves liver." She took a roast beef morsel and dunked it into the water.

Meanwhile, Dilly caught all he could get. There were so many hands going on, he could eat and nobody noticed. Finally he rose from his chair and told them pleasantly, "Actually, I think I'll bid you all a very good night. In the morning, I'll visit a pet shop and purchase some food he can't ignore."

MATCH THE WOOD....

Phil could see the lumbering figure of Knarr a couple blocks behind him. Lit by streetlamps, car lights and store windows, it moved after Phil like a nightmare. "I have to lose him," Phil panted. He looked around desperately, "Where can I go?"

The cars sleeted by in the rain. There was a building across the street. Colonnades and yellow windows, it was some kind of old fashioned hall. Phil ran in the weather, up the stairs, heaved open the door and went in.

It was a meeting hall. There was an empty auditorium before him filled with the rounded backs of black chairs facing a blank ghostly stage. He stared around wildly and saw stairs running up to another floor—maybe to a balcony—so he raced towards them. He jumped a braided rope that slung over low and he climbed the bright red stairway.

On the new floor, everything was silhouette wallpaper. He sought the dark curtain that floated like a dried up ghost against a column support and he hid in its waves. "Oh God," he prayed, "Don't let me be caught! I don't want to be torn apart. I didn't mean to do what I did. It wasn't my fault that things went wrong in that lab. Please let me through this to the next day."

The place was so calm. He tried to quiet down to make his breath match that of the wood.

DOWN THE STAIRS FORMS A TRAIL...

So much time passed Phil felt certain it must be safe for him to move. He pushed the curtain aside and walked back into the aisle. Apparently he escaped being followed. Anyway, he hoped so.

He followed the carpet to where the opposite set of stairs chopped back down to the lobby.

The stairs were bright red, a lurid fact he paid little attention to.

His walk on them made a sort of wet sound.

Curious, he guessed.

Around an elbow in the architecture, Phil descended the last flight and he stopped.

Strung across the final stair was a yellow rope with a dangling square sign, its message written on the opposite side.

He muttered, "What's that?"

He took the last of the steps, stretched valiantly over the rope onto the carpet of the ground floor. There he turned around to read the plaque.

Wet Paint.

He realized that he stood on their carpet with red footprints. The stairs he'd come down were plainly indented by his shoe size and stride.

"Oh no!" He raised a shoe and saw it was true. It was time to escape again. He ran across the lobby to the doors, leaving the most obvious trail that any fool could follow.

A GIANT CHARLIE CHAN...

To get out of the rain, Phil left the street into a movie theater. There were a lot of people in the lobby, forming lines and whirlpooling around. Phil kept looking over his shoulder suspiciously, as he drifted through and opened the first door he saw.

The bathroom...He remembered the time at the Martian Society and it made him stop hesitantly.

He took a couple steps onto the polished tiles, the door swung closed. He barely registered the mirror and sink and toilet stall, just the back of the person at the paper towel dispenser. Long blonde hair flowed gracefully like Veronica Lake.

"Oh, I'm sorry!" he gulped. "I'm in the wrong room!"

A beet red Phil Ticks leaped from the door labeled MEN and he retreated across the carpet to the next bathroom. It was quiet. His footsteps still left little coppery smudges as he went to the sink. His haggard image grew larger in the mirror. He stopped a foot away from the glass. His eyes were telling him in the desperate stare to go home and sleep. He ran some water out of the faucet. It splashed around in a swirl that slowly got warmer.

I have to rest.

He turned off the water and went into the narrow stall. Locking the door with a silver latch, he leaned against the stall wall and sighed. After a minute of staring at his paint splattered shoes, he drifted his attention to the wall.

Graffiti quilted it. If he was a flower, he would have wilted for the night. He couldn't believe his eyes, the things someone had written about a person named Barry. Oh well...He looked back at the floor to see the faint marks of his painted feet. He shook his head. "These shoes want to give me away."

Suddenly Phil held his breath—the bathroom door had opened, someone entered. He listened to the clicking pace that led over to his stall.

The locked door shook, "Hello?" asked a wisp of a voice.

"I'll be right out," Phil answered. He quickly stood and opened the door.

A woman shrieked, "What the—?!"

Once again, he threw himself out into the lobby. I have to keep moving, he knew, the whole place was like a carnival fun house. And dangerous too—there could be a killer looking for him. I have to lose myself in the crowd, he decided. I still have my ticket, the movie is playing. I'll go up the balcony ramp and hide in there.

Past the curtain door, the big room was lit in the purple and gray of the old movie. Phil looked uncertainly for a seat until the voice from the screen spoke to him, "Excuse please..."

Phil did a double-take. He laughed at the giant vision of Charlie Chan and he said, "Finally a friend." Happily, he took off his wet coat and sat down.

For the rest of the picture, Phil's jaw hung open and his eyes were two watery pools, filling up with every drop of plot. Charlie handled it all so surely. Like the conductor of a symphony, Sidney Toler led every nuance and shade to resolve at the end.

The houselights sunrised.

People came alive, standing in front of the white screen, and the surge moved towards the exit signs.

Phil grew restless too. He didn't want to leave though. There was a second picture starting soon.

Then he remembered something. He reached into the deep of his coat pocket. After a blind search, he pulled out a little spool of thread and from another pocket, a roll of tape and a dollar bill. It was just a dumb fishing game he liked to play. It was good for passing the time. On the table of his lap he stuck the end of thread to the dollar. He spidered it tentatively like a yo-yo, looked over his shoulder to make sure the coast was clear, then he cast the bill out into the aisle. Because of the dimness maybe, a few people went by without noticing. Phil gave his bait a tug. That was enough.

An old woman appeared. She slowly bent down to pick it up. Her hand opened an inch away from it, but suddenly, the money was gone. Bewildered, she creaked upright again.

Phil was winding string around his finger when a heavy paw landed on his shoulder. He jumped two feet in his seat.

"Here it is, ma'am!" thundered the man holding Phil—a giant dressed in a scout master's uniform. A crowd of boy scouts peered about him curiously. The gigantic Samaritan snapped the dollar off the string.

Phil winced and coughed unpleasantly. He looked away.

"Breeze must have blown it over here," the scout master said. He tensed and released his grip, squinting one eye like a bear trap in Phil's direction.

The old woman beamed, "Oh thank you, sir!" She took Phil's money and crept with an escort of uniforms towards the screen.

A soft dulled gong rang in the air, the second feature was about to begin.

Phil waited until it was dark and between the flicker river of the threading film, he got up and hurried for the green lit exit.

THE CONFEDERACY...

Sure he crossed the street. Phil went as fast as he could to the stopping bus. It hissed, letting him in the parted doors. He paid the driver and continued up the aisle, to find an empty seat. He found one in the middle, next to a woman drying her eyes in a bestseller book. Phil sat down. The windows shined as the city passed by.

He watched the night. Luckily he got out of the clutches of Knarr and the Martian Society. On the other hand—he turned to look out the other side of the bus—what was he going to tell the Davenport heirs? It looked like maybe he blew up their last hope.

Phil stared at his feet...Ragged old rusty battered cracked wing tips.

Maybe it wasn't too late to start over again.

The bus stopped. The woman pushed by his knees and left. He kept looking at the floor for another minute. Then he noticed that she had left her bestseller book on the plastic seat.

The title was *Pigment Fragrance*, a novel of lust and strife set in civil war America. He grabbed the paperback and pulled the cord to stop the bus.

Transformed into a Southern Gentleman, Phil Ticks ran off onto the shadowy sidewalk. He couldn't see her though, just lights of cars and the greenish latenight tint of closed stores.

"Too late..." he sighed. He pushed the book into his coat pocket sadly. Now he had to walk all the way home. He would go to sleep with another failure on his mind.

BLAME DARWIN...

In the morning, the goldfish brought Dilly to the water. He carried the fishbowl and a book under his arm. The book was so thick it pulled his shoulders over in a slant. Still, he walked with a determined pace, his eyes screwed to the distant green rattling sight of the park.

Along the neighborhood's gray sidewalk, in front of the rows of windows housed together, he clicked his cane and strained to hold the weight on his other arm. The goldfish spun. The sunlight caught gilded paper edges and the embossed title on the spine, *Darwin's Origin of Species*.

The pathway of the city ended in leaves pouring overhead. As he stepped under them, he breathed a sigh of relief. His journey was nearly complete.

He followed a grainy path. It led in eventual loop to a lake of sorts. The cement dipped into curbed water. The lake rippled with ducks and a few floating bottles over to a small island.

Dilly walked all the way to the edge where a bench awaited him. There he rested, set the fishbowl beside him, and opened the heavy book to a page marked by a tatter of newsprint bookmark. The old words told of iguanas and birds and fish. A theory began to derive that Dilly could relate to this modern situation.

He read only a little, looked up and stood. With fish and book in hand, his mind raced further on. His movement toward the water attracted the attention of the people fumbling around the lake. A woman feeding pigeons stopped and watched him. An old man got distracted and let his dog disappear in the leaves. A loopy pair of lovers held their waists together, as Dilly left port to explore.

Every step took him deeper into the green thick water. The waves went over his knees. It was alright though, he held Darwin's book higher as he went towards the island in the middle. It wasn't that far away.

After rising over his waist the water began to go down. With

381

his cane, he pushed a pirate bottle aside, muttering, "What an indigestion. Such pollution…"

He didn't presume to be adding to it, as he allowed the goldfish bowl to submerge. The lucky fish was on its own. It was as described, survival of the fittest.

Dilly emerged from the moat and came ashore onto the island. The ground was nothing but sand. The birds of the island had eaten every blade of grass and fern until the ground was bare. There were a couple trees, but they were only there like question marks.

"Very interesting," he mumbled and patted Darwin's book. "It seems evolution has developed even upon this little island. Just like the finches of Galapagos, every bird has found its place." He took notice of all the different looking ducks. The sly orange billed geese ganged on the shore to watch him. Little things paddled nervously. A grand idea was agreed in his mind. To put it down in words had changed the world.

"Hey!" someone threatened, just as he started to write. "Hey you!"

The interruption shook the thought away. It fled like doves, way past his head towards Xanadu.

"What could you possibly want?!" Dilly shouted across the water.

A police officer was standing on the beach. "That island is off limits! You're trespassing!"

"What?!"

"Come back here so I can arrest you!"

It took another hour for a truck to arrive with a rowboat so three officers could go across the moat and handcuff Dilly.

THE FIRST PAGE...

The first page of Phil's manuscript curled out of the type-writer. A stack of more white paper waited to go into the rusty machine, an Oliver from the early 1900s. The desk was a leaven toss of idea scraps and a clock, paperbacks, mysteries and good luck charms. A bean plant spun from a tall pile of magazines growing on the table corner. Everything was cast in green light and rich shadows.

Night meant the window was the green color of a dead tele-vision set. The faint buzz of the parking lot lamps could be heard like mosquitoes. Pushed against the darkest part of the room, the bed squeaked as Phil Ticks rolled over. He mumbled something in his sleep laconically. His dreamworld was a place in the city where he was dizzy and always struggling against lead. His eyes opened.

The room fizzed in reptile green. For a while Phil lay staring at the ceiling. The real world of Cynthia Villa had broken the spell of his dream. Just as well, he was feeling inspired. He got up and went over to the table. For inspiration he set an *American Detective* magazine facing him before he sat down and typed:

Don't let the name fool you, Cynthia Villa is a rugged affair. You only have to see it to know. Made in the 1950s, it's a crooked tow-er that's turned rotten gray. The floors of the Villa stack like lopsided mattresses above the street. The crazy wind blows it around. More than a few windows are broken. Pigeons go back and forth like doomed prisoners.

What a place. Such a prevailing feeling of doom, but it's nothing new to me. I'm used to it. Being a detective, I can stand the sight of Cynthia Villa day after day only because I live there.

THE KAMA SUTRA INCIDENT...

How can I tell her that I blew up the Martian Society? Phil paced back and forth in the slanted window rays. It's morning...She'll be here any minute and I don't know...I don't know what I can say.

He rehearsed to the city frame, "Ahh, Ms. Davenport...Remember that society you wanted me to investigate?" He cleared his throat, "Well, they aren't there anymore..."

No, that won't do.

Too dramatic...Sounds like I'm Captain America.

A wooden knock surprised him.

Someone was at his door.

"Yeah?!"

It wasn't locked. Slowly the door creaked open and a familiar woman entered. She was alone this time. "Hello?" she blinked into the strange gloaming.

"Oh!" Phil startled. "Ms. Davenport!" He looked quickly to make sure he was wearing his suit this time. "Come in, I was just trying to figure out what to say. I mean, that place you sent me to, don't worry about it. It's a memory now."

She stood before a chair that was tiered with books and papers and things. "What?"

"Oh, ah..." he garbled, "Let me clear that off for you." With both hands, he swiped the chair clear and allowed her to sit. Looking down her legs to the floor, he noticed his bare feet planted next to her. His bluish ivory feet gnarled opposite her streamlined pumps. "I'll be right back!"

"Where are you going?"

"I'll be right back," he repeated. In the bathroom he found his wingtips thrown against the side of the tub. Stuffing them on in a hurry, he came back out and continued, "The Martian Society has been thoroughly investigated, madam." But Phil couldn't move. Ms. Davenport had found a book amid all the chaos of his room. What fantastic chance guided her to that?

Her fingers held to the lurid Indian paperback, while her eyes darted back and forth, ingesting the contents of a weathered red love letter stuffed inside.

"I forgot about that—" Phil took a hesitant step towards her with his hand outstretched.

She jumped. "Stay back!" She threw the letter back onto his mildewed desk. She crumpled her brow, "I...I..." she struggled to speak.

"Look, Ms. Davenport," he flushed. "That letter means nothing. I used to be young and foolish. I haven't had those thoughts in a hundred years."

"Mister Ticks," she hissed, "I have *children!*" She tugged her coat tighter, "I am appalled! I apparently wasn't aware of who I was dealing with. I'm afraid I need the assistance of a different kind of detective."

"Awww, wait a minute!"

"No! Don't move! I'm quite sure!" Like a gazelle caught at the watering hole, she made for the door. "I don't need you anymore!" And in the quick flash of open and closed, she was gone.

Phil scratched the shin of his plaid covered leg. "What next?" he asked the unseen above. "Is this the beginning of more bad luck or what?"

In answer, the phone rang.

Why not? He grabbed it on the second ring. "Hello?"

"Is this Phil Ticks?"

"Yes."

"Figures…This is Officer O'Marty at the precinct. We have a friend of yours here. Name of Dilly Diamond."

THE GOAT...

"Just outrageous!" Dilly repeated. He and Phil sat in the booth of a little Mexican diner, not far from the gray block tower of the police precinct. "A man can't even unravel the mysteries of nature without the intrusion of the iron gauntlet of police harassment."

"Slow down, Dilly," Phil cooled him, "For crying out loud, try your lunch."

Dilly allowed himself to spoon at it hesitantly.

"You think you got it bad, Dilly...My life is so completely in shambles, I don't know where to turn."

"Not bad!" Dilly's face lit up. "This food is sensational!" He wolfed another bite.

Phil nodded his gaze out the window, "Yeah." He took in the skyscrapers and cloud piles, fighting birds.

"Waiter!" Dilly piped. "Excuse me, sir." He beamed at the waiter who now appeared, "Tell me, what is this I'm eating?"

The waiter looked uncertain, he drew his hands in the chalkboard air, "I'm not sure what you call it in English...A little...It's a small animal." He remembered, "The dog!"

"Dog?!"

"Yes, I think so..." The waiter watched Dilly deflate. "I'm sorry. It might not be the dog. You get milk from it?...Let me see..." He hurried away.

Dilly held onto the table weakly. "Phil," he gurgled. "I don't feel especially well."

Phil was still watching the downtown beehive. It didn't seem possible that so much had happened. Maybe the land had flipped over like a coin and landed upside down. Underneath, out of sight, grew the old beautiful world of forest lakes and fields.

The waiter returned with another man and excitedly explained, "The word was wrong, senor. I tell you the dog, but I meant to say the goat. The special today is the goat. Thank you,

I'm glad you like it."

As the waiter inched away, the other man unfolded his arms to reveal the bat-like cape he wore. With a flowering of wings, he announced, "I am here to perform magic!"

Dilly rested his fork on his plate and even Phil was drawn aback.

"Ladies and gentlemen…From the halls of Montezuma to the shores of Tripoli, I have brought the ancient art of the third eye."

There was a family next to him, mother and father and their two daughters and the magician grew close to them to speak. "Here," he offered a rose from his sleeve to the woman, "from Houdini."

Turning to attract everyone's attention, he went on, "I have a simple show I wish you to enjoy. By a miracle, we will discover a fortune." With all eyes on him, he continued to the littlest girl there at the table, producing a white handkerchief from his pocket. It was all knotted in folds and he handed it to her. "This could be nothing more than a scrap, a throw away. Doesn't it seem that way? If you please child, tell me what you find."

When she opened it, a silver coin fell out.

"Look at that!" he agreed with her smiles. "John F. Kennedy! Sometimes it happens that way."

"Surely it was in there to begin with," Dilly whispered.

"I would like you to draw a card," the magician smiled at the other seated girl. "Don't show it to me. Set it on top of the pack. Very good! Now in just a moment, I will tell you what it is."

Seated in back of him, Dilly watched in amazement as the card hitched up the magician's sleeve and hung at the edge of the cuff. "I can see the card!" he hissed to Phil. "It's right there!"

The sound of cards were shuffling loudly like parrot wings. "Now…" The magician held the pack and turned his wrist awkwardly, "I believe this is your card."

Dilly clapped riotously.

"Shhh!" Phil hissed.

"Thank you," the magician bowed. He searched behind him and proclaimed the next startle. "This is a top hat."

"Oh no," Dilly leaned towards Phil, "Don't tell me it's hiding a rabbit! What a perfectly preposterous ending."

"This is no ordinary top hat though." The magician's gloved hands turned it so everyone could see the patches in the worn black. "It once belonged in the world of gypsies and conjurers. Even I am sometimes surprised by its powers."

With another bite of food Dilly hummed pleasantly.

"May I set this down here?" the magician asked the family. "Thank you." He draped a marbled cloth over the upturned hat opening. "Could you whisper a magic word?" he asked the small girl. When she did, he thanked her, and with a nod he flapped the cloth away. Eyes shut, he put his hand inside the hat, until he seemed to feel a shock. "This is a mystery," he told his audience as he pulled it out. All the way out into the restaurant light, three feet of English carved wood emerged.

"That's my cane!" Dilly stood, "How did you—?!"

The applause of the room was like an ocean as the magician bowed once again. He passed the cane with a last smile to Dilly then he went through swinging doors to the silvery kitchen sounds beyond.

NORMAN ROCKWELL VS. VIRGINIA-NOT-SO-SLIM...

After that, they had no choice but to leave in a kind of grim fever, with Dilly leading the way, tapping quickly out the door onto the pavement, going west.

"What a strange and flustering matter! Phil, I think we should make it top priority to get back to Cynthia Villa intact."

"I know, I know," Phil mumbled. He felt the loose change in his pocket. "You got fare for the bus?"

"Me?"

"No, Norman Rockwell. Yes you! It's been a bad day. I spent my last dollar at that cafe."

"I certainly don't have any money. The barbarians at that police establishment went over me like leeches."

"Well, we'll have to hoof it then."

"Unheard of!" Dilly protested.

"Why not? We've walked across the city plenty of times. That's nothing new."

"But now you must think of your dignity. You're a detective! Be seen as royalty."

Phil sighed, "Yeah, well I'm broke and nothing is going my way."

"I won't hear it. What would Sherlock Holmes say? We'll find a way." Dilly pointed, "Ahah! Providence!"

Miserably, Phil looked across the street, down two blocks, at a neon sign that burnt its missing bulbs frantically. "A pool hall?"

"I was rather good at the game in my day," Dilly beamed. "I'll wager our way home..." he brought his cane up like a cue and invisibly tapped the eight ball into the pocket. "Just like that!"

Phil grabbed his arm, "I've never seen you play pool! That place is probably full of sharks. You know they break bones if you lose."

389

When Dilly smiled and took a step into the street, the confidence was really more than Phil could withstand.

"Sometimes Watson proved invaluable," Dilly called over his shoulder. "He wasn't without talent of his own. Come along, I'll be the one to outwit them this time."

Phil caught up with him, only to get tangled in a gray newspaper in front of the door as they entered. It resembled a dark barn where green pool tables were lit like swimming pools. The crack of the balls clacked bones all around the room. Taking in the scene, the eyes that twitched their way, Phil's immediate reaction was to run. Unfortunately the door had already swung solidly shut.

Dilly was fast at work though. He took off through the jukebox blues for the far wall rack of cues. Each one was carefully weighed in his hands, rolled in the cup of his palm, shaken, inspected like a Robin Hood bow. By trial of elimination, he at last discovered the suitable one.

For the last time Phil pleaded, "Do you really think we should?"

But Dilly was the Flying Circus, intent on a victim in the sky blue swirl of smoky air. There were plenty to choose from too. The room was full of competition angling over the tables. His eyes rested on one ballooning shape.

"Good afternoon, sir," Dilly said. He nodded to the velvet green surface, "Would you care for a tournament?"

A slow pair of eyes sized him up. "Hmmm," the man let out.

"I had supposed we could corroborate for a gentlemanly game of winner take all?"

"You want to play for money?"

"Indeed," Dilly nodded.

"What? Does that mean yes?" He threw his short arms to the side, rolled his eyes and implored, "Could someone tell me what he's talking about?"

Phil was forced into the picture to translate, "Yes, he would like to play you for money."

The man chuckled so deeply his entire continent seemed to roll. "Well, well, well," he laughed. "I guess you know what you're doing." He set up the rack in its pyramid spot and one after one the solid and striped fell in sparkling like eyes. He kept the eight ball rolling slightly in his hand, and asked, "So how much will it be?"

"I thought we should start small." Dilly rattled their loose change in his pocket, trying to make it sound like more. "What's the point of being largesse? How about...Oh say, eighty five cents?"

"Say what?! You must be—"

"It's merely a preliminary! To grease the wheel unto further treasure! I like to begin with sand, as in the days of the Egyptians."

"Awww..."

Dilly watched him hopefully.

The eight ball pieced into the triangle and the game was on.

"Say," their competition said, "You got a lot of nerve, you know that? What do they call you anyway? Cheapskate?"

"My name is Dilly Diamond," he bowed.

His opponent shook his head in disbelief. "Well, if eighty five cents is all you got, I'll take it just the same, cause I'm Virginia-Not-So-Slim and I'm a champion!"

LOST SHIRTS...

"Alright, I concede! It wasn't my fault though, how was I supposed to know?" Dilly clutched his arms across his bare chest. The five o'clock shift of light was beginning. Cold shadows formed the streets.

"With a name like that! *Virginia-Not-So-Slim*!? That's a pool hustler's name for God's sake!" Phil shivered. "That guy took my best coat!"

Dilly was silent. The buildings they walked by bent down with the toil of years. No one seemed to notice them anyway.

"I'm not going to walk home like this," Phil said. "You're the one who said I've got to appear royally. I should have listened to myself! If I walked to begin with, I would have been home already. I could have been in bed."

Dilly stopped suddenly in the yellow lamp light. "In all the archives of recorded exploits and human adversity, there are lost chapter laid down like shipwrecks, wherein the heroes are defeated. And this...alas...was one of them." He took a breath of cold air to elucidate.

"Wait a minute," Phil paused at the entrance to an alley. A lopsided cloth plop of color lay next to the green dumpster.

"No!" Dilly held up both his bare arms, "I must protest! You're going too far if you expect me to—"

"It's the answer to a prayer," Phil interrupted. He bent down and chose a zebra patterned shirt. Buttoning it, with a look of wonder he exclaimed, "It even fits!"

"You know you're deranged if you think I'm going to wear those sordid clothes."

"There's even a coat!" Phil pulled it out of the pile to try on.

Dilly stood there as a freezing sentinel for as long as he could, watching. Finally, he gave in with a tentative question, "What's that?" He pointed as Phil dug through. "That black item with the gold buttons."

Phil held it up. "It looks good, Dilly. You could wear this."

"Yes, well perhaps. If only to stave off pneumonia...Let me see it."

DILLY DIAMOND DARJEELING...

"I've been thinking about the case." Phil took another sip of the hot tea concoction Dilly had made. A taste rushed...Mesopotamia, Alexandria, the tilled climbs of Peru. He grimaced and continued, "I think they were on to me, testing me from the very beginning, starting with the stolen letter off my door...I think that Martian Society was a setup. I think I was on to something big and I got cut off."

"Of course!" Dilly agreed.

Phil continued to pace back and forth in front of the window slats, "I don't care what they tell me, I'm going to find out what really happened. They can't scare me off. I can't leave a mystery unsolved!"

Dilly laughed, "And when we do solve it, we'll have a ticker-tape parade in Washington D.C! Magnificent!"

With an exhausted sigh, Phil collapsed in the broken down chair by the window. "They thought they had me. But I'll make sense of it. All I have to do is concentrate." He put his hands to his temple and grew still.

"I can't wait," Dilly said, "When it's over, our memoirs will feed the jackals." He admitted, "I've always wanted to be a hero."

Phil swam above the current of the street, the ticking clocks, cheap Casio Classical music, car alarms...all the rumbling pond in and around the shores of Cynthia Villa. When Dilly made tea it was an invocation to another dimension. He caught the cloud passing by. Phil opened his eyes and decided, "I'll have to return to the ruins of the Martian Society. As of tomorrow, we're back on the case!"

THE MORNING OF OUR RETURN...

"Say no to those company bosses!" the man barked in Dilly's ear. Safeway was really a throng this morning. There were leaflets all over the pavement, scattered like stepping stones.

"I just want some orange juice," Dilly explained. He was surprised to see him here, away from the easy lanes of the college where they never seemed to leave.

"Let me tell you something, mister! Do the Panamanians have orange juice in the morning?"

"I'm well aware of the hypocrisy of our so-called democracy," Dilly told him. "As a matter of fact, I've spent all my life struggling like a fly in the amber web of America." He accepted the leaflet and passed through the mechanical doors. Every aisle was clogged with traffic. "What a miasma..."

Joining in the slow cough of dodge towards the back of the store, Dilly stopped in front of the juice row. They all danced together. "What am I looking for?" He couldn't believe he came all this way to be mindboggled. The cartons blurred into one jittering octave. Prices varying by only coins, brand names, block letters in battle. "Am I still holding this?" he noticed the leaflet pasted in his hand. He peeled it off to read the coupon. "This entitles you to one orange juice. Thank us when the revolution occurs." Dilly grabbed one of the bright orange cartons, "Well I certainly will!"

He found the line leading to the cashier and waited out the slow drain to the electric doors. Then, back in the wind, Dilly looked around for the missing revolutionaries. "No doubt retreated back to the warrens," he observed. "When you see them again," he told the rows of ninety nine cent primroses, "give my regards."

Moving briskly along the side of the grocery store, he tapped past a security guard hassling some teenagers. A car blasted its alarm. A parked shopping cart was full of plastic bags and cardboard, someone's pushcart home.

Dilly breathed in deeply though. Everything was just waiting for the change. "The perfect morning of our return."

THE WONDER OF THE CITY...

Meanwhile, dawn had come to Phil long ago on the stagger outlines of buildings caught in his window. In the sky an airplane wandered to some distant collapse.

He had been waiting all through a restless sleep for the new day to begin. Now that it appeared, he jumped out of bed filled with joy. He waved off the covers to get out.

It was morning and it felt like it.

Phil hurried over to his waiting clothes. "The Case of the Martian Society," he chuckled. He put on a cold shirt and asked himself in a reporter's voice, "Why do you do it, Detective Ticks? What drives you into such a dangerous world?"

Smiling at the question, Phil paused between shirt buttons to answer, "Because it's a mystery." Yes, he thought, I like that. I'll write that down for my book. In the gray shadows forming his desk top, he found a pencil and scratched the words.

"That reminds me!" he caught himself. "I have to leave Dilly a note before I leave."

Hopping on one leg, he stepped into his pants and tucked his shirt in. There was a frayed caterpillar green sweater to pull on too, then his socks and shoes. His coat as usual lay in broken folds on the floor.

That's it. That's all it took for this famous detective to be ready and reaching for the door.

He was pleased with himself.

"Oh!" he knocked wood on his forehead. "I forgot the note!"

PROGRESS...

Tony Toledo would have his way. The entire lot would be filled in with rides and booths, roofed by strings of flashing colored lights. It would be the most beautiful little Coney Island. It was his neighborhood, he was the King, and this was his way of showing his appreciation.

Though it was only morning, Tony stepped out of his chauffeured silver car to examine the progress. He held a styrofoam cup of coffee in one hand and a cigar in his other. Smoke rose from both. He eyed the Laurel and Hardy antics of two men setting up a ladder, pinwheel grazing the scratchy hawthorn branches.

"Hey!" Tony called.

They dropped the ladder. The bigger one cried out and grabbed his squashed foot.

"When I come back, I want to see some progress." He cracked his knuckles like a walnut tree snapping in the breeze.

A DETECTIVE IN REALITY...

Phil paid the fee and cheerfully told the bus driver, "Thanks," as he stepped off. The pallid city accepted his entrance. He noticed the telephone wire weighted down with a line of starlings. He was all excited to start the day with the beginning of an adventure. Feeling like royalty, as Dilly had told him to, he was prepared for marvelous things as he walked on the sidewalk next to the busy street. But, "Oh no..." not this time.

As the hill fell before him, there was a police car waiting below, a crowd, and a stalled long truck bed. The sight made Phil groan, "What now?"

Getting closer showed it clearly. In front of a diner, spiderwebbed with wires and bent boom microphones, an old car was parked. It was the kind of car that made you think of the old movies with thrilling detective stories. An entire film crew and all the barnacles were attached around its shiny metal. Feigning ignorance as he walked past, Phil was sure, any second now I'll hear the Hollywood voice of the director say, "Wait! Cut! Who's that?! Sign him on! He's perfect for this film!" Then I'll turn around slowly and tell them I'm already a detective in reality.

It didn't happen. Phil kept on walking and nobody noticed him go.

"Hollywood!" he laughed to himself. They've forgotten what's real. They film the same old thing over and over. I can picture better movies in my head.

Phil turned the corner down a cross street. He expected the derelict scene he was used to, the same one he'd run from when he left the burning remains of the Martian Society.

This just seemed to be the wrong time for him.

The gates of the old wall were blown open. The lot was being transformed into the mechanical wizardry of a carnival fair. If "The Case of the Martian Society" was supposed to start here, it had already begun without his knowing. He was so in the dark he let himself be drawn the way of a moth.

TEN PACES AWAY TOO FAR...

Dilly was almost back to the rust covered doors of Cynthia Villa, ten paces away, when a gargoyle detached itself from the cement wall and crossed the sidewalk in his direction.

Knarr grabbed Dilly around the waist and lifted him into the air like a doll. "You come with me," he growled.

Dilly couldn't speak or breathe. The universe kaleidoscoped in tribal, swirling colors.

Into the alley between buildings, Knarr carried him to a parked limousine. The dark window unrolled a few inches and the voice from in there said, "That isn't him. That's his friend."

Knarr's brow made waves as he shook Dilly. He thought and said, "Bait?"

"No," the voice growled. "We want the genuine article."

Knarr was confused. He shook the mummified Dilly.

"Dump that creep." The window went back up, leaving Ophelia reflections swimming on the black glass.

A smile broke on Knarr's face as wordlessly he obeyed, bending into a catapult, and with a snap he let Dilly fly.

UNDER THE METEOR SHOWER...

A meteor flashed overhead in the blink of an eye, so fast only a camera could catch it. Phil only saw the crowded hammering scene, that's all. The ramble plot of foggy land that he used to know was being transformed into something out of a science fiction nightmare. What else could he do but stare? It was crazy! He remembered a garden yesterday. Now it was going, going, gone.

"Looking for something, buddy?"

Startled, Phil garbled, "What's going on?"

"We're setting up the Saturn Circus."

"Of course," Phil observed. Some of them lived at Cynthia Villa too.

"Look here," interrupted the front half of the ladder, "Could you step aside and let us through."

Phil moved dreamily.

As the ladder went by, the smaller man on the end tipped his hat and smiled.

Was the whole world changing into unreal? Maybe, Phil decided. Why not? I shouldn't follow dead memories anyway, I have to start anew. If it wants to be this way, I should open myself to it. Phil caught up with the ladder crew and asked, "Do you need any help with the circus? Could I get a job?"

"See that trailer over there? Ask in there."

"Thanks." Phil straightened his collar and tie.

Not far away, the little tin building was surrounded by creamy gray Dumbo elephants waiting to be attached to the whirly-go-round ride. With a job, Phil realized, I'll be free to explore in the perfect disguise. He took a step and stopped. That reminded him. Before he got any closer, he reached in his pocket and took out a mangy looking stage beard.

UPSTAIRS...

Fiery trees broke his fall. The leaves were turned to dry yellow and orange stars. Dilly landed upstairs in the branches of a tall maple. "Ohhh..." he groaned, so foggy he couldn't tell if he was on another planet or not. Complex vision, like what a fly sees, hypnotized him with a web of streaked violets. He groaned again, louder.

"Hey!"

Dilly heard the voice coming from below him. He asked scratchily, "Am I in the air?"

"Hey you! Hey pal!"

Painfully, Dilly turned to look through the crayon scribbles. The ground formed a choppy sea of grass, dirt and fallen autumn leaves.

The doll sized person waved up at him and yelled, "Could you get my kite down?!"

Will I have to move? Can I move? Dilly's body crumpled like a nest in the crook of trunk and limb. With effort, he popped his leg out and he was shifted to a new view. In the frame presented to him was a blue kite caught in the fingers of his tree.

"Can you reach my kite?!" the yell came again.

It was out in the fine limbs. All Dilly could do was shake the branch he was on. Tremors were sent from him. Hand shaped leaves let go and spiraled. "Not unless it wants me to," Dilly replied in a quiet voice.

That's when he became aware that the tree had a strength all its own. The commotion he had started had triggered it. Now the tree was sending its own waves to get rid of him.

Dilly turned bright colors before he lost his grasp and fell.

THE INTERVIEW...

Tony Toledo poured a cup of coffee and stirred in the disappearing traces of three spoonfuls of sugar. Then he turned and faced the applicant seated in front of him. "So tell me..." he searched for the name on the form.

"I'm Phil. Phil Bricks." He nervously touched the beard stuck on his chin.

"Tell me, Phil Bricks, why do you want this job?" He paused to watch the reaction.

"It's always been my dream." A nervous laugh. "Ever since I was a kid, I've always wanted to work for the circus."

Tony set the cup onto the table and looked through a pocket for a fresh cigarette. He gave it life and breathed smoke. "How would you describe your approach to work?"

"Beyond needing it to pay the bills? Well, let's see...Work... Okay, it centers me," he tried. Phil had experience with job interviews, he was well versed. "I grow with it. In other words, I feel that every day requires my attention. I have fashioned this day on Earth."

Tony tapped his cigarette. "Alright," he said. He was getting the picture. "Let's get down to brass tacks. What do you know about selling lizards?"

"Lizards..." a pause could have grown to more before Phil answered, "I'm strongly in favor of selling lizards. Just look at evolution. We started with them, but we've progressed. We're past that stage, we've mastered it. I'm sure I can sell lizards as well as I've sold other commodity. Better, in fact. Allow me to prove it to you."

Tony let a cloud of smoke go. He collected the notes of a quarter hour. After another few waits, he shuffled them all together and allowed, "For minimum wage I'll let you join the Saturn Circus, but only for today. There's nothing certain for you beyond that. Understand?"

"Oh thank you," the new employee rose like a fast spring

driven flower.

THE LEAVES WERE CARDS...

This time the leaves were cards spread the same as him, flat on the ground. Dilly surprised himself by being able to move. Somehow the fall from the tree hadn't been the end of him. Inch after inch—it must have been the way a wounded chestnut would grow—he stood up.

The leaves shook with the applause of another falling object. His cane stuck into the grass like an arrow.

"Ah," a smile crossed his face and gave him strength to reach. He even laughed as he walked because it was amazing that he was alive. A miracle was at play.

Humming the new day song, he explored wherever he was. It was apparently a park. The last thing he remembered was being thrown. Pausing, he could still feel and hear the rumble of the cars and machines at work grinding a city. He continued past the heavy trees, scuffing leaves, breathing the earthy smell, pretending he was in a forest, when the maples stopped on the edge of a grassy hill. Dilly left the tree cover, using his cane to climb to see where he'd be next.

What if it's another land? he mused. I could have stepped out of the old America to somewhere really free!

An ancient cement bridge formed ahead of him. It was arched over what sounded like a rushing river. Dilly approached as though he would behold a wonderland and...

Cars below—by the hundreds, they went shocking underneath the bridge. They were blinks of sound. He stopped and rested on the gray railing to look over the edge and watch them hurry. There were two lanes going opposite ways, zippers up and down. He couldn't keep track and it made him dizzy to watch. So he tapped his way to the other end of the concrete where the land took over again.

Trees grew around the path. He was surprised how easily he thought he was in another world, far from civilization. With his back to the bridge, it sounded like a river again, but now he

407

knew.

Dilly allowed it and kept going until the path hit a mesh fence. Silver crisscrossed up ten feet into scrambled barbed wire stretching along either way. On the other side of it was a darker looking scratch. Who knew what lurked in there?

He continued to walk next to the prison-like fence. He tried not to slip into the confused shrubs and bottles that crumbled on the ridge above the freeway. He didn't know what, but something called for him on the other side of the tall fence. You could feel that draw, a hot fiery center. He was following instinct on the clouds of stepping stones. Maybe the fall out of the tree had bumped him senseless.

Then Dilly stopped in front of an amazing situation. Through the fence, not more than fifty feet away, an elephant was poised. The elephant watched Dilly shiver. It took a half minute of bewilderment in which Dilly's mind seemed to free fall like an octopus grabbing at clouds before he recalled why there was an elephant in the city. "It's the zoo!" he laughed. He could release his clinging fingers from the fence. "Now I know where I am."

CLUES OF YESTERDAY...

The more Phil scurried around trying to find the clues of yesterday, the faster his prey disappeared. Already:

1...The stone wall over there where Dilly had stood guard with the goldfish was gone. In its place was a row of tall black wooden posts with canvas sails nailed in between.

2...The mysterious garden and yard had been rolled over by a carpet of sparkly gravel and Saturn Circus allure.

3...And all the former space that clung with trees and vines had strangers putting up carnival machines. By afternoon the stage was set firm, the Saturn Circus had made the place its home.

Phil was over the site of the old Martian Society's laboratory, bumping against the crowded stalls of throw-the-ball and shoot-the-gun and pinball, intently watching the curious swing of the pendulum dangling from his hand.

"It's got powers," one of the citizens of Cynthia Villa had told him months ago.

Usually a gold weight like that would go back and forth until physics wore it out, but this thing tugged like a dog on a leash.

"Would it be out of the ordinary to ask what you're doing?" a volcano boomed at him from behind.

Phil lost track and fizzled as he turned to discover his boss. Tony Toledo stood there with a note-taking liege in tow.

"Didn't I hire you to do a job?"

As quickly as possible, Phil pocketed the strange device, thinking up, "It's my ten minute break." He held up the bucket of lizards, "We were just relaxing."

"Do I pay you to relax?" Tony took his hand from his pocket causing Phil to jump, expecting a gun. Tony stabbed a finger at Phil, "What's going on here? I want progress. Proceed, proceed! It's my time you're on now!"

As Tony and his scribbling secretary left, Phil closed his eyes and breathed a sigh of relief. Wherever the Martian Society used to be, they were gone now. Something with more fear had taken its place. But there was an aura left behind, the pendulum didn't lie. Employed by the circus, he had the perfect chance to find it. Cloned as another yes-man, how would they know that he was digging to the root?

CRAZY...

"Phil!" Dilly shouted. He had his eyes pressed to the poked out knothole in the white fence surrounding the fairground. "Phil! What are you doing in there?"

Phil looked around in circles. "Dilly?"

"Over here! The fence!" Dilly rapped on the plywood.

Phil obediently made his way over until he could see the eye.

"So you finally ran away with the circus?" it blinked.

"Dilly," Phil hushed him, "I'm undercover."

"I guess that explains the whiskers."

"This is where the Martian Society used to be. I got a job with the carnival so I could look for clues."

Suddenly Tony's voice boomed from behind Phil, "Oh, this is rich! Are my eyes playing tricks on me?! Is he talking to the wall? Someone tell me?"

"Yes Mister Toledo," his minion nodded furiously.

"Talking to a wall..." Tony walked up to Phil and lay a heavy crushing hand on his shoulder. "Some people do that, don't they? Some people talk to walls, some talk to trees, to rocks and water." He squeezed. "You know what I call those people?" he asked Phil.

Phil winced a syllable.

"Crazy!" Tony blurted. He shoved Phil against the wall. "Crazy people don't work for me! You're finished. Get out of here!"

Phil paused. His boss steamed in his face like a bull. "I forget where the exit is..."

"Then let me remind you!" were Tony Toledo's last words as he grabbed Phil and sent him up and over the circus fence.

411

WHERE WE WILL LAND...

Phil and Dilly were staring at the mirror of what the day had done, looking at each other across the table.

"We seem to be in dangerous territory," Dilly said at the end of a long silence.

"I know. There should be a limit to how much we endure." Phil took another sip of the coffee, bitterly continuing, "I'm not sure if it's worth going any further with this."

Dilly choked on his tea, "Do you mean to surrender?"

"No, I wouldn't say that. I'm just thinking out loud. Maybe we could go back to Cynthia Villa and just resume where we left off. It wasn't this bad to be in a world of our own. Stuck in there you never had to go past daydreams."

"You changed your door," Dilly reminded him. "You became a detective when you wanted something more than the old day-to-day routine…Your wish was granted. At this precise moment, we just can't predict where we will land."

Phil was despondent. He turned the canvas sounding pages of the newspaper classifieds. "I'm thinking of something that won't be as dangerous as detective work." Magically, it appeared in the print. Sometimes, no matter what he was going through, he seemed to be protected and guided. "Like this!" he brightened.

"What is it?"

Phil was already ripping the newspaper into a fragment that he could put in his pocket. "It's something I've been wanting for the longest time."

THE WORLD OF ART...

The clock showed him ten minutes early and the room only had a few people there, mostly old women, clustered and talking in loud nervous voices in the front row of seats.

Phil went instinctively to the back wall and sat down against its yellow pale. He slid his coat off over the wooden chair. Now what am I going to do?

The only window showed bare dark branches outside. That's all there was out there, besides the white sky. Facing him far away was a chalkboard smeared with a gray resembling pollution.

From the sloped height of the back of the room, Phil watched the rest of them enter and stumble to their seats; not many, but enough to make a barrier.

Phil marked the wait by drawing on the page of his notebook. One line was followed by another.

"Ahhhh..." a man announced as he entered. He closed the door and went to the pedestal awaiting him. Everyone was silent as he climbed before his audience. He looked them over too, putting his hand over his brow to spot Phil Ticks way up in the back. "Welcome to Beginner's Art. I'm your instructor, Mister Lent. Ahhhh..." he drawled, "I trust you've brought your notebooks and assorted drawing pencils? Your artist tools...Because we're going to dive right into the world of art."

Phil looked down and saw how out of control his sketch had got. He tore off the page and crumpled it.

Jiggling the spectacles located on the tip of his nose, the teacher continued, "Ahhhh..." He shuffled the loose pages of notes on his podium, "I'd like you all to take off one of your shoes. The right or the left, it's your choice."

The giggling assortment in the front rows obeyed immediately, bending down and bringing up their orthopedics: white, black and teal blue.

Phil looked down at his ratty wingtips. Could it be this was

413

the setup to a joke? Probably...Anyway, he peeled off his shoe and set it on the wooden desk armrest. Then he waited like everyone else for the cymbal crash.

"Wonderful!" Lent said. "Now take out your paper and draw. Ahhhh...From any angle you wish."

Phil kept watching from the teacher to the class. Any second it had to come...the laugh at their expense. But Lent was doodling or else fading out while the pencils scratched away.

Phil's bare foot was getting cold. Maybe it wasn't a joke, he thought, is this what art classes really do? His shoe looked like a tenement doomed to the wrecking ball. If I draw it the way it is, all full of holes and breaking creases, it would never be considered art. So he started to make it the streamlined boot an astronaut would wear.

Fifteen minutes into that venture, Mr. Lent cleared his throat, "Ahhhh...That should be long enough. Now I'd like to turn your attention to the interpretation of the human form."

On cue, the door fell open and a man wearing a towel walked in. Even before he crossed the room and dropped his covering to sit on the stool, Phil was frozen with recognition. The old ladies exhaled a quiver too.

Knarr struck the classic nude pose of The Thinker statue.

THE RETURN OF THE ALBATROSS...

"I can't escape from it," Phil told Dilly. "I thought I could get out of the detective racket by opening the most opposite door, but no...It keeps after me."

"It's beyond reasoning," Dilly said. "We're stuck in it, you have to admit. The only reprieve is in solving it."

"I know. Maybe I can solve this if I'm lucky, if I don't get my brains smashed again."

"Either way it's bound to become an albatross around your neck."

Well, Phil thought, the world revolves on that predicament. He could have continued rebounding with Dilly for another hour, but what was the use? Thinking beyond it all, a knock on the door broke their state.

A muffled woman called, "Detective Ticks? Are you in there?"

He had an idea who it was before he opened the door, but he was wrong. Ms. Davenport stood there. She bowed her head as if to speak solemnly.

"I guess you better come in," Phil stepped aside. She passed him quickly and steered her way by the piles of objects towards a chair that seemed to be empty. "That's my assistant," Phil waved at the figure lounging against the warped venetian blinds.

"Dilly Diamond," he waved a salutation.

Nonplussed, she burst, "Detective Ticks, I need you to follow a clue for me. I discovered where the Martian Society relocated."

Phil shrugged, "What else can I do?" When caught in amber...

From a purse near the pleats of her blouse sails, she pulled a soft-as-cloth paper map. It folded around her hands. "This is where the family fortune is being drawn. As a contestant to the will, I'm not allowed to go there. I need you to make a visit and find out what's happening."

Phil was biting his finger nail.

"I've already bought a bus ticket for you," she continued.

415

"And I've made a hotel reservation."

"In that case we better relent," Dilly spoke up. "Assuming of course that you included me in the deal?"

"Every detective has a partner," Phil said.

Dilly explained, "It tends to weigh the odds of survival in his favor, if someone can look over his shoulder for danger, or follow a random shadow."

"Alright," Ms. Davenport agreed. "Both of you can go. Just find out what's happening and make it stop."

WAR AND PEACE IN HALF AN HOUR...

That morning six inches of snow crumpled over the sidewalk, parked cars, skeleton trees and all the building elbows and corners.

Phil and Dilly had no idea what the weather would be as they stepped out of Cynthia Villa into the arctic. They rushed to the bus station in their best pressed suits.

And even though the bus had been driving for a half hour they were still freezing. The heater gasped out a trace of warmth up the side of the window.

Phil reached into the overhead luggage rack and pulled down his suitcase. Wedding cake slices of snow fell onto his chest. His numb fingers fumbled with the icy latches until the top unwarped.

Dilly was curled up on his seat like a sparrow in its nest. Over the tweed sleeves he watched Phil worm into two more shirts. That was all he had packed, unless he was going to try putting on another pair of pants too. A strange wrinkled piece of paper resembling a treasure map caught Dilly's eye. "What's that parchment?"

Phil had stuck two frayed socks on his hands. "This?" He had a hard time passing it to Dilly. "It's a drawing I made in class."

Dilly unrolled it flat on his knees.

"My shoe," Phil explained.

"Remarkable."

Phil scoffed. "You can have it."

"Thank you." Dilly put it in one of his pockets.

Phil closed the suitcase and dropped it on the floor. For a while he looked at the snowy city and the clouds sewn to match. "Say, you got a book I could read?" he asked Dilly.

"I had Darwin's noble effort, but it was bad luck. I disposed of it in a duck moat."

"I'm going to look for something to read. A magazine at least, maybe there's a crossword puzzle on board."

The bus was finally starting to pick up speed on the freeway. There were hundreds of miles to go, states to travel through, the journey was supposed to last days. Phil, caught in the swell of bus motion, made his way down the aisle searching hopefully. It didn't look promising...Statue after statue filled the seats, then life! Phil stopped next to a man with an open briefcase.

There were shiny book covers stacked inside like a checkers board. The man noticed as the shadow fell over them. "Hiya!" he said in a radio announcer's familiar tone.

Phil could only point mutely in disbelief.

"Yep! This is my bread and butter." He threw out his hand, "Name's Jer Pettigrew. I sell books."

"It's a long ride," Phil edged into the monologue. "I was try-ing to find a book to read."

The salesman laughed, "Isn't that a riot? And here I am with a bag full of books!" He turned the briefcase towards Phil, "You're an intellectual man. You deserve a good book. I deliver these from coast to coast, so why not to you? I happen to have an ex-cellent selection with me today. Real page turners. Look here," he rattled them off, "*Catcher In The Rye, Death Of A Salesman, Moll Flanders, Gulliver's Travels, Paradise Lost, The Iliad*...Am I getting warm?"

Phil took out one of the stapled brochures to examine. "They're so small though. I remember this book being a lot longer."

This was cause for another windy laugh from the salesman. "That's a good one! Listen, these are like program notes. Ev-erything that happens in the actual book—action, characters, plot—chapter by chapter, it's all arranged in everyday language you can understand without all the unnecessary words in be-tween. See here," he held a book, "remember this one from school? Boring!!" He shook his head sadly, "It went on and on, remember! Well now you can read this version and get all the points and understand what's trying to be said. It's a modern day miracle!"

"I don't know…"

"Okay, okay," the salesman tarried, smiled, "Listen, we're on the same bus together right? Let's be like brothers. Here—" he offered a handful of books, "I like you. Take these and read them. I insist! If you like them, if you want to purchase any, wonderful! If not, consider me a library."

THE FIRST MISTAKE...

Pavement. If there's one thing that goes on forever in America, the ingredients are simple: soil, chemicals, lime, cement, bitumen, gravel and other mineral materials. It spans everywhere. The Roman aqueducts only moved water in the empire. U.S.A had fashioned them a whole new way.

"Las Vegas!" the bus driver said.

Morning was brown and an orange sun blistered on the horizon. The buildings, still beating with the neon bloodstream, stuck against the desert flat.

"All ashore who's going ashore!" The driver stopped the bus against a saddle-looking building, leathery paint peeling off the walls, a wicked slump bent in the roof.

"Phil," Dilly shook his sleeping form. "We're there."

A slick paper fountain hit the seat, the floor, into the aisle, as the book brochures poured from Phil. He and Dilly slid all over them getting to the door.

The driver stood on the cement curb smoking a cigarette, watching as they dragged themselves out. "You two be careful," he told them. "This ain't no Disneyland." His eyes followed them, across the pavement into the swinging door of the restaurant hugging the station.

"That's your first mistake!" he shook his head at them.

$500 OATMEAL...

A cup of coffee and a cup of tea sat between them on the cracked counter top. They were waiting for breakfast.

Phil carefully unfolded the Davenport map. "It's not that far, maybe we can hitch a ride out there." He yawned and reached for his coffee. "I'm just so tired though."

Dilly said, "Perhaps we could seek lodging before we begin. Establish a home base."

"That makes sense to me." Phil stretched out and his back cracked approvingly. "Those buses aren't made for sleeping."

"Oatmeal," the waitress announced, with her arm extended holding the bowl.

"That's mine," Phil said.

"So this must be yours," she decided. She set a loud plate of toast and sliced pears before Dilly. "Continental breakfast."

"Indeed ."

"This oatmeal's going to knock me out. I hope."

"It certainly appears capable." Dilly spooned a pear onto his toast. "However, I prefer a light yet energetic meal in the morning."

"Yeah, well I'm so hungry I could eat a horse," Phil dug into the thick porridge, "and it's shoes too."

Dilly almost spit out the dry board of toast.

Phil could have laughed if the oatmeal hadn't clogged him. "Awff!" he gasped and tossed back a gulp of coffee. The bitter hot battery acid taste funneled the mash down. He coughed hoarsely, "Oh no! This is awful."

As discreetly as possible, Dilly was releasing his mouthful into the folds of a napkin. He crumpled it into a ball and set it on the plate. About to suggest retreat, he was startled by the waitress who hurried up to them and robbed his words.

"Excuse me," she leaned close to Phil. "There's been a slight mistake in making your oatmeal."

"I'll say!" Phil clutched his stomach.

421

She started to dig through the murky contents in the bowl.

Dilly gasped, "What in the name of—?"

Oatmeal squished through her fingers. "I'm looking for something."

She tipped the bowl over and spread out the gluey mixture. Nothing disturbed its texture of rough sawdust-like glop. "Where is it?" She was near tears, then, "Don't tell me..." she looked fiercely at Phil, "Did you already eat some?"

"How else can you explain this man's bleak composure?" Dilly burst. "Of course he did! We've both been persecuted with the worst breakfast since the days of Golgotha."

She seized Phil by the shoulders. "Stick out your tongue!"

"Awhh..." he sickly answered.

Looking down in there she began to cry. "It's gone now!" With a tortured expression, she raised her eyes to the rotten ceiling tiles.

"What did I eat?" Phil croaked.

"My ring!" she sobbed. "A diamond this big! It's been in my family for longer than I remember." She covered her face in her apron and cried.

Phil tried to stand to comfort her, but he didn't have the strength. "Look," he said. But one word had taken its toll. He had to rest to continue.

"We'll simply have to compensate you," Dilly offered in a soothing gentlemanly tone. He slid out of the booth and opened his wallet. "There, there," he touched her shoulder. "Here, this ought to make amends."

She tugged the money out of his hand and quickly slipped away to the kitchen.

"We should leave, Phil." Dilly attempted to free him from the counter top.

Phil winced and slowly stood, "What happened?"

"Everything's commendable, my friend. We're leaving. We'll get you accommodation so you can rest. In the afternoon we'll investigate."

Phil had to lean heavily on Dilly's support as they left the restaurant. They stopped at the curb. Phil teetered for a second.

"By the way, how much funds are you in possession of?" Dilly asked him. He scanned the traffic for a cab.

"Me? You're holding all Davenport's cash. She gave us five hundred dollars travel expenses."

Dilly was silent. "But do you have anything in the way of petty cash?"

"Wait a minute," Phil became very alert, "How much money did you give the waitress?"

Dilly spoke hesitantly, "I estimated the cost of her family heirloom, a diamond ring set in gold, plus the irreplaceable sentimental value..."

"Don't tell me..."

"I had to, Phil!"

"No," he staggered away, "This can't be happening. We were going to play it safe from now on." He wasn't watching, only seeing in his mind's eye their impending doom.

"Phil!"

He wasn't watching where he walked, without knowing, straight into a stop sign pole and then the world obliged him by snapping out.

UNDERWATER...

Was it the ocean?

The sound of waves?

One after the other they rushed, crashed and simmered away into another one coming.

Phil was reviving. He was laying on damp cold. It must be the beach. Where am I? The question made him open his eyes.

Way past afternoon, with evening setting in, he was outside on the ground, staring up. Some darker beam rode across the sky. A bridge...I'm under a bridge, he realized. His fingers dug a little into the dirt. There were some rocks biting into his back. Dizzily, he sat up and looked down the embankment. A little creek gurgled below. Cars echoed loudly above, making that sound of waves. He could feel a pain across his face.

"Phil!" came a familiar voice. "You're awake!"

He saw a man near the water, carrying a bundle of sticks and newspaper scraps. Phil let himself recline to stop the pain. Just by listening he could feel the footsteps get closer through the spaces in the noise of the cars.

"Phil! I'm so glad you're awake! Are you alright? Can you talk?"

He cleared his throat to make a sound, to speak softly. "Are we back on the street?" he asked sorrowfully.

"No!" Dilly grabbed him. "This was the only place we could go where you could sleep. I'm going to make a fire to keep you warm. I found some money in your coat. Not much, but enough. I'm going to the casinos."

"I don't think that's a good idea. Remember the pool hall? Remember Virginia-Not-So-Slim?" He tried to sit up, but the ocean was too much; he was hit by a wave and back he went, underwater.

AN OLD ACQUAINTANCE...

Phil woke up cold, in the dark. The fire had turned into the little orange windows of distant towns. This time he sat up slowly and he was able to stand. He made his way out of the bridge shadows. The night sky was murky with the neon watercolor milk of the city.

Walking out of the gulley, he found himself standing on a road facing the not so far away strip of downtown lights. If he was lucky, maybe he could find Dilly.

Along the way, he passed others walking their way out, dismal characters who lost it all and couldn't speak. Phil hurried. It would take all his skill of premonition to follow Dilly's trail. The first place he came to, a roadhouse, he didn't even bother to look inside. There wasn't anything magical about it. Phil knew Dilly would be heading for those jewels glowing brightest.

A few more blocks though and he was starting to get confused. The sidewalk was crowded with strange people, music, the bristling calls of casino doormen. It was all starting to blur, like trying to follow one horse in a merry-go-round.

He edged out of the crowd to get some air on the curb. Phil had to admit, Dilly could be anywhere. It would take a miracle to reveal his destination.

Car brakes screeched in the street. The doors of a black limousine flapped open and a man blundered out, freed like a rabid dog. Phil could see who he was, but it took another second to make his legs run.

Knarr was ten feet from him when Phil spun and dove into the crowd. The panic gave him the

push to run the obstacle course and dash into the first hiding place he could find.

THE MAGIC THEATER...

A Shinto pagoda shaped ticket booth stood in the middle of a green carpet. The rope cords led Phil into it.

Inside, only a white candle burned. Taped to the window were two movie stills and a card with only a few words he could read:

The Lost Snow Berry Island of Dragon's Land.
Noena as the Magic Princess.

Phil looked over his shoulder at the aqua colored glass doors. It was entirely possible that Knarr could come raging through them. "It's the third time he's chased me into a place like this," Phil stalled. But not for long—he could hear the film in progress, so he followed the sound, past the booth, along a carpet path that rivered to a drawn curtain. Silk parted around him.

There was enough light from the front of the theater to show him that he was the only one in the audience. Phil quickly took a seat and reclined.

He rubbed his eyes. Mysterious...Was he watching a stage or a screen? With his heart still beating madly from the run, he couldn't be quite sure of his vision. He thought it was supposed to be a movie, but then again, it had such depth, with shadows and space.

This city, he reminded himself, is made of illusions. It doesn't matter if it's a stage show or magic projection, just watch the story. So he did...

It was like looking into a box filled with thick smoky weather. Clouds crumpled into the front rows, spiraled and vanished in the air above the chairs.

Phil stared into the hypnotic swirl wishing for something to happen. The way the moments went by he couldn't be sure what was happening. Were they ever so slightly becoming transparent, to reveal a life beyond? A detective has to know.

He stood and moved closer to the front. Down the aisle he could feel the vapor of the clouds. It stung his bare skin. He chose a dark worn chair in the middle of the front row that creaked as he sat.

INVISIBLE GUIDANCE...

"Phil!" Dilly crashed among the dry stalks of foxglove. He sunk in the dirt and smudge underneath the bridge. "Phil!" He couldn't see anything but blackness. "Are you here?" He had to become a blind man to feel the darkness. "Phil?"

The place where he left Phil sleeping was smooth. Dilly lit a match and held it out. Like a bright sparking moth, it fluttered long enough to show him the sand and the charred ruins of the fire. No other sign of his friend remained. The match burned out against his fingers.

Dilly touched the shirt pocket over his heart. It held a hundred thousand dollar check. He had to announce it as if Phil was there. Since he left the casino he'd been dying to tell his friend, "It was unbelievable, Phil. Someone must have known about our desperate odds. From another dimension, they must have slipped through to invisibly guide that serendipitous roulette ball."

His smile sighed, "I don't know where you went Phil, but we don't have to stay here anymore. Our fortuitous situation calls for a grand hotel. Here—" he felt in his coat pocket, "I'll leave you a note." He unfolded a sheet of paper and wrote. By now his eyes were accustomed to the gloom of the underworld.

"My esteemed colleague. Don't suffer your soul here. There is room for you at the Bird of Paradise Hotel. Tell them you're with Dilly Diamond." He posted the note in the dirt bound to a stick of kindling. "Until morning then," he bowed to the absence. Then he dug his cane back in the clay incline and slipped away.

A few minutes went by. The bridge let a wave or two rattle the concrete beams before a curious pair came out of the darkest shadows. Like fish investigating out from the coral reef, they approached the note, circled it, slumped over it in their rags. They stopped to listen to the creeping dawn. It was quiet, the coast was clear and they were safe to examine the letter. You could wait your whole life for something like that to come true. An angel had visited them.

"The Bird of Paradise Hotel..." one of them read.

And the other replied, "Why not?"

PHIL TICKS IN DREAMS...

"Find him!" shrieked the telephone in his ear. A loud click followed.

Knarr set the black plastic receiver back in its cradle. His brow twisted with thoughts. "Every time," he had told the boss, "I chase and he gets away..." He even had nightmares about it: all of his strength and power turned to sluggish goo when he tried to get Phil Ticks in dreams.

"I'll get him this time!" Knarr snarled at the dial tone. "This time I will get him. Losing is not an option." He returned to the crowd, plowed a vicious path into them, leaving the crippled in his wake.

NOENA...

Optical illusions turned into reality as the clouds swerved aside for the vision of a green island in the midst of winter seas. The title in the lobby had already told him where he would be, so it wasn't a surprise. Green hills with caves, dragons breathing fog, burnt land and snow flowers pushing out leaves.

The vision settled upon the tallest hill about. White covered over the slope like a blanket. The theater had become cold. Phil drew up his knees and wrapped his arms around. He could see his breath making signatures. The chairs next to him were blown over with snow. The white was as bright in his eyes as the crown of the Himalayas.

The wind blew the music.

It was pleasant. The cold was becoming a drowsy warm. Phil watched the slope form the colors of a hearth. I must be delirious, he thought. Snow banks were all around him. Minus degrees, he slipped in, out, into a different state.

Footsteps could be heard. A figure appeared at the peak, wearing loose flags of cloth that blew aside to reveal her oval face.

The snow was so deep on Phil that he barely remained.

"You're finally here," her words came to him. "I was beginning to wonder when we would meet face to face."

He couldn't begin to say anything in reply.

"I've been keeping my eyes on you. I've always been here." She gave him a few seconds, "When you go back out, you can know, you'll be safe." The wind and snow got thick again and she was gone.

All the light seemed to go with her. The clouds poured across the snow. Cast over, the mountain disappeared and a haze returned the vision to a dark empty stage with tattered curtains.

A GUMBALL IN ATLANTIS...

The city had turned the seaweed colors of Atlantis. Phil would be coming out of the Magic Theater soon, but first the doors of The Bird of Paradise hotel swung open and Dilly entered the day. The doorman was giving directions, Dilly had slipped out unnoticed.

He paused, undecided on which way to go. Like a magnet toy, he let himself be drawn by another hand, moved by chance and luck towards the withered columns of an abandoned building. A puzzle among all the flash and boast, it had crooked old letters nailed to its callused balcony. Strings of burnt out lights draped the frame, giving it the look of some cobwebbed antique. As still in time as it looked, at that moment a gumball came tumbling out the door to land on the sidewalk.

"Phil!" Dilly ran to him. There was a pile of white around him. The great detective was covered in snow. Most surprising though was the look of bliss on his face. Dilly was almost afraid to startle him. He wanted to tell Phil the amazing news (he had challenged the dragon-like casino and made off with the loot), but he knew he shouldn't break that spell.

FREE RIDE...

A taxi passed the majestic Bird of Paradise where vagabonds were being evicted in shoals back to the sidewalks. The golden sun was shining electricity now.

The desert started to open its hands when Phil blinked awake. "Where are we going?"

"We're following the Davenport directions, off into the sand."

"In a taxi?" Phil only knew their last destitution.

"Phil, I've been telling you all morning. We're rich now! We can see this mystery out to the end and retire like kings!"

"In a taxi?" Phil repeated.

"An extravagance, I'll admit. But it just appeared as we were standing there and I thought, why not?" Dilly chuckled.

Phil was on edge though. Something crackled uneasily. More than the sight of cactus and barren hills, skull shaped rocks, he felt an ominous presence.

"Chalk one up for Watson," Dilly gloated, still oblivious.

The taxi hurtled along. The highway was theirs alone except for the occasional truck slashing past.

Suddenly Phil gasped for breath. What he had been so afraid of flew at him like a bat from the driver's rear view mirror. Those eyes looking back at him! Phil's first reaction was to grab the door handle.

"Don't do anything stupid," Knarr warned. He held up a pistol. "The boss don't want me to use this." It clicked. "But I might have an accident."

Dilly stared at Phil.

"You know that fortune you were talking about?" Phil asked him.

Dilly was silent.

The taxi sidled at a hostile rate through the growing desert.

"Don't give him a cent," Phil said.

THE COWBOY GRAVE...

For a half hour or more, the taxi rattled them deeper into the desert. Phil kept picturing the classic cowboy grave, a mound of gray dirt with a wooden cross, nobody knows. Distant bones of mountains stuck up off the plain, all he could see over the plow of the bulldozed trench they were driving in.

The taxi doors were locked, they couldn't escape. There was a gun in the front seat, and fifty miles per hour outside. The detectives in the movies would take a situation like this and turn it into a suspenseful fight with the driver. The taxi would swerve from lane to lane, ever closer to the plunge off the cliff, with Phil Ticks vs. Knarr battling to the end. What a show that would be! But Phil and Dilly knew there was nothing they could do but sit in the back seat and wait.

"Perhaps we can jump him when the cab stops," Dilly whispered.

"Don't even think it," Knarr replied. His voice dropped each word like railroad spikes.

Phil wondered if there were buzzards out there, or was that only in the Westerns? If they were lucky enough to survive the ride, they'd have a long walk in the heat waves over the dunes. What were the chances?

Dilly pulled Phil's sleeve and pointed at the apparition forming beyond the yellow hood of the car. They could see masts and looping metal structures, pylons and minarets.

As the car neared, the sight became clearer. The road trench was running like a dry river right for it.

"It looks like an amusement park," Dilly burst.

"Oh yeah..." Knarr answered. "You could call it that." His cabbage sized fist waved to a man sitting on a bulldozer. The man saluted them with a rifle.

Things were beginning to look very strange to Phil Ticks: so much activity out in the desert, the carnival scaffolding looming ahead, the submerged road.

435

Knarr braked the car in front of a barricade, turning up billows of red dust. He said, "Stay in the car," as he got out and approached the chain link fence.

"Phil, what are we going to do?"

"I'll think of something," Phil promised. He watched the clouded figure of Knarr shake the padlock on the gate. The giant didn't seem to have the key. He gave up and crushed the lock in his hand.

"Look!" Phil was staring at the painted sign becoming visible on the gate. "The Martian Society For Higher Technology!" he read it and turned, "We found it!"

BIG DREAMS...

"Well, well, well..." It was Tony Toledo. "I'm so glad you could make it here," he waved his hand, "My base of operations." Machines grinded away in the background...Tall, seemingly abandoned remnants of the Saturn Circus lurked and gangled uncertainly on and off of the sand. They formed a rusty dangerous playground. "You brought a friend too. That was nice of you. I'll see what I can do to accommodate." He stopped to light a cigarette.

"Look here," Dilly cried, "I'd like an explanation! What's going on around here?"

"Oh, I'll show you," Tony blew a cloud of white smoke his way. "Don't you worry, I'll show you. Follow me."

Knarr moved behind them like an elephant.

"We got big dreams," Tony explained. "And we been dreaming for a long time now, waiting and passing the time for our dreams to come true." He led them into the ghost town rides. There was dried popcorn strewn like chaff.

The four of them stopped next to a stilted roller coaster. It slumped and creaked every which way.

"Let's take a little ride."

Phil cleared his throat, "Ummm...I'd rather not...To tell you the truth, these things tend to make me seasick."

Tony stared at him. "Are you refusing my hospitality?"

Phil sized up the dinosaur profile of the whirligig, the demented face of the ringmaster, what else could he do? The time wasn't yet ripe for them to escape. Maybe the rollercoaster would plummet only enough to shake the mad Tony out, so that Dilly and he would be free. "Let the games begin," was all he could think of to say, and he knew it was a cliché.

Knarr pulled the seatbelts tight over them in their metal shelled cars. Tony talked over their shoulders, "When we get to the top, you'll see what's going on."

Gears caught the track under them and the cars began to

move, slowly, then gaining speed. Sparks and scrapes. They went clicking up a steep climb like a biplane. The land turned flat as map.

Tony laughed. He kept laughing behind them while the cars staggered upwards. At the peak, they stopped. The whole assembly rocked. "What do you see, Mr. Detective?"

Phil was barely able to put his head over the edge. Fortunately, Dilly could see and say, "The desert appears to be scratched in a regular quilted pattern. Are those streets drawn on the sand?"

Tony laughed, "We use canals to get everything here. Doesn't that look like something you've seen before?"

Phil struggled to breathe in the thin air, to see against the dizzy effects of vertigo. Before he closed his eyes and sank back, he had seen the world all red and channeled. "It looks like Mars," he mumbled.

"Bingo!" Tony applauded. "I thought you'd never guess! This is the start of Mars on Earth."

"Why?" Phil ran his sleeve over his sweaty face.

"Because it's time to leave." Tony pointed his cigarette at the sky. "It's time to switch planets."

"What?"

"Earth is dying. We're going to reseed Mars. All we needed was the right person to scatter on Mars to start the chain reaction. Our scientists have it all figured out…Superior DNA and all. They made quite a search for the right guy. Now he's been found." Tony waved at the hulking blob of Knarr waiting for them on the ground. "Take us down!"

A switch on the tracks clicked and like a banshee they plummeted back to Earth.

FLIGHT TO MARS...

Phil had lost control of his body. He slumped in the metal car with his mind skipping on nothing.

"He looks weak," Knarr said.

"Don't worry about that," Tony snapped, "Get him out. He's got a lot further to go."

Dilly pushed at the hands of the hired thug. "Where are you taking him?"

Knarr shoved him away and slung Phil over his shoulder.

Dilly landed in a crumple on the red dirt.

"Listen, Fancy Pants!" Tony growled. "There's nothing you can do, so stay out of our way!" He seized Dilly's fallen cane, "Unless you want to get busted in half!" With a sudden heave, Tony snapped the cane against his knee. And he shrieked, "Awwhhh!" He threw the undamaged cane at Dilly and limped after Knarr. "Let's get this over with!"

Phil could see the desert bounce with every step. There was Dilly marooned in the wake. It was so tiring he closed his eyes.

Tony Toledo hobbled like a pirate on a wooden leg trying to keep up with Knarr and their captive.

They shuffled and limped the rest of the way to the Flight To Mars ride. The front of the building bobbed with monster faces. A silver finned rocket ship sat on a rail that ramped into the shut doors.

"Knarr!" Tony yelled. "My knee's busted! Help me."

Holding an arm ready for him, Knarr scooped Tony up too and they continued.

"Warm up the engine!" Tony commanded the figures slouching around the rocket ride.

The motor whir in the air seemed to jolt Phil. Upside down, crunched over like a wet newspaper, he could see

439

the footsteps of Knarr crashing in the sand. From Knarr's other arm, Tony was held, cursing and dragging his foot in the dust.

The Flight To Mars was lit up with blinking stars. A chimney on the roof puffed out black smoke. Knarr stopped before the sight and released his boss.

Tony limped away from Knarr, grabbed one of the flagpoles and resumed authority. "Alright! Fasten him in the seat!"

Phil was dropped into the small confines of the riveted tube. He was just starting to return to life, enough to want to resist the belts strapping him in, when the canopy shut down, trapping him inside. Daylight came through a circle of glass. He could see the blue sky he was pointed at.

Muffled talk went with the screwdrivers, tightening the canopy.

"Wait a minute!" Phil spoke, "You're shooting me to Mars?!" He wrestled under the Houdini weight of chains and straps. "I'm not the one you want!" he yelled into the steel. "You can't send me to Mars! I'm afraid of heights!"

"Ready to go!" Knarr reported.

Tony leaned over to look into the porthole, "Fresh as a sardine!" He thumped the metal with his hand, "Alright! Let's send this rocket to Mars!"

YONDER...

A hundred feet away from the Flight To Mars, Tony huddled behind sand bags, with a pair of binoculars trained on the rocket.

It was sitting on the angled track that would run it through the building, going steeper and steeper out the other side where it would leave the Earth.

Tony wrapped thick black goggles over his eyes and smiled. "Pass me the detonator, Knarr."

Knarr gave him the dynamite plunger and put his hands back over his ears.

"Stop!" A blanket of dust was thrown off to reveal Dilly Diamond hurrying their way, waving his cane. "Cease fire!"

Tony laughed, pushed down, and sent the message through the wires. A bright sear of flame shot out the end of the rocket. It lurched forward.

Phil saw the passing images of frightening monsters and skeletons for a brief second, then blue spinning blue.

THERE GOES DILLY DIAMOND...

Tony pushed down Knarr's pointed gun. "Let him follow it," Tony laughed. "Where's he going to go? Mars?!" He laughed again. A black trail of hanging exhaust was slowly dissipating above them.

Across the desert, Dilly Diamond made his own dry wake of clouds as he scrambled afterwards. Stuck with cactus pins, he followed the little silver shooting star that left all that smoke.

THE MARTIAN...

A rainbow pool of oil spread leaking colors patterned around the crash site. The rocket was split open and the charred bent metal revealed Phil exposed in the middle.

He saw the galaxy displayed into the infinite. The midnight colored mountains grew against his right. His first Martian night...

He felt his shirt pocket breathe.

A small green lizard crawled out across the cloth. "Hello old friend," Phil said. So Mars had lizards too...He felt it go down his sleeve and then he lost sight of it as it flickered out of the rocket.

Phil tried to move, but he was still caught in tangle.

What do they want me to do? Just sit here on Mars until something happens?

Too bad the planet doesn't have crickets to keep me company...It must be up to me alone to start life on this world...

He found his voice and croaked, "What am I supposed to do?"

It hurt to talk.

All he could do was wait...

What else?

Time passed.

At last, a rumble grew out of the silence. Even the constellations seemed to shake, twirl and turn into mobiles at the approach.

There were lights.

It sounded like a door opened and footsteps crushed in the sand.

"Oh!" hushed the cry of woman. "You're still alive!" She wanted to reach inside but she was scared.

Phil wished he could talk.

She took in the fantastic sight of the rocket wrecked on their land. With sign language she pointed to herself, "My name is

Noena," she said, soft and slow as possible, "Are you a Martian?"

9:00 PM
January 2, 1997

JUPITER HILL

Originally, *Jupiter Hill* was to be the first part in a collection of three Bellingham novels titled, *Steeple & Gulley*. The book would comprise *Jupiter Hill, Jackson Ferocious*, and *Across the Street from the Holy Saint*. However, that trio never happened. *Jackson Ferocious* and *Across the Street from the Holy Saint* would appear in different Good Deed Rain editions many moons later.

In 1998, we moved back to the west coast from Ohio. I was thinking about those Ohio River valleys, where the factories were closed and the towns were drying up, an entire population thrown out of work. I was thinking about those people and I created Fled Magyar, a four-armed beehive worker made for the factory. He left Ohio with me and was the start of this book. By now we were living in Bellingham. I used to walk to work, from our little house on Grant Street, up Sehome Hill and through the arboretum forest. There was a view of the city from up there, perfectly framed between the fir and cedar. Once I had a vision of a big dark burning cloud drifting over the city. That was the start of this book that began on the hill. As I wrote, this apocalyptic scene came true in June when the Olympic gas pipeline exploded in Whatcom Creek, where my novel *Roosevelt* would later be set.

Contents

PART I

ANOTHER DAY

The sound of a loud splash and the two shadows lurked back down the dock into the darker waterfront.

Phil Ticks opened his eyes. He could see the stars overhead and the blue of the new day opening over the roofs and trees and mountain to the east. Pushing himself in the water, flapping his arms in the waves, he could breathe and laugh. Those two thugs didn't know anything about the natural laws! They dropped him off the end of the pier at low tide as if he would drown. He stopped laughing to peel a leaf of seaweed off his shoulder.

To get to shore, Phil had to swivel his cement blocked feet in slow portions towards the beach. He churned the water like a teapot for a while.

Someone from the dock above yelled down to him, "Okay Phil!" and turned off the film camera whirr. "That's good!"

A big fish went past him. It glided close under the surface, stirred up some waves while the tail cut out on the way away. Phil tried to hurry. The moonlight on the water showed the clouds of mud he swirled through.

ONTO JUPITER ROAD

The little film crew had gone on, lost along the docks looking for an indoor shot, breaking into some warehouse with nets hung on the wall and boxes surrounding. Phil was their stunt-man. He took the falls. The hero picked up where he landed. They said they would look for him later, when luck in the new reel was about to run out. For his trouble, Phil was left with a styrofoam cup, mostly empty of coffee and only half warm. He made the strangest sound as he walked, shuffling bricks where feet should be.

It was already dawn well begun. The robins had their song going, forklifts soaked through, the factory and the other morning sounds of the city too. Phil had to rest against a corner for a minute to wheeze. He touched the sweat on his forehead and rubbed the slip on his fingertips. He watched an alley full of cobblestones. No one else was around yet.

He got himself going again, moving his heavy encased shoes, thinking of the bed at home. This was a route he had travelled before. Turning out of the alley, he aimed himself for the tear in a chain link fence. Those weeds, some kind of phony gray wheat, brushed against his legs as he followed the path into the brush.

The path burred along past old wooden houses crooked behind blackberry crowds, backyard gardens and overgrowth. He saw a hen coop in one space under the arms of a madrona tree. The speckled chickens watched him climb the hill, not envying him. When the dirt path joined an alley again, he turned and continued. There were garbage cans piled beside worn garages and laurel scrubs, cardboard boxes warped by last night's brief rains. Phil could see the top of the hill. That's what he pulled for, the last climb of it that steeped onto Jupiter Road.

WAX

The room peaked its ceiling walls over him like a bending pair of cathedral hands. The window shade was made from a shirt of his, more than big enough to be a curtain. The light that came through it was a plaid movie, colored green and blue. He slept on the bed with his feet poking out the end of a knit blanket. He had managed to work them out of his shoes before he lay down. The socks kept some bits of cement knotted on the brown thread.

Someone somewhere outside was trying to start a car. The silences got longer and longer until they gave up. There was only one picture that clawed to the angled wall. It was a photocopy of a photograph from a hundred years ago, a woman at Coney Island, dancing on the pier.

Phil could have gone on sleeping wherever he was in his dreams if it wasn't for the surprising ring of the telephone coming to life on the floor.

He turned over and reached for it. He cleared his throat before he spoke into it. "Hello?"

A tin sort of laugh snaked over the telephone lines, followed by, "I bet you're still sleeping."

Phil recognized the words in his ear and cracked his eyes awake. "I was—"

"Never mind, pal. Listen Phil, I need you to come over right away."

Phil looked at the clock on the sloping table next to him. It tocked and the hands waved like an underwater creature.

"My other phone is ringing, Phil. Get out of bed and get over here. I need your expertise," he let the last word bend like wax before he hung up.

SUGAR

Phil sat on the edge of his bed. He was just getting ready to leave when a sound on the windowsill started to peck. He knew what it was. He rolled up the old shirt curtain to reveal the source.

A crow held onto the oak warp of the flower box outside.

"Good day," Phil smiled.

When a bird speaks our language, you must be close to hear. The crow whispered like water. "Their machines will not work. I came here to thank you."

Phil motioned to the sacks of sugar. Five of them were crumpled and mostly empty in the corner of the room. "The secret weapon against machines," he beamed. "Sugar in their gas tanks is like poison." The crow nodded. Then it bent its beak to lift something golden and shining off the ledge. "This treasure is for you," it sawed.

Phil stood and reached for it. "Oh..." he picked up the button and held it on his palm. "Thank you."

The words ran out, the bird returned to pantomime, held its shoulders in a hunched bow, then it flew away. Phil was left with the backyard view out the window. Morning glory climbed the telephone wire, poured over the fence, and the grass had grown so tall that it looked like a jungle below.

30% PHIL

Phil read the brass plate, "Rollo Van Sloat: Insurance and Deeds." Behind the closed door he could hear the monotonous tone on the cassette tape. It was the same self-hypnosis course that Rollo had been wearing out for months. Phil knocked when he heard the words pause and he opened the door.

"There you are!" Rollo boomed. He put his hands on a chair and pushed it across the floor towards Phil. "Take a seat. I'm about to ask you a favor."

Phil rested into the cushion.

"You're aware of the freeway construction..." Rollo began, as he sat on the corner of his desk. Now that the cassette player was off, he flipped open a cigarette case, seized one and took it out. A heavy black line had been penned around the middle of the cigarette. Pressing a button by the pen set on his desk made a sear of flame shoot from a brass fitting. "I don't need to remind you, everyone knows..." He lit the cigarette and sucked the smoke in.

"They're holding it up until after the vote," Phil said.

Rollo looked tired, "What vote?" He let the smoke go. "There's no vote."

"There are signs all over town. Initiative 20."

"Aww, that's just a joke! There's no vote, Phil! That's just a lot of paper waiting to fall in a slot. The reason they're waiting to

build more of the freeway is nothing will work. All their trucks and claws are sitting there frozen." His eyebrows raised as he drew in more smoke.

Phil edged nervously, "What do you want me to do?"

Rollo held up his hand and glanced at the cigarette, burning ever closer to the mark. "Here's the thing. They say it's because of that old lady's house.

They say she's a witch—that she put everything under a spell."

Phil couldn't help smiling in relief.

"I know it sounds crazy! Listen Phil, all I'm asking you to do is take a look. Maybe you can get her to sell. I've worked out a nice retirement package for her." He opened the desk and slid a packet of brochures across the shiny gray ceiling reflection.

"I can't do that, I'm not like you—"

"25%" Rollo interrupted. "I'll give you 25% of my commission if you do me this small favor."

"I don't know. Lately I've been working for someone else—"

"What kind of pay you getting?"

Phil was silent. The button was in his pocket. He wasn't going to explain.

"That's what I thought! I'm offering you 25% more than nothing!" He laughed at his joke until he looked at the cigarette. It had burned down to the mark. A hypnotized look came over him and he quickly stubbed it out. Then he returned to his laugh and repeated, "That's 25% more than nothing, Phil." His hand went for the cigarettes again. It crawled over the stack of brochures and pounced on the case, swiftly pulling out a filtered.

"Rollo, the thing is, I'm—"

"Alright then, 30% Phil." His words came through a puff of smoke. "And if you can get the old lady to move, I'll set you up in a sweet dream like this too." He tapped the brochures with his pinky ring. "Go see her Phil. I know you can do it."

FELIX'S FRY BREADS

A cool breeze, smelling of rain, came from the piled clouds. It felt good and Phil was glad he walked with that. He greeted the canoe and carved bear brushed around with ferns, he knew he was almost there. A Douglas fir hid the sight and then not.

Felix's truck was parked on the gravel road, with a stream of purple smoke coming out the chimney, threading over the green field of the school. Some students sat next to it on wooden benches. Phil hurried, mindful of the taste that was waiting.

"Hello Phil," said Felix. "I could see you on the way." The stoves sizzled. Felix passed a paper plate through the open window. A pair of hot fry breads, red jelly, butter and sweet syrup.

"Oh..." Phil sighed. He held the plate like a slate of pure gold.

Felix laughed at the way Phil dazed to a seat and became like the rest of his people, happy and away from all troubles for a while.

THE GOLD BUTTON

With another one of Felix's orders wrapped in paper and tucked in his coat, Phil followed the rest of the trees, to where the houses and backyards started over. In the border of that world again, Phil was crossing from the sumac and Oregon grape into a sort of gravel meadow.

A girl was walking not far ahead of him. At first, Phil thought she was planting seeds the way she was bending over to touch the ground every so often. She stopped when she heard him. She watched him curiously. Phil thought she could have been a time traveler the way she stared.

She nodded, "Have you seen something I lost?" She held her fingers into a round shape, "It's a button."

Phil blinked. "A crow gave me a gold one today." He showed her, "Here it is."

She sailed closer to him, then, "That's it!"

"Oh," he laughed. "What a coincidence. The crow must have wanted you to get it back." He turned his hand over and dropped it onto her palm.

She reached into the pocket of her sweater. What she took out was a puppet. It was all sewn together like a cloth balloon. Phil smiled. His own clothes looked so much like those of the doll. She placed the button where it had been before, and it sewed itself on, and stayed in place like magic.

THE THINGS IN A DREAM

They walked together the rest of the way, to where the gray highway cut into the neighborhood. Its coldness lay down like a wall, chopping the place in two. The houses on the other side of it seemed as far off as another map.

She brought Phil not quite to the end of construction, where she showed him a doorway. In the hedge of blackberry and dried copper ocean spray, a sort of tunnel was formed, made from scrapwood arches and tied leafy branches. "Follow me," she said.

They came out in a clearing beside the concrete, surrounded by the hiding bushes and scrub trees. Phil liked the funny house before him. It was made of discarded metal, wood and signs and election cardboards. A blue plastic tarp breathed and crackled on the sides.

"Come in," she said. "You should have some tea before you leave."

When he looked at her, she had grown older than the girl she had been in the field, or maybe it was only the shadows.

In the middle of her little home was a fire pit. A hot metal teapot sat on the stones. Some more puppets hung on the wall. The bright folded stage for their shows lay folded below. He never met her before, but seeing those puppets he remembered. One time, in a rainy cobblestone part of the city, he had seen them perform. Still, he wasn't sure he wasn't seeing the things in a dream.

A CARTER FAMILY RECORD

By now he could look in her eyes and not wonder if she was real. She was a woman and this was where she lived. He talked with her while she winded a Victrola and put on a Carter Family record. She brewed the tea, stirring the pot with roots, stems and flowers.

"You would never believe the things that got me here," he said. "You would think I'm from a fairy tale." He counted in air, "First, a crow asked me to stop the new road," he pointed in the direction of the stalled freeway. "So I did…And now, I'm supposed to ask a witch to let the road construction start again."

She sat beside him and offered him a clay bowl of tea. She smiled as he took it, smelled the steam and sighed. "What are you going to do?" she said.

He shook his head slowly. "When I think about all that happened, wouldn't it be perfect to end this way? With a peaceful stop to the construction…" He took a sip and felt the heat of the tea roll down into his heart.

ORANGE

When Phil left the orange light of her by the fire, he crawled up a plywood ladder onto the highway and travelled along the quiet structure of cement. It rode over the ground like an aqueduct, only the water wasn't running. It was strange to be on a road that doesn't work...only the wind and Phil's breathing. He looked deep into the way it had come, disappearing in perspective to a dot in the south. Turning around he faced the broken yellow machinery at the road's end. Beyond he could see the gables of houses and the tall redwood spire that he saved.

His feet made a clomping sound echoing toward the picture of it. When he had been here before with sugar, it had been in the nighttime. Now the tea must have been working warm potion in him—he never felt the world this way. He didn't stop at any of the wheels or caterpillar tracks. He walked to the very rim where the concrete and metal rods of the road broke off.

A drop from this height and Phil would fall into a backyard. Was this the source of the spell? Phil smiled. And all of their worries? Below him, Phil counted a few apple trees left over from the days of an orchard...a willow and rose bushes gently cared for by the old woman who moved in the shadows below.

He thought it funny and not surprising when he realized she was wearing the same green flowered dress and black sweater as the girl he first met, and the woman he had tea with. The three of them could have been the same person growing older in the space of a day.

There was nothing wrong with the way things were, he decided. He watched the old woman for a while as she ambled along. When the darkness started to fall, she lit orange candles one by one along the pickets and bramble bent fence.

SOME OTHER WAY

"So..." Rollo groaned. He extinguished another half cigarette sorrowfully. The blue ashtray was filled with them, each stopped and wrinkled at exactly the midway point. He reached in a cellophane pack for another. "Let me get this straight..." He held the cigarette up and lit it, tasted the flavor of the smoke and let out the next sentence, "You went up there and watched the sunset?"

Phil started to say something.

"No! It's alright, I understand." Rollo closed his eyes and shook his head all full of smoke again.

"She's not a witch, Rollo."

Rollo let go a cloud. "Every one of those machines just stopped dead on their own?" He shook his head, "No..." His eyes narrowed in on the tiny orange trace of light burning away at the tobacco. "I don't know why I expected it to happen the easy way. I was hoping you could get her to see what we have to do. Witch or not, she can't stop the progress of the highway. She can't! Nobody can, there's too much money in it. Now some other way will have to be used." He made a whistling noise and blew on the leaf so it flared. Suddenly, he snapped his look away from the life of a cigarette. They burned up so fast. He hated to see it go. "I appreciate your trying though, Phil. I just wish we didn't have to go to plan B."

BENEATH THE FUTURE

That left Phil in a sad state, walking the street towards home. He blamed himself. I guess I should have told her, or tried to let her know, what fate and Rollo and the others have in store. He rolled it over in his mind for a few blocks more. Finally, he sat down on a bench. While time slowed, he watched the world in front of him. Sparrows, in their own world, popped around a rain cloud puddle.

After a while, he remembered the extra fry bread Felix gave him. Just that second of thought alone brightened him and he took it out and opened the wrapped paper on his lap. He ripped off a piece of the sweet and couldn't wait to eat. But something stopped him.

The fry bread had been wrapped in words. Peeling the fry bread off, the rest of the paper revealed more, with a diagram of a place he recognized. In the picture, the tribal sacred land bled out from the reservation onto Jupiter Hill, where the redwood, the house and the highway all came together in a crash. He looked closer. Underneath the road something was drawn, words were written. He read through the jam and syrup and couldn't believe his eyes. It said, Oil Bomb, with a blob of ink like a viper, uncoiling beneath the future of a thousand trucks and driving cars.

ALL THE TIME IN THE WORLD

Phil ran back and forth along the wall of blackberry, looking for the way in. The tunnel must have collapsed. The hedge tangled locked thorns like the closed pages of *Grimms' Fairy Tales*. A blue jay screamed in surprise and bounced on a vine. Phil wiped his forehead with his sleeve. Besides everything else being threatened, he thought of her first, with her little cooking fire for tea so close to the buried danger.

He climbed up on the highway and looked for any signs of her nearby...puppet strings, buttons, flowers or herbs or anything. He followed the course of pavement to its end, then like a cartoon galleon that sailed to the edge of a map, he tipped around and went back.

Sitting on the black wheel of a grader, he tried to sift what he knew. He took out the clue Felix had given him and unpeeled it open. In front of him, the redwood shadowed the quiet end of the road. He wondered what he could do with what he knew.

Like fireflies coming to life in the dark, the old woman was lighting candles below.

But he didn't have time to call out to her.

The cab door of the grader behind his back snapped open suddenly and Phil turned to see a couple of hardboiled characters get out. "What's that?" they asked him and kept coming.

"What? Nothing..." Phil crumpled the map and as they reached for it, he trapped it in his mouth and chewed.

The two stopped, a foot from him. They waited for him to finish. They didn't care. They had all the time in the world. One said, "You must have been hungry." So they laughed for a few seconds then they got serious again. "Okay, let's go."

"I—" Phil looked around him. The far old woman was small as a doll under the trees.

"Come on."

Phil croaked, "Where are you taking me?" A starfish of a hand dropped onto his shoulder and squeezed.

467

"You like seafood?" and they laughed again.

THE PERFECT SET

Arms tied behind his back, Phil sat in a chair with his feet bound together, waiting in an empty rusted bucket. The ocean stirred as it rolled and unrolled under the floorboards. The sound of a seagull cried beyond the dark rafters. Beside a spigot, his two assailants were arguing about the correct cement mixture. Phil smiled; it was the perfect set. He spied for the camera. They hadn't given him the script for this or any cues, he guessed he'd have to play it quiet and wait. So Phil listened to them.

"It's a cup of water to a cup of the mix!"

"No, you're wrong!"

Phil wondered if he should help them out with the portion. He still remembered from the last time they filmed.

"Let's just dump it in. Go get the bucket."

Footsteps scuffed across to Phil. The bucket was pulled from his feet. Phil was preparing himself for the stunt. Would he plunge through a trapdoor to the sea glittering between the piers? He held himself ready for anything.

One poured in water and the other dumped in a cloud from the cement bag. They coughed. They slopped the heavy bucket by the handle back to him.

Phil lifted his feet and dropped them in obediently.

"That's good! He's cooperating!"

The starfish crushed Phil's shoulder again.

"Soon as that stuff gets hard, you can help us one last time." The tough guy paused like a vaudeville actor, "By sinking like a rock!" They laughed. Then they all got serious to watch the concrete set.

469

WAITING FOR THE CLIFFHANGER ENDING

Because Phil was waiting for the cliffhanger ending and the abrupt chance of luck that would save his life, it made sense to him and he was ready when it happened. He was abruptly lifted out of the cement and chair and swung free in the air like an angel.

His feet struck out at them, but they were already running for the door. These actors weren't very professional, Phil thought, watching the way they bumbled and slipped trying to get out. Must be for laughs…The door slammed and he was left hovering for a moment more.

He kept expecting "Cut!" to ring out in the warehouse. Until then, he held himself still and levitated for what must be the credits waterfalling.

A gentle force settled him back onto his chair. Above him he saw the girl's arms wave like a puppeteer. Her dark long hair shined past her face. He watched her climb down some skeleton stairs in the back of the room. She had a suitcase in one hand.

"Is it alright to talk now?" he whispered. He was just so happy to see her again that he risked spoiling the shot to speak. When she smiled, he did too. He said, "I've been looking and looking for you."

"You," she said. She gave him the most beautiful look. "You're the one I've been trying to find." A dream of this would visit him from time to time.

"I was worried about you being in trouble," he said. "I have to get you away from that freeway. We have to get far away."

Her eyes looked up at the shadows in the dark eaves. She was up there with them. She didn't answer as she untied him from the chair. The closeness of her was like the tea all over again.

When he was free, she held the suitcase in front of him. "You have to take this away from here." She opened the copper hinges. Inside were five puppets, made of the branches and paper and cloth she sewed. She closed it and pressed the handle into his hand. "Follow me," she said.

He would never forget how she led him across the boards that became the moonlight outside. Phil carried her suitcase along and it flicked the tips of the rubble weeds as they hurried to the water's edge.

"Don't worry," she told him with another forever look. "Watch them for me," she patted the suitcase. She put a gold button on his coat and it sewed itself on. "By and by," she promised. In one motion she put the rowboat to sea.

The distance between them kept growing like a motor was pushing them apart. It was quiet though. The waves slid around the hull and left a swerve of turned over water and moonlight.

Phil shifted on the wooden plank of a seat. The land was becoming a black line, the boat was still running him further out, and he had no idea how to stop it.

MILES AWAY

Something flew over him close enough to wake him. He sat up from the bow, still holding the suitcase glued in his hand. The big gray wings of a blue heron paged the air, disappearing slowly from him across the water. The dawn hour was calm, only a peaceful return of waves, a pale yellow and silver light on the ocean leaves.

But a clot of the night caught in the corner of his eye. He turned to look over the water. A monstrous black cloud was torn from the ground, into the heights of the sky. It made the world look like a burning toy. The boat rocked as he shocked, almost fell out.

He was miles away, but he knew the curve of the green hill. Behind it, the broken line of mountains and the winter pyramid of the tallest one. Nothing was the same though. A war had occurred and a dragon had taken roost.

"How does this boat move?" He peered around under the plank seats. There were no oars or motors. Phil reached under the wooden edges for hidden switches or controls. He followed the boards to their point of joining in the bow. As he searched, his look came up and over to notice the shore before him.

ANIMALS AND SPIRITS

The trees walked away from the rocks on the beach, into the clouds. An eagle worn in the crown of one was watching him. More animals and spirits lived in there too. Weathered and gray and leaning from time, they grew on totem poles.

Phil stepped over the boat into the soft give of the beach stones. A heartbeat line of seaweed showed the high water mark. The suitcase swung in his grip. Crows laughed in the shadows on the bark. They dared him in deeper to the forest, past the heather and sage. He breathed the green air. Over his shoulder, the sight of where he had been was already hidden by the overhang of fir needles and a wraith of morning fog.

A whisper called his name from a branch.

"Hello," said Phil as he caught sight of the crow. He scratched his hair and rubbed his chin. He paused. "I don't know what's happened. I feel a little lost I think."

The crow made a clucking noise. "You're looking for somewhere people are?"

"Is there a town or a road? Once I get back, I hope things will be okay."

The crow bunched its black shoulders. "Follow me." It hopped off the twig, left it bouncing, and glided ten yards ahead. Landing on the moss, it waited for Phil to pursue.

DREAM IN BETWEEN

Rain chattered down the waterspouts to drains, ran along the walls and windows, off the roofs. In the shelter of a gateway, Phil watched until the clouds were pushed off by the wind. The rays of sun returned, shining on even the smallest things like the drops caught in webs, or the bent tips of leaves.

Phil shook the rain off his hands. He set the suitcase flat on the ledge and opened the copper latches. The puppets were fitted in protecting the Victrola. There was a soft pocket for the records sewn across the inside lid.

Phil took out a yellow ball of string and he pulled it tight across the gate arch and tied the ends. Making a sort of a laundry line, he pulled off his coat and draped it over. It hung in the sunshine like a curtain from a lost circus ring. He smiled. He had the puppets, he knew their show, all he needed was a calliope now.

The Victrola had a silver shepherd crook to turn and windup the simple works.

Phil chose a thick wax record made in Hungary and set it under the bird-necked needle arm. It spun quickly. There wasn't much time to it, but there was enough for a song, a dream in between the beginning and end, to make a story for the puppets brought to life.

PART II

ALL THAT ONCE FANFARED

Fled Magyar left it behind him. The little house set in the hillside belonged to the ghosts. The other spirits watched from chimneys, tilted, piled up and down the steepness in the early morning. Starlings crackled the spidery tree above the sidewalk. Fled Magyar got into his white car. It pointed down the hill toward the factory's falling apart.

The engine started, rattled, the ropes lashed over it hummed like the strings of a musical instrument. He folded all his arms around the wheel, stepped on the brake. Turning around to look, the red lights gave him his last sight of the narrow street built on a slant.

He drove along Main Street of the town he lost, the shut-down stores, boarded windows, bars and the metal stairways never used anymore—all that once fanfared into a factory that no longer smoked and warmed and gave the town its life. Fled watched it for the last time. Someone in a long coat sort of shuffled along, and there was that poor crazy in the lawn-chair asking for names. Fled Magyar knew he was leaving ghosts, that he could have stayed on and been one too…It wasn't easy to drive to the gate and get out.

WORK

Ever since then, Fled's car had been rusting under blackberries, a blanket of them that just grew and grew as time went by. He lived in a house on another hill. On foggy days the ocean would ride up the air and fill up the beehive he rented. The window pane shook with the work going on in the backyard field.

It woke Fled up. He stared out the glass to watch that miniature factory the landlord had leased. Fled knew all about factory work—and not this kind that had been shrunk for the turns and gears of an automated box no bigger than one of the cars he used to make—where he was born, everyone had been a part of the factory. A generation had been created for it. He was part of that design. But who would have thought it would end and all those workers would be cast to the wind?

He watched the machine's progress. Green smoke charred out the factory stacks and vents as it tracked along. It cleared a path through the brambles and tall hay. For a couple days it had been chewing its way from the house, getting closer to the edge of Potter's Field. Fled took a ripening apple off the sill.

After eating it, a little sweet energy to start the day, he turned from the window and picked up the big basket full of fruit that was at his feet. He carried it over to the open door and put it in the wagon. Everything fit perfectly in it. He had made it out of wood scraps and the wheels from a grocery cart. It was painted like Noah's ark. He went back for his instruments, taking in his hands a clarinet, violin and celeste, before he closed the door and started off for work.

477

A SEA MONSTER

The old part of town clacked under the wheels. Cobblestones stuck out of the concrete street like rocks in a gray river. "Apples!" Fled called. "Plums, pears and blackberries!" Some bells on the sides of the cart made him sound like a gypsy caravan pushing by. Mostly the kids would look out from curtains at him. A dog or two would bark.

He looked up at the lines of clothes stringed in the air between the buildings. "Apples!" Just the end of the violin appeared from the black coat as he played a song and pushed the wagon along. It rocked into a puddle and he dropped a note as he heaved it free. The celeste and clarinet swung over his shoulder waiting their turn to play.

When he got to the fountain, he stopped and leaned the wooden corners up against the rocks. He sat down. Sooner or later some people would come down to see him. Against his back the water from a sea monster sculpture rained. There was a plaque with the names of those lost to the sea. Under the flows of his cloak, Fled set the three instruments in his arms and started to play for them.

FEATURING CHAIRS

The Hong Kong Cabin had the cheapest caffeine in town and featured chairs outside on the sidewalk if you were too tired to walk anymore. Fled's cart saddled up against one of the tables while he sipped and warmed two of his hands with a cup. He didn't need to think about anything. His eyes drifted over the mural painted on a wall across the street.

"Hey!" said a voice in a brown suit next to him. "How would you like to work for me?" The man scraped his chair closer. "Name's Rollo," he nodded and lit a cigarette.

Fled was quiet.

"Alright..." Rollo let go some smoke, "Say I buy that load of whatnot you're trucking around," he flipped out a hundred dollar bill, "and I ask you a favor in return?" He set the crisp money on the tabletop. "Suppose I do that?" He laughed. "All I need you to do is follow someone for me. Simple."

Fled peeled the money off a circle of water, held it across his palm like a calm light bird that startled, curled its wings over, and hid itself in his pocket.

THE OCTOBER BEES

So Fled Magyar waited and waited. When he was tired of sitting there on the curb with the ferns and chestnut tree, Fled took out the clarinet. Maybe that person Rollo described would never walk by and maybe it didn't matter. He had a hundred dollars and he smiled into the clarinet. Still, he kept it quiet, as if a sensitive cartoon caterpillar was tapping along the moss.

Before he appeared, Fled heard the dried coppery score of footsteps and knew it was him. Fled watched through the barrage of green and yellow leaves, and crunched onto his knees in the grass to make sure he wasn't seen as his objective passed. The man looked harmless enough. He really could have gone on with his world, undisturbed. But Rollo must have known somehow that Fled would keep his word.

Fled followed about a block behind him as they climbed the hill. The houses went by, not much was happening. A cow lowed, tied next to an old car without wheels. The point at which Fled lost him was a veil and really no fault of his own. A corner turned next to the remains of a redwood garage in the vines and then a thick island of blackberry land began where his quarry simply vanished. Fled felt like one of those October bees you see holding onto the cold cement when summer is really gone and winter is crashing down.

BLACKBERRY OIL

Fled Magyar waited. After picking cold blackberries for a while, he turned around and left the alley. The man he was following was gone.

Fled preferred to walk in the street beside the curb, sometimes you could find pennies in the gutter. A tree dropped a couple of yellow leaves for him. They looked like gold on the wet paving. The houses sat up on green lawns watching him. It was still early. At the height of the roofs, there was a ghostly fog looking for trees to sleep in.

Ahead, he could hear someone working on their car. He wandered across the street looking to help. Cars were something Fled knew about.

"I'm not going to get oil on my shirt!" a man yelled.

A woman's voice murmured back from the porch.

"I still have time! I'm just changing the tire!"

Stopping by the car, Fled dropped down to give a hand. With his four arms, he lifted the car so the old wheel tipped and rolled off onto the dirt.

The fellow stared like a photograph.

Fled took the new tire in one hand and tapped it onto the axle. The heavy car settled back, crunching gravel and popped chestnuts beneath. Nimble as the shoemaker in a story from the Black Forest, Fled tightened the wheel on. With his speed and ability, he could have been a match for that factory in his backyard. He patted the car hood then he tucked arms under his coat again, done.

The fellow was still speechless.

Fled stared at the house when the woman spoke.

"See!" she pointed the flowered sleeve of her yellow bathrobe. Blackberries had left leopard spots on Fled's coat.

"He's got oil all over him!"

THE SAINT OF SLOW MOTION

Fled was remembering the factory town. The music that came from that memory reeled around the fountain in a sad sort of smoke. But when he opened his eyes, he was surprised to see that a statue had been moved to life.

It had the familiar appearance of a saint, with a beard and long heavy robe. A while before, it was standing on the other side of the water—now it paled beside Fled like a white spirit waiting for the violin again.

Fled's shoulders dropped and his arms sawed and at paint by numbers speed, the saint of slow motion creaked. The progress was so slow that nobody would know if they didn't take the time to stop there and watch him go...A clockwork part of the world where everything moves in small degrees.

FROM TIME TO TIME

Fled wondered all the way back to his house, where on Earth had he seen the statue before? It could have been from some garden, or churchyard he used to glance at from time to time? It wasn't until he passed the old farmland fence of his backyard that he realized…

The miniature factory hadn't stopped at the end of the property. It had eaten the stone wall and was still riverboating, crunching its path through the cemetery, leaving tumbled stones and chalky flattened weeds and sod. That's where Fled had seen the saint! It was from that quiet, overgrowing green of Potter's Field. Like any other lost soul, it had been disturbed, the way a kite is drawn into the wind.

Fled listened to the distant noise speak down the hill to him. He opened the squeaking gate just enough and padded over the tall grass towards it.

THE HUM

A wind that couldn't be heard brushed the leaves, grass and even the dried flower bones stuck in jars. The ground in the cemetery shook from the hum of the factory. Apples were dropping off branches. Some rolled on the flat shiny roof between linnet bolts. The drills and pulleys inside mined for something as the heavy machinery pushed over graves.

Fled kept to the distance of the wounded fence. He could imagine souls being captured, pumped out like oil. But there was still the ghostly power in some to come back to this world and send for help. Like the statue he met, with only his pedestal left in the ruins. Fled knew the feeling: a factory forced him to run.

He turned from the sight. He picked up an apple. It was starting to rain and nothing it seemed was able to stop these new factories for now, only escape.

GREEN WINGS

The kitchen was set in the basement like the damp hull of a steamship. A small window cut above the sink looked out at sidewalk level. Fled poured water into a pan and set it to boil on the orange coils of the stove. Outside, the rain was trapping on the grass and mud. The water made a crack- ling log fire sound. Soon enough it was matched by the boiling in the pan. Fled put a handful of berries, honeycomb and plum paste in. He lowered the temperature, turning the dial and covered it with a lid.

When Fled turned around, he jumped.

Rollo Van Sloat was leaned back in a chair. He took his head- phones off and set them on his lap so the recorded voice could be heard faintly buzzing. "I'm a little disappointed…" Rollo said. "When I give someone a job, I like to get my money's worth."

Fled froze at the stove, with his back close to the bubbling.

"I've prepared an evaluation." Rollo started to take something out of his coat, but Fled stopped him before it appeared.

Fled dropped the hundred dollar bill on the table. It crum- pled like the wings of a green bat. "I don't need this. It comes and goes. It's okay," he said peacefully. "I still have music and the good things that keep me alive."

Fled turned from Rollo to pay attention to cooking, stirring the taste around, and when he was done, he wasn't surprised to discover that Rollo was gone.

EVERY CANDLE JUMPED

It was evening time and Fled had arranged along the kitchen counters a double row of jam jars, each filled and cooling. He had candles lit on the table where he sat, half asleep, in the orange and dark. Shadows and the sound of the rain down the drainpipe, trickling by the window in a creek, was a quiet record crackling from another room.

Footsteps chuffed into the wooden stairs behind the kitchen door and the familiar shuffle turned into the landlord. Every candle jumped as he entered. "Fled!"

He strolled into the room, laughing to himself, picked up a jar of jam, rolled it between his palms. "Still working for pennies, huh Fled?" He clinked it against the others. He came closer so the tiny flames of light glazed on his face. He chuckled, "That factory out there is going to make me a millionaire." He tapped his finger on the table whorl. "Oil…" His finger scratched at the spot. "The factory knows where there's oil and it's going to find it for me." Beaming like a pumpkin, he laughed half in a whisper, "On Jupiter Hill.

THE LAST PART OF HERE

When the pictures came off the wall, they left corners of taped paper on the blue paint. Fled put them in the suitcase on top of the clothes, closed it, and tied its sides together with yellow rope. That was the last part of here he put in the cart.

Night blew around him. The leaves next to the house rattled. "The sheik of Jupiter Hill," he said. He looked from the house to the rubbled wake the factory had left behind. Moonlight revealed it like a scar. He shook his head, "Goodbye," to wherever it went.

The cart shook over the stones. The bell jars and the wood sides rubbed like the seams of a strange animal. He would have played some music but he needed to push the cart against the wind with all four arms.

November 7, 1999

WHITE POND

Phil Ticks returns to the detective racket. I had been reading Stephen King and my memories of Maine propelled this book along. There had to be snow, there had to be The Mammoth Mart (long since gone) and it had to be scary. Just look what was happening to America when I wrote this.

I also had in mind that old black and white television program, *The Fugitive*. Aaron and I were devoted fans of David Jannsen's struggle to survive. I even borrowed the format of the QM Production, with a dramatic intro followed by Acts. (The traditional epilogue is missing, but when you're writing about zombies, something has to get eaten).

"So, this is going to be one of those escaped zombies on the run type stories?"

"No, no. Not at all. We know exactly where he went."

"Where?"

"Hoboken."

For a detective, Phil Ticks was on shaky ground from the beginning. None of this made any sense yet. He took a deep breath then stared at the guard's beady set of eyes. "Okay… Let me get this straight…You let a maximum security inmate escape to Hoboken?"

"Oh, we didn't let him. He was bought and paid for. Aww, what's that face for?" the guard shook his head in mock sympathy. "Do you know how tough it is to run a place like this? Hey, if someone puts the dough upfront for a zombie, what are we going to do? This place can spare a few of them. It pays the bills." The guard filled his mouth with coffee from styrofoam. "Oh, come on," he hissed and continued sarcastically, "Do you really think we're here to rehabilitate them so they can contribute to society?"

"No, they're—"

"Zombies!" the guard spat. "We keep them here so they don't mess up the pretty outdoors. Nobody wants that. We all know what happens then."

"Since you've got things under control, I'm just wondering what you want me to do."

The guard downed some more bitter coffee then scratched under his right ear. "Listen…When things happen like this, it doesn't look good." He sat down in a plastic chair. All the items on his belt scratched the molded backing. "Here, pull up a chair. I'll tell you the reason you're here."

"Begeal!!"

The guard snapped to attention.

A wiry old man with two assistants entered the room. The old man creaked his way to the video console. He rested against the row of lit buttons and controls and told Phil, "I'm sorry I couldn't be here sooner. The Center demands a great deal of my time."

"I was just telling him about Hoboken," the guard hurried.

"I know that Begeal. Did you forget these walls have ears?" He chuckled then turned his attention to the detective. "What Mr. Begeal so routinely pointed out is true, Mr. Ticks. It's not uncommon for a prisoner to fetch release if it meets an acceptable price." The old man tottered and his assistants leaned him into a chair. "That's better," he said. "Join me, Mr. Ticks. There's no need to be that way. Have a seat, let me explain."

So Phil did, and so he heard.

"After the extinction alerts, we gathered what we could. We are the collectors of very rare creatures. Because of our efforts, as of today there are 517 zombies inside our walls." The old man wetted his lips and continued. "Do you remember the buffalos that roamed over America's plains and the passenger pigeons that packed the sky?" He chuckled wryly, "Well, of course you wouldn't, that was a long time ago, but it's all part of a pattern. Knowing history gives you an advantage over the simpletons. I saw the zombie war that way and because of the visionary work of the Center, I'm proud to say, if someone wants to know about zombies, the knowledge resides here."

"I appreciate everything you're saying," Phil said. "I like this place, really. If I was a zombie, what more could I ask for? But why do you need me?"

The old man looked genuinely sad. Phil watched his hand garble over his tie. "When we sell one of our specimens, it's with the greatest amount of caution…Honestly. Only this time, the buyer was unprepared. What happened in Hoboken rarely happens."

"So what happened?"

"That zombie ate everyone in the house!"

"And got away," Phil concluded.

"It's unusually clever, Mr. Ticks. That's why we're hiring you. This is a chance for you to match minds." He croaked, "I am prepared to hire you on the spot, provided you accept my condition."

"Which is?"

"If anything should go wrong, we don't know you."

Phil shrugged. "You still haven't told me what you want me to do."

"Kill it," the old man rasped.

Phil stared. "A strange request, coming from a man dedicated to sheltering zombies."

"If word of this gets out, it could be very damaging, dangerous, to the Center. We could be facing a full scale revolt here. I'll tell you plain, Mr. Ticks. It's a common misconception that zombies are unreasoning, shambling monsters. They're not. This one especially has me worried, this one is adapting very well to the outside world. It seems to be getting everything it wants on a silver platter." Then the old man held out his hand flat like a waiter carrying a tray. The man on his right placed an envelope on the old palm. "This should cover expenses, Mr. Ticks. The rest of your payment will be provided upon successful completion of extermination."

Calmly, Phil took the envelope. It seemed to be stuffed with money. He stopped a smile from forming.

"I must say," the old man gleamed, "I half envy you. The hunt is on."

ACT I

Riding east in a Greyhound bus, Phil had plenty of time to think. The little towns that sprung up out of the leafless forests were cold looking, gray, clung to by the patches of snow. He hadn't prepared very well for this trip, going into a winter a lot colder than the one out west. The money wasn't as much as he thought either. Once he paid off some IOUs, the rent on his apartment, and other sundry debts, it all added up. He had wanted to fly, but realized if he did, once he got to White Pond, he wouldn't have much money left. Also, Phil didn't know how long it would take to track the zombie down and take him out. He was cautious by nature and prone to worst case scenarios. So he bought a one-way bus ticket and the window was a movie screen that played for days.

After he took the money envelope, the old man told Phil they lost contact with the last detective they sent out, admitting he was probably dead.

"Thanks for telling me," Phil told him.

The old man burst into a rattling laugh. Phil knew he would never forget that sound.

He watched mountains, fields, water towers over towns, city train yards at night. And he thought about what he would do when he got to White Pond. He took a deep breath. For the hundredth time he was thinking about how he was going to kill the zombie. He wanted to be discreet. A gun was out. Just thinking about a gun, his foot shrank back under the chair rest, seeking cover. He still had the scar. When he was a boy, he'd put a hole in his foot with a .22. Ever since then, he couldn't carry a gun. If a client demanded he have one, Phil had a holster he would wear under his coat. Padded with newspaper, it assumed the shape of a gun. No, he hoped the opportunity would arise where he could dispose of the zombie without a gun.

There were plenty of other weapons to choose from, explosives, flammables, and wouldn't poison work? Probably…He looked out the window again.

All of America was becoming a rush of little towns and gray black cities and the blur in between filled by scratchy looking trees. Finally, one morning as the bus eased into the sight of the next nowhere town, he wondered groggily, "Where are we now?"

"White Pond," the driver cried.

All at once Phil was electrified. For days he waited for those words. He leaped up, almost bumping his head on the luggage rack, as he reached to take his bags down.

"I half envy you," the old man at the Center had cackled. Well, here I go, Phil thought. Let it begin.

Outside of the bus it was frigid. The cold went right through his lean coat and Hawaiian shirt. That shirt was his last clean shirt. He needed to find a laundromat. After breakfast though, his stomach reminded him.

The bus let him off in a parking lot in front of a wooden house that served as the town's bus station. The curtains were all drawn and a sign on the door said Closed. He turned to watch the bus leave to his left and he actually felt thankful for the belching exhaust. It was warm.

White Pond wasn't much. Walking on a crust of crunching ice, he carefully headed towards a diner planted on the corner and oh what a relief to get there.

The waitress showed Phil to a booth as he quickly ordered coffee. He tossed his bags down next to him, and in a minute his hands cupped about a porcelain mug full of hot black coffee. Once he was warmed, he got up and bought a newspaper from the stack at the register. *The White Pond Herald*. With a sigh, Phil sat back down and unfurled it.

He didn't have to read between the lines. There on the front page was the zombie. Not caught in the act, tearing into skin, the picture showed Mayor Ambrose Fleischer. "Mayor?" Phil mumbled in surprise. "Unbelievable…" And after a sip, he continued to read.

Newly elected Mayor Ambrose Fleischer vowed yesterday to put a stop to the recent attacks on local pets and livestock. The partially eaten remains of ten dogs, sixteen cats and one and a half dairy cows have been discovered this past week.

"Your breakfast," the waitress interrupted. She set down a heavy plate of ham and eggs, toast and potatoes.

"Ahh…" Phil sighed. "Delicious."

"You in town on business or pleasure?" she asked him.

"Oh…Business," Phil said. He grabbed his fork. "I'm starving." He grinned.

He ate it in a couple minutes. Dabbing at his mouth with a paper napkin, he remembered a chilling film he had seen. A water buffalo was trying to cross the Amazon in grainy black and white footage. In the same amount of time that Phil had consumed his Breakfast Special #7, unseen piranhas had turned the agonized cow into a skeleton. He didn't like that thought… He didn't like the way it had jumped into his head and he didn't like the way the waitress was staring at him either.

Phil took some money from the envelope in his coat pocket and gathered up his bags. Better get going.

Soon he was right back where he started, on a freezing street in a town he didn't know. He looked down the road both ways. He got the feeling this was it…White Pond was this one main street which probably fed a few dozen lanes before turning back into pinewoods.

Luckily, he didn't miss the neon sign of the motel. It was past the gas station, it wasn't far.

He hobbled on what felt like plastic shoes. He would have to get some warmer clothes once he was settled into a room. He'd been a fool not to bring winter clothing. He was never good at packing.

White Pond was written in white letters on the sign. *Motel* was written in blood red neon. He slipped on the doorstep, but clung to the handle and opened the door.

He knew it wasn't a good sign: the office was filled with dead animals, on the walls, on the counter, a bobcat by the brochures, a bear skin not far from his feet. But the bell had rung and it brought a pallid man from another room where a TV was playing. It sounded like a Western, plenty of shooting going on.

"You looking for a room?" the wraithlike man asked. He was so frail, he looked like you could pick him up and fly him like a paper airplane.

Phil asked, "You do taxidermy too?"

"Yes," the manager waved about him. "It pays the bills when business is slow."

Phil stared in horror at the claw protruding from the end of the man's long black sleeve where a hand should be.

"Oh!" A thin smile sketched itself across the manager's pale face. "This is from a wolverine. My latest project…" He set the claw onto the countertop. Below it were shelves stocked with dead loons and wood ducks.

Phil took a deep breath and asked, "Do you have any rooms available."

"Sure." The manager moved the paw and set out a coppery key.

While Phil fished out his envelope again, the manager asked, "You come here on the bus?"

"Yes. How'd you know?"

"I don't see no car out there." He took Phil's money and re-counted it. "What's your business? If I may ask."

"I'm a…salesman."

"Salesman? A traveling sales-man?"

"Yes." Phil thought quickly. "I sell toothbrushes."

"Hah!" The manager laughed like a creaking hinge. "You came all the way here by bus to sell toothbrushes? Why White Pond?"

"It's a test market," Phil said.

That laugh again. The manager pressed his weight on the glass counter so it squeaked and Phil feared it would snap into shards. "I don't know if you're aware, but we've been brushing our teeth in White Pond for years. I think we know what we're doing." He picked up the claw again, still wheezing.

Phil fired off a question before the manager left back to his television and formaldehyde, "I was reading about Mayor Fleischer in the paper. Do you know him?"

That stopped the manager dead in his tracks.

Phil continued, "How did he get to be mayor so fast? Didn't he just get here?"

Like some Medieval mechanical creature locked in a clock tower, the manager turned and shuffled back to the counter. He let out a steam of breath and said, "It all goes back to the night he showed up in town."

"Let me guess," Phil couldn't resist, "Was it dark and stormy?"

"Actually, it was. A car drove off the road into the river, about a half mile from here. The driver and his wife, nobody seen since…must have been swept downstream. But when the sheriff arrived on the scene, there was Ambrose down there waist deep in the rapids holding up the only survivor…A five year old boy. Sheriff told me that was the bravest man he ever saw, Ambrose jumped right into that cold raging water to save a child." The manager shook his head in awe. "That's how he became mayor, I guess. We all voted him in without knowing it."

"They haven't found the parents?"

"That was a terrible storm that night. They're probably washed deep into some bog somewhere. Maybe spring will uncover them."

"Weird," Phil said. "Interesting story though. Your mayor would be a fascinating person to meet while I'm here."

"You can see him today if you're not busy." He took the *Herald* off the stool beside him. "Hmmm, it's in here somewhere…" He flipped back and forth between the twenty or so pages. "Oh, here…Mayor Ambrose Fleischer will address an assembly at White Pond High School at 11 o'clock sharp." He folded the paper. "You should try to make it to that. Those poor kids—" He choked up.

For a few seconds, the office became darkened by the life lost out of all the animals that used to be.

"What?" Phil said. "What happened?"

"The mayor's talking to those poor kids."

"What do you mean?"

"They lost two freshmen."

"Really?"

"Oh yeah. White Pond's hit hard times. Mayor Ambrose arrived like a prayer."

Phil nodded. It made sense. It reminded him of the book *Dracula* that his mother made him read. That was her favorite book. Sure, he could understand how something so dark could sweep into a nowhere town like this and take over. There was a wooden clock on the wall near a gloomy dead deer. "How do I get to the high school?"

"From here it's easy." The manager pointed out the grimed window. "Just walk back of Mammoth Mart and go on through the cemetery. School's on the other side there."

"Cemetery?"

"It's okay. Folks pass over it every day. Don't worry," he grinned.

"Well, I'll—I'll just go to my room first. I still have time for a nap maybe."

"You do what you need to do, mister."

"You can call me Phil."

"Okay Phil." The manager put out a hand from the sleeve that held the wolverine. "You can call me Bill."

The hallway from there was only twenty feet, a couple rooms

on either side, then the door that matched his key number. Phil dropped all the bags and the folded *Herald* on the carpeted floor while he worked on unlocking it.

His room for the rest of his stay in White Pond opened without a push. Winter light filled it. Sleepy air drew him in. He tossed his armful of things beside his bed. He saw the door swing closed. He kicked off his shoes. He thought how wonderful it was to lay on a bed. Then he was asleep.

When he woke up, he jumped as if startled by science fiction electricity. The clock next to the bed read 10:34.

Phil threw off the cover. He still had time to see the assembly if he hurried. He hoped. He caught a glimpse of himself in the mirror and tried to avoid it. He left everything else where it was, bags on the floor, and took his coat off the door hook. He knew he was still wearing a foolish combination of clothing, Hawaiian shirt and trench coat, but what could he do? All the other clothes were dirty, kept in plastic bags until he went to a laundromat. Okay, that was another thing he had to do—go to a laundromat. The list went on and on…Never ending.

He thought about Ambrose Fleischer. That froze him. No, he jerked on his coat. He had to kill the zombie first, get it over with and get on with whatever was next.

Phil left the room, gaining confidence by steps. He walked through the dead looks of the office without raising the manager. Probably busy with his wolverine, Phil decided.

On the street, in the cold, Phil looked like someone drawn in a cartoon. He battered up his arms and hurried on towards the big sign with the elephant.

Mammoth Mart was where a crop of pine had fallen to let tar take over. It seemed an acre of cars must arrive every day.

Phil walked along the poured concrete pathway. He knew he should go in there to look for some warmer clothes. He chattered and wondered if he had time for that. But he went on past the simple white painted wall of Mammoth Mart.

The cars on this side were probably the employees', parked

near the gray doors on the back wall. Phil bet there was a time-clock to punch just inside. He remembered one of the first jobs he had. He was always rushing to get there before the hour started. Not anymore, now he could pick from the jobs that came his way.

Phil walked close along the file of surviving pines. If something crazy happened, if the mayor leaped out at him—Phil stopped himself—surely he could outrun a zombie. He didn't have far to go, he could already see where the trees took over at the end of the parking lot. That's where the cemetery must be, and then the school somewhere beyond that.

It was too cold though! That made up his mind. He had to go back and get warm clothes first.

Jogging, he returned to the huge building. Like a ship in the Arctic, it massed out of the shards of ice and patchy snow. By the time he got back around to the front sliding doors, he was shivering like a maniac.

Inside was an oasis though. How could they keep so much heat clamshelled? He grabbed on to a grocery buggy just so he could lean on something for support. But before Phil had gone ten more feet, he drifted over to Mammoth Mart's Express Deli. He bought a hotdog and a large cup of coffee. That got him going again.

Now he could shop. He pushed on down the aisle like a Spanish galleon. The sultry fabrics of women's lingerie floated, bright colored ABCs of baby clothes, and he turned to steer towards where he needed to be. Large square banners of plaid descended from the ceiling above the men's clothing section.

Phil parked his buggy next to the thick winter coats, seized a big brown one and threw it on board. He got some flannel shirts, some corduroys that must have been half an inch thick, socks, and finally a pair of black boots. He felt great about the piled loot.

When a teenager wearing the store uniform walked by, Phil asked her, "Excuse me. Is it okay if I change my clothes into

504

these before I pay?"

"Whatever," she said. "Tell the cashier."

So Phil veered for the dressing rooms. He took in everything except the coat. He knew it would fit. He could put that on in the entryway on the way out.

The changing room was cramped as a coffin, but he hurried to take off the old and put on new. What a relief. He grabbed up what he couldn't wear and hurried out the door.

Phil didn't notice him yet, but before Phil had gone another two aisles, the security guard caught up with him.

"Excuse me, sir."

"What?" Phil whirled around.

"What's that you're wearing, sir?"

Phil stared at the uniformed kid, young enough to be playing Frisbee, or running after fireflies.

"You're wearing unpaid for merchandise."

Phil said, "It's okay, I have all the tags. I wanted to dress warm before I go outside again. Look," he showed him the bunch of barcode cards. "I won't pull anything on you. It's cold out there."

"I think I better follow you anyway. There's rules you know."

"I know, I know. I'm sorry you feel that way. Follow me, you'll see."

With the security guard trailing him, Phil got to where everyone jockeyed for cashiers. Phil aimed for the lighted cube 4, but the security guard pulled his shoulder to number 6.

"Excuse me Deborah, this customer wants to pay for what he's got on."

Even though Deborah had seen face after face like a daisy chain, she smiled at Phil and said, "Okay."

Phil handed her the deck of price tags. "I couldn't resist wearing them."

"It's wicked cold," she agreed.

The price sprung up on the register and Phil patted his shirt pocket. The look on his face was what the guard had been waiting for.

"Yeah," the guard said, "That's what I thought."

"No," Phil told him, "My money's in my other shirt." He pawed into his old clothes, found his Hawaiian shirt and with considerable relief took out the thinned envelope. "Here you are."

Deborah got it all charged, rang the register bell and told him, "Stay warm."

"I will. Oh, could I put these old clothes in a bag?"

"Sure." She gave him a light blue plastic bag with a pink smiling elephant on it.

"See you later."

"I'm keeping my eye on you," the kid security guard barked after him.

Phil waved and left. The hissing doors threw the cold into him. It was even snowing a little bit, strayed white dots across the parking lot colors. It didn't matter now, Phil was zipped in a thick down coat and he swung the Mammoth Mart bag with a mitten hand.

At the end of the pavement, the fence buckled open to allow entrance to the cemetery. A holly branch scratched his parka as he ducked through. Some chickadees feeding on the fresh snow scattered at his approach. He must have looked like a monster, waving his thick arms, his breath coming out gray billows.

Cemeteries held no terrors for Phil. He'd seen his share of them. He had plenty of friends underground. Cemeteries were memory gardens, that's all.

He passed a tall stalk of red plastic flowers that rattled in a vase beside a headstone.

The snow was making rills on top of all the graves and dusting over the marble names planted flat on the grass.

Barely visible ahead through the trees, he saw some kids he guessed were skipping out from the high school. All the kids were dressed in black and hunched around in a circle like feeding crows. Were they cooking something? He thought he saw smoke. When they saw him, they all stood up quickly and watched. Their arms hung by their sides, their sleeves could have been filled with sand.

Phil passed a hundred feet from them. They didn't return his wave. They reminded him of animals tensed to go.

He found a path that wore out of the cemetery between a torn mesh fence. It dropped him onto the grounds of White Pond High School.

He saw five flat glassy cold buildings with an American flag towering in between. On the far end of the parking lot was a taller square building. He guessed that was the gym, where they would have an assembly most likely, where he'd catch his first glimpse of the zombie.

Phil tried to shake off thoughts of his own high school, but it was all too easy to feel those teenage fears and dramas all around him again.

The classroom windows showed no signs of students. Everyone had to be at the gym. Yes, just then he heard a muffled orchestrated roar of voices. What in God's name was that zombie telling them? Phil hurried the last few yards. Can zombies even speak intelligently, he wondered? He didn't think so, but maybe they didn't need to. On the bus journey, he read the 384 page zombie guidebook. There were details he hadn't known. They could cloud your mind, make you crazy with fear, you could see things that weren't there.

Getting to the big closed metal door, he paused a moment to listen. There was a sudden blast of applause and screaming cheers, then a brass band turned on like a blender full of tin. Phil opened the door and tried to press inside.

He pushed against a wall of people, students and teachers in motion. Over the shoulders, past their heads, he could see cheerleaders leaping, a lectern out on the glossy basketball court. For a second he saw a large man in a black suit with his right arm outstretched, reaching towards the crowded bleachers, before the surge shoved Phil back out the door.

The crowd shoved him from the door as more and more students steamed out like opening the hood of a racing car. Phil backed off to a cement flowerbox where he stopped. He watched the river of them all. If he hadn't gone to Mammoth Mart, he surely would have heard the zombie's pep talk. What an effect the creature had—every face coming out of there wore the same look.

Phil swung his pink and blue plastic bag conspicuously. He could stand there in the cold, or he could go. With a cloudy sigh, he chose the latter.

The classroom windows were filling up. Phil walked past them like a man at an aquarium, as he shuffled to the parking lot again. There was the forest that protected the cemetery. He stepped around the tear in the fence. Dark pines scratched out the sky. He didn't see those students who were there before.

He switched the bag to the other hand. He felt like shelving it amongst the crumble of a broken log and snow. He was tired of carrying it anyway. He thought of taking his old clothes out of it and laying them piece by piece on the cold ground. It would look like he turned invisible, or been eaten right out of them. Okay, he decided he didn't like that last thought…He switched the bag to the other hand.

Where was he? This wasn't the way he came earlier. Snow covered branches curtained around rocks in a clearing. He walked that direction so he could look at something catching his attention.

In the middle of a pond, standing out of it, was a guitar. It looked like a wooden statue.

That's when he got spooked. It started with a rusty metal creaking sound like a hundred old sewing machines prickling the bare branches overhead. On every inch of the trees popped an agitated starling screeching at him. When he took a step, they swooped.

He began to run around gravestones, slipped on someone's name in the snow. The birds followed, screeching obscenely, tracking him like a cloud. Phil broke through a skeleton stand of birches as they attacked him. At first it sounded like thousands of leaves, but as the birds fell, whirled in a thick storm around him, he was hit again and again.

With a scream, Phil bolted from the trees. He ran with his arms over his face. His leg struck an upright stone marker, spinning him. He kept on his feet and churned through the hailstorm of birds.

Then, when Phil toppled down a steep embankment out of the graveyard, the starlings were gone. If it wasn't for his steaming gasping breath, it would be stone quiet.

He lay with his back against the embankment, his legs stretched before him, feet on the edge of some back road. He thought he could see the blue rooftop of Mammoth Mart off to his left riding the pines. Phil let out a groan and held up his arms to look at his coat. The new fabric was slashed by beaks and claws. It looked like he fell in a piranha pool.

There was nothing in the sky now except the fitful snow. Still, he couldn't get up quite yet. He touched a scratch on his face and checked his fingertip for blood.

Off to his right began the slow approaching crackle of car tires on the icy road. He drew his knees up as a black Cadillac neared. The windows were tinted, he couldn't see the driver, but as it passed him Phil could easily see the man in the backseat. The window was rolled all the way down and there was no doubt about it. The zombie's hair stood icily on end, his eyes burned red like a poorly developed snapshot portrait and on his pale ghastly face his mouth was open wide. The car passed by, pulling a freezing wake.

Phil waited until the sound of it died, then he pushed himself upright, to go find the warmth of the White Pond Motel.

ACT II

Returning to his room, Phil threw the coat off onto the red carpet floor. A few of the scratches had gone through to his plaid shirt. He took that off too, went to the bathroom and examined his arms and torso. He roughed some soap on the small red lines and hoped that was good enough. Oh brother, he groaned at the bubbled soap on his gooseflesh dirty skin. He had been on a bus for a week, he could use a shower.

After that, he walked out into the room again in a cloud of steam, wrapped in a towel. He eyed the pink Mammoth Mart bag dropped on the floor. He regretted not buying more clothes, but he didn't want to be in White Pond much longer. He wanted to get the job over and done with.

Reluctantly, he pawed into the bag and took out his Hawaiian shirt again. His new pants were muddy from the fall, so he had to get back into his thin suit pants too. Well, he thought, the motel might have a washing machine he could use.

I saw him, he recalled with a jolt. Ambrose Fleischer.

Phil sat down on the edge of the bed. What a monster!

The motel did have a washer and dryer. Phil even bought a White Pond t-shirt when he got his quarters for the machines. In less than an hour, he had returned to his room. He carried the stack of clean clothes to the dresser under the drawn window shades. Opening the top drawer, he froze and dropped the clothes in terror.

The long narrow interior of the drawer was packed neatly with the dead body of a man. His arms and legs had been chopped to fit neatly on either side. And pinned to his blue shirt was a note that said, *Hiya Buddy.*

Phil backed off until he hit the bed, and fell onto the bristling red carpet. He swallowed against the rising feeling of being ill.

The feeling passed, but left a damp sweat on his face like oil.

Slowly, he used the bed to stand up. He steeled himself and approached the drawer.

511

It was empty. No, not empty, there was a black Bible pushed in the corner. That was it though. He remembered what the zombie guidebook on the bus warned. They can cloud your mind, make you crazy with fear, see things that aren't there.

That face in the drawer had been torn right from the portfolio the Center gave him for the job. It was the face of the last man they sent to do this job. Drawing the manila folder from the zippered pouch in his suitcase, Phil collapsed onto the bed. Propped against two pillows, he found the page. Jeff Triffid. Sure enough, those were the eyes. That was his predecessor, chopped up like kindling.

Phil closed the folder.

Ambrose Fleischer had corralled this town and would eat them all one by one. A black car driving the streets, the back window rolled all the way down to let the screaming winter wind funnel in.

"No!" Phil shouted. His voice bounced like a wrecking ball off the wallpaper. That cleared his head. I'll get him, Phil vowed. I just need to control my thinking. It's my mind he's after first.

His stomach rumbled reminding him that he missed lunch. A picture formed of the diner, home of the surly waitress. It was also home of food so good he had wolfed it like a zombie this morning. He put on his shredded jacket and left the room. There were things to do in this town. The town was waiting for him to get it done.

ACT III

The diner hadn't changed much since morning, there were still the four old men in the corner booth jawing it over, the same songs playing with tinny echo from the kitchen, the same waitress giving him the same look of disdain. Phil even sat in the same booth. The only thing missing was the newspaper, but he thought maybe he'd get one when his meal arrived. It was easy to decide on that, he wanted a bowl of soup and a grilled sandwich. He just had to wait for her to care.

After a long minute, she crossed the linoleum and stopped. "Back again?"

"Yeah, I got hungry again."

"Mmhmmm." She chewed on the sound like a bite she wanted to spit into a napkin.

"Could I get a bowl of tomato soup, some fries and a grilled chicken sandwich?"

She wrote it the way an officer would take down a crime scene report.

"Oh, and a coffee too, please."

That got stabbed onto the little notepad at the end.

"Thanks," Phil said to her turned and retreating pale yellow dress.

As long as the food's good, he didn't care. It didn't matter what she thought of him, he didn't care. Feelings didn't matter, he was just here for the food. He couldn't dwell on her. She and the Mammoth Mart security guard were probably related.

It wasn't long before the plates and bowls arrived. When she set the coffee down with a clack, it spilled black into the saucer.

Phil smiled, grabbed the ketchup from its place beside the salt and pepper and tipped the bottle. It poured red as blood onto the fries. He paused and stopped its flow. He didn't like the look of it.

But it got worse. As he stared at the red pool in the soup bowl, the face looking back wasn't his reflection.

Jeff Triffid was back.

Phil wasn't surprised though. "What happened to you?" he asked the bowl. "Tell me how to stop him."

"You can't stop him."

"Why? What went wrong?"

The face croaked, "Now it's your turn."

A big hand landed on the tabletop with a sharp bang. The chef bristled at Phil, "I want you out of here."

"What—?"

"Out!"

Phil stared back at the table frantically. It was splattered like a butcher's block, tomato soup and ketchup.

The cook grabbed Phil by the scruff of his cutup coat and he looked close and deep into Phil's shifting eyes. "What are you doing here anyway, mister?" He pulled Phil to the door and seethed, "I'm not the only one watching you!" Then he tossed Phil out the door.

Phil landed and slid almost comically on his new rubber soled boots, not falling, gliding for ten feet, away from the slammed door.

He was starting to feel unwanted in this town. He would have to act fast if he didn't want to end up run out of town, or thrown in the slammer. Maybe he would call the Center and ask for more money. If he could have foreseen this, he never would have taken this job. Zombies were supposed to be walking zucchini.

A snowball hit the back of his coat with a heavy splat. "What?!" He whirled.

Another snowball spun by his face. A boy was throwing them at Phil. He was down packing another one together.

"What's the matter with you, kid?" Phil guessed he must be in 4th or 5th grade. School must have let out.

The next snowball loped slowly over Phil's head.

This was ridiculous. Phil turned his back and walked away from the diner. He didn't care when a snowball narrowly missed him.

He spotted the library. That was where he would go for some answers.

As he crossed the street, three snowballs flew over him, another one scattered on the road.

Phil looked over his shoulder and saw five schoolboys. Their next hail of snow sailed all around him.

Phil hurried onto the sidewalk. More snow missed him. He reached the library as snow spattered the brick wall like birdshot. One snowball glanced off his leg.

Up the steps, Phil turned the cold brass handle and opened the door.

The White Pond Public Library probably hadn't changed in fifty years. There was a big wooden globe on top of the card catalog, stuffed chairs by the fireplace, bookshelves on every wall, a spiral stairway that corkscrewed to the balcony. A girl on a ladder was shelving a book. The librarian at a wooden hulled checkout desk in the center of the room helped an old man load books into his plastic bag.

515

The fireplace was calling Phil. There was a chair open. That's what he wanted to do, sit and get warm, try to come up with a plan.

When he stared at the fire long enough to feel thawed out, he got up. He had to see if any books could help him.

The teenage girl who was on the ladder a while ago was shelving books nearby. She reminded him of the high school students he saw in the cemetery woods. All her clothes were black. She noticed him before he got to her. She wore an unsurprised look.

"Excuse me," Phil started. Once he got close he was quieter, "Does the library have any books on zombies?"

She could have smiled. He couldn't quite tell, but one eyebrow had bent a little. "You have an interest in zombies?" she said.

They both jumped as the lights in the library dimmed, then brightened. From the intercom the librarian announced, "The library will be closing in ten minutes. Please bring any materials you wish to check out to the counter. Thank you."

Before she turned back to her cart, Phil said quickly, "There's something strange going on in this town."

"I'm done in ten minutes," she said. "If you want, we can meet at the Chinese restaurant. We can talk. I'm starving." Then she pushed the book cart down the row.

Phil crossed the library floor. He hoped he would be allowed into another restaurant. He wondered how fast the news about him was traveling.

It wasn't snowing outside, but it was bitter.

He looked down the street both ways. It wasn't much of an avenue. Old buildings made of bricks, cold windows above a lot of closed shops. To his left Phil did notice the green and red neon sign, a dragon, Chinese Takeout. He went down the library stairs. He remembered the school kids and kept an eye out for them.

Nothing happened to him on the sidewalk though. He made it to the restaurant and went inside.

A Chinese woman and her young son sat at a table. The boy was doing his homework, opened book, pencil in hand. They both looked at him. Four other tables stood behind them, from the ceiling hung paper lanterns. There was a green clock on the wall, set in a landscape photograph of water that seemed to move, some trick of electricity current. The woman stood, pressed down her black dress and nodded at him.

"Hi," Phil waved. "I'll be meeting someone here for dinner."

The woman nodded. "You can choose your table."

"Thanks." Not surprisingly, Phil took the table below the intriguing clock.

"Would you like some tea?"

"Yes please. That would be great." Phil rubbed his hands together. He picked at the white fluff coming out of his coat. What a shame. It had been brand new this morning.

The woman placed a copper kettle of tea next to the plastic flowers on his table, along with two delicate white cups.

"Thanks."

"Sure. The menu's posted on the wall. Just tell me when you're ready."

"We will."

She went back to the table with her son. The boy was leaning into writing something.

Phil poured a bit of the orange colored tea. The cup didn't hold much, he could have poured it into an egg, but it warmed his hands wrapped around.

While Phil was lost, looking at the rippling wave effect above him, the frosted door opened.

"Hello Karen," the woman said and, "Hi," the boy added.

"Hello, hello." The girl from the library spotted Phil and waved. "What's this?" she stopped beside the boy.

"Geography."

"Oh yeah, I remember studying geography." She patted his shoulder. "If you need to find where I am, I'll be sitting over there."

The boy laughed at her joke.

Phil poured tea for her, stood and sat down with her. "I guess we should introduce ourselves. My name's Phil."

"Karen." They shook hands, his warm from porcelain. "Did you order yet? The chow mein is great. That's what I always get. Lily already knows."

"Oh, I'm okay with just tea. I'm not really that hungry." To tell the truth, he didn't even like the thought of food.

"Well, I'm starved." She turned around in her chair.

Lily waved to her and went to the kitchen, followed by her son.

"This is a good place to talk," Karen said. "Nobody from town comes here." She held the tea close to her mouth. "You were asking about zombies? What I'd like to know is your reason for asking. If you don't mind."

"Fair enough. At this point, I don't mind being honest to someone about it. I've been sent here to find one and I have. Your mayor is a zombie."

The girl gave him a hard look.

"It's no secret is it? I mean, it's so obvious. You only have to *look* at the guy. Doesn't everyone know?"

She drew a deep breath. "They probably do. They should. Deep inside, they should know." She rubbed her hands together. Phil could hear the little clinking scratch of the silver rings worn on all her fingers. "Or maybe they're just fools." She took hold of her little china cup. "I knew it the moment I saw him."

"Well—what the hell?"

"He just…He kind of appeared at a time when…It happened so fast. There were all these weird disappearances of animals and mutilations. People were on edge, nobody knew what was going on except that something violent and terrible was loose. Then the storm hit when our last mayor drove into the river with his family. Everybody talks about Ambrose Fleischer being the hero of that tragedy."

Phil nodded, "The motel manager told me."

"But *nobody* ever found the bodies of the mayor and his wife. How strange, right? And there he is, Ambrose Fleischer, caught in the sheriff's flashlight with that little boy held up to his face…"

"You think he was going to eat him?"

"You can ask the boy yourself. His name is Saroyan Green. He's over at St. Benedict's hospital. Ughhh!" she rolled her eyes. "It's awful."

"I know. It is. But I'm here now. I'll be able to take care of that zombie."

"Really? You think you can stop him?"

"Listen. I've been doing this for a long time. Not just him. I can handle it. What he's trying to do to me right now is typical mind control, throw me into fear, make me drop into hopelessness, make me think, 'Oh there's nothing I can do to change this, I'm cowering under a cloud.' I'm not. I understand what's going on. You do too."

She swallowed a sip of tea and said, "He's very strong here. He's thinking for everyone and now that he's mayor he's making the rules for the town. He's taking control." She set her cup down, "Did you know that after tomorrow there won't be any more bus service to White Pond?"

"What?"

"Yes. So I wonder how long it will be before he cuts the telephone wires down. Or blocks off the roads, or fences everyone in. Then he's got his farm all prepared. I'm not taking any chances, Phil. I'm getting on the bus tomorrow and I'm gone."

Lily arrived with the chow mein. "Enjoy."

"Oh wow!" Karen brightened at once. "Thanks Lily." She sunk a fork in and brought it to her mouth.

"Well…" Phil took a look into his disappearing tea instead. He couldn't watch food being eaten. "I don't mean to sound like I'm underestimating him. If it was that easy for him to take over this town, who knows what he has planned next. The state? The whole country? We'd be right back in the zombie war again.

That's why I have to be stronger than him and stop him quick."

"What are—?" she stopped to finish the food she was chewing. "What are you going to use to stop him?"

"I can't say yet." Actually, he didn't know.

"There's a good store across the street. You might find what you need. There's pretty much everything in there."

"Thanks Karen. If I didn't meet you, I would have thought all of White Pond was a mean nightmare."

"You better catch that bus tomorrow."

"I'll try. We'll see how it goes"

"Can I save you a seat?"

"I'll try my best to be there at the station with you, but if you don't see me, don't think twice, get on." He finished his tea. "Anyway, I should get going before that store closes."

"Be careful, Phil."

"Thanks." That was it. That was the last time he would see her, she was gone. That's what it felt like.

He stopped next to Lily on the way out and gave her some money. "Thanks for the tea."

"You're welcome." Then she took something out of her pocket. "Here…" It was a fortune cookie, wrapped in clear plastic.

He thanked her, put it in his pocket and left into the dark.

Cars and trucks were passing on the street, the jobs had all let out. People were going home. On a cold night like this, he could have wished he was one of them. It was almost blinding to stare into the headlights. They seemed to cut into his eyes. He went to the crosswalk and waited for the signal. The snowing had become a light dry sand that brushed across his skin.

In a minute, he crossed the street. He hoped no maniac would gun the icy crosswalk to run him down, he hadn't made that many enemies yet he hoped. But what would happen when he killed their mayor? Would they be freed from their curse? Or would he have to run for his life to grab the last Greyhound ever out of town? Tomorrow knew—all the clocks were just counting down.

Phil saw the store Karen had told him about. Two big windows glowed yellow onto the sidewalk. *Fetchits*, the letters painted on the glass read. It really did look like he could get something there. Phil pushed on the door and let himself in.

He didn't know where to start. He stood confused in front of a manikin wearing hip-waders, holding a fly rod hooked to a stringed wooden puppet. The place was filled with shelves, barrels and bins and a wide stairway led to more upstairs.

"Can I help you find something?"

Phil waved awkwardly at the man behind the counter. "Uhh, not yet. I think I'll take a look around."

"Fine with me." The man went back to the chess game he was playing against a computer. Its robot arm shifted a piece precisely on the board. "You give a yell if you need help."

"Okay, I will."

Phil walked past the wall of toys. They wouldn't be of any use against a zombie, except in a surrealistic slapstick world.

There was a red motorcycle helmet. That could be useful. He went by an alcove of record albums and 45 singles. Eventually he had toured all of the downstairs to no avail, so he headed upstairs.

The steps creaked. What was he looking for anyway? A bazooka? What he needed was a gun—that's what they used in the war—he just couldn't do it though.

Fortunately, rising into sight at the top of the stairs was what he needed, in the arms of another manikin. This one was dressed in a sea diver suit with oxygen tanks and snorkel and mask, and balanced in its plastic hold was a deadly looking spear-gun. Attached comically to the spear end was a sign that read, *More This Way*.

Phil examined the terrible weapon. It was a gun, but it wasn't. It had a short metal stock, trigger guard, and a spear with coiled line. He reached for it. He was able to grasp it and lift it from the diver. Phil fought back a wave of bitter memory as his hand fit around the grip and his finger tensed over the trigger. It's not a gun, he commanded his head. He pictured Ambrose Fleischer standing in front of him. This is what I need to do it.

But it wasn't like he could just walk up to the zombie carrying this. Phil knew he couldn't hide it under his already battered coat either.

That's when that new problem was answered by the plaid, awkward looking object leaning nearby. It was a golf bag. There were a couple clubs periscoping out, their ends covered with what looked like mittens. It was perfect for disguising the arrow when he fit the spear-gun down inside.

He hurried over and tried it out and to his delight, the effect was better than dreamed. The stock of the weapon was hidden down in the tartan and the spear that stuck out when covered by a mitten really did look just like another golf iron. Phil chuckled and hefted the bag onto his shoulder, securing it with a leather strap. He was ready.

ACT IV

The walk to the motel was in biting cold. The town leered up gray from the frozen ground into the black of night. Phil was shaking when he got back to his room and locked himself in. He shook the thin sheen of snow off of himself, threw the coat onto a padded chair and leaned the golf bag against the wall.

He sought the thermostat and gave it a crank. Wind rattled the glass pane hidden behind the blood red curtains.

It hadn't been a wasted first day in White Pond, Phil ruminated. Actually, quite a lot had happened. It had been a day of tracking, he reassured himself, a day of setting the trap. Tomorrow it would be sprung.

Heat was venting in the room noisily. Phil got onto the bed and grabbed the remote off the nightstand. He clicked the round red power button and across from his feet the television turned on. Through the usual mirage of images, he looked for a movie. The channels were filled with food, commercials, cooking shows, and all the food visions were making him feel ill. He wondered if he caught something at the diner. He pictured a tapeworm, scouring him. He turned channels frantically. Finally he landed on the familiar terrain of a black and white planet.

An astronaut staggered across the crumbling landscape, mountainous crags, deep valleys, steep hills littered with scree. Phil vaguely recalled seeing the film a long time ago.

He marveled at the feelings he still had, resurfacing while he watched. Long afternoons pretending to be astronauts on strange worlds, climbing the laurel tree, running around the block, in and out of breaks in the neighborhood fences, games that would be reality, so true they would live in them for hours.

All at once, the astronaut was surrounded by enemies and with a gleeful start Phil vividly recalled their name, "The hungry ghosts!" he said aloud. They were pathetic looking creatures, cheap sci-fi puppets, laughable, but even so they had terrified him as a child. With huge pot bellies, they waddled around

523

the astronaut, their tiny mouths attempted to eat him but they could not. They bounced harmlessly off him like bowling pins. The sound they made! Phil clenched his hands at the recall. There were so many times he had heard that while the years sanded away the source. It was a sort of rusty animal sound, a car braking on seagulls.

He couldn't remember where the film went next or how it ended. As it turned out, it would stay a mystery. The movie stopped as a deep voice intoned over the shadow of a ticking clock.

"Tonight's classic, *Hungry Ghost Planet* will be back after this short commercial break."

The screen popped with the color appearance of a parking lot. "How would you like to make an easy ten grand?" asked the man in a black suit. "It's easy! Just bring your car into White Pond Auto and I'll give you this," a cartoon pile of money spun in a circle, "Ten thousand dollars!" The car dealer held his hands out sheepishly, "What do you need a car for anyway? Where do you need to go?" A family stepped out of their van and gave the keys to the man. They all chanted happily into the camera, "Ten thousand dollars!"

Phil pressed the power button. How could he watch any more of that? Karen was right. Ambrose Fleischer was closing the net. Soon, anyone who remained here and tried to escape would have to run on foot.

A weird wave went into Phil. For a couple seconds he clung to the bedspread. It almost felt like an earthquake and it was only when it passed, when he realized he had not cracked or fallen to the floor with debris, that he knew it had only been inside of him. Was it a symptom of hunger? He only ate once at the diner. A lightheaded swoon almost, that's all it was. Still, the thought of eating didn't appeal to him at all.

In a lucid moment, his mind railed at him, "Of course!" Ambrose Fleischer wants to weaken and starve me out! I'll be so weak when I try to move into action tomorrow, I'll only

manage to grasp at straws. He can stalk right up to me and crack the spear-gun over his knee, throw the pieces at me and rip into my flesh. That's it, I'll be done. Then White Pond will go on, spreading to the next town and beyond.

Phil sat up and let his feet find the floor. There was a phonebook planted next to the TV. He grabbed it and brought it back to the bed.

He flipped through the soft pulp pages. It was like preening the feathers of a magical bird. At this hour it would have to be delivery food.

Pizza. That should be good. There were two places listed. He chose Leonard's because they delivered. There was a brown phone waiting on the bed stand where the remote was. He un-cradled it and called.

"Leonard's Pizza."

"Hi there. I'm at the White Pond Motel, I'd like to have a pizza sent here."

"Sure mister, what would you like?"

Phil told him mechanically from memory. He honestly wasn't hungry, but he knew what to say and how to say it.

When he hung up, all he had to do was wait.

No more TV though. He didn't want to see the eyes of Ambrose Fleischer shriek into him. Besides, Phil had a feeling that machine was probably set up to watch him.

He let his eyes glide around the dull room. The motel didn't want to offend anyone. The one framed print on the wall was a landscape Phil had seen reprinted a million times before. It was

525

a favorite well known work of art.

He reached into his pocket to get that well worn envelope. A pizza would be about the end of it. Maybe he could beg his way onto the bus tomorrow. He took what he needed. The Center would pay off when the job was done anyway.

Pocketing the cash with the room key, Phil left into the dim hall and went to the motel foyer. It was quiet in there. He sat down and picked up a *Field & Stream*. The pages felt slick as a fish. He turned them, looking for something to read.

"Mr. Ticks?"

Phil turned at the sound of the manager. "Yes?"

"You see our mayor today?" The manager veered ghoulishly along the counter. He held a splay of bird feathers fanned in his hand. "At the high school?"

"At the high school? No…No, I missed him."

"You get yourself another chance tomorrow. He'll be at the ice skating rink for the Boy's Junior Hockey League." He added with satisfaction, "We got a good team this year."

Phil nodded and looked down at an article on bow hunting.

He didn't want the guy to think he was overly interested, but he said, "What kind of place does he live in? A mansion or something?"

The manager guffawed. "I guess you could call it that. He bought the old armory. You probably haven't seen that." He puffed like a tourist guide, "It was built in 1910 for the National Guard. It's been leased out for the last twenty years to the sanitation board. They've been storing stuff there. Then it got so nobody wanted it and it just stood there."

"He lives in it?"

"You won't see the lights on, but that's where he calls home."

"Weird."

The manager's face tightened. "I imagine it has its charms." He stared closely at one of the feathers. "When I was a boy we used to go there for roller skating. It had a beautiful wooden floor with a balcony, a stain glass window like a church. Of course I haven't been inside there for years."

Phil clucked a sound of mild interest. He dropped his gaze to the *Field & Stream*, but he felt like laughing, unbolting like a lunatic. He had the option of spearing the zombie at a roller skating rink, or at an ice skating rink. Absurd!

The front door opened and a short kid wearing a red and blue uniform entered with a pizza box.

"I got a pizza for Paul Tacks."

"Phil Ticks. That's me."

"Sorry." The blushing kid handed him the box at an angle, a knee bent like a Medieval squire.

Phil gave him the money and took the pizza box. "Ohhh," he groaned and sat down again. The smell of it was too much. What had he been thinking? He was at the end of his money too.

"You okay, Mr. Ticks?" the manager said.

"I—I don't think I want a pizza after all." He knew what he would see if he opened that cardboard lid. It wouldn't be tomato sauce and Canadian bacon. He could see it plainly, like the box was made of glass, the skin was stretched like a drum, it was splattered with gore. "You can have it if you want," he managed to croak. If he didn't get back to his room, Phil was going to scream or pass out.

Movement was slowed to a dream. Phil pushed against a weight in the air, but he made it back to his room. He locked the door with the gold chain and just hit the bed as his vision began.

The whole town was a spider web. The night streets all radiated white lights out from the armory building in the center. Cars traveled on the webs like bolts of dew. Spiraling in like a fly or a floating ghost, he passed over or through. The cold moon sparked on the white parking lots and backyards. He dipped under the glinting telephone wires, cutting them as he passed, so they curled and lay down across the snow. He poured up to the armory and the giant bolted oak door opened obediently.

It was black inside but he didn't need to see. Cobwebs clutched him, his feet crunched on broken glass. He followed the water-seeped, moldering hallway further than anyone dared. He ducked a fallen beam and went through a hole punched in the wall. The room he was in tightened around him. All the light and life had been sucked out. He sat down heavily. Next to him, he could smell it, a midnight snack. He reached to rip an arm off the body laying there.

Phil leaped from the dream or whatever had been playing in his mind. That was Ambrose Fleischer! Phil knew it. And he could taste the blood on his lips.

He sat up. He was lucky. It was morning. He wouldn't have to try to go back to sleep.

The gray light of a new day was slitting the curtain. He mopped his forehead with his shirt sleeve. The heat was blasting in the room. No wonder, he forgot to turn the thermostat down.

"My last day in White Pond," Phil said. "It better be…"

The red numbers of the digital clock read 6:50. He rubbed his eyes. He wondered if he had any dreams. He couldn't remember any. Out like a light, he supposed.

Phil stretched and got up. A wave of dizziness swirled around him. Yesterday morning was the last meal he had, but he didn't think of eating, he only let the moment pass. He waited then he stood up.

He was okay this time. Phil saw the golf bag, his battle-worn parka and boots waiting for him. This was the big day alright. The showdown…

What are you supposed to do waking up alone in a motel? He didn't want to turn on the TV. It felt too much like an eye that would blink open at him. Of course he had his portfolio, all his zombic reading, but he didn't want to go over that again.

So he put on his shoes. The motel had a pool. Why not? A swim would be a good way to wake up. He grabbed a towel from the bathroom and went to see what it was like.

The pool was down the hall to the left, then a right. He

opened the door and what do you know? There was a machine he'd never seen before.

It was some sort of a vending machine, tall, black, with a glass front. Disposable Bathing Suits, read the sign on the front. Phil wanted to laugh. He dug into his flannel pocket though and got a dollar bill. The machine had a slot to eat it. He pressed the button for MAN and out it came, a plastic ball dropped into the tray.

Phil popped it open and uncreased the bunched cloth. A pale green pair of swimming trunks appeared like magic. He did laugh at that.

He took them to the men's room and went inside to put them on. They fit like a handkerchief. He rolled up his clothes and stuffed them in a metal locker. Another door took him to the pool.

This was the crowning achievement of the town, a hidden wonder of the world. Phil was in a room lined with palm trees, real or plastic, surrounding a pale blue colored pool. The ceiling was glass windows powdered with snow. A faint whirl of heat skirled across the water top.

Phil muttered, "Ohhh," as he padded to where the marble

curled in. He sat down there and put his legs in. It was heavenly. Who would have known?

He let himself slide. He went underwater. He sunk until his feet touched the bottom, then with a spring, he launched himself up to the surface. Opening his eyes, he saw green palm fronds as he paddled in the warm. It was wonderful.

He started a breast stroke, pumping his legs in time with the swoop of his arms. It felt so good to kick everything off. He got to the other end and turned.

A black fin cut the water, went down.

Phil scrambled for the side of the pool. It was all automatic survival. When he hit the edge, he kicked himself up, threw his body over the marble edge. Gasping, coughing, his eyes buried in his soft forearms, he rode the panic to the end.

It's only the zombie, he told himself. He's awake again. Look! Sure enough, when he turned he saw that heavenly swimming pool with the scribbling, peaceful waves. No shark in sight.

Phil unstuck himself and stood. His feet slapped the tiles on his way to the changing room. Enough...

ACT V

Five minutes later, Phil was in the motel lobby. He held a paperback book. It was one of those books people leave behind, but he was holding it tight, trying to keep his thoughts on the pages of *The Foolproof Loser*. So far, the story was obvious. He was starting to skip paragraphs, hoping it would end soon.

"Morning, Mr. Ticks," the manager said, loud enough to make the stuffed birds on pegs jump.

Phil caught the book closed on a finger. "Hello."

"You're up early. Care to join me in some coffee?"

"Oh. I guess so."

The manager brayed, "You guess so? How long you been awake?"

"An hour or two."

"Mmhmm." The manager shifted, "I'm not surprised you didn't get much sleep. I guess I better tell you upfront. I was playing a trick on you, Mr. Ticks. I gave you a haunted room."

"What do you mean?"

"I'm sorry," he came clean. "I guess I do it for kicks. Every once in a while I give the haunted room to some poor out-of-town sucker. I'm sorry it had to be you."

"Don't worry about it. I don't mind."

The manager shook his head in disbelief, "Mister, I don't know what to say."

"Forget about it." Phil took the styrofoam cup of coffee from him. "What time does that hockey game start?"

"Oh yeah. That's at ten. You can go with me if you want. I love hockey."

"Okay. I want to meet him then, if I can." Phil took a sip of the coffee. It stuck in his mouth. What the?!—he brought the cup back to his mouth and spit it out.

The manager didn't notice though. He was busy brushing down the black shoulder feathers of a raven next to the register. "You want something for breakfast? You can have the continental breakfast special if you want. My treat."

"That's okay. I'm alright." Phil opened the book again. "I'll take you up on that ride though. Tell me when you want to leave." He brought the book back up so he could read it. "I'll be right here."

He was on page 28 of *The Foolproof Loser*, turning the pages but nothing was sinking in. For a bizarre moment he wondered what the hell was going on.

Phil managed to grasp it after a while, and he was in the middle of page 53 when the manager returned to the counter.

"You ready to go?"

"Almost," Phil said. "I'll get my coat." He tossed the paperback on the table. He was done with it.

Back in his room, Phil put on the coat and shouldered the golf bag. He left the rest of his stuff. If he survived, he would be back for it afterwards, to grab everything and run for the last bus. That was the plan. The golf bag was heavy enough.

The manager gave Phil the prize idiot look, "I said hockey! We're not going to a golf course!"

"I know. Afterward I thought I could practice my swing."

The manager shook his head as if he'd heard a bad joke.

Phil held the door open for him. Sometime during the night a fresh layer of snow had fallen. Phil really did look the fool with his tartan golf bag slung on his back, wearing his coat the starlings tore.

Their boots crumped across the new snow, around the side of the motel to where a yellow station wagon hid under white. Phil stopped next to its passenger side door, where *White Pond Motel* was painted on.

"We're not taking that!" The manager told him, "The arena's

only a block away. Besides, that car won't run."

Phil joined him again. "You should tow it to White Pond Auto. They'll give you ten thousand dollars."

"I know, I know." The manager sighed. "I guess I'm keeping it for sentiment. Besides, the rate cars are getting turned in there, this might be the last one left. Who knows, I might need to get it running again."

"That's true."

They crossed the street behind the motel. The tall elephant of an elm stomped on the corner.

"This way, down this alley, then we'll be there." Between two brick warehouses, they sunk into the untrampled snow. The buildings looked very old, the bricks were scarred black. Some of the windows were broken.

Phil was noticing the infinitesimal dots of soot in the powder when there was a crash of splintering wood and glass. Some huge shadow swept down on top of the manager, thrown over him like a black blanket.

Before Phil could react, the shape of Ambrose Fleischer stood up, clutching the dangling dead manager, holding his broken neck in his mouth. Eyes flitted at Phil, then the mayor leaped, back through the torn window. Inside the dark warehouse, the sound of the zombie faded across crunching and splintering debris.

Phil stood there next to the red snow and listened until it was quiet. Finally, he had to step over that red splash. Another dizzy spell roared over him. With his hand propping him against the blackened wall, he rode it out. The golf bag had slipped off his shoulder. Phil reeled. Who knew the mayor could move that fast?! Was it all a trap? Did the zombie know we would come this way? Did he read it in our minds?

Phil took the spear-gun out and pointed the weapon at the ground. He armed it by pulling the surgical tubing back from the spear to the firing pin. He would have to be ready to shoot instantly. The golf bag was too cumbersome, unless he could make some adjustments. He searched the ruined side of the wall where the window blew out wood and glass and very carefully picked out a thick, jagged shard. He scraped a spot at the bottom of the golf bag to cut the cloth. He made a hole big enough to fit his arm in. Balancing the front of the bag with his left arm, he muscled his right arm inside, found the grip and kept a finger on the guard. Now he could point the bag and be ready to fire.

Wobbling, Phil made his way out of the alley. The motel manager was dead, Phil reflected with cold truth—and that could have been me. Of course! No wonder this town didn't say or do anything about Ambrose Fleischer—they were petrified! Phil, like them, was alive for now, he was lucky to stay that way. The golf bag was pointed like a cannon, all Phil needed was a clear shot to end this town's madness. One shot was all he would get.

As he moved along the parking lot, he pivoted like a gunslinger.

Every car could hide an ambush, the zombie could spring eight feet from a grill, or off a snowy roof rack. The cars surrounded the drum shaped ice skating rink.

Phil made it to the glass doors. He watched his reflection, making sure he wasn't jumped from behind, reaching a hand off the bag to open the door. His reflection was a disturbing sight. Not only was his coat slashed, now it was splattered with the manager's blood. But he pushed on. He had a job to finish.

Rock music rumbled from the speakers and beyond the lobby he could see the zamboni slowly circling on the ice. A tier of bleachers rowed up from the floor on the left and on the right.

Where was the mayor? He searched the crowd. Had the whole town shown up? There were balloons and so much excitement he couldn't tell. Every time the zamboni passed, the crowd would wave and yell and the driver would wave back and flash the truck's lights for the children standing at the plexiglass wall.

Phil moved ahead, keeping his back to the wall. Teenagers

passed him devouring pizza. The zamboni horn bleated going by. How long would it take Ambrose Fleischer to eat the manager? Phil wondered. Maybe he would be a while getting here. There had to be a special section for the mayor though. Phil looked for bunting or flags, something patriotic…

Finding himself going behind the bleachers, Phil followed the wall. He could see through the slats, the legs and feet. Where was that monster hiding?

"Ladies and gentlemen," the speakers switched from the rock n roll. "Ladies and gentlemen, welcome to the White Pond Junior Boy's Hockey League!" There was a roar and applause and the zamboni's shrill horn. "I know you all know this man standing next to me." The feet on the bleacher slats suddenly began to stomp. "I don't need to introduce him." The bleacher structure was swaying, shaking more and more as the whole town stomped feet on the metal.

Phil moved swiftly, brushing the wall, craning his neck. He couldn't hear the microphone anymore. The arena had become a pounding drum.

Then there was a break. Phil was between two sets of bleachers and there was a gap of ten feet. An aisle led right up to the plexiglass edge of the ice where Ambrose Fleischer towered huge on the other side, his arms held up, his fingers wriggling in the air.

Phil bolted. He charged his target and pulled the trigger five feet from him. The spear shot out whipping a trail of polymer rope.

The seconds of that played to the dull heavy beat of a heart. Seconds never moved so slowly. The spear cut through space at a weird angle. The zombie spun like a toreador, looked down as the spear ripped past his chest. The rope followed in a sleek blurred yellow line.

Phil was yanked off his feet, the golf bag cinched around his shoulder and neck as he was pulled. A big flower of exploding plexiglass, diamonds of it, sprayed everywhere.

The zombie snapped teeth at Phil as he soared by, out the jagged hole in the glass wall. The deep cuts from it, he didn't feel. The spear hit the zamboni rear bumper and stuck. Phil was flung hard on the white ice and dragged in the steaming wake.

He was done. He knew it. With relief, Phil was allowed the merciful realization that it was all tied to the beating of his heart…everything…and it was time for it to stop.

Written
January 10, 2008—February 7, 2008

SUN MTN. GROCERY

After that last adventure, I just had to give Phil Ticks a break. You can't blame me, can you? I couldn't leave him that way. So here he is, back for a curtain call and a final bow.

Contents

A MIRACLE

A silver propeller plane fought through a slanting snowy wind. The freakish patch of weather wasn't on any radar scope. It had pounced on the plane out of nowhere. The aircraft pitched violently, as the pilot inside fought every move of the air. His intense expression seemed riveted on keeping the thing flying.

City lights bristled below. The exhaust of cars never seemed to go away, they colored the atmosphere. Where a concrete apartment scraped through, a window lit the swirls of city fog, and a man could be seen in there.

It was a miracle he could move. He was thankful for that. Phil Ticks walked with a limp but he was okay. The scars wouldn't stop him. He stopped at the window and looked out.

What a beautiful jewel the night skyline pretended to be. He had been close enough to evil to know how good life was now.

There was a newspaper clipping taped to the wallpaper by the window. The stark gray photo said it all. The town of White Pond had been destroyed by an air force bomb. The article maintained it had been dropped accidentally. The whole place was wiped out.

Phil limped back from there. When he thought about what happened, what he tried to keep from happening there, the fear returned. What could he do? As long as he lived, it would be with him. His last assignment wouldn't let him go.

Phil couldn't understand how he arrived in the city again. Somehow he ended up back home. His first awareness was awakening in the hospital with the warm winter west coast sun on the window. What he couldn't fathom was why Ambrose Fleischer let him leave alive. The hospital staff couldn't answer his questions. A nurse showed him the receipt of receivership. He had been express mailed in a box from White Pond.

He rubbed his hands together. Why didn't Ambrose Fleischer eat him? Why did he let him go? At last, a terrible thought occurred to Phil. It seemed a real possibility in light of all the horror he had seen—Ambrose Fleischer was seeding him out. Ambrose set him free so he could watch him. Phil had seen the power of the zombie's mind control. The fear wouldn't let go. Even after the air force bomb, Phil didn't know.

Three feet from the window, he sat down in the wooden chair parked beside the kitchen stove. On the little formica table cramped there, the teapot waited. A crumpled packet of cellophane was balled next to his cup. As he poured, he watched the serpentine steam. His medicine turned and roiled in the cup. Sooner or later, his hand would have to move, to down the bitter stuff.

It was his last packet of tea, the end of a two week treatment he bought at Sun Mtn. Grocery. It was also the end of his money. Tomorrow morning he had to hit the pavement again and work on getting work. It didn't look promising. What prospects were there for a limping, cane wielding detective?

He sighed and folded his fingers around the tea cup. The tea was made from roots and flowers grown at the top of the world. It had powers, Phil had been assured. The old man at the grocery grinded the ingredients into powder and divided that into fourteen packets, while Phil looked round and round at the mystic potions and paraphernalia that clung to every shelf and space on the walls.

Phil gulped the tea. He felt ripped from his chair, shaken in the muzzle of a fearsome dog. When that passed, he filled his cup again. He was ready for the Tibetan superpowers to flow into him. Tomorrow he would need them. He listened to the quiet and let the tea do its work. Then he closed his eyes and went looking for sleep.

A JOB

Morning woke him knocking on his door. He threw off the thin blanket covering and pulled on the robe pinned to the hook of the bedroom door.

"Hey Ticks! You in there?"

"I'm coming," he said and walked towards the sound.

Phil realized he wasn't using his cane as he reached for the front door. He made it all the way there on his own. He paused. Maybe he didn't need the cane anymore?

"Open up, Ticks. You got a phone call."

"Oh. Okay. Thanks."

Still trying out his balance, Phil unlocked the apartment door. He was in time to see the back of his neighbor Mr. Timburr going back to his room.

The phone was on the wall in the hall. The receiver hung from it, left on the floor at a taught end of cord.

"Thanks."

Mr. Timburr shrugged and returned to his room.

Phil bent so easily, without pain, smiling, as he picked up the telephone and said, "Hello."

It sounded like a wind was trying to blow through the phone. Further away in the distorted gale, he heard a little voice bleating. "Down!" Phil heard a miniature yell. Was someone calling him from the bottom of a pit? It seemed hopeless, Phil was about to hang up when the shrill voice rebounded. "That's it—right, that's right. Good job! Thank you, Bertha." Then Phil heard his name, "Hello? Is Phil Ticks there?"

"Yes."

"I apologize for that. Bertha took the phone away. I'd like to speak to Phil Ticks."

"Speaking."

"Fantastic! I heard you were looking for a job."

"You did?" Phil had been testing his balance, switching his weight from one leg to the other. Miraculously, he could do it easily. Now he stopped with both feet planted, holding him up straight. "How'd you know about that?"

"We've got an expert at knowing things."

"What kind of help do you need?"

"Well...I think you should see in person, Mr. Ticks. No, Bertha!" the man shouted, "Put me down!"

Phil was listening to a struggle. The man's voice was distant again, shouting like a genie in a bottle.

"I don't know if I'm ready for your job." Phil wasn't sure if he was getting through, "I'm still healing from my last assignment. I think I need to take it easy. Thanks though." He hung the phone up on the struggling sound. I need a job that won't kill me, he thought, like a monotonous file clerk job. He tried to picture himself in an office, getting paid to type on square orange cards that got indexed away. The quiet of a job like that appealed to him. No more vampires or werewolves or—.

The phone rang. He took it off the wall. "Hello?"

"Mr. Ticks?"

"Yesss."

"I'm sorry about that. Bertha's tied up now. Listen, I really need your help here."

"Why me?"

"This is your kind of job, that's why."

The vision of an office somewhere was starting to fade.

"Just come to the Saturn Circus. We're on the waterfront, you know where we are. I'll show you why I need your help."

There was a shadow pooled at Phil's feet. It was an imaginary office job turned to dust and waiting to be swept away.

The man added, "The fortune teller told me you won't regret it."

"Okay," Phil sighed, "I'll be there in a little while."

"Great! Great! When you get here, just ask for Button Deen."

"Okay. I'll see you." Phil hung up the phone. He stepped over the stained carpet to go back to his room. Walking felt good. Things were looking up. He might actually be ready for the new job.

A LEPRECHAUN

Button Deen was still having trouble with Bertha when Phil arrived at the circus. A clown pointed at the little man held kicking in the air and told Phil, "That's Button Deen."

"Thanks," Phil said and wondered, is this what he wants me to help him with? I don't know much about elephants.

Phil lingered beside a lilac tent line and waited.

Button Deen had the Fay Wray act down good, arms and legs fluttering, shrieking in a high pitch. Button was kept bleating in the air until Bertha was ready to lower him. When she did, her trunk released him lightly and recoiled.

Phil swore the elephant was grinning.

While Button caught his breath, Phil stood still, listening to the flap of the colored flags.

It turned out Button had been aware of Phil all along. As soon as he could, the little man waved and gasped, "Hello, Mr. Ticks."

Phil nodded. He took a step. The way he could walk without any pain was magical. He smiled, thinking he had to get back to Sun Mtn. today and thank the grocer. If there was time after helping Button…How long would it take to train an elephant? It shouldn't take all day. "Button Deen?"

"That's me." There was so much straw stuck to his shoes it looked like Button was walking on doormats. "Come on over to my trailer, Mister Ticks."

"Okay."

The circus unfolded around them.

Button stopped at the silver metal door of an Airstream trailer. "I sure am glad you could make it here. I'm a big fan. I didn't want to say it on the phone. You know how fans sound."

"No..."

Button Deen was still a little man, even let down out of the air and dropped from perspective, but he moved quickly, sprightly. Phil couldn't help thinking of a leprechaun. "Welcome to my humble abode." Button opened the shiny door.

Surprisingly, Phil stepped into a room far tidier than his own. In fact, there was nothing there. They were in a stainless steel shell, like being in an abalone.

"Hope you don't mind, it's a little nondescript in here. I'm still settling in."

Phil got right to the point, "Do you need help with an elephant?"

"An elephant? You mean Bertha? Oh sure, she bothers me, but I have a bigger problem. You ever tour the Curiosity Tent?"

"No. I've never been to this circus before."

Button stared at him with a genuinely stunned look.

"No offence," Phil added.

"I'm just...surprised."

"Sorry. That's the way I am I guess."

Button continued, "There's an exhibit in there you have to see. Correction—" he held up a pointed finger, "There *was* an exhibit in there. It's gone. That's why I need your help."

Though not much interest stirred in Phil's voice, he asked, "What's the exhibit?" It was his turn to be surprised.

"An invisible yeti."

"What?!" Phil's astonished echo clanged the chrome walls.

"Yeah," Button held up his hands to quiet Phil, "I don't want anyone to know about it though. You're the only one I've told, so keep it quiet please."

"An invisible yeti," Phil repeated steadily. "I haven't had much experience with invisible beings. Ghosts, of course, but they tend to make themselves known."

"I can show you the scene of the crime."

Phil shrugged. He needed a job today. There were bills waiting for him. "I don't mind."

A VISION

`"First thing I have to ask you…" Phil said, as he stared at the glass display case and read the white card on it, *Invisible Yeti,* "How do you know it's gone?"

Button Deen sighed and knotted his hands together. "Because last night, when I was turning the lights off, I saw the lid move." He touched the thin metal seam on top. "I reached in and I didn't feel anything at all. The yeti got out and I don't have the slightest idea how to find him." He gripped the display. It seemed to be holding him from falling.

Phil had an idea. It was like a vision. He didn't want to say, but he saw the yeti's hideout clearly. "What happens if I go out and find this yeti? How do I get him back to you?"

"All you have to do is soothe him. He likes music. It puts him in a state. If you play him music, you could lead him across a tightrope wire."

"I'll find him. I'll play music. I'll take his invisible paw and he'll follow me back to you."

Button beamed.

Phil shook his small hand.

It was simple.

Simple as getting on the next bus from the circus, simple as going where a gut feeling told him a yeti might be. *A VISION*

`"First thing I have to ask you…" Phil said, as he stared at the glass display case and read the white card on it, *Invisible Yeti,* "How do you know it's gone?"

Button Deen sighed and knotted his hands together. "Because last night, when I was turning the lights off, I saw the lid move." He touched the thin metal seam on top. "I reached in and I didn't feel anything at all. The yeti got out and I don't have the slightest idea how to find him." He gripped the display. It seemed to be holding him from falling.

Phil had an idea. It was like a vision. He didn't want to say,

553

but he saw the yeti's hideout clearly. "What happens if I go out and find this yeti? How do I get him back to you?"

"All you have to do is soothe him. He likes music. It puts him in a state. If you play him music, you could lead him across a tightrope wire."

"I'll find him. I'll play music. I'll take his invisible paw and he'll follow me back to you."

Button beamed.

Phil shook his small hand.

It was simple.

Simple as getting on the next bus from the circus, simple as going where a gut feeling told him a yeti might be.

A SUNNY DAY

Phil got off the bus at Buchanan Street and started to walk. It was still winter but the weather wasn't bad. In fact it was nice… Blue sky…Sunshine. He could have gone without a coat. It was a good mild day to track down a yeti.

He still felt a little uneasy about birds. He couldn't help it. White Pond left him with some fear. He kept an eye on the telephone wire across the street where a songline of starlings held on. They were all talking back and forth watching him, moving, bobbing, slashing wings sometimes.

That was White Pond haunting him.

That whole town had been under a spell. But he survived, Phil told himself. What happened there wouldn't follow him here.

It was a sunny day and he was alive.

Where Phil was going, the vision he had recognized, wasn't far away. He walked along a block wall of windows cramped together, and past the last apartment, he followed the grade of land, as it turned into hill. A path made of crushed seashells sparkled under him. It reminded him of walking at White Pond, where it never stopped being winter. Phil whistled. All he had to do was find an invisible yeti. And he already knew where it was. He was almost there.

A REST

Come on, he urged himself, there's the entrance, but his legs were sore. They walked him to a black iron park bench instead. Phil needed to rest. He knew he would need strength when he got to the caves.

He shifted his backpack off his shoulders and let the bag slump beside him. It was filled with heavy yellow coils of rope, enough he hoped to bind the yeti when he found it.

He may have been sore, but the pains of White Pond were mostly washed away. He reminded himself to stop by Sun Mtn. Grocery. The tea had made him new.

Motion on the rhododendron leaf pointed over the bench made him look. It was a yellow spider, beautiful as a beach agate, waving a long moon colored leg bent like a fishing pole in the wind. Below, in the city, he heard the noon whistle blow.

Well, he could have sat a long time in that warming March sun, but he had to get up, sling the backpack on. The yeti was waiting for him.

A KNOT

It didn't take long to get to the cave. Cold air exhaled from the rocky mouth. Phil read the sandwich board sign standing there.

Ice Orchestra Rehearsal.
Your Quiet Is Appreciated.

Phil stepped around the sign and entered the ice cave. It got cold quickly. Soon he had his hands in his pockets. Why was he always underdressed for these monster hunts? He wished he could look for a mummy instead. That search might take him to hot Egyptian sands.

Music from the orchestra spun louder down the rounded tunnel towards him. Blue light bulbs had been strung on a wire fixed to the wall.

When he got to the domed chamber room where the orchestra played, the vision he had seen enveloped him. This was the place. Where else would a Himalayan yeti go?

Phil scanned the bundled musicians. All their instruments were carved from ice, blue white violins, cellos and shining brass. Cut into the wall, behind a harp, a doorway went into darkness.

"Bingo," Phil whispered.

The cold had him limping again. His bones were birch trees. He went to the doorway as quickly and softly as he could.

As Phil eased beside the harp, the harpist gave him a glare from the depths of her muffler, mittens on the strings.

Phil responded with an a-okay signal then stepped into the dark room.

With the last of the blue light on his back, he felt like a diver about to plunge into a deeper blacker layer. First though, he unzipped his backpack and took out the rope. He made a loop, took a step and stopped.

Against the purr of music moving in the other room, he heard a growling snore. It was close.

Phil shuffled towards the sound and the unmistakable reek of wet yak fur. That smell alone could reveal the invisible.

Phil touched the yeti. While it slept on, lulled by Brahms, Phil wrapped the thick line around its arms and chest, around its legs, and tied the rope with a double half hitch knot. That's it, he thought. Job's done.

A TAXI

He left the yeti and returned to the blue lit ice orchestra. Tapping the heavy wool shoulder of the harpist who was waiting out a wave of violins, Phil whispered, "Hey," and, "Is there a phone around here?"

The bundled musician nodded and pointed to the ragged wall behind the timpani.

Phil nodded and crept along the glassy cut shimmer of frozen rock. He hoped the orchestra wouldn't stop before he heaved the monster out.

He dropped two quarters into the phone box and quietly told the operator, "Can I get a taxi cab?"

"Which kind?"

"One of the yellow ones I guess."

"Alright sir." The receiver clicked through to the next voice. "Yellow Taxi."

"I'd like to get a taxi."

"Where are you? Where do you want to go?"

"I'm at the ice caves. I need to get to the circus."

The dispatcher rolled that over in his mind and said, "What is this, a crank call?"

Phil smiled and said, "No, it's legitimate. Also, I need some help getting my uhhh…luggage…in the trunk too."

"The ice caves?"

"Yeah. Is that okay?"

"Okay…Ride's on the way."

The call was done.

Phil was pretty sure the cabbie would arrive to find a full-out brawl in the ice caves, with the wakened yeti raging, furiously tossing chairs and shards of snapped instruments, throwing musicians out of its way like pillows.

But it didn't happen that way.

A RADIO

Ten minutes later the cabbie stepped into the blue light, looking like an actor on stage. He chewed the end of a cigar. He had a transistor radio clamped in his right hand. When he got to the harp, he asked, "You know who wanted a cab?"

Phil caught his attention and crooked his finger towards the dark antechamber.

The cabbie's radio faintly played a ball game, the announcer's voice and crowd burred away.

Phil was glad the taxi driver looked able to lift his half of a yeti. That was a bonus.

"Okay," Phil said and he led the way into the darkness to where the ropes spun tightly in midair.

"Is this a magic act?"

"Nope." Phil patted his hands on the snowman's broad shoulders. "It's invisible. I have to get it back to the circus. Give me a hand, would you?"

The cabbie acted like he'd seen it all, until he reached out and fingers hit the yeti.

Phil told him, "I need your help getting this into the taxi."

"What is it? A guy wrapped in a carpet? Why can't I see him?"

"It's a yeti. Don't worry. As long as it hears music, it won't wake up." Then Phil realized how lucky things turned out. "Hey, you've got a radio! That's just what we need. Put some music on. When we get out of here we'll need that."

"I'm listening to the game!"

"I know. But if you want to keep your arms from getting ripped off, you better switch the station."

"I got money riding on this game!"

"Of course we could take a chance on waking him up. I imagine he'll be angry though…"

With a long oath muttered under his breath, the cabbie spun the radio dial from the game to flamenco guitar.

"That's good," Phil said. "You get that end."

561

"This better not be the biting end."

"Just be careful." Phil grasped under two hairy feet and lifted. "And keep that music going."

A ROSARY

The next few minutes were spent in a Laurel & Hardy routine, keeping the yeti from falling, getting past the orchestra. In the tunnel, the radio took over as the soundtrack. It was John Lee Hooker. The yeti slept on.

They got it outside and fitted into the backseat of the taxi. The thing was a sound sleeper. Phil supposed it could have crawled into the ice cave to hibernate like a bear. That made sense.

Phil collapsed onto the front seat. The yeti was stacked in back.

The driver patted his brow with a handkerchief. "Circus, right?"

Phil nodded.

The cab started. The driver spun the car radio from sports to the first song he found. When he rolled the window down, it wasn't so he could share the sounds of the Grand Ole Opry, he needed fresh air. "That thing stinks! Hey, reach in the glove compartment."

Phil opened the latch.

"Hand me that air freshener."

Phil took out the green tree shape. It was tied by a white string to another one, and another one like a row of firecrackers.

The driver held his hand out for them. "Yeah, pass me all of them."

He roped them over the rear view mirror like a rosary, or a vampire repelling garland of garlic.

The car winded to sea level, and a song later they got to the circus.

A DREAM

The driver slowed and stopped and gasped, "What happened here?"

A tent had been ripped in half. Two men were running after an ostrich, someone was hammering rope stakes back into the ground. Everything was dust and litter. Around the crowds rode a white dog on back of a panicked horse.

"Oh no…" Phil got out of the stopped taxi, paid the fare, and got in the thick of it.

Button Deen was gathering alligator eggs spilled in the grass, putting them carefully in his felt hat.

Phil pointed, "Your yeti is tied up over there."

Button Deen jumped. He looked at Phil, then he spotted the taxi driver sitting next to a hoop of rope, holding a radio on his knee. "Here, take this," he told Phil, passing him the hatful of eggs, as he hurried over to the invisible yeti.

Phil waited. Maybe that job went okay. He hadn't been maimed or worse. The scene around him though was troubling. He watched an elephant—it might have been Bertha—trunking water onto a small fire. It looked like a cyclone had hit and ripped a path across the circus. "What happened?" he asked a woman with a goldfish bowl.

"She ran off."

"Who did?"

"That little giant girl."

Phil knew he was being drawn in, it was happening again, but what could he do? He pictured running back to the taxi, taking it back to his apartment where he could pretend the day had been a dream. But he knew this would catch up with him somehow.

He didn't have a chance to ask the woman more, she was gone. He didn't see Button Deen either, or the roped yeti. That taxi was gone too. The excitement over, what had happened was dying down like a coal.

There didn't seem to be a reason to stay and wait for orders. It was time to go. He was part of something that never stopped happening.

Phil took a step.

He didn't have to open the gate. Some powerful force had bent it down.

Every ten paces, Phil walked into a huge footstep.

It wasn't hard to follow her path.

She led him straight towards the blue ragged hills north of town.

Author with dog and time machine, shortly before the journey that led to writing *Sitting On A Bomb*.

Books by Allen Frost

Ohio Trio (Bottom Dog Press 2001)

Bowl of Water (Bottom Dog Press 2003)

Another Life (Bird Dog Publishing 2007)

Home Recordings (Bird Dog Publishing 2009)

The Mermaid Translation (Bird Dog Publishing 2010)

The Selected Correspondence of Kenneth Patchen
    edited by Allen Frost (Bottom Dog Press 2012)

The Wonderful Stupid Man (Bird Dog Publishing 2012)

Saint Lemonade (Good Deed Rain 2014)

Playground (Good Deed Rain 2014)

Roosevelt (Good Deed Rain 2015)

5 Novels (Good Deed Rain 2015)

The Sylvan Moore Show (Good Deed Rain 2015)

Town in a Cloud (Good Deed Rain 2015)

A Flutter of Birds Passing Through Heaven:
    A Tribute To Robert Sund
    edited by Allen Frost and Paul Piper (Good Deed Rain 2016)

At the Edge of America (Good Deed Rain 2016)

Lake Erie Submarine (Good Deed Rain 2016)

The Book of Ticks (Good Deed Rain 2017)

www.ingramcontent.com/pod-product-compliance
Lightning Source LLC
Chambersburg PA
CBHW050059120726
47904CB00004B/1143